W9-BNB-284

THE FIFTH DOCTRINE

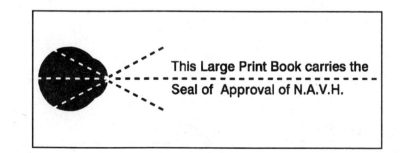

This Large Print Book carries the
Seal of Approval of N.A.V.H.

THE FIFTH DOCTRINE

KAREN ROBARDS

WHEELER PUBLISHING
A part of Gale, a Cengage Company

Farmington Hills, Mich • San Francisco • New York • Waterville, Maine
Meriden, Conn • Mason, Ohio • Chicago

LIBRARY OF CONGRESS CIP DATA ON FILE.
CATALOGUING IN PUBLICATION FOR THIS BOOK
IS AVAILABLE FROM THE LIBRARY OF CONGRESS

ISBN-13: 978-1-4328-6264-0 (hardcover alk. paper)

Published in 2019 by arrangement with Harlequin Books S.A.

Printed in Mexico
1 2 3 4 5 6 7 23 22 21 20 19

Jack, my love, this book is for you, in honor of your graduation from college. I am so proud of you! Christopher, this book is also for you, to celebrate your graduation from medical school. Dr. Robards, I'm so proud of you, too! And Peter, I couldn't have written this book without you. Your contributions were invaluable. Proud times three! The only thing I can say about you guys is — Wow! Did your dad and I do a good job, or what?

1

Friday, December 13th
3:50 a.m.

I am not a traitor.

Like a neon warning sign, the words flashed through Lynette Holbrook's increasingly chaotic thoughts in time to the accelerated beating of her heart.

But then again, maybe she was. If she went through with this. Maybe she should stop, right now, before —

"Finish up, people." Jim Cillizza, her supervisor, stood in the middle of the fluorescent-lit, two-car-garage-sized room, looking around at the twenty-four employees of NSA contractor Crane Bernard Sherman, of whom Lynette was one. A portly, balding and good-natured fifty-seven-year-old, Jim had rolled the sleeves of his blue dress shirt up to the elbows because, despite the freezing temperatures of the mid-December night outside, the enclosed space was stuffy and hot. "Ten minutes."

Ten minutes to finish what she was doing and sign out of the program forever. Ten minutes to get the last of the information into the system.

Ten minutes to decide the course of the rest of her life.

It was 3:50 a.m. By four, when she lined up with the others to exit the room, the die would be cast.

Her throat was dry and her palms were damp with sweat as her fingers flew over the keys, typing in the last few pages of what had been document after document containing some of the United States' most highly protected military secrets. The files were ECI — exceptionally controlled information, material so sensitive that it was not kept online, not uploaded to the cloud, and only existed as hard copies stored in safes.

Until now.

Now all those files had been transferred to a closed computer system located in a SCIF, or sensitive compartmented information facility. This particular one was a state-of-the-art underground bunker beneath a deceptively nondescript office building in DC. The walls were steel-reinforced concrete. There were no windows, and the only door was both constantly monitored via camera and under armed guard. The room had been specially outfitted with the latest anti-surveillance and anti-intrusion technology. The computers themselves were linked to the others in the room, but not to any outside source so as to eliminate the possibility that the system could be hacked. The transfer was being undertaken to make the tens of thousands of pages searchable by the few who had sufficiently high-level clearance to gain access to the room.

For now, those few were augmented by herself and the other employees of Crane Bernard Sherman who had been brought in for this task. Like herself, her coworkers all sat in front of computers busily inputting the last of the files. The click-click-click of computer keys formed a muted backdrop to the hiss of the antiquated heating system. After tonight, the project would be finished and they, the subcontractors, would be gone.

And if she did what she planned, what she'd come in to work tonight intending to do, soon afterward all the terrible secrets, all the lies, all the deadly information contained in those files would be exposed for the entire world to examine and, hopefully, do something about.

Only she was starting to get cold feet.

I am not a traitor.

So why did she feel like one?

"We're talking the fucking apocalypse here! But we can stop it. *You* can stop it. You'll be a goddamned hero, baby," Cory Allen, her boyfriend, interrupted, rounding on her even before she'd finished voicing her concerns to him. That had been exactly three weeks ago last night. As he'd listened to her, he'd run his hands through his hair with agitation and paced the combination living/dining space of her small apartment. Notwithstanding her security clearance and the nondisclosure agreement that was part of the terms of her employment, she'd found herself unable to keep the enormity of what she'd learned to herself and had told him some of the truly terrifying things in the documents she'd been typing into the system. Not everything, just the worst of it, the parts that had started keeping her awake nights.

The end-of-the-world parts.

"How?" she'd asked, looking up at him from the spot where she sat with her jeans-clad legs and stocking feet tucked up beside her on her well-worn couch. Cory was so good-looking, tall and well built and even a little adorably nerdy with his ratty cardigan and wire-rimmed glasses, that sometimes she found it hard to believe that he was actually hers. She was a bit of a nerd girl herself, plumpish with ordinary brown hair, unremarkable features and her own black-framed glasses with thick lenses that had earned her the nickname Mrs. Magoo in high school. When he'd slid onto the stool beside her in the bar where she'd gone to meet a potential match from a dating site who'd never shown up, she'd been so sure he couldn't be interested in her that when he'd asked if he could buy her a drink she'd said a curt *no,* and kept on nursing her strawberry daiquiri. But when it came time to pay her bill and she'd discovered that her wallet was missing from her purse, and he'd offered to pay for her, she'd let him. After that, one thing had led to another, and here they were. He'd come into her life not long after her mother's death, when everything had been gray and sad and she'd been so, so lonely. Sometimes she wondered if her mother, from wherever she was now, had steered him in her direction. In the two short months they'd been together, he'd made her happier than she'd ever been. She was hoping — fingers crossed, toes crossed, everything crossed — to spend the rest of her life with him.

Assuming that she, and an untold number of other inhabitants of the planet Earth, *had* a rest of her life.

Because Cory was right. The secrets in those papers painted a bloodcurdling picture of a looming apocalypse. One that a select few in power knew was hanging over them all like the sword of Damocles, while no one else did.

Unless somebody did something. Somebody like her.

All it takes for evil to triumph is for good men (or in her case, a woman) to do nothing.

Cory had said that to her. He'd also, in answer to her question of *how?*, told her exactly what she could do to maybe stop the worst from happening. And from that moment on they'd talked about it, analyzed it, argued about it, agonized over it, until she'd accepted that it was on her to do something, because there was no one else.

So here she was. Doing what she had to do.

Only she was starting to feel that maybe she shouldn't. Maybe the tightness of her chest and the knot in her stomach were trying to tell her something.

Like, *walk away.*

"Five minutes," Cillizza boomed from right behind her. She jumped, then gave a self-conscious little laugh as he said, "Sorry, didn't mean to startle you," and leaned over her shoulder to scrutinize her monitor.

Her heart gave a wild thump. Her fingers froze on the keys for just a fraction of a second — *Can he tell? Will he know?* — then resumed typing as she forced herself to carry on, to look at the printed page she was copying, to key in the words, to *act like nothing was wrong.*

"That the last page?" Cillizza asked. His face was close enough so that she could feel his breath stirring her hair. He was still studying her monitor, watching with unnerving attention as letters coalesced into words behind a blinking cursor —

What's he looking at? What does he see?

She could feel sweat pop out on her forehead.

Please don't let him notice anything.

"One more." Her throat was so tight she sounded like she was being strangled, but he appeared to notice nothing amiss because he straightened and, to her enormous relief, moved away.

"Three minutes. Everybody should be finishing up," Cillizza said to the group at large. "Chop-chop. Let's get it done."

Lynette barely managed not to collapse in a puddle of flop sweat on the floor beside her chair. She kept typing, her fingers skimming the keys, her mind barely registering the words. She was all too conscious, horribly conscious, of what she had done, of what was happening, of what she intended to do.

The spyder she'd introduced into the system was invisible as it scraped data out of it. The web crawler software was designed to search, index and collate into a single file certain information identified by a series of key words. It was an automated process, and all she had to do to make it work was keep the small flash drive in place in the USB port until the download could be completed.

Which was taking place *now,* even as Cillizza had leaned over to look at her screen, even as she finished up the last of her work, even as minutes turned into seconds and counted down.

Her sweater, which she'd removed presumably because of the room's heat, was a fluffy pale gray cardigan with a knitted-in pattern of huge pink cabbage roses. Puddled on the desk beside her, it hid the flash drive from view. But she was terrified that there was something on the monitor, some small symbol that would give the spyder's presence away that she might have missed but

Cillizza could have spotted. She was terrified that the system itself might detect the presence of an intruder, and could even now be sending out a silent scream to whatever scary government entity monitored such things. She —

"Okay, time's up. Log out. We got to go," Cillizza announced from the center of the room. They'd arrived at 9:00 p.m. and were leaving at 4:00 a.m. so as to avoid having anyone know they were there. The workers in the building above, the cleaning and janitorial staff, even building security, were unaware of the project taking place in the sub-basement bunker, just as they were almost certainly unaware of the existence of the bunker itself. Crane Bernard Sherman personnel would exit as they had entered, through a tunnel that opened into the basement of another government building nearby where they were part of the night shift keying in data for the Fed.

Having finished typing in the last of the document seconds before, she began the logout process. At the same time, she cast a furtive glance around to check that she was unobserved — *impossible to be sure* — and slid a hand beneath her sweater. In use, the flash drive looked like a ChapStick with its cap off. Pulling it from the USB port, she pushed it back into its lid and slipped what now looked like an ordinary tube into the pocket of her sweater. There was nowhere else to conceal it: for security purposes, they weren't allowed to bring anything like coats, purses, cell phones, etc., into the room.

All the while, her heart raced like a frightened rabbit's.

No one yelled, *What are you doing?* No one grabbed her hand or her sweater or the flash drive. No one did anything at all out of the ordinary.

But maybe they were even now tracking the intrusion into the system. Maybe they were tracing it to her workstation, to *her.* Maybe they were on their way —

Her logout complete, the screen went dark.

Fighting rising panic, she stood up, pulled on her sweater, got in line with the others and dutifully shuffled forward as, one by one, her group was processed out the door. Exiting the SCIF was a lot like passing through airport security. Everyone went single file through a portable body-scan machine under the eagle eye of an armed guard. Random pat-downs were conducted by more armed guards. Their belongings, kept in bins just outside the security area, were then returned to them. Once everyone was cleared, they were escorted in a group through the tunnel that took them away from the building.

Tonight the process felt excruciatingly slow.

She realized that she was watching for some sign of a disturbance, listening for the sound of — what? An army of approaching footsteps? An alarm? A phone call?

"Anybody got tickets to the 'Skins game on Sunday?" Dan Turner, a wiry fortyish former math teacher who was two people in front of her in line, turned to ask the group at large as they waited their turn to go through the scanner. No fan of football in general, or the Washington Redskins in particular, Lynette tried to look politely interested as someone behind her replied in the affirmative.

She only hoped no one could tell that, beneath her neat gray slacks, her legs were shaking.

"Doing anything exciting this weekend?" Amy Berkowitz, immediately ahead of her in line, was in the process of untwisting her long dark hair from the ballerina bun she'd wound it into for work as she met Lynette's gaze. Near her own age, Amy was a friend, sort of, of the casual office relationship type that consisted mainly of the two of them grabbing a coffee on the way out of work now and then.

Out of the corner of her eye, Lynette saw Dan reach the body scanner. Covertly watching as he went through the procedure, she tried not to let the sudden explosion of butterflies in her stomach show.

"Going to the grocery. Cleaning the apartment," she replied.

Dan was through. Amy was up.

"Sounds like my weekend," Amy said over her shoulder as she stepped into the machine, turned sideways and lifted her arms over her head. The slight whirring noise as the machine revolved around her made Lynette want to throw up. "Full of fun, fun, fun."

Amy stepped out. It was her turn.

Her heart jackhammered. The pounding of her pulse in her ears was so loud she feared the whole world would hear it.

She stepped into the scanner.

The best way to hide something is in plain sight. Cory had told her that. Together they'd practiced what she would do when she got to the machine.

Reaching into her pocket, she pulled out the ersatz ChapStick, waggled it at the guard and then held it over her head as she lifted her hands. *Nothing to see here, folks.*

18

No big deal, just a girl with a ChapStick.
Standing there, with the hard evidence of
what she had done so casually displayed,
she was so antsy she was practically jumping out of her skin. Her mouth went dry as
she waited to see if the guard would call her
on it. It was all she could do not to wet her
lips, not to swallow.

I could lose my job. I could lose everything.
I could go to jail for the rest of my life. I —

The machine whirred.

The guard, a no-nonsense-looking woman
in a blue uniform with a holstered gun on
her hip, beckoned her out.

Their eyes met. The guard looked stern.
Lynette's stomach went into free fall. The
ChapStick felt like a red-hot, pulsing,
impossible-to-miss smoking gun in her
hand.

"Love your sweater," the guard said.

"Thanks." She managed a smile.

The guard's gaze moved on to whoever
was next in line.

Pocketing the ChapStick, Lynette all but
tottered away.

Her subsequent walk through the curved
concrete dimness of the tunnel felt like
something out of *The Green Mile*. Sweating
bullets and praying no one noticed, she
chatted with Amy, listened to Dan and a

couple of others talking football, and waited for a hand on her shoulder, a guard to confront her, a siren to go off, something, anything, to stop her from leaving, to announce that they *knew*.

Nothing happened. She made it into the other building, rode the elevator up, pulled on her coat, wound her knit scarf around her head and neck, and exited onto the sidewalk. The air smelled of snow. The frigid wind slapped her in the face. The cold felt even worse because she was so sweaty. A few fat snowflakes swirled through the light of the pale halogens that illuminated the street. Beyond the lights, the night was black.

She had to clench her teeth to keep them from chattering. She was cold to her bone marrow. And the weather had nothing to do with it.

Was she really going to be able to just walk away?

Or would a cop car come screeching up at any minute? Or maybe it would be the FBI. Or the CIA. Or the NSA. Or — somebody. They would jump out and arrest her, take her away.

The thought made her insides quake.

She was breathing way too fast. She did her best to slow that down.

A group of them headed to the McPherson Square station, where they boarded the Metro. Lynette was the only one to get off at her home stop. She trudged up the steps to street level, glanced nervously around. It was still spitting snow, still night-black beyond the streetlights although it was getting close to 5:00 a.m. One other person was in sight, a man, no more than a dark shape on the sidewalk at a distance of about half a block. He headed down a cross street even as she spotted him. The area was working-class residential, tree-shaded, considered safe. Her building was five blocks away.

What will happen to me if I get caught?

The sudden sour taste in her mouth was, she realized, fear.

Ducking her head against the cold and snow, she started walking, long strides that were nevertheless careful because of the icy patches on the sidewalk. The ChapStick was still in the pocket of her sweater, snug beneath her coat. It felt radioactive. Doubt, regret — a whole host of unpleasant emotions shook her.

Maybe I'm not cut out to be a hero.

Cory knew somebody who knew somebody who knew the guy at WikiLeaks. That was the plan — they would get the information she'd stolen from the files to him, and it would be published on the web for everybody to see. There would be an outcry. A media frenzy.

Edward Snowden had done something similar. Edward Snowden was spending the rest of his life in Russia. If he was lucky.

It occurred to her that she didn't have to go through with it. There was still time. She could pull the ChapStick from her pocket right now and drop it down a gutter grate, toss it into a dumpster, throw it away —

"Hey." A hand grabbed her arm. It startled her so badly that she jumped and screeched as she yanked free. "Jeez, baby, it's me."

Cory.

"Oh my God, you scared me." He was wearing his ancient green army jacket and a knit hat pulled down over his forehead all the way to the edge of his glasses. She was so glad to see him, so relieved to no longer be in this alone — but his presence meant that time was up. She had to decide. She could tell him that she'd been assigned to a different task for the night, or that the system had been down, or —

"You do it?" Cory wrapped an arm around her shoulders as he guided her toward his beater Chevy Malibu, parked a few yards farther on, at the curb. It was running;

exhaust puffed out in small clouds of white smoke. He looked at her, his expression excited, expectant.

All her doubts, fears, misgivings — they didn't just vanish. But she couldn't disappoint him.

"Yes." Her teeth chattered.

"Good job! Any problems?" His arm was snug around her shoulders. She was glad of the support, glad of his body heat. She leaned into him, wrapped an arm around his waist. She felt light-headed, weak-kneed. Frightened. But glad, too. Glad that she'd been brave. Glad that she'd come through for him. For them. For everybody.

"No," she said.

"That's awesome."

"What are you doing here?"

"Think I'd let you walk home in the cold?"

She smiled at him as they reached the Malibu. He pulled open the passenger door for her. She climbed in, subsided against the faded cloth seat. It was warm inside the car and smelled faintly of coffee. A downward glance revealed an empty take-out coffee cup in the cup holder. Cory got in, but instead of starting the car, he reached into the back seat and pulled his ancient messenger bag into the front.

"What are you doing?" She watched him

23

extract his laptop from the bag.

"Where is it?"

She knew what he was referring to. Wordlessly she unzipped her coat, pulled the ChapStick from her sweater pocket and held it up for him to see. He took it from her, pulled off the cap and inserted the flash drive into the USB port. She understood: he was checking to see that the spyder had collected what they needed.

An image appeared on the screen. Her stomach clenched and her heart started pounding a mile a minute as he scrolled down through page after page of text, diagrams, pictures.

"It's all here. Everything." His tone was exultant.

"What if someone finds out it was me?" Heat blasted from the vents, but she was still bone cold. Once again she found herself wondering if this was her body telling her she was making a terrible mistake.

"They won't." He sounded so sure. Closing the laptop, he tucked the flash drive into the breast pocket of his coat and stowed the laptop away in the messenger bag, which he thrust into the back.

"But what if they do?" she persisted as he pulled away from the curb. "There weren't that many of us in that room and —"

"Don't worry about it."

"I'm just wondering if maybe we should —"

"I *said,* don't worry about it."

His unusual edginess silenced her. She sat there, chewing her lip and staring unseeingly out into the night until he turned a corner onto a side street she didn't recognize. It was dark, deserted. He pulled over, put the car in Park.

"Why are we stopping?" She didn't want him to think she was overly sensitive, didn't want him to know that his abruptness had hurt her feelings, so she tried to make the question sound casual.

Turning off the engine without replying, he opened the door and got out. A frigid blast of air complete with swirling snowflakes blew past him into the car.

"Cory —"

He leaned down to look in at her. His hand slid into the pocket of his coat, reappeared holding a gun. She blinked at it in surprise.

He screwed something onto the tip.

"Sorry, baby," he said. "Loose lips sink ships."

That made no sense, just like the gun in his hand made no sense. Frowning, she was just lifting her eyes to his when his hand jerked up and he aimed at her face.

She never even felt the impact of the bullet that killed her.

Dead, she went limp, then slithered down so that most of her body was folded into the foot well. Her eyes stayed open, staring sightlessly up at him in an accusing way that bothered him not at all. There was a dime-sized black hole in her forehead, but very little blood.

She'd known him as Cory. His actual name was Grant Norton. In the course of his work as a deep cover CIA agent, he'd seen, and done, far worse.

He felt no guilt: she'd signed her own death warrant by stealing secrets from her country. He might have trolled the ranks of the worker bees for the most vulnerable and chosen her for her obvious isolation. He might have gone to work on her as systematically and ruthlessly as a tiger culling a weak antelope from the herd. He might have put the idea that it was her duty to alert mankind to the looming threat facing it in her head, then petted and persuaded her until she did it, but in the end the choice had been hers.

She had betrayed her country.

For which the penalty was death.

Even if he'd wanted to leave her alive, there was too much at stake to chance it. Lives, maybe millions of them, were on the line.

Any collateral damage left behind by this operation was a small price to pay for what it could accomplish.

He shut the door, locked it, walked away. Someone else would be along to drive the car to the junkyard where it would be crushed — the girl crushed with it. Both would then disappear.

"It's done," he said into the burner phone he'd been provided with for precisely this call.

"Excellent work," replied the man on the other end. His name was Edward Mulhaney, and he was head of NCS, the National Clandestine Service. Mulhaney's voice grew faintly muffled as he said to someone who was apparently in the room with him, "Part A is complete. Operation Fifth Doctrine is a go."

2

Bianca St. Ives prided herself on her poker face.

Too bad life wasn't poker.

Impossible as it seemed, Colin Rogan stood right there in front of her. *In her private office.* On the opposite side of the room, but still. To say he was too close was the understatement of the century.

He swung around to face her as she walked through the door, turning his back to the tall, steel-framed windows that overlooked the muddy Savannah River fifteen stories below. The pale December daylight streamed in around him so that, at first glance, he appeared as little more than a dark silhouette against the gray sky. Not even that was enough to mask his identity. Thirty-two years old, six foot three, leanly muscular in a well-tailored blue suit. Wavy black hair. Hard, handsome face. Eyes narrowed with satisfaction as they collided with hers.

Not even the slightest chance of a mistake.

The shock of his presence hit her like a body blow. A spontaneous glad bubble of recognition — she kinda/sorta liked the guy, she was attracted to him, they had a brief but volatile history — was immediately swamped by horror. Fear widened her eyes, parted her lips. Her breath caught. Her heart lurched.

Her mind screamed, *Danger.*

Then her face froze.

Just that heartbeat too late to — what? Pretend she didn't know him? That she was somebody else — her own twin? A doppelgänger?

Like that was going to work.

Some people had awful, no good, very bad days. She was having an awful, no good, very bad year.

He said, "Hello, Bianca."

And smiled at her. Bianca read all kinds of evil intentions in that smile.

Her world shook to its foundation.

Considering that the last time she and the former MI6 agent-turned-mercenary had met she'd drugged him and left him passed out cold on a bed in a hotel room in Moscow, that he might be upset with her was not exactly surprising.

What was surprising was — how *the hell* had he found her?

In sleepy, out-of-the-way Savannah. Her safe place. Her bolt-hole.

Not anymore.

He'd called her Bianca. Beth was the last in the string of fake names he'd known her by, the one she'd sworn to him was her real, true name. Beth McAlister.

Not Bianca. Not ever.

Bianca St. Ives was her real name. Or at least, the realest name she possessed. The one she used in her real life. The life she'd made for herself here in Savannah, as the owner of Guardian Consulting, the thriving private security firm that she'd founded as a hedge against the dark side of her existence. The life that nobody in the criminal world, or the CIA, or Interpol, or anyone else who might be hunting her, knew about.

Only now, obviously, *he* did.

Finding people is part of what I do: he'd said that to her, once.

He knows my name. He knows where I live. Oh, God, what else *does he know?*

As she met that opaque gaze, the thought that he might have learned her deepest, darkest secret in the course of hunting her

30

down exploded in her head. Lightning bolts of dread blasted through her system. She had only recently discovered the staggering truth herself, and she was still having trouble coming to terms with it. If he now knew what she was — a genetically altered scientific experiment, a high-tech Frankenstein's monster engineered by a clandestine branch of the US government as part of their top secret, long-abandoned effort to create a strain of supersoldiers, a *thing* labeled by her creator (and, no, she wasn't talking God here) as Nomad 44 — she didn't think she could bear it.

With that giant question mark hanging over their — she wasn't going to call it a relationship — their *acquaintance,* she felt suddenly, hideously vulnerable. Exposed.

Ashamed.

A shiver slid down her spine.

Her fingers itched to touch the small ridged scar beneath her jaw, the one that had resulted from the removal of the tattoo she'd been given as a newborn: the number 44. Marking her, they'd thought for life, as one of theirs.

Good thing she couldn't seem to catch her breath, or she'd probably start hyperventilating about now.

It doesn't matter what he thinks about me.

But it did. *It did.*

"Did you enjoy the boat parade, Mr. Tower?" Evie asked from behind her. Bianca welcomed the question as a chance to get reoriented, to catch her breath. It was a reference to the procession of barges done up like holiday floats that the Westin across the river put on daily at 3:30 p.m. sharp for their guests. Its toot-toot-tooted boat horn version of "Jingle Bells," audible even at this distance, had just signaled its conclusion. Bianca's office windows afforded a perfect view of the spectacle. From her tone, it was clear that Evie — Evangeline Talmadge, Bianca's longtime best friend and recently hired office manager — had advised him to watch while he waited.

"I did," he answered.

Evie had alerted her to the presence of a client waiting in her office as Bianca had returned, laden with just-purchased Christmas gifts, from a long and late lunch. Mildly intrigued — she'd had no scheduled appointments for that time and in any case it was unusual for a client to be shown into her private office without her — she'd still missed what was, in retrospect, an obvious red flag and blindly walked in to the life-destroying catastrophe that was Colin, here.

Evie wasn't to blame. She knew nothing

32

about any of it. Who Colin was. Who Bianca was, for that matter. What she did when she wasn't being Bianca St. Ives.

Evie didn't have the slightest clue about the existence of the deadly forces that Colin represented, much less that his presence meant that they had somehow managed to run her to earth here, where she'd thought, hoped, prayed, no one could ever find her.

Evie had no clue that Bianca's life — maybe all their lives — now trembled in the balance.

Bianca only then realized that she'd come to a dead stop a few strides inside the room. That her eyes were glued to Colin. Luckily, Evie couldn't see her face.

Get it together, Bianca ordered herself. Managing to take a breath — at last! — she said, "Mr. Tower." Her tone might be wooden, but it was the best she could manage by way of the kind of polite greeting that Evie would be expecting to hear from her.

The only substitute for good manners was fast reflexes, and since she'd already blown the hell out of the fast reflexes thing, she had to fall back on what was left.

She resumed walking, carefully putting one sleek black high heel in front of the other as she headed toward her desk. Her legs, slim in sheer black stockings, felt unsteady as she stepped from the smooth white marble that floored the entire building onto the blue-and-gray contemporary carpet that covered the center of the room and lay beneath her desk. Walking, talking, hanging on to her packages, functioning in general, all required an icy dichotomy, her body going through the motions while her mind reeled.

To cross her office toward Colin like he was nothing more than another client, like he was welcome, like having him show up here in the city where she had gone to ground wasn't a cataclysmic disaster, was one of the hardest things she had ever done.

But she did it.

The obvious Step One in the plan she was scrambling to pull together was to jettison the packages that filled her arms.

"I would have called, but I wanted to surprise you." He sounded remorseful, a sentiment she knew was about as real as his name.

Mr. Tower — Evie had said that the man waiting for her in her office was from Tower Consulting, so in that context the name made sense — was clearly a pseudonym. Unless Colin Rogan, the name he'd given her during their last fraught encounter, was the pseudonym. Or maybe they both were. After all, every other name he'd ever given her was fake. Just because there was a wealth of information about Colin Rogan and his spy-for-hire company, Cambridge Solutions, Ltd., available in the public arena didn't mean that any of it was true.

Lies upon lies: her stock-in-trade, and apparently his, too.

"You succeeded," she said. Brittle had replaced wooden, but at least she was managing to string coherent words together. He was armed, of course. She was familiar with the pistol he carried in an ankle holster. Her eyes slid over him. No sign of a shoulder holster under his sleek suit, but that didn't mean it, or multiple other concealed weapons, wasn't present.

Colin's gaze was fixed on her now, just as her gaze had been riveted to him from the moment she'd stepped into the room. As their eyes met and held, an invisible current surged between them, tangible as an electrical charge. There was chemistry, of course — they'd struck sexual sparks off each other since their first encounter. Add in anger, wariness, distrust, and the volatile mixture all but crackled in the air.

She knew what he saw: a twenty-six-year-old, five-foot-six-inch blonde (five-nine in her custom-made shoes) wearing a long-sleeved, high-necked, knee-length, snugly belted crimson dress that relied for its knock-'em-dead quotient on the way its knit fabric hugged her slender figure. Her shoulder-length hair was brushed back from a delicately featured, high-cheekboned face that was dominated by a pair of large crystalline blue eyes. Her mouth was lipsticked the same vibrant shade as her dress.

The overall impression she gave was of slightly fragile, high-maintenance femininity. She cultivated it deliberately. It was the polar opposite of what she was, and the problem was he knew it. With their history, catching him by surprise with what she could do just wasn't going to happen.

Which meant she was going to have to wait for the right moment to take him out.

"Can I get you some coffee?" Evie asked him.

As Bianca reached her desk and started off-loading the bags onto it, he glanced away from her at last to focus on Evie.

"Or we have tea, if you'd prefer. Hot or iced," Evie added. "Or water. Or eggnog."

Curiosity was coming off Evie in waves. Bianca could feel it. Evie knew her well enough to pick up on whatever freaked-out vibes she must be giving off. Fortunately,

Colin was a good-looking guy and Evie was an inveterate matchmaker. The way Evie's mind worked, she was probably putting Bianca's reaction and the impossible-to-miss tension in the air down to some kind of mysterious romantic past between them.

Please, God.

The good news was, there was no possible way Evie could guess the truth. The bad news was, there *was* a romantic past between them. A very abbreviated one. A few shared kisses, mostly staged by one or the other of them to further their respective up-to-no-good agendas.

No need to dwell on the fact that the heat generated by those kisses had been 100 percent real. Or that she'd been deliberately kissing Colin mindless when the drug she'd given him had finally kicked in and he'd passed out on that Moscow hotel room bed.

Yes, it was a good bet that he *might* still be a little mad about that.

"*And* we have Christmas cookies," Evie added, her tone that of one offering up a deal clincher.

In the act of disentangling the strings of a Santa Claus–themed gift bag from one sporting snowflakes, both of which dangled from her wrist, Bianca glanced around at Evie to find her giving Colin a warm smile.

Warm was Evie's thing, which was one reason she was such a surprisingly big success in this, the poor little rich girl's first paid job. Evie was five foot two, with big brown eyes, shoulder-length chocolate-brown curls and a round, pretty face. The former Savannah Deb of the Year was a rich man's daughter, a rich man's (soon-to-be ex) wife, a Southern aristocrat to her toes. She and Bianca had been besties since they were ten years old, when they'd met at the exclusive Swiss boarding school they'd both been shunted off to. Taking this job was an essential part of the first act of rebellion Evie had ever engaged in, which was leaving her cheating scumbag of a husband. Like Bianca, today she was dressed for the fancy dinner of appreciation that Guardian Consulting was throwing for their best customers after work, because Christmas was less than two weeks away and showing appreciation at the holidays was what successful businesses did.

Evie looked like one of Santa's more upscale elves in a loose emerald velvet sheath that skimmed her beach-ball-sized belly. It had long sleeves, an emerald satin Peter Pan collar, and was worn with a matching headband and flats that Evie had reluctantly chosen over the heels she normally preferred because her feet had a distressing tendency to swell.

Evie was almost six months pregnant.

She couldn't have looked more wholesome if she'd tried.

"Cookies?" Colin responded with interest. He was, Bianca was aghast to discover, now right beside her. A big guy for all his appearance of leanness, he loomed more than half a head taller, and his shoulders were twice as wide as hers. It was all she could do not to jump as she discovered him not an arm's length away. He'd moved as silently as a shadow, and she was reminded once again of the deadly skills he possessed. As an operative, he was nearly — *nearly* being the key word here — her equal. At such close quarters, she could feel his energy, feel his strength, feel the voltage he gave off. She was sensitized to it, she supposed, because her every nerve ending was rubbed raw by his presence.

"Let me help," he said to her as Evie nodded affirmatively in reply to his cookies query. His caramel-brown eyes glinted with malicious enjoyment as they collided with Bianca's. He obviously knew how much his presence was rattling her and was getting a kick out of it. Without waiting for an answer, he started lifting the uppermost layer of packages from her arms and stacking them on her desk.

Bianca was torn between equally strong impulses to back away from him and drop him to the floor with a side kick to the kneecap.

All too conscious of Evie watching them, she did neither.

"Thank you." Her tone was almost normal now. Credit that to a lifetime's worth of training kicking in. Succeeding in freeing the entwined bags at last, she slid them over her hand and deposited them on her desk. Colin solicitously moved a few gaily wrapped boxes to make room. It was all she could do not to jerk away as his fingers brushed hers. Instead she absorbed the static-electricity-style jolt without outwardly reacting, then sidled a strategic few steps to one side.

"What kind of cookies?" he asked Evie, seemingly unaware of any defensive repositioning on Bianca's part. Bianca wasn't fooled: he knew exactly, precisely, to the inch how much distance she'd put between them.

And he was enjoying the game. *Cat, meet mouse.*

"Snickerdoodles, thumbprints, gingersnaps, sugar cookies and iced Santa Clauses and Christmas trees." Evie ticked the types of available cookies off on her fingers as she spoke. "I could bring in the tray and let you choose."

"That would be fantastic. A Christmas cookie with coffee is exactly what I wanted." His eyes met Bianca's again as he lifted more packages from her arms. "It's almost like you were expecting me."

The thing was, the faint undertone of mockery notwithstanding, Colin sounded perfectly normal, too. He *looked* perfectly normal, just one more (okay, maybe exceptionally hot) businessman with a possible need for Guardian Consulting's services. Nothing about him, his words, his body language, his expression, came across as the least bit scary. Nobody who didn't know could have guessed what he was. What his presence meant. It was all Bianca could do not to shudder as the ramifications revolved through her mind in a heart-stopping slide-show. Bottom line, she was caught, exposed, possibly arrested, maybe even dead.

"If only." She said it before she thought, and watched Colin's eyes flicker as he registered the not-all-that-well-hidden meaning: if she'd known he was coming, she would have prepared a reception that he'd never forget.

No stranger to the tartness of her tone, and clearly recognizing it for the harbinger of worse things to come that it usually was, Evie frowned at her.

For Evie's sake, Bianca tried to cover up, adding lightly, "For one thing, I'd have gotten in some tea cakes and scones."

Evie brightened. "Oh, are you British?" she asked Colin.

"Partly. Like most people, I'm a bit of a mixed bag." He smiled at Evie, then glanced at Bianca. There was something in his face — a slight contraction of his brows, a quirk at the corner of his mouth — that caused her pulse to quicken with alarm. Once more she was made to wonder, *Does he know?* "A little of this, a little of that."

Was that aimed at her? Did he mean, a little of this, a little of that, like her own, like Nomad 44's, doctored biology?

Flustered wasn't something she did, but her reaction closely resembled it. Knocked off balance by the idea that he might be seeing her as something other than human, she busied herself yanking one more crammed-to-overflowing shopping bag down her arm while she fought to get her suddenly pathetically thin-skinned act together.

"Looks like somebody's going to have a big Christmas." Colin relieved her of the heavy bag as she lifted it free.

"Tomorrow we do Dare-To-Care," Evie said when Bianca didn't reply. At Colin's inquiring look Evie explained: "It's a party we throw with other local businesses to provide gifts for children who otherwise wouldn't get very much for Christmas."

Oh, God, the party. The dinner tonight. Her plans for the weekend. Her plans for her *life*. At the thought that it was now all blown to smithereens, Bianca felt her insides twist.

"That's great," he replied. "It's nice to know that Guardian Consulting is so dedicated to the community. That's the kind of company we like to do business with."

Evie smiled, but Bianca had to physically bite her tongue to keep from snapping *Bullshit*.

Okay, pencil in a nervous breakdown for later. For now, take control of the situation. First order of business: protect the innocent.

"Evie," she began, meaning to send her friend away so that she could go ahead and confront Colin already and find out exactly what she was facing, then broke off as another terrible thought hit her.

Is he alone?

The possibility that he might not be made her blood run cold.

A swift glance out at the overcast sky beyond the wall of windows reminded her that one very important reason she had selected this particular riverside penthouse office suite to be her new company's head-quarters was because none of the windows afforded a sight line for a sniper shot.

So she didn't have to worry about having her head blown off at any second. Didn't mean there weren't all kinds of other un-pleasant surprises out there waiting for her.

One thing she knew for sure: she had to deal with Colin before the whole house of cards that was her life came crashing down.

Whatever it took.

"Yes?" Evie looked at her with some surprise. Breaking off in the middle of a sentence to gaze blankly out a window wasn't something Bianca did.

Until now. Damn Colin anyway.

"Do I have any more appointments this afternoon?" Ordinarily she would have known. She *did* know. She just couldn't think.

"Triad Services at four thirty." Evie shot her a questioning look — Bianca never forgot appointments — before refocusing on Colin. "About that coffee. Cream and sugar or . . . ?"

"Black, please," Colin replied.

"Reschedule that appointment," Bianca said. "I'm done for the day."

"Okay." Evie wasn't quite able to keep the bemusement out of her voice: Bianca never rescheduled client appointments — and she was almost never abrupt, which that request had been. "You want coffee, Bee?" No need for Evie to ask how she took her coffee, because she knew: black. One more thing, Bianca reflected grimly, that she apparently had in common with Colin.

She didn't like acknowledging a single one of them.

"Yes, thanks."

She placed the last of the packages — a small red gift bag containing the latest handheld game system for Quincy Pack, a young neighbor — on her desk. Immediately she felt better. With her hands free and her arms unencumbered, she was more than Colin's match. If it came down to hand-to-hand combat, she would back herself against him anytime.

But she was conscious of a terrible certainty that this wasn't going to be resolved with something as uncomplicated as hand-to-hand combat.

Colin and Evie were talking — something about the merits of Dark Roast Arabica Coffee from Koffee Kult (which Evie swore by and bought for the office) versus plain old Folgers — and he seemingly paid no attention as she set her purse down beside the gift bag.

Once again, she wasn't fooled. He was aware of her every move.

"I look forward to trying it," Colin said to Evie. His deep voice with its slight trace of an accent — not British but Irish, as Bianca had discovered while reviewing his background, presuming that what the research had turned up was accurate — was utterly charming. The smile he gave Evie was far different from the wolfish one with which he'd greeted her. She hoped it meant that he'd realized that Evie was harmless. And clueless. An innocent noncombatant in their war.

On the other hand, innocent noncombatants made excellent shields — and weapons.

Would Colin really stoop so low as to use Evie to gain an advantage over her?

Bianca didn't even have to think about it: yes, he would.

I need to get her out of here. The idea of Evie as collateral damage zapped the last of Bianca's shock. She could feel herself morphing into warrior mode, feel the familiar cold calm descending as her head cleared and her body readied itself for action.

"Be right back." Evie beamed at him and headed for the door. Bianca followed her, meaning to close it behind her while welcoming the excuse to put a strategic amount of distance between herself and Colin.

It was always better to launch the kind of attack she was considering from at least a couple of yards away.

First, though, she needed a private word with him.

Before she made the call on whether or not she had to kill him.

3

"Uh, boss, you need help with anything?"
Doc — Miles Davis Zeigler, Guardian
Consulting's pudgy, baby-faced computer
expert — loomed in the doorway, blocking
Evie's exit, causing both her and Bianca,
who was some four paces behind her, to
stop where they were. A close cap of frizzy
black curls sprouted from his recently
buzzed scalp. His maroon dress shirt was
rumpled, his candy-cane striped tie was
askew, his black polyester pants drooped.
He was paler even than usual, with beads of
sweat visible around his hairline. He darted
a speaking glance past her at Colin, who
was blocked from getting a good look at him
because of the position of the door. His dark
eyes were alive with alarm.

Unlike Evie, Doc knew exactly who and
what Colin was.

Last time the two had encountered each
other, Doc had slammed Colin over the

head with a heavy bronze statue and knocked him cold. And Colin knew it.

Given their history, today's reunion couldn't have been a happy one. Doc's horror at Colin's presence had to be nearly as great as her own.

With her head full of Christmas shopping and that night's party and a hundred other things, she'd been oblivious to what, in hindsight, had been his desperate attempts to clue her in to the disaster that had befallen them.

Colin hadn't hurt Doc or done anything else to him (like having him cuffed and carted off), which she had to take as meaning that, for the moment at least, he had a different agenda.

Potentially valuable information. She just didn't see, yet, how she could use it to her advantage.

"I'm fine." She remembered the text she'd ignored while exiting the elevator because her hands were too full to allow her to access her phone. Dollars to doughnuts it had come from Doc. His frantic expression as she'd headed toward her office, his hand slashing across his throat in an age-old gesture of dire warning, should have told her something.

What was it they said about hindsight?

"What are you doing with that? It's for Hay." Folding her arms over her chest, Evie glommed in on something Doc clearly was trying to hide behind his back.

Bianca saw that it was — she had to look closer at the place where Doc's fingers curled around the object's wooden neck to be sure — a baseball bat. The effort he was putting into concealing the thing told her that he was hoping to keep Colin from spotting it, probably with the goal of reprising the sneak-up-and-brain-him tactic that had worked so well before. She didn't need Evie's accusing tone to recognize the bat as the one Evie had had signed by Georgia Tech's entire Ramblin' Wreck team for überfan Hay's Christmas gift, then hidden in the cabinet behind her desk until she could wrap and give it to him. Hay being Haywood Long, former cop and Bianca's second in command at Guardian Consulting. In the thank-God-for-small-favors department, Hay was currently out overseeing a job. In that same department Bianca now placed the fact that she had banned guns from the office. If Doc had had ready access to one, she had no doubt at all that he'd be holding it right now instead of a bat.

That way lay disaster. Like milk and

lemon juice, Doc and guns was one of those combinations that just wasn't meant to be.

"I — uh — opened the cabinet and it fell out. Probably you should think about hiding it somewhere else." Doc blinked nervously at Evie.

Bianca couldn't see Colin's expression, or Evie's, but her own mouth twisted with derision. As lies went, that one stank.

He'd snatched the baseball bat up in case he needed to come to her defense. She knew it. She had little doubt that Colin knew it. A nice thought on Doc's part, although in practice it would be laughably ineffective against someone as highly trained as Colin — unless he was fatally distracted by, say, her half-naked body sprawled on the floor, trapped beneath an unconscious mountain of human flesh, as had been the case when Doc had gotten the drop on him before.

She was pretty sure Doc wasn't going to get that lucky twice.

To Doc, Colin said, "Keeping things hidden is hard."

Bianca couldn't help it: at the (spurious) sympathy in his voice she glanced around at him. He'd moved, perching on the corner of her desk with one well-shod foot swinging. His expression as he looked at Doc, whom he could now see perfectly well, was bland. Doc, on the other hand, was looking right back at him with the desperate resolve of a trapped animal. After everything they'd been through together she was family to Doc now, just like he was family to her. She was absolutely certain that he couldn't take Colin out, but she was just as certain that for her sake he was prepared to try.

The knowledge would have been heartwarming if it hadn't been so terrifying.

Doc needed to be gotten out of the way along with Evie. God only knew how this was going to play out, but the last thing she wanted was for anyone she cared about to be at ground zero if (when) the situation went south.

"Give that to me." Evie marched toward Doc, who backed out of the doorway and her way. Snatching the bat from him as she passed, Evie headed toward the small kitchen with a reproving look for Doc and a brisk "I'll just be a minute with that coffee" thrown over her shoulder at Bianca and Colin.

Bianca narrowed her eyes warningly at Doc, who stood a few feet away in the reception area while she was still inside her office. Empty-handed now, he looked back at her with transparent horror. Everything from his twitching fingers to his too-rapid blinking betrayed his consternation.

"Did you get the Lifson proposal finished?" she asked, referring to the cybersecurity recommendations they were drawing up for Lifson Industries.

Doc took a deep breath. She could almost see the mental shift required for him to think about work. "Yes."

"Good. I need you to print it out and hand-carry it over to their office." Her tone was brisk, no-nonsense: the verbal equivalent of a shock-busting slap in the face.

"I was going to email it."

"Do both. Now. I want the hard copy in their hands by five."

"Now?" He looked aghast.

"*Now.* Don Lifson is heading for the Middle East tonight and he's afraid he won't have a reliable internet connection for the next week or so. We're going to make approving this proposal easy for him." That Lifson had concerns about internet connectivity was true — he'd told her so in a phone call earlier, adding that for that reason it would probably be a couple of weeks at the soonest before he could get back to her about the proposal — but the idea of taking him over a hard copy was brand-new as of this minute, meant to get Doc out of there.

Tell the truth until you can't: it was one of the rules she'd been raised to live by. Just like *don't get close.* If she'd followed that one, she wouldn't be worried about Evie or Doc or anyone else right now, because she wouldn't have let them matter to her. No emotional connections equaled one more layer of safety.

Because sooner or later the people you cared about became your Achilles' heel.

And you became their funeral.

"Boss —" Doc's reluctance to obey was obvious in his tone, his face and every rigid line of his less-than-rigid body.

The look Bianca gave him shut him up. Her unspoken message: *Go. I'll deal with this.* Doc protested with a violent screwing up of his face: *No way.* Bianca's brows snapped together: *Get out of here. I mean it.*

Doc looked distressed. Bianca gave him one last speaking glare — *do as you're told* — and closed her office door in his face.

"Alone at last," Colin said as the solid wood panel settled into its frame with a whoosh and a click. The sardonic undertone to his voice made Bianca's grip on the knob tighten. Her office was large and appeared even more so because of the uncluttered nature of the contemporary decor, but she had the sudden unpleasant sensation that the walls were closing in.

Turning to face him, she wrapped her fingers around the smooth, cool Lucite of the circular pendant that hung from her neck. It might look like an ordinary piece of jewelry, but its centerpiece was a gleaming silver throwing star. All she had to do to take Colin out now, this minute, was pop it free and hurl it at his throat.

Then what? Watch him bleed out on her polished marble floor?

Her lips compressed.

"What are you doing here?" she asked.

"You don't call, you don't write . . ."

His tone might be light, but his eyes were watchful as they met hers. For all his casual perch on the edge of her desk, she could sense the tension in his body, his readiness to react. Well, he knew her. Knew something of what she was capable of. Would be prepared for whatever she might be getting ready to throw (literally) at him.

Wait. Her hand dropped away from the pendant.

"Funny," she said.

"You know, if you're not careful you're going to make me think you're not happy to see me."

"I'm not."

"Now that just hurts my feelings."

55

"How to put this? Boo-hoo."

He smiled. It wasn't a nice smile. "For the record, I'm not a big fan of being roofied."

"Really? 'Cause I'm not a big fan of being stalked."

"Beautiful, what you're not a big fan of is being found."

Their eyes locked. The reluctant attraction that had blazed between them from the first was there in that exchange of hard stares, along with hostility and suspicion and a whole host of other less-than-positive emotions. Bianca felt a tightness in her chest. Once, she'd thought they might have the potential to be something special to each other. She'd even thought they might be falling in *lo-o-ove*. Much as she hated to admit it, for one brief, shining (delusional) moment, visions of hearts and flowers and rainbows and unicorns had danced in her head when she looked at him. Then he'd handcuffed her to a boat rail, she'd retaliated by throwing him overboard, and the rest, as they say, was history. Discovering what she was had, for her, put a permanent end to any thought that happily-ever-after — falling in love, marriage, children, the whole white-picket-fence nine yards — was ever going to be possible for her. All the normal things that made up the normal life

56

that was all she'd ever wanted were forever out of her reach. Truth was that she was something both more and less than human, and the knowledge scared as well as sickened her. The thought of reproducing, if she even could reproduce, brought a whole host of practical and ethical considerations with it that made her shudder. The thought that a man could love her, knowing the truth — well, she would never give anyone that chance. She might not like what she was — okay, she hated it — but facts were facts, however painful. Now what needed to be, and was, in her mind when she looked at Colin came down to *Is he my enemy?* Followed by *Am I going to have to kill him?*

If she wished things were different, well, if wishes were horses . . .

Her voice was stony as she said, "I repeat, what are you doing here?"

"Vacation?"

He'd given that ridiculous excuse for showing up in an unexpected place before. She hadn't liked it any better then.

She made an impatient sound. "How about you cut the crap and —"

A tap at the door interrupted them.

"Bee?" Evie called. "Could you open the door? My hands are full."

"Saved by the cookies," Colin murmured.

The look she shot him should have fried his eyeballs. Without replying, she opened the door.

"I canceled Triad Services," Evie said as she entered. She was carrying a large silver tray on which rested two steaming mugs of coffee and a plate with a selection of cookies.

"Thanks." Bianca body-blocked her from walking farther into the room even as a swift glance around the reception area revealed that Doc was nowhere in sight. The sound of the printer whirring in his office told her that he was presumably doing as directed and printing out the Lifson proposal.

One problem on its way to being solved. Next item on the agenda: get rid of Evie.

"I'll take care of this." She took the tray from Evie, who, clearly curious about her relationship with Guardian Consulting's newest prospective client, frowned at her. Ordinarily, by this time Bianca would have had the client sitting on the black leather couch against the wall while she occupied the matching adjacent chair. Evie had served refreshments on the glass-and-steel coffee table in front of that couch countless times. The number of times Bianca had met her at the door, taken the tray and kept Evie out of the room? Zero. Bianca avoided the

58

unspoken question in Evie's eyes by the simple expedient of looking down at the tray. Under better circumstances, she would have found the sight, to say nothing of the smells, of hot coffee and buttercream icing alluring. These were not better circumstances.

Evie said, "Hay called. He said he's running late and will meet us at the restaurant."

"Good," Bianca replied. She'd been worried about the possibility of Hay showing up at an inopportune moment. He would have been one more noncombatant to be gotten out of the way, and Hay, where she and Evie were concerned, tended to be a tad overprotective. At her tone, Evie's eyes sharpened on her face. Bianca gave herself a mental kick for sounding relieved. "Listen, I need you to run over to Celine's —" the florist-cum-gift shop in charge of decorations, etc., for that night's dinner "— and check out the gift bags for tonight. Make sure that they all have our discount card in them, and that the miniature paintings of the client's buildings are actually of their buildings, and —"

"You don't trust Janelle Nash to see to that?" Janelle Nash was Celine's general manager. Having used her for many a party, Evie swore by her.

"It's Friday the thirteenth, remember? Anything can go wrong. I want you to go over there and make sure nothing does. Those gift bags are important." Bianca tried not to let it bother her as Colin, having abandoned the desk, loomed beside her to pick up an iced Santa Claus from the plate. Having him standing so close made the hair stand up on the back of her neck. Attacks worked both ways, and she knew full well how good at martial arts he was. While she didn't expect him to make any immediate violent moves in her direction, her internal warning system clearly was not convinced. Besides, his proximity made taking him out that much more difficult if she decided to do it. A throwing star to the throat was far more impersonal, and thus doable, than, say, a palm heel strike to the nose. Ignoring him as best she could, she focused on Evie. "That's the kind of detail that can make or break a business."

Evie's answering look said, *Seriously?* "Since when have you been superstitious?"

"Evie, just do it."

"This looks delicious," Colin said, referring to the cookie he was holding. The blandness of his tone told Bianca that he'd found her exchange with Evie entertaining.

"You should try the coffee," Evie urged,

smiling at him. Bianca knew that smile: it meant she liked him.

Probably now was a good time to remind herself that Evie had really lousy instincts when it came to men.

"I will," Colin promised. His long fingers curled around the handle of a mug as he picked it up. A tactical mistake, Bianca judged: a cookie was one thing, but holding a full cup of coffee would definitely slow him down. He would be aware of that, though. Since she was all but certain that hurling hot coffee at her wasn't his style, that meant he had no intention of launching anything physical in her direction for at least the next few minutes.

Good to know.

Also, a good time for her to attack?

"Why don't you go ahead and take off for Celine's," Bianca said to Evie. "It's Friday, and the traffic will be horrendous. And once you're done there, you don't need to come back. I'll meet you at the restaurant at seven."

"But —" Evie's gaze moved from Bianca to Colin. A speculative look came into her eyes. Bianca could read the exact moment when she decided that she knew what was going on, and the exact thought that came into her head: *Oh my goodness, they want to be alone.*

Controlling an impulse to grimace, Bianca confirmed that with a barely-there wrinkle of her nose when Evie, face alight with interest, met her eyes again.

"Okay," Evie chirped, and said to Colin, "It was a pleasure meeting you."

"The pleasure's all mine."

"Lock up behind you," Bianca called after her as, with a final knowing look thrown her way, Evie exited. The last thing she needed to be worrying about was any reinforcements of Colin's entering the premises before she'd finished dealing with him. Having Evie lock up would slow that down, at least. "Oh, and make sure Doc's out the door before you leave, would you, please?"

"Will do."

There was a note in Evie's voice that told Bianca she was picturing a little Afternoon Delight between her friend and the hunky newcomer once they were alone.

Which was way better than having Evie suspect that a death match was potentially in the offing.

4

Nudging her office door closed with a foot, Bianca turned to find Colin standing right behind her. He was so close she had to tilt her head back to meet his eyes. His nearness triggered an immediate frisson of physical awareness: on some deep, visceral level, she realized, she had not quite let go of the connection between them. And she always tended to forget how much bigger than she he was.

Yeah, well, the point to focus on here was, *the bigger they are, the harder they fall.*

"Nice woman," he said. Now that they were alone, he seemed to take up way more than his fair share of space. She supposed it was because she was hyperaware of him.

"Yes, she is." Having her hands full of tray was a tactical disadvantage, but on the other hand, it provided an excellent excuse for her to put distance between them without advertising that that was what she was doing. Skirting him, she headed for the coffee table.

"She a secret ninja, too?" It was a gibe.

Bianca's brows snapped together. "No. She's just the receptionist. She knows nothing about anything."

"Glad to hear it. Unless that whole 'with child' thing she's got going on is a sham. In that case, hats off to whoever came up with it. It's a solid defensive tactic, I must admit."

"Trust me, Evie's really pregnant." Reaching the coffee table, she set the tray down and turned to face him.

He was watching her. "Beautiful, where you're concerned I've learned not to trust anything."

The security monitor on the wall beeped, letting her know that the outer office door had been locked and the alarm activated. She shot a glance in its direction, then looked back at Colin. With Evie and Doc both out of the way and her hands once again free and his full, she wasn't likely to get a better chance.

Carpe diem.

Maybe it would be better to first find out everything she could about the situation.

"Who else knows about me? My name, and that I'm here in Savannah?" Her throat felt almost as tight as her chest. Her voice had a certain raspy quality as a result. Her fingers started to stray toward her pendant, but she caught herself in time and redirected the movement into tucking a strand of hair behind her ear instead. She didn't want to focus his attention on the pendant. She didn't want him to realize what it was, unless and until it was time to use it.

If his answer was no one else, the smartest thing she could do was kill him now, before he had a chance to share her whereabouts with the dark forces that wanted her dead. The question was, would killing him be enough to keep herself safe? Or was it already too late?

"Legions." He was no longer looking at her. Instead, he turned his cookie this way and that, examining it.

She made an impatient sound. "I'm serious."

"So am I."

"Durand? Does Durand know?" Laurent Durand was a high-level Interpol official. He'd been hunting Mason Thayer for years, basically playing Captain Ahab to Mason's great white whale. Colin had been working for Durand and hunting Mason, too, at Durand's behest, when they'd met. Mason was the world-class thief and con man who'd raised her to be his partner in crime, the man she'd spent her whole life thinking was her father, Richard St. Ives, only to discover in the last few weeks that he was not — that he was, in fact, Mason Thayer, a former elite CIA assassin whose original mission had been to find and kill her and her mother before, for whatever murky reason, he'd experienced a change of heart and informally adopted her. The man who had recently both betrayed and semi ("semi" because his effort had been minimal and could have gone badly wrong, which would have left her *dead*) saved her.

The man whom she had loved as her father for her whole life, until she'd found out under the most brutal circumstances possible that he was not. The man who *hadn't* killed her, whom she now trusted about as much as she trusted that she would live to be a hundred. Her feelings for him were a jumbled knot of confusion and pain. Her discovery of the truth about him, about herself, about her whole life, had knocked her world off its axis.

She was still recovering.

Colin said, "If I said no, would you believe me?"

She would not. She —

Watching him, she lost her train of thought.

He was sniffing his coffee. Suspiciously.

The significance of that, coupled with the way he'd examined his cookie, burst upon her. Apparently the way they'd parted in Moscow had left a lasting impression on him.

She folded her arms over her chest. "Oh, for God's sake. The coffee's not drugged. Neither is the cookie."

He shrugged and shot a look at her. "Fool me once —"

"What, do you think I keep drugged refreshments on hand for chance visitors?"

"I must admit, the thought crossed my mind."

"Well, I don't."

"Forgive me if I choose not to chance it."

He set the mug and the cookie down on a corner of her desk.

Leaving his hands free. So much for her strategic advantage.

"Your loss," she said, nettled. "They're really good cookies." To illustrate, she picked up a Santa cookie identical to the one he'd rejected. Holding his gaze, she took a large bite and mimicked savoring the crumbly sweetness with exaggerated pleasure. "Mmm, yum."

He appeared unmoved. "I'll take your word for it."

Swallowing, she shot him an unfriendly look as she discarded the rest of the cookie. She really wasn't in the mood for crumbly sweetness.

"Mason's not anywhere in Savannah, if that's why you're here. And other than that, I have no idea where he is. Not that I'd tell you if I did." Colin had been trying to use her to get to Mason since they'd met. As ambivalent as she felt toward her former presumed father at the moment, she still wasn't about to aid in his capture. As she spoke, her hand found her pendant, curled around it. It would be so *easy* . . .

His eyes followed the movement, narrowed. "I'm not here for Thayer. I'm here for you."

A beat passed in which the world seemed to stand still. "At least you're honest."

"Unlike some people, I try to be. When I can."

"So what's the plan? You can't arrest me. You're a civilian contractor with no power to do anything except call the cops, or the feds. If you were going to do that, you would already have done it. My guess is that you don't want anybody official to know you're here. And if you think you can pull off some kind of rendition and hijack me away somewhere by force, or you're planning anything

68

else violent, well, good luck with that."

She could feel the pendant's beveled rim digging into her palm. One thrust of her thumb and the throwing star would be in her hand. A flip of her wrist and it would be streaking toward him. Their eyes met on the thought, and a grim smile just touched the corners of his mouth. It made her uneasy. Maybe something in the way she was holding the pendant, or her expression, or her body language, was a tell?

"I'm not going to have you arrested, I'm not going to try to hijack you, as you put it, and offering you violence is the furthest thing from my mind. And while we're on the subject of violence, you might as well quit fondling that throwing star because we both know you're not going to use it on me." The dry certainty of that last annoyed her almost as much as the realization that he'd made her weapon.

Dropping the pendant like it was hot, she bared her teeth at him. Nice that he was so sure. "I have no idea what you're talking about."

Walking to the window to give herself a moment to think, she smoothed her skirt in a kind of reflexive reaction that was the self-comforting equivalent of a child seeking out, say, a beloved blankie. Beneath the fine knit she could feel the outlines of the garter belt she wore. Custom-made, bristling with the tools of her secret criminal life, it was an essential part of the arsenal she now kept on her person at all times.

"And you can bet I'm going to notice if you start lifting your skirt." His caustic words caused her hand to freeze.

Unfortunately, he knew of her garter belt's existence — and had firsthand experience with the stun gun that was one of its components.

And, yes, she'd been thinking about hitting him with it — again. Probably now that he'd called her on it, a repeat performance wasn't in the cards.

Besides, that would merely serve as a temporary solution to a permanent problem. He knew her identity and where she lived. Zapping him into unconsciousness and, say, locking him up somewhere wasn't going to help, because at some point she would have to let him go or someone else would free him or he would escape and he'd still know what he knew. Bottom line: *can't unring a bell.*

Hmm.

A glance down at the river's churning brown water and what little bit of the rear parking lot she could see told her that, for most people, life was proceeding as usual.

He said, "Why not just face up to it? Short of killing me, there's nothing you can do to get rid of me. And I think we've already established that you're no killer."

Except when I have to be, she countered silently as she turned to face him. But what he didn't know worked in her favor. Although the barely digestible truth was, killing him wasn't something she was prepared to do if there was any possible way she could avoid it. The trick lay in coming up with some other solution to the threat he posed.

"If you're not here for Mason, what do you want from me?" she asked. "You didn't go to all this effort just because you missed me."

"I'm here to offer you a job."

Her brows came together. "What kind of job?"

"Top secret. Highly specialized. Government related."

One of the new rules of her existence was, she was staying as far away from anything government related as she could get. "Not interested. But thanks for thinking of me."

"I'd reconsider that if I were you. This may be your one chance to save your ass."

"I wasn't aware my ass needed saving."

"Weren't you?" That grim smile of his returned. "You really think CIA kill teams just give up and go away?"

5

Bianca's heart stuttered. It was her worst fear put into words. Because of what she was — the living proof of a clandestine program that certain elements of the government wanted to keep hidden forever — the CIA had dispatched a crack squad of assassins to eliminate the evidence, namely her. They'd tried and failed to kill her a number of times already. But she'd been hoping — was hoping, right up until this moment — that at last they'd given up, or that they didn't know she survived.

The only way to escape them is to die. Mason had told her that. She'd learned for herself that it was true.

Only as far as she was concerned, dying wasn't on today's to-do list. Or tomorrow's, either. And she'd tried fake dying, which clearly wasn't working for her.

"They're still hunting me." Her voice sounded hollow to her own ears. She'd known it all along, of course, however much she'd wanted to pretend it wasn't true. Probably she was still traumatized by the events of the last few weeks, and it was coloring her reactions. Immersing herself in the day-to-day running of her business, in Christmas shopping and the making of holiday plans and simply doing her best to feel normal, was her way of coping. It was the equivalent of an ostrich sticking its head in the sand, she knew. She hadn't wanted to see anything else that was terrible heading her way, and so she hadn't. Unfortunately, ignorance might be bliss, but it wasn't smart.

His nod was curt. "Hot on the trail. Probably now would be a good time to fess up to what you did to get them turned loose on you. Because that tale you tried to sell me about Prince Al Khalifa's missing millions being the reason doesn't cut it."

Her mouth twisted. So the Al Khalifa explanation had been a lie. So would anything else she told him, because the one thing she wasn't going to tell him was the truth. Personal considerations aside, if he ever found out she wasn't sure whose side he would be on. A genetic abomination couldn't count on having a whole lot of friends: ask Frankenstein's monster. Confession might be good for the soul, but she was pretty sure it was bad for the life expectancy.

"About a dozen murders, a few bombings, oh, and I robbed the Fed —"

"You're going to tell me the truth sooner or later," he interrupted. "Knowing you, I'm guessing it's something Thayer got you to do."

"See, the thing is you *don't* know me."

He regarded her intently. "So tell me, Sylvia/Cara/Kangana/Beth/Bianca, whatever your name really is. Tell me your story. I'm listening."

She hooted. "Thanks, Dr. Phil. You know, I would — if I had a story to tell."

"Dr. Phil can't get a CIA kill team called off. I can."

"How do I know that?"

"Trust me."

"I think we've been down this road before."

"Are we talking about right before you drugged me, which, by the way, was right after I saved your life from the multiple gunmen who were doing their best to blow multiple holes through you?"

"I saved my own life. The whole diving at the gunman thing and taking him down? That was me."

"Right, and the whole shooting back at all the other gunmen and dragging you out of the line of fire? I'm pretty sure that was me."

"Doesn't mean you saved my life."

"You're not dead, are you? Although with the CIA on the hunt for you, all I can say is, give it time."

She wet her lips. "How do you know they're still after me, anyway? You alphabet agency types keep in touch much?"

"Some."

Coupled with his expression, that was as good as an admission.

"What do you know that you're not telling me? Are they here already? Is that it?" The atmosphere in the room deteriorated in an instant. Open antagonism now crackled in the air, tangible as a low-pressure front before a coming storm. Her body went taut as a bowstring. Her fists clenched. Her eyes were hard on his face.

"Not to my knowledge. But they're coming. Could be today, could be tomorrow, could be next week. And I guarantee you they won't stop by your office for a chat first like I did. They'll just take you out where they find you."

"So what are you, the canary in the mine? Are they watching to see if you come back dead?" Everything she stood to lose — her home, her friends, the life she'd built for herself, her *life* — flashed before her eyes. It wasn't right. It wasn't *fair.* To be hunted to the death by her own government because of something they'd done to her in the first place — if she could have made them all fall down dead where they stood, every single one of them who'd had a hand in creating her, in killing her mother, in subjecting her to this nightmare, she would have done it with the snap of her fingers.

But that wasn't possible. Neither was tracking them down and eliminating them before they could get to her. There were too many of them, and she knew the identities of only a handful.

Her choices boiled down to two: she could run — or she could wait. And hope. And prepare.

Waiting and hoping weren't really her thing. And she *was* prepared. Just not, she feared, prepared enough. Given the capabilities of the enemy, she was beginning to think that it was impossible to be prepared enough. And any fight waged on her home turf carried with it the possibility that people she cared about would get hurt.

He said, "I doubt it. I'm sure they'd credit you with enough sense to dispose of my body where nobody could find it. By the way, in addition to getting the CIA kill team called off, I can get you full immunity for anything you've ever done. Think of it as the ultimate get-out-of-jail-free card."

It was clear that he actually believed he could do what he promised. Too bad she didn't. "What part of 'not interested' did you miss?"

"I probably should have told you from the beginning that this is one of those offers you can't refuse."

"Oh, woo, what are you going to do if I do? Kill me? Get in line."

He looked at her without answering.

She said, "First of all, give it your best shot, and second, think I don't know you wouldn't do it if you could? Which, believe me, you can't."

"How about, have your business shut down? For starters."

"And how would you go about doing that?"

"Well, let's see, the picture on Bianca St. Ives's business license application isn't actually of you. The fingerprints you submitted aren't yours, either. I think that comes under the heading of fraud. And that's just the beginning. Do you really want to invite the kind of investigation that would go along with a state agency digging into your past?"

They eyed one another measuringly.

He added, "The job pays fifty million dollars."

As far as carrots went, that was a big, juicy one. It caught her attention, as he'd no doubt intended.

"For that much money, what do you want me to do? Assassinate the Pope?"

"Impersonate somebody. I'll give you the details later, when we're in a more secure environment."

The thing was, she'd been promised an awful lot of money for the last couple of jobs she'd taken on. How much of the payout had she actually seen? So far, not one skinny silver dime. Although she was working on that.

"Pie in the sky," she scoffed.

"Half up front," he countered. "Before you put on your first wig."

"That's a real incentive, but — how to put this? No."

"You save your ass and your business and you get all that money. Plus you'll be doing vital, important work. Sounds like a no-brainer to me."

"No," she said again, and frowned. "How did you find me, anyway?"

He shrugged. "I'm good at what I do."

Obviously that was true: he'd hunted her,

and found her. Three times now.

Third time's a charm. Or in his case, maybe a death sentence. For him.

She was still making up her mind about that.

"Where'd you put the tracking device this time?" Because the last time he'd found her, that's what he'd done: planted one in her purse.

"I didn't need a tracking device. And neither will they. They'll come across something — a fingerprint, a public record, a snippet in a monitored phone conversation, could be anything — and it'll lead them here. It's just a matter of when. You know it as well as I do." He moved toward her. She watched warily, but he stopped while he was still a good three feet away. "You take this job, you'll be protected. The kill team will be called off. They'll leave you alone, because you'll be one of us — one of *them.* Safe under the umbrella of officialdom. Spooks don't hit other spooks, at least not ones playing for the same team."

But they did hit illegal government experiments that, alive, constituted evidence of their crimes. The fact that she *was* an illegal government experiment was a small but vital piece of information that, as it turned out, he didn't seem to know. On a personal level, she was glad. Not that it made a difference to the realities of her situation.

"What team is that? You're not even American."

"Five Eyes. Ever hear of it?"

It was a spy pact between the USA, Britain, Canada, Australia and New Zealand. Founded in the aftermath of World War II, the once top secret organization had evolved into one of the most complex and far-reaching intelligence and espionage alliances of all time.

"I have. So they're the ones paying you now?"

"That's right."

"Let's see, what does that make you? A mercenary?"

"Yep. Just like stealing makes you a thief. At least if you come to work for me you'll be doing bad things for a good cause."

"Now, that *is* tempting," she allowed, and smiled at him. Mockingly. "The answer's still no."

"They found you in Macau," he reminded her. "They found you in Moscow."

Bianca stared at him as a fragment of thought that had been twisting around the edges of her mind took form and shape and center stage.

"Or maybe what they found was *you*."

81

He'd been there, in Macau and Moscow, when the CIA kill team had done its best to take her out. She'd accused him of being with them, he'd sworn it wasn't true, and she'd believed him. Maybe she still believed him. Maybe he was even legitimately offering her a job with Five Eyes. Maybe he really did think that taking it was the best way out for her.

But even if all that was true, maybe he didn't know the full story of what was going down. She was all but certain now that he didn't know what she was. Maybe something else he didn't know was that the CIA was using him to find her.

Her stomach dropped clear to her toes. As answers went, that one hit it out of the park.

If they were tracking *him,* they could show up at any moment. She'd considered the possibility before, even if briefly and less than seriously, when he and the CIA kill team had both turned up in Moscow. Now she had a horrible, gut-wrenching feeling that it was true.

You never see the bullet that takes you down.

"Maybe they're watching *you* to find *me.*" Her tone was stark.

"Not a chance in hell."

"It makes sense." The possibility unnerved

her. If that was the case, they were *here.* She was already moving, already on the way out the door, on the thought. Her coat and purse were in the closet behind Evie's desk. She would grab them and head for the safe house she'd set up in another part of the city in case something like this ever happened and she couldn't go home. She would gather up the weapons and the bug-out bag she kept there, and get gone.

He who turns and runs away . . .

She would figure out how to combat the threat from somewhere else.

He said, "My company's countersurveillance capabilities are some of the best in the business. I'd know if I was being watched, or tailed, or monitored. I don't even carry a phone on me to keep anyone from tracking me through that. And nobody's leaking my whereabouts, because nobody knows where I am. *Nobody.*"

That would have been interesting to hear — a few minutes ago. Now she didn't trust it.

"How long have you been in Savannah?" She threw the question over her shoulder as she retrieved her coat and purse. The big silver letters of the Guardian Consulting sign that filled the wall behind Evie's desk caught her eye. Her business was dear to her: she'd worked hard to found and build it. But if something happened to her, or if something fake-happened to her, as it might have to if she was forced to disappear forever, the business would go to Hay, who would run it well and capably. The possibility that when she walked out the door she might never be coming back, might never be returning to Savannah, might never again see Hay or Evie or Doc or anyone else who mattered to Bianca St. Ives, brought a lump to her throat.

Get over it.

Never look back. It was one of the rules.

Hay's Christmas-gift baseball bat was once again tucked into a corner of the closet. Seeing it, Bianca had a brilliant flash of inspiration and snatched it up.

"About two and a half hours, give or take. Where are you going?" He followed her as she headed for the door.

"Home. Didn't you hear? I have a dinner party to go to tonight. I have to change." She wasn't about to share her real intentions with him. She hadn't quite labeled him an enemy, but her coalescing plan was strictly need to know, and he didn't. Besides, the first phase of her plan involved ditching him.

"You need to trust me on this. You need

to take the job."

"Beautiful, where you're concerned I've learned not to trust anything." She threw his words back at him. Shrugging into her coat, a sleek black rainproof trench, she tied the belt, hoisted her purse over her shoulder and tucked Hay's bat under one arm.

"Your life is on the line here."

She knew how serious he was by the fact that he ignored that provocative "beautiful." "There's a news flash."

"Bianca — is that even your name? — this is your only path forward. I'm begging you. Take it."

"Begging? Really? I like a man who begs." Pausing by the keypad next to the door, she threw a mock-flirtatious look back at him before punching in the code to turn off the alarm and unlock the door. "Fine. I'll do it. But you need to keep your promise and pony up half the money. Before I leave Savannah." Now, *that* sounded believable.

Lull them into a sense of complacency. It was another rule.

"Done," he said.

"You must really want me for this job."

"I wouldn't be here if I didn't."

"I'll give you an account number to wire the money into."

"Five minutes after you do, the money will

85

be in the account. You're going to have to give your parties a miss, though. We need to leave ASAP. And what's with the bat?"

The alarm beeped as he spoke, signaling the all clear. Bianca punched in the code a second time, which gave them forty-five seconds to exit before the alarm reset and the door automatically locked again.

"It's a Christmas gift for my partner. Evie's planning to give it to him tonight. She must have forgotten it. If we really have to leave right away, I'll drop it off at my place, which is a lot closer to the restaurant, and let Evie know where it is. I assume I have time to pack a few things?" If Colin knew her real name, and about Guardian Consulting, she assumed he also knew where she lived. What could be more natural than stopping by her home?

Not that she meant to. Any place where the enemy knew you habitually went was a dangerous place to go. But if Colin thought that was her plan, it would provide a useful red herring for him to target when she slipped out of his reach.

"You won't need anything. It's all taken care of," Colin said. He was right behind her as she stepped out into the hall.

"I'm going to need some things." Her voice was firm.

Her neighbor, Fred Dunn from the business she shared the floor with, was already out in the hall waiting for the elevator. He lifted a hand in greeting.

"Hey, Bianca."

"Hey, Fred." She waved back. With Fred was a man she didn't know. Instantly, instinctively, she sized the second guy up even as the elevator dinged to announce its arrival on their floor.

No threat was her assessment.

"Don't hold the elevator. I forgot something. I have to go back in," she called as the men stepped into it.

"See you Monday," Fred called back in answer.

"See you," she echoed, and thought *I wish.*

As the elevator doors closed, she and Colin turned as one toward the stairs.

Because in times of danger elevators are potential death traps, as every operative worthy of the name knew.

Bianca recognized that, once again, they were on the same page of the survival handbook. Also once again, she didn't like it. The more he thought like her, the more likely he was to anticipate her moves.

"You don't want to go by your apartment," Colin said as they jogged down the stairs. "If anyone should be in town looking

87

for you, that's one of the first places they'll visit."

Snap. But she didn't say it.

"I presume we're talking CIA kill team? I thought taking this job was supposed to make them back off."

"It will, just as soon as the word gets out."

"So how about you get the word out?"

"The minute I have access to secure communications."

With the possibility that Colin had been followed at the forefront of her mind, Bianca was moving fast. At the same time she was busy off-loading essential items like her wallet and her car keys from her purse into the patch pockets of her coat, while trying to be subtle about it so that he wouldn't notice. He stayed right behind her, moving as quickly and purposefully as she was herself. Fortunately, she was in excellent shape, because fifteen floors, even going down, added up to a lot of stairs. Especially given that she was wearing heels. The concrete walls, the metal steps, the closed security doors all created an echo chamber in which the clatter of their footsteps sounded unnaturally loud. The thought that someone — like, say, a gang of professional killers — might already be on the premises and able to locate them by the noise they were making gave her the willies.

On the other hand, trying to run down the stairs in her slippery stocking feet was liable to wind up with her lying dead at the bottom of them. And since staying alive was the whole point of the exercise, she opted to keep on clattering.

"You know, despite your warning I'm going to chance stopping by my condo. I'm going to need clothes." She threw the remark over her shoulder.

"No, you won't. At least, not your own clothes. Like I said, you're going to be impersonating someone."

"Who?"

"Fill you in on the plane."

"Plane?"

"Private jet waiting at Lowcountry Airport."

The region's largest general aviation airport.

Bianca's stomach tightened. She thought of the elaborate stratagems she used to throw potential pursuers off her trail when heading into or out of Savannah. Clearly now all blown to hell. "You couldn't have used an airport farther away?"

"Stop worrying. The plane's registered to the Canadian Cattleman's Association. There's a Beef USA convention going on in

Hilton Head as we speak, and our plane is one of many that flew in for it. No reason for anyone to think anything different."

She reached the ground floor and exited the stairwell with him following. The emergency stairs opened into a little-used side hallway that allowed them to bypass the lobby, which, judging from the sounds that reached her ears, was busy. The side hallway had been designed to provide direct access to the rear parking lot for occupants of the building forced to evacuate by way of the stairs. A set of double push-through metal doors at the end of the hallway opened outward into a small vestibule that, in turn, opened into the rear parking lot.

Her getaway car was parked in the rear lot.

A couple of steps before she reached the double doors, Bianca lost her grip on her purse.

It hit the floor with a soft plop. She strode on, apparently unaware.

Behind her, Colin said, "Hey —"

She pushed through the double doors.

"— you dropped your bag."

To all intents and purposes, she didn't hear a thing.

As the doors started to swing shut behind her, she pivoted to face them. The move gave her a good look at Colin bending to scoop up her purse.

He straightened, purse in hand, just in time to meet her eyes through the diminishing gap as she leaped after the closing doors. Awareness flashed across his face and he lunged toward the doors as well. Too late: they clanged shut in his face.

Bianca was right behind them, shoving the bat through the D-shaped twin steel handles on her side of the doors. As far as securing outward-opening double doors went, that was about as effective an exit-blocker as it was possible to come up with on the fly.

Thump. The door convulsed as he tried to push through. *Thump. THUMP.*

By that last thump it was obvious he was putting his shoulder into it.

"Bloody hell."

Even muffled by two-inch-thick solid metal doors, he sounded pissed.

The slight smile that curved her lips as she sprinted for the parking lot was a tiny bright spot in what had been, so far, one more terrible, horrible, no good, very bad day.

6

"I'm going to be away for a while." Bianca had her cell on speaker as she drove with controlled speed toward the nearest parking lot exit. The phone itself, a burner she carried for just such emergencies as this so that it couldn't be tracked, was tucked into the open console between the seats, out of her way as it allowed her to talk hands-free. She'd left her usual phone behind in her purse, after pushing a button that triggered an app that wiped its memory, a precaution she'd had Doc install for her. She hoped Colin appreciated the gift. The problem with her attempted speedy exit was that, on this, a Friday so close to Christmas, lots of people seemed to be leaving work early and the rear parking lot's two exits were backed up. On River Street, which she was aiming for, traffic grew heavier by the minute. A side glance at the rows of sweet gum trees and ornamental fencing ringing the parking lot reconfirmed what she already knew: the exits were the only way out. No off-roading it for her. "I'm heading for Europe tonight. I left Evie a message that my father's been hospitalized and I'm rushing to his side. I'll tell Hay the same thing when I hang up with you."

The part about Europe was one more lie, designed to further throw Colin off the scent should he manage to weasel or coerce her supposed destination out of those she was leaving behind.

"What'd you do to James Bond?" Doc, on the other end of the call, was referring to Colin, she knew.

"Nothing. Ditched him."

"He's not going to like that."

"Too bad. What's he going to do?"

"Uh, arrest *me*?"

"For what? You haven't committed any crimes. At least, as far as he can prove. Anyway, he can't. He doesn't have any legal authority to arrest anybody. And he's not about to call in the locals. As soon as he does that, the feds will be all over this and he'll lose any power he has." She was in line now, three cars back from it being her turn to pull out. Once she was through the bottleneck, she would be in the wind. All too aware that by now Colin would be coming after her like a terrier after a rat, she felt like rolling down her window to scream at the people in front of her to hurry. Since that would be worse than useless, outwardly she remained calm. It helped to remind herself that, to catch up to her, Colin had to go back the way they had come and exit through the lobby. That would put him at the front of the building. He would next have to run all the way around the building and through the large front parking lot, shared with the retail shops next door, before reaching the smaller rear parking lot. He then had to beat her to the exit she'd chosen, which was at the lot's farthest edge. And in order to do all those things, he had to first know where she was. And what car she was in, because the Jeep Cherokee she was currently driving was not the car she generally drove, not the blue Acura she'd driven to work that morning and back to the office from lunch and left in her reserved spot in the front parking lot. This was the just-in-case vehicle she'd kept in the rear lot since she'd made it back alive to Savannah, because one of the new, ongoing principles of her life was *shit happens*. So unless he'd planted another tracking device on her person, which she'd taken good care hadn't happened, finding her was going to be difficult — especially if the people in front of her would just freaking *move.*

She added, "Anyway, he said he was prepared to overlook the fact that you clonked him over the head in Macau."

"Yeah, well, he said 'later' to me after I showed him into your office. Since he did that finger-gun thing and pointed it at me when he said it, I don't think we're gonna be hugging it out anytime soon. You really going to Europe?"

"Maybe," she answered. "I won't be answering my phone or any of my usual emails, so if you need to contact me use the fail-safe." The fail-safe was a completely new false identity, complete with phone and email, that, like the Jeep, she'd put in place for just such a situation as she was now facing. It was strictly for communication with Doc in an emergency. She would use it for as long as she could, and then, if she had to disappear, she would cut that last tether to Bianca St. Ives as completely as she left behind everything else.

She refused to allow herself to acknowledge how her heart bled at the prospect.

"That bad, huh?" Doc sounded glum. "Maybe I should come with you."

"I wish you could." She was surprised by how much she meant it. But survival meant that cutting ties, if that was what she ended up having to do, had to be final and absolute. No post-partem Christmas cards allowed. "Where are you?"

"Still at Lifson's. In Mr. Lifson's private office, to be precise, sitting at his desk checking out his computer for him while he finishes up a staff meeting. Seems he's been having trouble connecting to the internet, among other things, and who better to solve his problem than Guardian Consulting's head computer geek? Since I was here anyway. Gives him a chance to evaluate the quality of our work before shelling out for a big contract."

Despite everything, she smiled at Doc's tone. "Is that what he said?"

"Yep. Turns out his wireless router was unplugged. I'm still checking his computer out, but I'd say that was his problem with connecting with the internet."

"Good job. Way to represent!"

Doc's reply was lost as the two cars at the front of the line exited at the same time, shooting out one after the other through a tiny gap in the traffic to the accompaniment of much indignant horn-blaring from the drivers on the street. Bianca felt like hailing that bold move with a congratulatory *woo-hoo.* She was now only one car back and —

Bam.

The sound made her jump. It was caused, she saw with a startled glance in her rear-view mirror, by a large masculine fist slamming into the back of the Jeep.

Her eyes widened as she caught a glimpse of the tall man in a suit that the angry fist belonged to.

Colin.

"Damn it." Her heart jumped. Her hands clenched around the wheel. She couldn't believe it: he was *there,* racing up beside the car, bending to glare at her through the front passenger window. The wind blowing in off the river ruffled his black hair. His expression was several degrees less than friendly.

"What?" Doc demanded. She ignored him; her focus was all on Colin.

Who, she saw, gripped what was approximately three-quarters of the now-broken bat. The barrel was intact but the cap was missing, leaving jagged shards of wood to bear witness to the atrocity that had befallen it.

A glimmer of respect for Colin's physical strength infused her shocked surprise as she registered the fact that he must have caught up with her so fast by smashing through the double doors, which she'd thought was all but impossible given the presence of the (very sturdy) bat. Having managed to do that, he'd clearly rushed out the same exit she'd used then spotted her in the parking lot and given chase.

"Nice try," he told her through the window. "Let me in."

She would have instantly goosed the gas to escape, but there was nowhere to go. The Jeep was hemmed in on all sides.

"Go away," she snapped.

He rattled the handle, smacked the glass with his palm. "Unlock the door."

"No." Once she was through the bottleneck, she could still lose him, she calculated. Unless he was prepared to jump on the hood and cling like a bug, in which case she would do her best *Fast and Furious* imitation until she shook him off. A glance at the street in front of her made her grimace: a solid wall of traffic blocked the exit. Much as she might wish it was otherwise, *Fast and Furious* wasn't happening anytime soon.

"What's going on?" Doc asked in alarm.

"Rogan," Bianca responded, then, much louder and to Colin, "Get away from the car. I'm not letting you in."

His eyes narrowed. His mouth went thin. His jaw hardened.

"Oh, yes, you are." His sheer size, to say

nothing of the steely look he fixed on her, made him appear unexpectedly formidable. Or at least, as formidable as a man in what she guessed was at least a thousand-dollar suit accessorized with a (her) very feminine-looking, fringed and beaded shoulder bag and carrying a broken baseball bat could look. The gesture with which he underlined his words made it clear that if she didn't comply, he intended to use the remains of the bat to smash the window and let himself in.

She gave him a derisive smile. What he didn't know, but was about to find out, was that even slamming the bat into the window with every bit of strength culled from every one of his many manly muscles wouldn't do diddly-squat. Among other reinforcements to her getaway car, she'd had bulletproof glass installed. Because the possibility of snipers had recently become one of the realities of her existence, and she was a big believer in the Girl Scout motto of *be prepared.*

"Boss? Are you okay?" Doc sounded almost as agitated as she felt.

"Fine," she said.

"Last chance. Unlock the door." Colin drew the bat back threateningly. The rounded business end was aimed at the window. She smirked at him in anticipation. "I'm going to give you to the count of three. One —"

A woman walking through the parking lot looked wide-eyed in his direction. So did a pair of teenagers two rows over who were just exiting their vehicle. Bianca could see the driver of the car in front of her checking out the action in his rearview mirror.

"— two —"

A glance in her rearview mirror told her that the female driver of the car behind her was watching Colin with her mouth agape. No doubt there were a number of other witnesses as well. As sure as God made little green apples, if he started beating her car window with a baseball bat one of them would call 911.

"— th —"

Bianca thought of the explanations the arrival of the police would entail, spit out an ugly word and unlocked the door.

"Good call." Colin got in, slammed the door and tossed the broken bat into the back seat. A blast of river-scented air came with him. A big guy, he seemed to fill the car as he settled in beside her. "You dropped your bag." The sarcasm was rife. Her purse followed the bat into the back seat.

"Jackass."

"I bet you say that to all the guys."

"Only the really shitty ones."

The car in front of her scooted away, leaving her first in line. Of course it did, *now.* Was that the way life worked, or what?

He said, "You really think you could lose me that easily?"

She shot him a poisonous look. "A girl can dream."

"Sweet bug-out car, by the way. Where were you heading in it?"

"I told you I had to go home to get ready for tonight's dinner party. That's where I'm heading."

"And I told you that you'd have to give the party a miss because of the time-is-of-the-essence nature of your new job. So how about you head for Lowcountry Airport instead."

"In case you haven't figured it out, that back there with the bat and the doors was me saying I quit."

A gap appeared in the traffic. She smashed her foot down on the gas with real relish, hung a left to the tune of her own squealing tires and in the teeth of the oncoming wall of honking vehicles, and then slammed on the brakes to drop back down to a snail's pace as she joined the gridlock crawling along the river. The heavy gray sky and the muddy dreariness of the rolling water exactly matched her mood: dark. On one side, a long, low-slung warehouse partially blocked her view of a giant barge chugging toward the ocean. On her other side, Colin had been jolted forward by her maneuver and was now casting her a black look as he sat back and dragged his seat belt across himself.

Shoving it closed with an audible *click,* he said, "You can't quit."

"I just did." She changed lanes as she worked feverishly to come up with a new plan. If she took him to her apartment, she could possibly lose him there. She could say she needed to change clothes, go into her bathroom — he couldn't very well follow her into the bathroom, could he? — and make use of the emergency exit she'd fashioned for herself there. But what if a squad of assassins was already at her building, lying in wait?

"Offering you a job was the easy way to do this. Try dumping me again, and we'll do it the hard way."

"Ooh, you're scaring me now."

"You should be scared."

She made a scoffing sound. "Of you? Give me a break. We both know I can take you out with one hand tied behind my back."

"Beautiful, just so we're clear, I've been pulling my punches with you since we met."

"Oh, really? Ever occur to you that maybe *I've* been pulling my punches with *you*?"

"What are you trying to say with that? That you like me? You really, really like me?"

Good one. If she'd been the blushing type, she realized to her horror, that's what she would be doing. Fortunately, she wasn't. "That I'm not scared of you, so don't bother threatening me."

"I wasn't saying you should be scared of me. I was saying you should be scared of *them.* You blow this off, sooner or later they'll kill you. My bet's on sooner."

Okay, so maybe she was a little bit scared. The thought of CIA assassins gave her the willies. It had her casting wary glances at the occupants of nearby cars, at windows and rooflines and even pedestrians, because, while the car windows might be bulletproof, there were other things a good hit squad could try. Like bombs. Or missiles. Or a "runaway" semi. Not that she would ever let so much as a flicker of fear show.

"I'll take my chances." Her response was equal parts bravado and lack of options.

"Not on my watch." His tone was grim.

"This isn't your watch. This isn't your anything. It's me, my life, my decision, and

I'm telling you straight-out, you can take your job and shove it."

"Why?"

"What do you mean, why?"

"Just what I said. Why? Explain it to me."

She threw him a hostile look. "You really want me to spell it out? Fine. I don't want to work for you. I don't want to work for Five Eyes. If that's even really who sent you. See the problem? I don't believe a word you say. For all I know it was Durand, and he and you think you can use me to find Mason."

"Anybody ever tell you you have major trust issues?"

She laughed. The sound was not filled with amusement. "That's it, isn't it? You're hoping to use me to find Mason. Well, it's not going to work. To begin with, I have no idea where he is." The thing was, a lot of those trust issues Colin referred to came from her recent interactions with Mason. The man she'd spent most of her life thinking was her father had sold her out to the CIA. Yes, he'd given her the key to saving herself, and, yes, she hadn't died, but the betrayal was what stuck with her.

"This is not about Thayer. This is about you." Colin said the words slowly and with emphasis, as if talking to a particularly dense child. "When this job came up, I knew you were the perfect choice for it. I ran it by some people, they agreed, and here I am. Take the damned job. It's your only way out."

"No."

"How bloody pigheaded can you be? I'm trying to save your life here."

"I don't need you to save my life. I need you to get out of it. Go away and stay away."

"Not gonna happen."

"You might as well, because I'm not going anywhere with you."

"Looks to me like you are." His gesture encompassed the car.

"Anywhere besides my apartment, where you're getting out and getting lost."

"I don't think so. Here's the deal — you're coming with me if I have to handcuff you and frog-march you aboard that plane."

"Like handcuffing me worked out so well for you the last time."

"Last time I was thrown off guard by the sexy way you kissed me. That was then, this is now."

"That kiss get under your skin? Guess that explains why you keep stalking me."

"If I was stalking you, believe me, you'd never know it."

Because she was busy keeping an eye out

for possible assassins while at the same time running through various escape plans — taking him to a public place, like a crowded bar for a drink, supposedly to talk, and losing him there was where her head was currently at — she didn't reply. Somewhere in the midst of all her calculations it occurred to her that hitting him with her throwing star/knife/various other lethal weapons hadn't figured in any of the scenarios she'd come up with. That was when she knew: for her, for now at least, killing him was indeed off the table.

The knowledge was galling.

He said, "You want to tell me why you'd rather face a CIA kill team on your own than come with me?"

"Maybe because I think I have a better chance of surviving on my own than with you?"

"Bollocks." His eyes narrowed. "You planning to run to somebody else for help? To Thayer? Is that it?"

She threw him an angry glance. "Is that what you're trying to do? Scare me into running to him so you can follow me?" A possibility made her stiffen. "Is there even really a CIA kill team still hunting me? Or is this all a ploy to get to Mason?"

"You know better than that."

"No, I actually don't."

"Like I said, major trust issues."

"Yeah, well, maybe I have trust issues because you have lying issues."

"Right back at you, beautiful."

They'd reached the busiest part of River Street. The uneven pavers of the cobblestoned street made the steering wheel vibrate slightly beneath Bianca's hands. Ringing bells from Salvation Army kettle workers, "Silent Night" from a costumed troupe of carolers strolling past the shops, and the clip-clop of a horse-drawn carriage full of tourists as it passed them joined the more ordinary purr of car engines and jumbled voices. Traffic was bumper to bumper. Shoppers crowded the sidewalks. Christmas lights were strung along the rooftops and hung in festoons from the balconies of the historic buildings nestled along the waterfront. The lights blinked to life just as the Jeep passed a busy open-air market. The twinkly explosion of multicolored bulbs felt incongruously festive under the circumstances. That they came on at just that moment drew the gathering twilight to her attention, and alerted her to how close nightfall was. That was underlined when the Jeep's headlights, set to automatic, came on as well.

"And, yes, Virginia, there really is a CIA kill team hunting you." His tone was dry.

"Like at this point I'd believe anything you say."

In the near distance, Talmadge Memorial Bridge was already lit up. It made a spectacular display against the darkening sky. Longer than San Francisco's Golden Gate Bridge, it spanned the river from Savannah to Hutchinson Island, and with its cables decked out in white Christmas lights it was breathtaking.

She was going to miss it. She was going to miss Savannah.

Tell it to somebody who cares.

He said, "If you didn't believe me, you wouldn't be running."

"I'm not running. I'm heading to my apartment. To get ready for my party."

"Uh-huh. And you tried to lock me in your building because . . . ?"

"I really, really *don't* like you?"

She saw an opening, swerved into the far lane and managed to speed up as the spider-web of city streets siphoned cars in other directions. The increasing darkness had given her her plan.

Simple was always best.

At the earliest opportunity, say, the next red light, she would surprise him with a side

108

chop to the G-spot — as in, gotcha spot, her term for a particularly vulnerable part of the neck — that would, as long as he didn't see it coming and manage to counter it, render him instantly unconscious. She would follow that up with a jolt from her stun gun, which would have been her first choice to lay him out with except for the twin facts that he knew she had it and she was pretty sure that in the confined space of the car he was going to notice if she went for it. Once he was unconscious, she would park, drag him out of the car, leave him, rush to the safe house, grab what she needed and *go.*

The key to success lay in the means she used to distract him while she launched the neck chop. She had a feeling he might suspect a rat if she suddenly came out with something along the lines of "Look! Over there!"

The traffic light at the upcoming intersection turned yellow. Braking, she tensed ever so slightly, preparing to make her move.

He said, "Two blocks up, you want to hang a right. That'll take us to I-95 North."

Which would take them to Lowcountry Airport, a little less than an hour's drive away.

Uh-uh. No.

She thought about pretending she was giving up, was prepared to do what he wanted, to take the job he offered.

He won't fall for it. Not after the fiasco with the doors and the baseball bat. And other things.

In that case, might as well be brutally honest.

"You know you're wasting your time, right?"

"I don't think so."

"Ever hear that old saying about how you can lead a horse to water but you can't make it drink?"

"What about it?"

"Even if you somehow managed to scare or blackmail or shanghai me to wherever, there's no way you can make me impersonate whoever it is you want me to impersonate."

"Think not?"

"I *know* not."

The Jeep stopped. They were the first car in line at the light. Traffic shot out in front of them from the cross street. The gloomy-gray interior of the Jeep was bathed in a kaleidoscope of changing colors caused by a combination of the red light, the Christmas lights and a procession of headlights flashing past. Something about the constantly changing nature of the light made it almost as concealing as total darkness would have been.

He said, "What if I told you this job is a matter of national security? *International* security?"

'Time to make her move.

"Wow! That does make a difference, except — I don't care."

The threat of a sniper was real. The chance that a sniper would be in position exactly there, at that red light, at that moment, ready to take her out, was, she judged, remote.

Go for it.

Colin's face had hardened. He was saying, "— don't think you fully understand the situation. I *own* you. You don't do what I tell you, I'll have you arrested. Hit you with —"

While looking at him with what she hoped came off as mocking attention, she nudged the button on her door that controlled his window.

"— the full 'international criminal' rap. The investigation will involve your business, your friends. They —"

Whir. His window came down. As she'd known he must, he jerked a look toward it even as (because there was no sense in tempting fate more than she had to) it started to go back up again.

Quick as a striking cobra, she let loose with a side chop to his neck.

7

Only to have the blow deflected and her hand grabbed right out of the air.

Bianca froze. Her instant reaction: *Crap, he's fast.*

The only outward indication of surprise she gave was the slight widening of her eyes.

She and Colin stared at each other over their locked hands. Antagonism sparked between them. His hand was warm, slightly rough and way bigger than hers. It utterly engulfed her palm and slender fingers. His grip was steely. Any impartial observer would be justified in thinking that he could crush her hand at will.

She had no doubt whatsoever about her ability to break his grip.

The question was, was it smart to go full-on supersoldier on him now?

Her foot, of necessity, stayed on the brake. In a pitched battle, it would certainly shift. The cramped interior of the Jeep was less than ideal for the kind of down and dirty fight she would have to wage to defeat him. They were surrounded by other vehicles, complete with drivers and passengers, and pedestrians, also known as witnesses with cell phones and 911 at their fingertips. And if there really was a CIA kill team in the vicinity, stopping traffic in the middle of a busy intersection for the length of the epic battle that would be forthcoming if she persevered was probably a really good way to draw their attention.

The thing to do was back down. For the time being.

"Close but no cigar." He tightened his grip on her hand with the goal, she surmised, of letting her feel his superior strength. She managed not to smirk at him. "Think I can't read your tells by this time?"

That took care of her impulse to smirk. Tells? She'd given him a tell?

"You're good." She said it grudgingly, like she was chagrined over being bested. Which, indeed, she was, temporary as the setback might be. The burning question she was left with was, what was the tell?

"You're right," he said.

Whir.

His window went down again.

"You really going to try that twice?" he

asked with disgust, and released her hand. The window went back up.

The thing was, the hand he hadn't been holding was flattened against her stomach. The hand he had been holding — well, he'd been holding it.

She frowned at the window.

Swish, swish. Swish, swish.

The windshield wipers activated, swiping frantically across the dry-as-dust windshield.

She blinked at them. Then she tried to turn them off.

She couldn't.

The monitor in the center of the dashboard, the one that displayed the outside temperature and a number of other bits of un-vital information, flickered, then went black.

The radio came on, blaring the R&B-flavored Latin pop of Camila Cabello's "Havana."

His eyes narrowed at her. "What the hell are you doing?"

She punched the radio button, trying to turn it off. *Nada.*

"I'm not doing anything. The radio, the windshield wipers, came on by themselves. I can't turn them off." She had to raise her voice to be heard over the sexy wail of the song. She was still trying, punching the radio button, twisting the windshield wiper control, frowning at the dark monitor, achieving nothing.

He stabbed at the radio's control button with an impatient forefinger. His try wasn't any more successful than hers. "Forget it, whatever you're up to. It's not going to wor—"

He broke off as the Jeep jumped forward, surging past the car waiting in the lane beside it. There it stopped, for just about long enough for him to turn his head and look at her. It then began to slowly roll toward the red light and the busy intersection with complete disregard for the rush of cross-street traffic zooming out in front of them.

"Damn it to hell, Bianca!"

"It's not me!"

Pulse leaping, eyes on the explosion of cars in their path, Bianca ground the foot she already had smashed down on the brakes practically through the floor.

"The brakes aren't working!"

Bracing a hand against the dashboard, his eyes on the speeding cars in front of them, too, Colin yelped, "For God's sake, *knock it off*!"

"It's not me! I can't!" She demonstrated

by lifting her foot and jamming it back down on the brake as hard as she could. Several times. They were yards away from disaster. "I swear it's not me!"

"Then what the hell is it?" He lunged into her space to punch the keyless ignition button in an attempt to shut down the engine. Still nada. He repeatedly jammed the heel of his hand against the small black rectangle. "Damned thing won't turn off."

She scrabbled at the door handle, pushed at the door, ready to roll out onto the pavement to escape. The door wouldn't open. She jabbed at the lock, then pulled at it. It stayed locked. Her mouth went dry. Her stomach cramped. "The lock's stuck!"

"Try the key." Eyes glued to the jet stream of vehicles now only feet in front of them, Colin grabbed the gearshift, yanked it down into Neutral. Nothing.

"I am." She'd already scooped the key out of the console and was pressing her thumb down frantically on each of the tiny buttons in hopes of turning the car off, unlocking the door, something. At the same time she jerked the steering wheel to the left in an attempt to turn the Jeep into the flow of traffic and thus avoid being T-boned. *"Nothing's working."*

She practically stood on the brake as a

bus-sized RV rattled past, way too close for comfort.

The Jeep kept moving. The radio mourned *Ha-va-a-na.* The wipers went s*wish, swish.*

A terrible suspicion reared its ugly head. Her stomach turned inside out. If she was right, the CIA kill team was there for real.

"Steer away from the cars!" Colin's voice was harsh.

"Ya think?" Still frantically pumping the brakes, she spun the wheel in the opposite direction as the prospect of imminent death in a car crash made her heart jackhammer. Meanwhile he was cursing a blue streak as he tried to open his door without success. Suspicion jelled into certainty, and she faced the horrible truth. "It's Boston brakes. It's got to be."

The words squeaked out of her fear-tightened throat.

"What?" He threw the question at her as they worked in a tightly controlled frenzy to find some way to stop the car, open the doors, something.

"Boston brakes!" She shrieked it at him this time. The words bounced off the hard surfaces of the metal eggshell in which they were trapped.

"Shit!" That was Colin's explosive acknowledgment of her conclusion, uttered as he

tried, and failed, to force his door open. Their eyes met in a split second of mutual comprehension. This time she was glad they were on the same page of the operative handbook. She didn't have to explain what she meant by Boston brakes: he knew as well as she did that the CIA had the ability to remotely seize control of a vehicle, a capability that (like so much else) they consistently denied. It was a form of cyber-attack, a super-hacking, if you would, that was supposed to be impossible and was way beyond top secret and had been used in a number of intelligence-service-organized assassinations disguised as accidents. As common as they were, car crashes offered the Agency the ultimate in deniability. Unless they could find a way to prevent it, this would be just one more regrettable fatal accident.

His tone held a degree of grim satisfaction as he added, "Believe me about the CIA kill team now?"

"Are you really choosing this moment to say *I told you so?*" Bianca gripped the steering wheel so hard her fingers hurt. Dread made her chest feel tight as she realized how helpless she actually was. Then a thought occurred, and she shot an accusing look at him. "You! *You* can stop this! They must not realize you're in the car with me! You need to let them know *now.*" She scrabbled in the console for the phone.

"What? You think I can just — *Hang on.*" Colin gave a vicious yank to the wheel that did no good whatsoever. As the wheel was torn from her one-handed grip on it, Bianca snapped a look at the tsunami of oncoming vehicles, forgot the phone and went rigid, instinctively steeling for a collision as the Jeep plowed straight ahead into oncoming traffic.

Brakes screamed. Headlights skewered them. Cars swerved, drove off the road, rear-ended each other. The din of shrieking horns was loud enough to drown out even the blaring radio. A horn blasted a strident warning as a UPS truck barreling through the intersection apparently only spotted them at the last minute. Slamming on its brakes, the truck skidded sideways, tires squealing, in a desperate attempt to avoid running them down.

"*Ah!*" Wide-eyed with fear, Bianca grabbed the wheel, turned it (nothing) and pressed back against the seat as tightly as she could as the truck hurtled toward them.

"Fuck, fuck, *fuck,*" Colin yelled.

Bianca cringed as the huge brown blur spun past with inches to spare then jumped the curb on the opposite side of the intersection and smashed into a storefront. The impact sent glass flying everywhere. It sounded like a bomb going off.

"Oh no! Oh my God!" Her thoughts flew to the patrons inside the store as smoke started to billow from the truck.

Brakes squealed as approaching cars stopped. Drivers leaped out, presumably to help. Witnesses on the sidewalk, having scattered, started running back. Shoppers spilled out of the surrounding stores. A dazed-looking woman staggered out of the shop the truck had hit. The acrid smell of smoke was strong, making Bianca fear an imminent fire.

She remembered the phone in the console, grabbed it, thrust it at Colin. *Call them off.*

"You think there's some kind of 1-800-Spooks-R-Us number? I can't just call them off. I'm not with them. Remember them shooting at me in Moscow?"

"They were shooting at me. You just got in the way. And you said —"

"Boss! Boss, can you hear me?" Doc: she'd forgotten Doc. He was still on speakerphone, his voice a tinny thread amid the uproar. From his tone, this wasn't the first time he'd called out to her. She only heard him now because the phone was in her hand.

"Yes. *Yes.* I can hear you." Ridiculous as it was, the phone felt like a lifeline. Chaos replaced the steady stream of traffic around them as vehicles slammed to a stop, changed lanes, swerved to avoid each other. The Jeep continued to roll, cutting through the barrage of opposing traffic like it wasn't even there.

"I need the VIN number." Doc's voice was high-pitched with urgency.

"What?"

"The VIN number! You got Boston brakes, right? I need the VIN number to get the Jeep's IP address to maybe turn it off."

Doc had clearly heard everything. She wasn't about to waste time trying to remember exactly what "everything" entailed, or in peppering him with questions. She'd seen him work too many hacking-related miracles.

"Okay." Her hand tightened on the phone as she tried to think. The VIN number was stamped on the dashboard — in a spot that could only be seen from outside the car. It was —

"Who the hell are you talking to?" Colin roared. He was running his fingers along the junction of the roof and his door frame, clearly hoping to find a weak spot.

"Doc." She threw the answer at him as an aside as she frantically reviewed all the places the VIN number could be found. On the engine —

"Look out!"

At Colin's hoarse cry her head snapped toward him.

Crash.

"Oh!" Bianca was thrown sideways. Her head bumped hard against the window beside her. Seeing stars from the impact, she blinked at a yellow MINI Cooper skidding by. Two screaming women in the front seat looked back at her with terror in their faces as the little car, having just rammed into the Jeep's front passenger-side fender, flew past.

The Jeep corrected course with a jerk and kept going.

"You okay?" Colin's voice was harsh. His arm was in front of her now, stretched out at shoulder level, hard with muscle beneath his expensive jacket as it pinned her to the seat. He'd thrust it out to protect her, she realized, and grimaced at all that the gesture implied. There was no time at the moment to process her feelings, but she wasn't used to being protected.

"Yes. Don't hang up." She shoved Colin's

arm out of the way and pushed the phone into his hand at the same time as she released her seat belt and jackknifed across his legs to yank the glove compartment open. She'd remembered —

"Boss, the VIN number," Doc shrieked.

"One minute," she responded, yelling to make sure he heard. She'd remembered the one obvious, accessible place to find the VIN number. The glove compartment light came on; she could see a corner of the rectangular slip of paper that was the registration down under the owner's manual. Grabbing it, she pulled it free and, still bent across Colin's legs to take advantage of the light, snatched the phone out of his hand and read the VIN number off the registration.

"Got it," Doc crowed. "Game on, you mothers!"

Bianca guessed the target of that last was whoever was Boston braking the Jeep.

Primed to face the next horror, she snapped upright to find that the barrage of cars careening past them had vanished. A glance in her rearview mirror told her why: the light had changed. The cross traffic had stopped. The Jeep continued to roll, but now they were through the gauntlet, disgorged into a connecting street with relatively few vehicles, all of which were going their way. The Jeep was just one more unremarkable blip in the traffic.

They were alive, and basically unharmed.

"Oh my God. We survived." She felt light-headed with relief — or maybe from the blow to her head. It was hard to tell. Taking a much-needed deep breath, she glanced around, her eyes raking the activity sliding past outside the windows. A service station on one side, a 7-Eleven on the other —

In all the excitement her foot had slipped from the brake. She slammed it back down, once more grinding the pedal into the floor.

The Jeep didn't stop. It didn't slow.

Her pulse raced anew as she faced the hideous truth. The CIA kill team was still out there, still operative, still controlling the Jeep. They could be anywhere. In the white van pulling away from the 7-Eleven. In the black SUV two cars up. In the Domino's Pizza delivery car behind them.

Or maybe they were working remotely. Maybe they were using satellites. Or drones. It wouldn't be the first time. Bianca caught herself peering up through the swishing wipers at the night sky. Other than a whole lot of darkness, there was nothing to see. Not even the moon, or any stars.

"They're not finished with us," she said.

Her mouth tasted sour with fear. The Jeep rolled past a strip mall, closed office buildings, a used-car lot. Multiple sirens screamed in the distance as, presumably, emergency responders headed for the mess they'd left behind. On the radio, "Havana" had been swapped out for somebody singing about thunder. Imagine Dragons — with the tiny part of her brain that wasn't wholly occupied with fighting off terror, she recognized the song.

"Probably not," Colin agreed. The very evenness of his voice told her how on edge he still was. "Put your seat belt on."

Then, releasing his, twisting around in his seat so that he was once again encroaching head and shoulders into her space, he lifted one long, powerful-looking leg and slammed his foot into his window with what looked like all his might.

The glass didn't break. It didn't even shiver.

"Bulletproof glass," she told him.

"Of course it is. *Fuck.*"

Her insides twisted as she played connect-the-dots with what was happening. Maybe getting them killed in a car crash at that intersection hadn't been the endgame here. Maybe —

"We're being taken somewhere," she said.

8

"Yeah."

At that flat rejoinder, which told her Colin had come to the same conclusion — blame the blow to her head if he'd gotten there before she did — Bianca felt goose bumps spring to prickly life all over her skin. She remembered the fate the CIA had planned for her the last time they'd had her in their clutches: they'd been in the process of trying to drown her in a vat of preservative liquid when she'd managed to escape.

She was, she discovered, still holding the phone. She spoke urgently into it. "Doc?"

"On it." He sounded abstracted. She pictured him feverishly working his computer magic — on Lifson's computer, she had no doubt — and realized that the best thing she could do was leave him alone to do his thing.

"Great," she said. And hoped her voice didn't sound as hollow to him as it did to her. The knot in her stomach was now boulder-sized. She had to work to keep her breathing even. She had great faith in Doc, she really did. But —

Praise the Lord, but pass the ammunition: a favorite saying of the grizzled former Army Ranger who'd trained her in wilderness survival, that was what popped into her mind in this moment of extremis. In other words, waiting for rescue was all well and good, but if you wanted to live you'd best get busy saving yourself.

"This your buddy who knocked me out?" Colin took the phone from her.

Bianca nodded. And bent double, twisting herself into a pretzel as she wormed her way down to reach the gas pedal in a quest to see if, perhaps, lifting/prying it up would close the throttle valve — stepping on the gas makes a car go forward because it depresses the mechanism that opens up the throttle valve, which lets air into the engine to mix with the gas — thus stopping the car. But the gas pedal was up, the throttle valve mechanism was in the closed position and impossible to manipulate without going through the metal floor, and the Jeep was still moving.

And picking up speed. At least, she thought it was. The vibration, the hum of the tires, the sensation of hurtling along, was intensified by her being wedged into the foot well. The faint smell of exhaust seeping through the floorboard made her nauseous.

Or maybe what was making her nauseous was burgeoning fear.

"You find a way to stop this thing and we're quits, brother," Colin said into the phone. That's when she knew for sure that he was as alarmed about their potential fate as she was.

"Doing my best." Doc's reply was barely audible. Again Bianca pictured him at Lifson's computer. Popping up, taking a steadying breath of fresher air, she turned the steering wheel — nothing — hit the gas as well as the brakes just to *see* — nothing. Absolutely no change. The Jeep was driving itself, or, rather, being driven remotely by someone unseen, zipping along and dodging the few cars in front of it as if it had eyes and could see.

And, yes, they were picking up speed. A glance at the speedometer showed her that it was creeping toward forty. On a street with a thirty-five-mile-per-hour limit, that was fast.

Not good.

"Doc?" Her thumb hovered above the

disconnect button. She hated to cut off contact.

"Yeah?"

"I'm hanging up," she told him. "Call me back if something comes up."

"Yeah."

She hated to do it, but she disconnected. Then she held the phone out to Colin. "I'm taking your job offer, okay? You said the kill team would be called off when you got the word out. So get the word out. I'm in."

"You know I know you're lying, right?"

"Does it matter? Make the damned call."

He took the phone from her, but shook his head. "You think the people I work for take calls from any random cell phone? That's not the way they operate. We communicate through authorized channels only."

"You have a phone number to call, don't you?" His expression told her that he did. *"Try."*

His mouth twisted. Then he punched in a number, hit the speaker button. The phone rang once, twice. A click as the call was picked up made Bianca's pulse quicken with hope. Then a voice recording said, "We're sorry. You have reached a number that is disconnected or that is no longer in service. If you feel you have reached this recording in error, please hang up and —"

He disconnected. "I can keep trying, use other numbers even, but the result's not going to change, and we don't have that kind of time."

Disappointment felt thick in her throat. Well, she should have known that nothing was ever that easy. She gave a nod of reluctant acceptance.

"You armed?" she asked as he dropped the phone back into the console. "With anything besides the Glock 17 in your ankle holster, I mean?"

He gave her a narrow-eyed look. "A knife in my shoe."

"That's it?"

"Sorry, I left my AK-47 at home. What about you? Besides the throwing star necklace, that is. That sexy garter belt got anything lethal in it?"

"A switchblade. A garrote. My earrings are *bo-shuriken.*" Her favorites for special occasions when she had reason to fear for her safety, they were long, dangly crystal dazzlers with needlelike centers. He frowned at them. "Japanese throwing darts," she explained.

"I know what *bo-shuriken* are." His eyes slid over her. "No gun?"

"You know, when I got dressed this morning, I didn't know you were coming. If I'd known, the answer might be different, but as it is, the throwing star and the rest are it."

"So we're facing a well-armed, highly trained and extremely lethal CIA kill team with one gun, two knives and some jewelry between us."

"When you put it like that —" She broke off as their eyes met.

"Piece of cake," he said.

She had to smile.

"They don't need to get up close and personal to kill us," he said.

This time the look they exchanged was grim.

"We need to get out of the car," she said.

"Yep." Clambering to his knees, holding on to the seat backs for balance against the Jeep's rocking, he shimmied/squeezed into the back seat. At any other time, watching him lever his six-foot-three-inch frame through the few inches of space available to him would have made her laugh. This was not that time.

"How long do you think we have?" She couldn't quite keep the tension out of her voice.

"They'll want as few witnesses as possible,

so at a guess we've got till we're out of the city."

Roughly fifteen minutes, then, was her estimate, and she thanked God for urban sprawl. Fifteen minutes she could work with.

The Jeep changed lanes again as it dodged a gray sedan emerging from a McDonald's. Grimacing, she looked ahead for possible obstacles: some cars, a few red lights. She knew this street — there were warehouses and a dock down at the end of it, complete with security fences and guards. The river was to the left; Talmadge Bridge was coming up. To the right was the entire city of Savannah. And beyond that — the world.

Bottom line was, they could be headed anywhere. She wet her lips as anxiety dried her mouth. Realizing that she was glad Colin was trapped with her didn't make her feel any better. He was, of course, a second trained body to fight, but that wasn't entirely it, and she didn't care to speculate on exactly what the rest of *it* was. Survive first, soul search later, she ordered herself.

"This isn't aimed at you. It's aimed at me." She spoke with far more sangfroid than she was feeling as she studied the interior of the door. No way to wedge even the slimmest tool between the door and the

133

window to hit the lock mechanism; thanks to the bulletproofing, the fit was too tight.

"Looks to me like we're in it together."

A glance in the rearview mirror revealed that he was trying the door handles and the window switches.

"Just think, if you'd minded your own business and left me alone, *you* wouldn't be in this fix."

"And if you weren't so bloody pigheaded, we'd both be on a plane right now and neither one of us would be in this fix."

"Like being in your power and the power of whoever you're working for would be so much better."

"Five Eyes. I told you. And in case you haven't quite picked up on what's happening, somebody's trying to kill us here. How much bloody worse could it get?"

"Who knows? You already threatened my friends and my business."

"Anything I could do to them beats the hell out of us being dead."

Fair point. She didn't say it. Instead her response was a scornful grunt as she ran her hands searchingly over the hard, smooth plastic of the door panel.

The ironic thing was, she could break into just about any car ever made in a matter of minutes. Breaking out of a car, however, was trickier, because the locks providing easy access were on the outside of the doors. To get to them from the inside without being able to use some kind of makeshift slim-jim would require digging into the door itself: doable but time-consuming. Especially given all the custom reinforcements she'd added to the Jeep.

What could she say? It had seemed like a good idea at the time.

She went for something potentially quicker, reaching up under her skirt to yank the knife from her garter belt then grabbing every wire she could find. If she was lucky, she might be able to kill the flow of electricity to the battery or fuel pump, which would in theory cause the car to stop.

In a series of quick, fierce movements she sliced through wire after wire.

At the same time Colin kicked savagely at the rear windows and doors. *Smash, smash, smash, smash.*

The radio shut off right in the middle of Neil Diamond's ode to Sweet Caroline. The windshield wipers stopped midswish. In the back seat, Colin muttered, "Ow!"

From the disgruntled tone of that pained *ow*, she gathered that he'd come to the conclusion that brute strength wasn't the answer. Just as she'd figured out that cutting every last wire she could reach — which she'd done — wasn't going to accomplish anything much besides stilling the windshield wipers and silencing Neil Diamond.

Small mercies, maybe, but no real help.

"Hurt your leg?" she asked, with no more than the barest hint of snark. After trying the brake, steering wheel and gearshift again in a series of quick, hopeful actions without any apparent change in anything, she freed the lock pick from her garter belt and used it to attack the door handle in hopes of going through that vulnerable spot to access the door's locking mechanism.

"Having any luck with your undie armory?" he fired back.

The door handle broke away from the door. Beneath it was a small hole penetrating a layer of insulation — and a solid steel panel, courtesy of the bulletproofing she'd had done to the Jeep. The hole was too small for the pick to even fit inside.

"Damn it," she said.

"I take that as a 'no.' " He was in the process of letting down a seat so that he could more easily access the rear cargo area.

Grimacing by way of an answer, she grabbed the phone with the intention of calling 911 and reporting a kidnapping in progress, namely theirs. Whatever the repercussions of dealing with the police might be, it couldn't be as bad as what the CIA had in store for them. Although what could the police do — set up a roadblock for the Jeep to smash into? Not good with the speedometer approaching (she looked and winced) forty-five and no way to stop; shoot out the tires? That was a terrible wreck waiting to happen — she wasn't quite sure. Anything, though, was better than what they were currently doing, which was going not-so-gently into that good night.

Smash. Smash. Colin kicked savagely at the cargo door window as she started to punch in the emergency number.

"Who bulletproofs their damned windows?"

She paused, glancing back at him. "Oh, I don't know — the person everybody is trying to kill? The same person who armor-plates the chassis, by the way, which added extra weight to the doors, which meant the locks had to be reinforced, which is why kicking at everything is just not going to work."

"What?"

"Yeah," she confirmed, and turned her attention back to the phone in her hand. Before she could punch in the final 1, it rang. Only one person had that number.

Answering, she said, "Doc?" Then when he didn't answer added anxiously, "Doc? Are you there?"

"God *damn* it." Colin slammed one more vicious kick at the cargo door with predictable results. "You couldn't have told me that sooner?"

"Need to know." She threw that at him before saying "Doc?" again into the phone.

Colin's less-than-polite answer was lost to posterity as Doc's disembodied voice came at her.

"I screwed up. They're onto me." The shrill words tumbling over each other riveted her attention to the phone in her hand, and never mind the large and irate man cursing under his breath in the back. "Boss, they've got an intrusion detection system I never saw coming and it made me. I'm trying to pop your door locks but they're erasing my code as fast as I can write it and I —"

His voice dissolved into an incomprehensible garble.

"Doc? *Doc?*" Even as she called to him, the screen went black except for a blue circle swirling in the middle. "Get out of there! Can you hear me? *Run!*"

Visions of a team of government assassins storming Lifson's office to take out Doc made Bianca sweat. Calling his name while frantically punching buttons did nothing but make her crazy. There was no reply, the phone itself didn't make a sound and the blue circle stayed on the black screen. She had little doubt that the call was being jammed. There was no way she could get to him, nothing she could do. Glancing back at Colin, she said, "Did you hear what Doc said?" Her voice sounded harsh from being kept so tightly under control. Giving way to emotion did no one any good.

He responded with an affirmative grunt. "At least we don't have to worry about the call being tracked and leading them to us. They already know where we are."

That display of pure self-interest narrowed her eyes. "Really? That's what you're concerned about?"

Crouched in the cargo area, he was pulling up his pant leg to, she saw, access the gun in his ankle holster.

"If you're worried about your friend, I wouldn't. He doesn't strike me as being stupid enough to just sit there and let himself be found."

Good point. A lightning review of Doc's handiness with computers raised a fair degree of certainty that he would have put safeguards in place to prevent his work from being traced back to a specific location. And the fact that Colin now had weapon in hand proved a potent distraction.

"What are you doing?"

He pivoted to face the cargo door. "Getting ready to shoot the fuck out of the bloody lock."

"No! Wait! Stop! Steel panels in the doors! *Ricochet!*" She sang out the urgent warning as the Jeep hung a sharp left onto a four-lane street. The unexpected move threw her against the door and knocked him on his ass. The Jeep picked up speed. The speedometer read fifty with a steady upward crawl. The light spilling into the interior changed character, grew dimmer and colder —

It was the glow of white Christmas lights.

Bianca had shed her coat and was scrambling into the back seat as the import of that registered. A comprehensive glance out the windows confirmed that they were zooming up the access ramp to Talmadge Bridge at the approximate speed of a bullet train. The thing was, the other end of this section of the bridge, the one that led into South Carolina, was temporarily closed for repairs. The only place they were going right now was Hutchinson Island, where, because it was a — wait for it — island, their ride would of necessity shortly be over. The question was, where exactly would they end up? Besides the Westin and the convention center, there was an unfinished motorsport track and a fair number of abandoned buildings and lots of parcels of undeveloped land.

The better to murder you in, my dear.

What felt like a cold hand dug its claws into her chest.

She said, "We're going over the bridge. Only thing it leads to right now is a little speck of an island in the middle of the river."

"You trying to tell me that the end is near?" He crouched on the balls of his feet. His weapon was in his hand. The slight quirk at the corner of his mouth alerted her that that was supposed to be a joke. She was so wired she couldn't even smile.

"Yes." Crawling past him into the cargo area, she fought to maintain her balance as the Jeep whipped around a gray Hyundai and ran right up on the rear of a red Chevy Malibu that at the last minute moved over to let them pass. "Put the damned gun away and help me."

"Help you what?" He dropped the pistol into his jacket pocket.

"Kick the door open. If we both do it together —" She sat on the cargo area floor with her back wedged against the remaining upright second-row seat for leverage and let her words trail off. The implication was that their combined strength just might do the trick. Truth was, much as she hated to face it, extreme strength had been built into her DNA. If ever there was a moment to test what degree of strength they were talking about, she figured this was it. Having him help her kick provided cover if she did manage to break the door open. And it was always possible that the additional strength he brought to the table might be the little extra bit of oomph that did the trick.

With a nod he positioned himself beside her. Their arms bumped as the Jeep bounced and swayed. Both of them sat flat on the rough pile of the carpet, legs bent, right feet ready, hands braced beside them for support. Her black pump with its hidden spike in the heel looked positively dainty next to his black lace-up oxford, which was probably the one with the concealed knife. Her slender, black-stockinged leg looked fragile next to the muscular, trouser-clad length of his.

What was it they said about appearances?

"On three. Get ready to jump." Colin's voice was tight. He knew as well as she did that jumping from a moving vehicle, especially one traveling as fast as the Jeep was, was perilously close to suicidal. Like hers, his eyes were on the dark expanse of asphalt unspooling behind the car. Following cars posed a danger, too, although there was enough distance between them and the closest vehicle that in theory it should be possible to roll to the side of the road without getting flattened. The Jeep was on the bridge proper now, speeding toward the apex, which was a good eighteen stories above the ribbon of black water that was the river. Outlined by the soaring cables with their wrapping of twinkly white lights, the view encompassed the lit-up waterfront and the city and even the bay beyond and was spectacular.

Too bad she wasn't in the right frame of mind to appreciate it.

"On three," she agreed.

Colin said, "One —"

Or, rather, he started to say it. He didn't even get the word all the way out before all four doors plus the cargo door popped open. A vortex of chilly, river-scented air swirled through the Jeep. It caught Bianca's hair, whipped it around her face. The unexpected blinding, coupled with the sudden onslaught of sound — the swoosh of the wind, the growl of the tires, the rattle of the flapping doors — was momentarily disorienting.

"Doc." Pushing her hair out of her face, Bianca acknowledged the probable architect of their deliverance with a gasp of relief: it had to mean that he was alive, free and functioning.

Then the Jeep, with a fresh burst of speed, made a sharp right turn, careened across the adjacent lane, hit the low concrete barrier separating the road from a whole lot of nothing and flipped skyward, sailing between the twinkling cables like a Falcons' football being kicked through the goalposts for the extra point.

Thrown head over heels, Bianca saw a jumble of Christmas lights and thick black clouds and gray carpet and seat backs and Colin, with a yell, being ejected through the open cargo door. In the dizzying moment before reality took hold and she fully understood what was happening, she smashed into the corner between the upright seat and the wall — and felt the Jeep tilt nose-down and plummet like a stone toward the river.

9

Bianca's heart shot into her throat. Her stomach went into free fall right along with the Jeep. She grabbed on to a wall-hung seat belt to stop herself from being sucked out, clung for dear life and screamed like a steam whistle.

Not all the souped-up DNA in the world was enough to enable her to survive an eighteen-story fall, she feared.

The headlong plunge was interrupted by a violent jerk. She bounced into the wall before falling back against the seat behind her. The Jeep's death drop slowed then stopped abruptly as its back end seemed to get hung up on something. Amid metallic groaning and ripping sounds the Jeep swung through the air in a slow, terrifying arc. Whatever was happening, she knew with a bone-deep certainty that she had no more than fractions of a second in which to act.

Using the wall beside her for a foothold,

nails digging into the carpet, she surged toward where the cargo door opened to the night.

A quick look around as she reached the edge confirmed the danger: the river waiting far below was shiny black, already collecting wisps of fog that would be thick soon, outlined by the lights along the banks. The Jeep's headlights speared down into the darkness, illuminating the trajectory of its swing only to peter out long before reaching the surface of the water. Closer at hand, she saw that the rear bumper was caught in a tangle of still-twinkling Christmas lights. Suspended nose-down in empty space, the Jeep swayed precariously as the bumper slowly ripped away.

Glancing up revealed that she was some twenty-five feet below the bottom of the bridge. Everywhere in her immediate vicinity she saw nothing but air. The resulting butterfly stampede in her stomach underlined exactly how much trouble she was in.

"Jump!" Colin roared. Bianca spotted him hanging by both hands from one of the under-bridge girders and was conscious of a glad little tingle because he wasn't dead. She —

Rrrip.

Just like that, with no more warning than

a shriek of rending metal, the bumper gave way. The Jeep fell. Galvanized by fear, she launched herself skyward and barely managed to grab on to a single twisted strand of the net of cords that still held the now-detached bumper. Swinging wildly through space as the Jeep nose-dived into the river, she watched the splashdown and shuddered.

If she'd still been in that car, she would have died.

Which wasn't to say she was safe where she was.

Sniper. A burst of adrenaline raced like speed through her veins as every instinct she possessed screamed the warning. The team behind the Boston brakes had to be close by to have reacted so swiftly to Doc's opening of the doors. They would have seen the Jeep go over. They might have seen her jump out. They could be targeting her even now.

Doing the Tarzan thing with the Christmas lights as she was, she was a sitting duck. She did an instantaneous, horrified reconnoiter: no telltale red dot on her person gave warning of an incoming round; the bridge was the only viable vantage point for a gunman. She looked up —

Snap. Snap. Snap.

She dropped about five feet and almost lost her grip. Her heart hammered. Her breath caught. The wire cut into her palms. Her feet dangled in thin air. Hanging on desperately, she swung in a slow circle as the weight of the bumper plus her body generated unwanted momentum. Instinctively she glanced down: the drop was dizzying, terrifying. Forcing herself to look away, she very gingerly tried pulling herself up hand over hand, which was difficult because her palms were sweaty with fear and the plastic-coated wire was thin and slippery. To add to the problem, she had to maneuver around the tangled-up bumper before bringing her legs and feet into play. Attempting anything too athletic or too vigorous was out of the question: she was afraid the wire might break.

So she hung and swung and inched carefully upward, while at the same time looking to the bridge in an attempt to identify what had caused the snapping sounds and her subsequent sudden drop. She saw Colin executing an athletic maneuver of his own that, if successful, would put him on top of the beam that had saved him. And she saw —

Her heart skipped a beat.

Forget worrying about a sniper. The

Christmas lights that were her lifeline were pulling away from their moorings on the suspension cables. Whatever had secured them was never meant to withstand the weight of a human being and a bumper dangling from them, much less a car crashing through them. Even as she oscillated like a pendulum some three stories beneath the bridge, the trusses anchoring the strands cradling the bumper — and the one to which she clung — were giving up the ghost one by one.

Snap. Snap.

She dropped another foot, swung wildly. Dislodged, the bumper fell, just missing her as it hurtled down into the darkness below.

A section of lights, including the strand she was clinging to, went dark.

Afraid every second that the remaining moorings would rip away, Bianca threw caution to the wind and swarmed up the wires like a monkey on a vine.

Not to the surface, not to the roadway from whence the Jeep had fallen and where the CIA kill team might very well be lying in wait. She reached the bridge's underside, the web of I-beams and girders that underlay the concrete, used her body weight to whip up enough momentum to allow her to swing toward them and leaped onto a steel beam. Landing on her hands and the balls of her feet, she grabbed on to the cold metal edges of the beam and went to her knees. Gusts of winds buffeted her, whistling softly as they curled back on themselves against the bottom of the bridge then hurtled down. She braced herself against their force. The slippery perch was no more than a foot wide. There was nothing nearby with which to steady herself. A fall would mean certain death.

So don't fall.

Movement in the shadows made her heart lurch as she caught it out of the corner of her eye. It was, thank God, only Colin. Having managed to pull himself up onto the beam he'd been hanging from, he was bent nearly double as he crept cautiously along it. He acknowledged her with a raised hand, but didn't call out to her. He, too, must be thinking that the hunters couldn't be far away.

She stayed where she was for a moment, getting her balance, pulling herself together. Her heart thumped. Her pulse pounded in her ears. She was short of breath, shaken, bruised — but she was alive, which was the important part. Taking a deep, controlled breath and then another, she consciously worked to slow her heart rate and pulse, regulate her breathing.

Go. Go. Go.

Thank God that her shoes were designed to be versatile! Twisting the heels to one side, she pulled them off and stuck the spikes in her belt, leaving herself in a pair of rubber-soled flats that she was profoundly thankful for, given that the beam was slimy with moss and dew and God only knew what else. She got her feet squarely beneath her. Then, bent over so that she could hold on to the rough metal edges with both hands, she scuttled along the beam like a hunchbacked spider.

"You all right?" Colin reached the junction of their beams a moment before she did. A large, dark shape in the gloom, he waited for her to catch up to him.

"Yes," she replied. "You?"

He nodded and moved off in rough approximation of an offensive lineman's four-point stance. She followed in spider mode until they reached the bridge's front apron, where, still concealed from view by the concrete drop, they were able to straighten to their full heights. Using the support beams embedded in the bridge's floor as a makeshift handrail, they cautiously side-stepped toward solid ground.

Neither of them had to say what they both

knew: they didn't have much time in which to make a getaway. The kill team would be coming after them hard.

The knowledge made her breathing quicken.

Vibrations and traffic sounds from the bridge confirmed that it continued in use, but shouts overhead told Bianca that at least some of the cars above them had stopped, that the Jeep's plunge into the water had been seen, that people were leaning over the side at that moment, looking down into the river. Were their would-be murderers among them? There wasn't any way to know. She had no doubt that help had been summoned, that police were on the way. Police boats would be coming, too, as would, almost certainly, a boat containing members of the CIA kill team.

The good news was that, unless a Black Hawk suddenly swooped down out of nowhere, or members of the kill team rappelled over the side of the bridge, which wasn't likely given the number of potential witnesses, they were relatively safe for the moment. With only minimal illumination from the Christmas lights and the distant waterfront reaching the grid of beams, they were hidden by darkness and sheltered beneath the bridge. Absent the Black Hawk, a sniper's only possible shot was from the river, would have to be made with the aid of night-vision equipment and be angled almost straight up. The shooter would need a boat or a Jet Ski or something similar to reach any viable spot to launch an attack. Since she was almost 100 percent sure that the Jeep's detour over the side had been precipitated by Doc's opening of the doors and not planned in advance, a sniper in a boat would not already be in place.

Looking down — mistake; it made her dizzy, so that one glance was all she allowed herself — she saw the *Georgia Queen* riverboat, appearing not much larger than a matchbox car from that height, identifiable by its lights and distinctive shape as it steamed across the river; a barge with its accompanying tugboat coming upriver from the bay; docked pleasure craft and fishing boats and all manner of water-going vessels along the banks; lots of lights and activity, but no apparent immediate threat.

In a perfect world, the kill team would not have seen her leap from the Jeep. They would presume that she had plunged with it into the river and died.

If anyone lived in a perfect world, it certainly wasn't her.

Negotiating the places where the beams

connected was the hardest part. Her fingers grew cold and stiff from hanging on so tightly. Her clothing was, she discovered, all wrong for the occasion. The wind bit through the thin knit of her dress. The short hemline left most of her legs exposed, and her stockings were soon in tatters and provided no protection whatsoever for her skin. Edging around a vertical post in her figure-hugging skirt was awkward — and dangerous. Put a foot wrong, and she was dead. She tried not to watch Colin. He was much bigger than she was, clearly lacked her gymnastics training and, despite the fact that he was at least wearing pants, several times seemed like a prime candidate for escapee most likely to plunge to his death. Since there was nothing she could do to help him — not that she particularly wanted to help him, she reminded herself severely — she did her best to keep her focus on their surroundings.

Screaming sirens approached at speed. She had little doubt that they belonged to first responders racing to the scene, which made it even more imperative that they get out of there fast. Now that it appeared she had a reasonable chance of escaping the kill team, she had no intention of complicating the situation by bringing in the local PD, some of whom she knew and all of whom would ask endless questions.

What scared her most was imagining what the kill team must be doing right at that moment. Unless the takeover of the Jeep had been via satellite or drone from some distant location, they were on the scene. By now at least some of them should have found a boat and be heading for where the Jeep had hit the water. The stripe of darkened lights running up the bridge marked the spot where the Jeep had gone over, which should make its location in the river easy to pinpoint. They would search, or they would watch the official police search, until they were satisfied as to her fate.

Or not.

If they'd seen her jump, they would come looking under the bridge. And not just looking: bringing every high-tech tool the best-equipped intelligence service in the world had at its disposal.

Thermal imaging, anyone?

That was the thought that sent an icy finger of dread running down her spine.

Hurry, hurry, hurry. Fortunately, she didn't have to say it aloud. When it came to the need for speed, she and Colin were clearly of one mind.

Toward the end, the bridge and the beams

supporting it slanted steeply downward, making it harder than ever not to lose her footing. The brackish smell of the water grew strong. The river was over a mile wide, and a thickening layer of fog now floated above it so that it was impossible to identify anything very far out with any degree of accuracy. A flotilla of boat lights that, seen through the fog, looked like a swarm of fireflies seemed to be converging on the approximate place where the Jeep had disappeared beneath the water. But so far it appeared that no organized effort was under way to search the river or the banks for possible survivors.

She had no doubt at all that the clock was ticking down on that.

We've got to get out of here.

Colin hit the ground first, his long body unfolding from the beam while they were still at a height of maybe fifteen feet. He hung from his hands and let go, his feet crunching on a carpet of small rocks and scrub grass as he landed. She would have done the same thing, although given the difference in their heights she would have done it several yards farther along where the drop would have been shorter, because she really didn't want to risk a sprained ankle. But he immediately stepped beneath where she still sidestepped along the beam and held up his hands to her.

"Come here," he said. Even to her, his voice was barely audible above the lapping of the river and the rumble of overhead traffic. Farther away but approaching quickly, the screaming sirens eliminated the possibility that anyone outside their immediate vicinity could hear him. Still she tensed: ears that were high-tech enough could pick up the drop of a pin on Mars.

In the interest of getting out of there as quickly as possible she swung down into his arms.

10

Colin caught her around the waist, steadying her as she dropped. As Bianca found her feet, she looked up at him. The Christmas lights cast the hard planes and angles of his face into sharp relief. His mouth looked grim, his eyes black. He was handsome, familiar, a welcome presence in the dark. She felt a pull of connection, of affinity: *we're in this together.* For the briefest of moments, they stood chest to chest, her hands on his shoulders, his on her waist. She could feel the size and strength of his hands through her dress, and she was reminded that she liked the way they felt. Now that she was wearing flats, the top of her head just about reached his chin and she liked the difference in their heights, too. The width of his shoulders and the solid muscularity of his arms and chest appealed to her. So did his ripped abs and the powerful length of his legs. He was built the way she liked men to be built: tall and hard and spare, like weapons. As their bodies pressed close, the electric awareness that had existed between them from the beginning flared, activating that part of her that was instinctively, atavistically female. It was obvious — their bodies were *very* close — that she was having a reciprocal effect on him.

No point in trying to hide from the fact that she was still majorly attracted to him. The thing was, it didn't matter. That fierce sexual tug was a residual from her old life that was no longer valid. Given what she now knew about herself, getting involved with him was never going to happen. It was not a life choice that was open to her any longer.

A dark trickle of what could only be blood ran down the left side of his forehead. Her gaze flicked to that instead of meeting his eyes, which were searching her face.

"Your head's bleeding." Her tone was brusque as she pulled out of his arms.

"Is it? I must have caught a sharp edge." He dashed a forearm across the wound.

She was already walking away from him, moving swiftly toward the gravel service road that led to a ramshackle dry dock and boat storage facility. Guardian Consulting had provided security for a nearby, now-defunct sailing club once upon a time, so she was familiar with the area. It was December: the boatyard was closed. If she was lucky, there was a pickup truck she could steal, the one that the workers used to tow runabouts from the river. It was very old, which was just what she wanted. And that would be because, thanks to her late, unlamented most recent brush with death, she'd had it with any vehicle with onboard electronics.

According to everything she'd been taught, the thing to do in this situation was rush immediately toward the heavily populated tourist area and try to hide among the crowd. The problem was, that was exactly what every operative was taught, and what the kill team, assuming they didn't think she was dead, would expect her to do.

So she was doing the opposite. If they knew she lived, they'd soon be scouring the riverbank. But she was gambling with her life that their first action would be to post lookouts along the routes heading away from the river toward the crowds.

When they expect you to zig, zag.

The first swampy shoals of the river began maybe a hundred feet to her left. Coffee-colored water slurped against the muddy shore. The huge black rectangle of the barge she had spotted earlier nosed silently beneath the bridge. The fact that she could see all its running lights through the fog told her that there were no vessels between her and it. What she'd been concerned about was that the kill team might be running a boat without lights, but if so, it wasn't between the bank where they were and the barge. By this time the screaming sirens were on the bridge, and traffic was backing up in the surrounding streets. The stroboscopic flash from the police cruisers gave the darkness a hellish quality. Bianca peered suspiciously into the shadowy area where the bank rose steeply before flattening out into the streets and shops of the tourist area: lots of weeds, trash, bottles and what appeared to be a homeless man wrapped in a blanket lying fast asleep. No physical threat but — a potential witness to their survival? From the look of him, a bomb could have gone off beside him and he would have slept on.

A more committed operative would undoubtedly have killed him just to make sure he could never talk about what he probably hadn't even seen.

Bianca looked away. In her mind, she could almost hear Mason, her not-father, jeer.

"Your knees are bleeding." Colin caught up. She didn't even glance at him. Now that they had survived, she hadn't yet made up her mind what her next move should be as far as he was concerned. Ditch him and go her own way — or not?

"I'll live." She flicked a look down to verify that, yes, her knees were exposed through the gaping holes their escape had torn in her stockings, and, yes, they had scrapes on them that were dark with blood. She hadn't even noticed that they stung until he'd pointed out the damage.

"This time." He dropped something — his jacket, she discovered as it settled around her — over her shoulders. It was fine wool, silk-lined, warm from his body, and smelled faintly of soap and some kind of woodsy aftershave. She didn't like that she liked the smell. She also didn't like that he had given her his jacket. Having a man, especially this man, take care of her was not, repeat *not*, the dream. She didn't want it. She didn't need it.

But keeping him thinking of her as a woman he needed to protect was probably to her advantage. Also, she *was* cold. In the spirit of not looking a gift horse in the mouth she accepted the gesture with no more than a satiric murmur of "Aren't you the gentleman?" even as she thrust her arms into the sleeves for ease of movement. She flipped the cuffs back to free her hands, and, not coincidentally, stuck her hand in the pocket for the weapon he'd dropped in there earlier.

It was missing. A sideways glance found that he was carrying it, held straight down by his side in a way that would allow him to snap it up and fire at a split second's notice.

She would have found that reassuring, except for the fact that a pistol was basically useless against most of what she suspected the kill team would throw at them if they were spotted.

"I try." They were moving together now, striding along the gravel road, keeping their heads down as the bright blue bursts from the police cars lit up the night. The dampness of the rising fog twined around her lower body like a cat.

The thickening mist was welcome in that it helped conceal them. Unfortunately, it also helped conceal anyone who might be coming after them.

On that thought, suddenly every unidentifiable shape took on a sinister cast.

She was, she realized, glad she wasn't alone. And that was bad.

She flicked a look at him. "You can take

off now, you know. They're not after you. They're after me. Anything happens to you, it's just collateral damage."

He snorted. She took that as an *I'm not going anywhere.* Hard to face the fact that she was relieved.

He said, "How about we put our heads together and come up with a plan that gets us both the hell out of here?"

"I have a plan."

"Oh, yeah? No collaborative effort, no 'what do you think we ought to do'? Just 'I have a plan'?"

"I'm the one they're trying to kill. That means I'm the one who gets to call the shots."

"So what's your plan?"

"Steal a car. Get gone."

"I like that. Short and sweet." He paused, glancing around. The area they were walking through was dark, deserted, swampy and full of weeds. The gravel road was the only solid ground. The good news was, there really wasn't anywhere in the near vicinity for a wannabe assassin to launch an attack. The bad news was, the attack didn't have to be launched from the near vicinity. "You happen to know where you're going to find a car to steal?"

"I do happen to know that, yes."

"I was betting you did."

By now the bridge was crawling with cops. Fire trucks raced up the ramp. A searchlight raked the river, its white beam sweeping the dark water, making Bianca shiver. She'd come so close to dying in that river tonight. She still *could* die tonight.

Thwap. Thwap. Thwap. Thwap.

Her heart leaped into her throat as the heavy beat of a helicopter's rotors reached her ears. She instinctively glanced around even before the aircraft, sleek and dark against the glittery Savannah skyline, came into view. She looked forward again and down so that the pale oval of her face wouldn't be immediately visible to anyone inside the chopper. It was flying low as it passed almost directly above them, heading toward the river. The sound of the rotors drowned out everything else. Its searchlight missed them by maybe twenty feet. Every nerve ending she possessed screamed *run.* Training won out: she didn't.

Don't so much as flinch. If anyone looking out the chopper windows saw them, they were just two people walking along the river. In the dark. In a neglected area with nothing touristy around.

Okay. Now she was just psyching herself out.

"Steady." Colin grabbed her hand, held tight. She figured her sudden attack of jitters must have somehow communicated themselves to him. Flicking a look at him, her eyes widened. His white shirt was dirty and torn, but — white. Would someone in the helicopter notice it, notice them? A sniper with a silenced weapon positioned inside the chopper could take them both out in less than ten seconds without anyone on the ground even realizing. Trying to cover it up by, say, giving him back his coat would only draw more attention if anyone was watching, so, gritting her teeth, she wrapped her fingers around his and kept walking. Two people, a guy and a girl, out for a romantic stroll in the moonlight. Except there was no moonlight. There was fog. And — *Stop it.*

"Police chopper," she breathed when the thing was out over the water and turning toward the bridge. The logo on the side made her briefly giddy with relief. Moments later they rounded a bend and the boatyard came into sight. She wiggled the fingers of the hand he was gripping. "You can let go now."

"So you can try ditching me again?" His voice was cool. His hand was firm and warm. "I don't think so."

"If I wanted to ditch you, you'd be ditched."

But she didn't make an issue of it, and in any case he had to let go when they reached the six-foot-tall chain-link fence that enclosed the boatyard. Rusty and decrepit, it sported a tired double gate that was secured with a heavy chain and padlock. Bianca wouldn't have bothered to pick the lock — vaulting one of the sagging spots in the fence would have been faster — but when they left they were going to have to exit through that gate, so she did. In a matter of seconds, which elicited an admiring if under-the-breath whistle from Colin.

"You're good."

"I know. Leave it open," she said, referring to the gate as he followed her inside.

"Yes, ma'am."

A single light above the door of the shed-like office building left most of the lot in darkness. The truck was parked beside the building. Just inside the pool of light.

Of course it was. It had been that kind of day.

It took her approximately twenty seconds to get the ancient Ford F-150's door open. The whole time that she was standing there bathed in the bluish glow of the mercury vapor fixture the skin between her shoulder blades prickled in anticipation of taking a bullet. The thing about stealing this particular truck was, due to the boatyard's inactivity in winter, it might not be missed for weeks.

The keys were tucked above the driver's sun flap: second place she looked after under the floor mat. She shut the door, started the engine.

Colin slid onto the other end of the peeling brown vinyl bench seat while she wrestled with the clutch and balky stick shift. Which worked for her, really, because having him on board before she had a chance to drive away at least temporarily solved the problem of whether or not she should take off and leave him. Disappearing into the ether of criminal connections she'd grown up in was tempting. The question to ponder was, could she really disappear?

They'd found her in Macau, they'd found her in Moscow, and now they'd found her in Savannah.

Bumping out onto the gravel road, she reflected that she liked that Colin didn't give her any macho crap about wanting to drive, until it occurred to her that as long as she was driving he didn't have to worry about her jumping out of the truck and taking off at, say, the first red light.

She gave him some side-eye, wondering if that was really his motivation.

"Lights?" His tone questioned her choice to turn on the headlights. Given that the truck was the only vehicle on the gravel road, the lights seemed especially conspicuous.

She'd debated it, too. "If anyone spots the truck driving without lights, they'll *know* it's us."

For the same reason, she was careful not to drive too fast. No squealing tires or spurting gravel for her. Just an ordinary couple out for an ordinary Friday night in their junker of a pickup.

He grunted acceptance of her reasoning.

"Head for I-95 North," he said when they left the gravel behind for an actual paved street, which happened to be Lathrop Avenue.

She looked at him, raised her brows. They were driving toward the city center, and she made no move to change directions. The street wasn't particularly busy, but there were enough other vehicles to provide cover. Unless they were really unlucky, no one would be looking for a battered pickup.

"You're not still going to give me grief about this, are you?" His face tightened with impatience. "I'm going to say this one more time. You have to take the job. They almost succeeded in killing you tonight, and unless we can back them off they won't quit until they do succeed. And now that they know where you live, they won't just be coming after you. They'll be coming after everybody you love. They'll hurt anybody they have to hurt, and kill anybody they have to kill, to get to you."

As much as she hated to face it, she knew it was true.

"I'm thinking about it," she said.

"If I were you, I'd think fast." His voice was grim. "They could find us again at any time."

She knew he was right. The prospect made her insides twist. Lightning images of Doc and Evie and Hay spun through her head. She remembered how the CIA had kidnapped Marin and Margery, Mason's seven-year-old daughter and his wife, and held them captive to force him to reveal himself. They would have killed them, too, along with Mason and Bianca, at that black site in Heiligenblut, Austria, if she and Mason hadn't managed to turn the tables on them and rescue his family and escape.

She remembered the other Nomads — the dead little babies in the tubes. Twice now she'd barely escaped joining them.

Bottom line was, she really didn't want to die. She didn't want anyone she loved to die.

Alexander Groton, the recently deceased former head of the Defense Advance Research Projects Agency (DARPA), had wanted her to come and work for them. He'd actually issued the job offer while holding her at gunpoint. The alternative to agreeing was he would shoot her on the spot like a rabid dog.

She'd said no and lived to tell the tale. So far.

But the hard truth was, having a CIA kill team on her trail made her long-term survival unlikely.

One of the reasons she'd so vehemently refused Groton's offer was that she didn't trust him or the CIA. She didn't trust those agents of her own government not to lie to her, not to use her until they had no more use for her and then kill her. She was beyond wary of putting herself within their reach.

But she did, to a certain extent, trust Colin. Call it a working trust. Or trust in progress. Subject to change at any time.

She didn't know Five Eyes. But Five Eyes was not the CIA. Five Eyes had not killed her mother, had not murdered forty-seven little babies and their gestational mothers. Five Eyes had not initiated the experiment that had made her what she was.

Going to work for them might, in fact, be her best weapon against the CIA, and her best shot at staying alive. Unless and until she could figure something else out.

"Fine," she said. "I'm on board. For real this time. I'll take the job."

"Hallelujah. She sees the light at last." Glancing around, he pointed at the next intersection. "Take a right up here, and head for I-95."

Reaching the intersection, she hung the requested right, then cast him a sour look. "And just for the record, you don't *own* me. Not in any way, shape or form. Are we clear?"

The merest suspicion of a smile touched the corners of his mouth.

"As glass," he said.

11

An hour later, the Gulfstream V was wheels up and Colin was accessing the plane's secure communications channel to brief his employer.

"I've acquired the asset," he said when Jeffrey Bowling, Britain's Director of GCHQ (Government Communications Headquarters), came on the line. Knowing what he knew — that there were eager would-be listeners out there, and that every communication channel, even one as secure as this, had the potential for being breached — he didn't want to get more specific.

Bowling had been one of the tight cabal of Five Eye spymasters who had contracted with Cambridge Solutions for this operation, and that had been because none of them wanted to get their or their agency's hands dirty. Outsourcing possibly problematic missions was a time-honored tradition with intelligence services in general, and

British intelligence in particular. In fact, 80 percent of the free world's intelligence operations were now in the hands of private companies, in part because outsourcing prevented those who were burdened with government accountability from breaking any laws and also furnished them with plausible deniability if anything should go wrong. Picture it as the government version of a kid breaking a lamp, throwing up his hands and saying *It wasn't me.* The heads-will-roll mentality of many oversight committees coupled with the ever-present threat of exposure in this new era of WikiLeaks had infected many governments with the same paranoia, and had thus created a vast and lucrative shadow world of spies-for-hire of which Cambridge Solutions was a part.

Bowling himself had subsequently green-lighted Colin's choice for a female operative to participate in Part B of this mission; Part A had been under the purview of the Americans. And that separation was in place because the name of the game when it came to minimizing the chances of a leak was *compartmentalize.* If the left hand didn't know what the right hand was doing, the left hand couldn't tell anyone about it.

When Colin referred to "the asset," therefore, Bowling would know whom he meant.

Within minutes of the conversation's conclusion, the information that Beth McAlister/Bianca St. Ives was now one of them would be circulated throughout Five Eyes' ultra-secret STONEGHOST network, without anyone outside their tight little circle knowing precisely what she had been brought on board to do. The CIA would be forced to back the fuck off her.

"Any difficulty?" Bowling's plummy voice conjured up a picture of him as Colin had last seen him: a large, rumpled man in his late sixties, ruddy-faced and heavy-jowled, seated with cigar in hand behind his oversize desk in The Doughnut, as the GCHQ building was known due to its distinctive circle-with-a-hole-in-the-middle shape, which was located in the unremarkable suburbs of Cheltenham.

"Our American cousins arrived right after I did. They did their best to take her out." He'd already briefed Bowling on an edited version of what he knew of her background. For the director's consumption, he'd attributed the CIA's lethal interest in her to her long-standing association with Mason Thayer. Now there, they both had agreed, was a target for assassination everybody could get behind.

Bowling said, "I find it extraordinary that

175

a team like that didn't succeed."

"I'm sure they do, too. Heartwarming if you think about it."

"Quite." Bowling's voice reflected the smile that the thought of the Americans' discomfiture must have brought to his face. "You're sure she's the right person for this job?"

"I am. As I told you, she's one of the best I've ever seen." He heard the note of pride in his own voice and hoped Bowling missed it. The last thing he wanted was for Bowling or anyone else in officialdom to start thinking that his interest in their newly acquired asset was personal.

"I defer to your judgment." Implicit in the words was that Colin would pay a price if things didn't work out. "You know how important this mission is. I don't exaggerate when I tell you that the fate of the free world may well hang in the balance."

"I understand."

"Then get the job done."

Bowling rang off.

Leaning back in the contoured leather chair in the partitioned-off work area in the tail section, Colin stared unseeingly at the blinking banks of computer and communication equipment facing him. The round windows had their shades drawn against the

176

night, and looked for all the world like closed eyes. The tan leather walls and the tan carpet were soothing, as were the low-level lighting and the gentle hum of the plane in flight. He should have felt exhausted, but he didn't: he felt energized.

He'd saved a woman from death at the hands of a CIA kill team, he'd gained the operative he wanted for this job, and, as an added bonus, he'd baited a trap for Thayer, who, if history was a map to the future, would show up in her vicinity again sooner or later. Cambridge Solutions had a contract with Interpol, and he'd made a personal pact with his old friend and mentor Laurent Durand, head of Interpol's Organized and Emerging Crime Program, to bring Thayer in. Like the Mounties, he prided himself on always getting his man. Sometimes it just took a little longer.

So he had in effect killed three birds with one stone, which meant he could chalk it up as a successful day.

Colin opened a drawer and retrieved the specially configured cell phone he'd left there. It was a state-of-the-art "black" phone meant to be used when the communication made over it absolutely, positively had to be secure. It was, among other unique features, totally untrackable. He'd left it behind on the plane out of an excess of caution, because even the best security measures weren't 100 percent foolproof. Ironic to think that he hadn't wanted to risk bringing trouble down on his target's head, given how much trouble had found her anyway. He'd also had a not totally unreasonable fear that she would do something like insist on patting him down, find the phone and have enough knowledge to get past its encryption to discover who and what it was connected to, which he knew would screw the pooch as far as gaining her cooperation was concerned.

The message he needed to send over it now wasn't anything he wanted going out over official channels. He didn't want Bowling or anyone else in the intelligence community picking it up.

I have her, he typed, and hit Send. The message was to Durand, who would know what he meant.

Then he pocketed the phone. Next order of business: bring his new associate up to speed. He'd left her strapped into a forward seat as the plane took off.

He stood up and walked out of the work area. Except for the pilot and copilot, who knew not to leave the cockpit, he and she were alone on the plane. He didn't want anyone else to know exactly who was on board, or to get a look at her.

The success of the operation hinged on her ability to become someone else.

He saw her the instant he started toward the front of the plane. Once he did, she was all he could see.

She sat on the cream-colored leather couch that filled part of one wall. Her head was bent so that a curtain of silky blond hair hid her face. Her red dress clung with loving attention to every one of her killer curves. Its hem was hiked way — *way* — up past midthigh.

Her knees were scraped. That wasn't what he noticed.

She was peeling a torn black stocking down one of her long, slim, impossibly sexy legs.

He was human. He watched. His body responded as male bodies were designed to do.

Damn it.

She pulled the stocking all the way off.

Her skin was tanned and smooth. Like her legs, her feet were long and slim. Her ankles were delicate. Her toenails were painted the same vivid crimson as her fingernails, as her dress.

His pulse kicked it up a notch. Or three.

Damn it.

She wadded her discarded stocking into a ball, tucked it into one of her now-reconstituted high heels that she'd placed side by side near her feet, glanced up and saw him.

"So did you get the word out?" she asked. If he'd just been hit by a sexual thunderbolt, she obviously had not. Her voice was as cool and untroubled as if she took her stockings off in front of him every day.

He realized that he'd paused to watch her and resumed walking, stopping in the aisle a few feet away. To keep his balance against the yawing of the plane, his hand rested on the back of one of the plush leather chairs.

"I did. And by the way, you've officially started work for Five Eyes."

"Oh, yay." She looked up at him with big blue eyes that seemed guileless and, as he knew from experience, were as deceptive as nearly everything else about her. "If I'm a spy now, I want my decoder ring."

That made him smile. She made a face at him. Then she reached up under her skirt to unclip the other stocking from her garter belt (speaking of deceptive, discovering the truth behind that provocative scrap of lingerie had been an eye-opener). As he watched her slender fingers work the clasp

180

that attached the narrow black satin strap to the silky black band that circled her thigh, his smile died.

She pushed that stocking down her leg with as much unconcern for his presence as she'd removed the other one.

Damn it.

Flames licked at his skin. He felt his blood flash-heat to boiling point. He had to consciously *not* clench his jaw. His fingers tightened on the cool smooth leather beneath them before he forced them to relax.

So maybe he did have a personal interest in her.

Maybe he'd gone hunting for her after waking up from her dirty trick in Moscow not just because he was royally pissed, not just because his company had gotten this job and he'd realized that she possessed the precise skills needed to successfully pull it off, but because he was desperate to keep her from being killed by the people who were after her, otherwise known as the CIA.

Whatever his motivation might or might not have been, it didn't matter. The fact was she was perfect for the job, and as her handler he could be as objective about her as he needed to be.

She rolled that stocking down, tucked it into her shoe just like she'd done with the other one and stood up.

That brought her close enough to touch.

He didn't. He kept his hands to himself, inhaled the faint flowery fragrance of — what? her shampoo? — only because he couldn't help it and responded with a nod when she said, "I'm just going to go clean up my knees."

Then he watched her walk away. Barefoot. A little unsteady as the plane vibrated through a patch of rough air.

And found himself staring at her truly world-class ass.

Damn it.

While they were on the job, his policy toward her had to be strictly hands off. And eyes open. Even after the job was finished he was a fool if he didn't just walk away. He was fairly confident that she wouldn't stick a knife in his ribs when he wasn't paying attention, but other than that all bets were off. How far could he trust her? The answer had to be, about as far as it took her to walk out of his sight. So far in their acquaintance she'd lied to him just about every time she'd opened her mouth. She'd employed every means in her power to escape him. She'd zapped him with a stun gun, thrown him overboard into a shark-infested bay, had him knocked unconscious by an associate and drugged him into a twenty-four-hour stupor. Among other, lesser, things.

She was a thief, a con artist, a trained, skilled operative.

She was loyal to Mason Thayer.

Enough said.

By the time she returned from the lavatory, he was sitting in one of the pair of chairs across from the couch, thumbing through the file he meant to go over with her.

He looked up as she approached. She'd washed her face, slicked back her hair.

Makeup free, she was beautiful. He caught himself looking at her mouth and glanced back down at the file in his hands.

"Here," she said, which caused him to look up again. She was holding a Band-Aid and — he squinted — an antiseptic wipe still in its foil packet out to him.

"For your head." She indicated a spot up near his hairline above his left eyebrow as he took the items. "There was a first-aid kit in the bathroom."

"Thank you." Truth was, he'd forgotten all about the cut, which had quit bleeding some time ago and which he knew to be minor. Still, he tore the packet open and swiped the towelette across it. "Youch!"

Stung like a bitch. His eyes watered.

She smiled. He grimaced in wry response. Then he ripped the Band-Aid open, pulled off the plastic tabs that protected the adhesive and realized, as he lifted it toward his head, that placing it by following the stinging sensation and his vague sense of where the cut was could go ridiculously wrong.

"Give it to me." Her tone was resigned. He silently held the Band-Aid out to her. She took it, brushed his hair back away from the cut and plastered the thing on his forehead.

The feel of her fingers moving in his hair and against his skin had his body reacting all over again.

Damn it.

"We've got about an hour and a half of flight time left," he said. His voice was even, businesslike, which under the circumstances was something he could congratulate himself on. She wasn't looking at him. She was gathering up the Band-Aid debris from the table beside him and dropping it in the nearest trash receptacle. His eyes slid over her as she moved with what he had come to recognize as her own singular brand of grace.

"Sit down and I'll give you the details of what you'll be doing." So maybe his voice was a little gruff. At least he was talking.

"Where are we going?" She obediently sat on the couch, crossed her legs. He swiveled to face her and tried not to notice that, disarmingly, she'd applied Band-Aids to both knees.

"Newark. You'll be taking a commercial flight to Paris that leaves first thing in the morning."

"*I* will be?"

"I'll be on the plane, but we won't be traveling together. To all outward appearances, you'll be alone."

She nodded, waited.

"Your name is Lynette Holbrook. You live in Washington, DC. You're a computer data specialist. You work for NSA contractor Crane Bernard Sherman. In that job, you've been computerizing top secret US government files and last night — you've been working nights lately — you stole some valuable information from those files. You're on your way to Paris to offer it for sale. A small group of NSA security experts is already aware of the theft, but they're trying to keep a lid on it while they determine exactly what was taken, who did it and where you are. Alarms are going off all over the place as the scope of the breach becomes clear. By the time you get to Paris word of a cybertheft of military secrets of enormous importance and magnitude will have spread throughout every dark corner of the intelligence community and beyond. Bad actors will be coming out of the woodwork like cockroaches when the lights go out to get hold of it. Our job is to make sure the information gets into the right hands."

"Whose hands are those?"

"The North Koreans'."

She looked at him without speaking for a moment.

"What kind of information did she — I — steal?"

"Details about operations the United States and its allies are currently running in North Korea. A virtual map of the allied spy network in that country, complete with names. Plans for a possible invasion, the seizure of their nukes, regime change, that kind of thing."

Her eyes widened. "And I'm just going to sell all this to the highest bidder?"

"That was the information Lynette Holbrook stole. That information, the real information, has been recovered. What you're going to sell is disinformation. The spies named in the material you'll pass on include some of the military's top commanders and the Supreme Leader's most trusted advisers. Operational plans, details on an invasion, candidates to replace the Supreme Leader, it's all in there and it's all false, all meant to make him turn on and probably purge his closest allies and prepare for an attack that bears no resemblance to anything that might really be in the works." He dug into a pocket in the file and held up what looked like a ChapStick tube. "This is the flash drive containing the information. It's identical to the one Lynette Holbrook used and managed to smuggle out of a secure facility. No one suspects a Chap-Stick, I guess. And, oh, yes, besides containing the disinformation, it has another function. The hope is that once it's in the hands of the North Koreans it will be given to the military for analysis and plugged into their system, which is air-gapped and not connected to the internet and thus is almost impossible to hack from the outside. If that happens, there's malware on it that will spread throughout the entire system. It should give us access to everything they have, plus enable us to locate their nukes. Once we know where they are, it gets a whole lot easier to take them out."

"But if the system's air-gapped, what difference will it make? Nobody on the outside will be able to access the information," she objected.

He smiled. "That's the beauty of it. There's a worm in the program that aggressively jumps into every device that's ever connected to the network. At some point a laptop will connect to it that will subsequently be taken to a place where it can connect to the internet, or a thumb drive or some peripheral will be plugged in to it that will also be used on a home computer or a laptop or tablet that *is* connected to the internet. The second that internet connection is made, the malware is programmed to do an E.T. and phone home. Every bit of information on their system will be downloaded onto ours."

She held up a hand to stop him. "Hold it right there. Let me make sure I'm understanding this. You're planning to use *me* to try to save the world from possible nuclear annihilation."

"Not just you. You and a ChapStick."

"Funny."

"Think of it like this. You're the Trojan horse. Well, you and the ChapStick."

"Just so you know, I'm still not laughing."

"Fair enough. Nuclear annihilation is not a funny subject."

The look she gave him was withering. She held out her hand for the flash drive, looked it over when he handed it to her. "And how, exactly, am I supposed to get this to the North Koreans? Last time I looked, Paris was a long way in the opposite direction."

"They have a surprisingly substantial community in France. A couple of left-leaning political parties. A study group that has maintained ties with Pyongyang for years. There's a France-Korea Friendship Association. They actually have a youth cultural exchange program. North Korean students from privileged backgrounds are sent to study architecture in Paris, political science in Le Havre, cookery at Le Cordon Bleu, that kind of thing. They stay for several years, with the idea that when they get back home they'll be able to use what they've learned for the glory of the regime."

"So what's the plan? Somehow I don't think putting an ad in *Le Monde* advertising North Korean invasion plans for sale is going to cut it."

"You're going to make direct contact with Park Il-hyeok and offer to sell the information to him. Park's supposedly a defector from North Korea who escaped to the South and then moved to Paris some years ago. In reality, he was sent to the South and to Paris, and is North Korea's top agent in France."

She narrowed her eyes at him. "And you know this how?"

"I'm a spy, beautiful. Knowing stuff is what us spies do. To make things even more interesting, the truth about Park was in the information Lynette Holbrook stole. It's one of the few pieces of true intelligence still on that flash drive. As Lynette, you have, of course, seen it."

Their eyes met in a moment of pure understanding. "And having me — Lynette — know who he is and contact him will validate all the other information — *dis*information — on the flash drive."

"Exactly."

"Not bad," she said. "So I pose as Lynette, sell this Park the flash drive, and that's it?"

"More or less."

She gave him a suspicious look, and he added, "Depending on conditions, we might have to make some field adjustments, but those are the broad strokes."

"Then what?"

"Then whatever you want. We'll probably need to keep you on Five Eyes' payroll on a consulting basis for a while just to make sure the CIA leaves you alone, but you won't have to take any job you don't want to take. Or any job at all."

"You swear." Her voice dripped skepticism.

"Cross my heart." He made the appropriate gesture.

"You didn't need me for this. Any woman around the right age who isn't on some kind of searchable special agent list could do it."

"You did hear me say that a lot of bad actors — and I mean really bad actors, not just government agents but rogue spies and international criminals and terrorists — will be coming after this information? I need you because I need someone who can stay alive long enough to get the information to Park."

"Oh," she said.

"Should be easy enough."

"Unless I die." Her voice was faintly caustic.

"There's that. But I have faith in you. And you've got me to play bodyguard. Besides, if there wasn't any danger, we wouldn't be offering you the big bucks."

"And when do I get these big bucks?"

"This is where most people would tell you that avariciousness is not an attractive trait."

"Most people don't have to worry about spending years on the run. A fugitive without money is dead in the water."

"You sound like you speak from experience." He kept it casual, a throwaway remark, but he was more than interested to hear her reply. It occurred to him that the bios he'd read on her and her many alter egos were probably all about as true as the information he was hoping to pass on to North Korea: in other words, not.

He found that he wanted to know the truth.

"Maybe," she replied. "And you didn't answer me."

This wasn't the moment to push her on her past. There was too much at stake.

"You get paid when you hand the flash drive to Park. And he passes you the money."

"What?"

"You're going to ask for fifty million US. And he's going to pay it."

"That's — that's —" she sputtered, her face pinkening with indignation.

He grinned.

"Smart," he said.

"A total *crock.*"

"It'll help sell it. Nobody takes this kind of risk for free."

"What about the half you offered to pay me when I agreed to accept the job? As in, now?"

"Now that the CIA kill team's found you,

transferring money into any of your bank accounts will just tell them that you're alive and where you are."

"They won't find my bank accounts."

"Ah, but can you be sure they won't find the bank account holding the clandestine slush fund the money was going to come out of? I'm fairly confident the CIA knows about most of them. And if they find the withdrawal, all they have to do is follow the money to you."

She stared at him. He could almost see her calculating the odds.

"You planned this all along," she said finally, accusingly.

He couldn't help it. He laughed, but shook his head. "Field adjustments, remember? Adapt or die."

"Easy for you to say."

"Look at this." He flipped the folder open to show her the pictures clipped to the inside front cover. Full face and profile, full body and full body profile. Nut-brown hair with bangs to the eyebrows. Grayish-blue eyes beneath black, thick-lensed glasses. Round cheeks, thin-lipped mouth, unremarkable nose. A little on the plump side, with none of the spectacular physical attributes of the woman sitting across from him. He would find it impossible to believe that she could pull off a convincing imper- sonation if he hadn't already seen for himself what she could do. "Lynette Hol- brook. There's a suitcase full of her clothes and everything else you'll need waiting for us at the safe house where we'll spend the night. Along with ID, passport, credit cards, the works. Oh, and her car will be left in the airport parking garage."

She frowned as she took the folder from him. "What about the real Lynette Hol- brook? She's not going to show up some- where like, say, Paris and blow this whole thing up, is she?"

He shook his head. "I've been assured that she's securely under wraps. Only a handful of agents know that she was caught and that you're taking her place. For this to work, it has to look real, and for it to look real, the spook network has to be lit up with the news that she's on the run with stolen, highly classified information. Once you get in contact with Park, he'll have his network check it out, believe me. Within a few hours, he'll know everything about Lynette Hol- brook down to her mother's hair color. So will a whole lot of others. The best of the best, and the worst of the worst, will be coming after her — you — full bore. We'll have about thirty-six hours after we arrive in Paris to make contact, make the sale and get out. After that it'll get too dangerous. Word will have spread. Criminals will be doing their best to get hold of the multimillion-dollar payday that you and the information you stole represent. Swarms of spooks will have located you and be descending on Paris to either arrest you — well, Lynette — or take you out. And since we can't ever reveal the charade we need to get you away before that happens."

She wrinkled her nose. "Ever?"

"Not if this is going to work."

"So if a criminal or an agent from a hostile government gets to me I'm probably going to get robbed and whacked. If an agent from a friendly government gets to me I'm looking at life in prison or the death penalty as Lynette Holbrook for stealing government secrets, and if I just get found without getting arrested I'm looking at something like a sniper hit."

"Pretty much sums it up."

She narrowed her eyes at him. "I'd never make it to prison, would I? If I get arrested I'll be dead before I ever see the inside of a cell."

"I'd say that's a fairly accurate assessment."

"And this is better than being in the

crosshairs of a CIA kill team how?"

"Because we're going to get you safely in and out of there. And you've got me to keep anyone from getting to you in the meantime."

"Oh, wow. Now I feel safe." Her brow furrowed. "Who else knows that I'm the one taking Lynette Holbrook's place?"

"You, specifically?"

She nodded.

"Strictly need to know. Which means me. The man who hired me. No more than half a dozen others, as far as actually knowing your identity is concerned. Maybe a couple of dozen more know that an operative will be impersonating Lynette Holbrook, but they don't know your name, or anything about who that operative is."

She bent her head, studying the photos. "Covering all the bases, hmm?"

"That's the job."

"I'm going to need contacts in her eye color. Acrylics and a dental mold so I can make a prosthesis to alter the shape of my cheeks. A recording of her voice so I can match it."

"Anything you need that's not already at the safe house we'll have brought in tonight. By the time we leave for the airport in the morning, you will be Lynette Holbrook and

Operation Fifth Doctrine will be up and running."

She closed the folder, gave him a skeptical look. "Okay, I'll bite. It's a catchy name. Does it actually mean something?"

"Sure it does. You think somebody would just pull a name for an operation like this out of their hat? US military doctrine recognizes five 'domains of war' for which the military are responsible. The first one is land, the second one is sea, the third one is air, the fourth one is space, and the last one, the fifth doctrine, is information. Kind of gives that whole 'war of words' thing a brand-new meaning."

"The web is mightier than the sword?"

He grinned. "There you go. That's it exactly."

12

Saturday, December 14th

CIA Special Agent Steve Hanes got the call at 6:00 a.m. He was already on-site, having driven in to the United States Army Regional Correctional Facility–Europe, located in Mannheim, Germany, from his temporary lodgings in that same city hours earlier in anticipation of this moment.

Outside, dawn's charcoal sky was lightening to the gray cloud cover that was typical of Mannheim in chilly December. Inside, the prison was also gray. Concrete walls, steel bars, gray tile floors, all of it bathed in the harsh light of industrial fluorescents.

When it rang at last, his encrypted cell phone was sitting right in front of him on his borrowed desk in a small office deep in the bowels of the prison. He'd kept it within reach because, as he had been all through the night, he was expecting word on the success, or not, of an operation. Among other things, a man's life hung on the answer.

The man in question was a former crack CIA operative gone rogue decades before. Elite assassin. Thief. Con man. Blackmailer. Bad Guy Extraordinaire. A fixture on Interpol's most wanted list for years. A fixture on a lot of other most wanted lists as well, some of them so secret that even Hanes had not known they existed before pulling this assignment.

His name was Mason Thayer. Sixty-four years old, six-one, a hundred ninety-three well-honed pounds, gray hair, blue eyes. Handsome features now partially concealed by a grizzled beard. Recent gunshot wound to the hip. Even more recent broken ribs, severe lacerations and burns to the left side as a result of a helicopter crash, courtesy of Hanes and crew, who'd shot down the one he was attempting to escape Macau in.

Thayer was at that moment sitting in a cell kept at a deliberately miserable 50 degrees, on a concrete bench built into the concrete rear wall. The floor was concrete, too, with a drain in the center. A steel toilet, lidless and bolted to the floor, was within his reach. Nothing else was, because word was that the man could make a weapon out of anything. The cell was finished off with three Plexiglas walls so that its occupant could be kept under constant observation, both by anyone in this adjacent office and by a camera mounted on the wall opposite the cell. His hands and feet were shackled, chained to the wall behind him. Except for a pair of army-issued blue boxers, he was naked.

He lounged back against that cold concrete wall as if it were a BarcaLounger in his living room.

Hanes was itching to get the go-ahead to shoot the SOB in the head. If the operation had gone as planned, this phone call should provide it.

As Hanes picked up the phone, his eyes met the prisoner's through the glass. Thayer knew the portent of the call, knew what had been going down on the other side of the world, knew that his own life hung in the balance, because Hanes had told him. Slowly and with a great deal of pleasure.

Thayer smiled at him.

Hanes flipped him the bird.

Hanes was SOG, or Special Operations Group. SOG was the United States' most secretive special operations force. An offshoot of the CIA's SAD, it was almost unknown to the public. The biggest, baddest, most covert of the covert intelligence operations being carried out at any given time around the world were by and large the work of the SOG. The Mannheim prison was equally big and bad, being the only US Department of Defense, Level 1 corrections facility in Europe. It held, and had held, some of the most heinous foreign criminals taken into custody abroad by the United States, from a trio of Benghazi plotters to the masterminds of the 9/11 attacks.

"We've got a problem," said the voice on the other end of the phone. No greeting, no preamble. Hanes's gut tightened. The speaker was Greg Wafford, Deputy Director of the National Clandestine Service, which oversaw the SOG. Wafford was Hanes's boss, and one of the few in the know about Thayer's capture. It was midnight in Langley, Virginia, where Wafford's office was tucked away deep in CIA headquarters, but the operation Hanes had been waiting to hear about was mission critical. Wafford wouldn't have left the building until the word had come down. "She got away."

She being Nomad 44, also known as Beth McAlister, also known by multiple aliases, the current one being Bianca St. Ives.

Remembering in time what a tight-ass Wafford was, Hanes swallowed a curse. "You found her? The intel was good?"

"It was. She was located right where you

told us she'd be. Unfortunately, they failed to kill her and she escaped." The heaviness of Wafford's voice told Hanes what a blow that failure was.

"She can't have gotten far. She was in Savannah, Georgia, for God's sake. Where could she go? The team can still get the job done. How hard can it be to kill one lone girl?" Hanes ran a hand over his face in frustration.

"There's where we have the problem. She's no longer alone. She's working for Five Eyes."

"*What?* How did that happen?"

"I have no idea. All I know is we failed to kill her, and she somehow hooked up with a contractor who hooked her up with Five Eyes. You know what that means."

"Our hands are tied." Hanes felt as if he'd been punched in the stomach.

"That's right. Under the terms of the UKUSA Agreement —" a pact for joint co-operation among the Five Eyes countries in signals intelligence, military intelligence and human intelligence, it was pronounced *yew-kew-zah* "— we're pledged to cooperate with each other. Which means we can't hit her. Officially."

Hanes absorbed both the words and the underlying meaning. Officially was out.

Unofficially, however, was still on the table. "I understand." He frowned as a sudden thought crystallized into a near certainty. "Would that contractor be Colin Rogan of Cambridge Solutions?"

"It would. You know him?"

"Our paths crossed in Macau. He was hunting Thayer." While Hanes had been hunting Nomad 44. "But he showed interest in the girl."

Wafford made a sound that might have denoted mild amusement. "Pity we can't contact Rogan and offer to trade Thayer for her."

"It is."

"We have an unacceptable degree of exposure in this matter that reaches into the very highest echelons of our government. The only way to eliminate it is to eliminate all traces of the Nomad program. Nomad 44 is living, breathing evidence of a project that should never have been undertaken in the first place. It was not only illegal, it was immoral. And you and I, who had nothing to do with creating it, are tasked with cleaning up the mess. Whatever it takes."

"Yes, sir."

"I can trust you to see to it?"

"You can."

"Good man. As expeditiously as possible.

And remember, no fingerprints. Nothing that can be traced back to us."

"No, sir."

"And we need the body. Intact."

"I understand."

"Then take care of it." Wafford disconnected.

Hanes looked up to find Thayer watching him. It was impossible that he could have heard the conversation, but there was a mocking twist to his mouth that made Hanes's own mouth thin.

Dropping the phone into his pocket, scooping up the iPad that lay on the desk near where the phone had been, Hanes headed for Thayer's cell. His weapon was practically burning a hole in its shoulder holster, he wanted to use it so bad.

One of the reasons he'd had Thayer placed in that particular cell was that, with its drain and the multiple recessed water nozzles built into the ceiling and wall, it was an ideal place to execute someone by gunshot without leaving a hell of a mess.

Thayer watched him enter without altering his position by so much as a twitch of a finger. The eggplant bruises covering his left side from shoulder to knee, the fading redness of still-healing burns, the jagged black lines of the sutures closing the cuts he'd suffered, seemed to bother him not at all.

"Trouble, Special Agent?" Thayer's tone was mocking.

"I brought you something," Hanes said. "A present."

Careful to stay well out of Thayer's reach, he turned on the iPad and held it out so the other man could see it as the screen came to life.

"Mummy, do you think Father Christmas will be able to find us here?" The speaker was Thayer's seven-year-old daughter, Marin. Round-faced with big brown eyes and chunky brown pigtails, the little girl plopped down in a wooden chair pulled up to a small square table in an outdated kitchen in a farmhouse near Mittenwald, Germany. She was wearing a pink hoodie with jeans and seemed about to tuck into a bowl of something that waited for her on the table. Seen through a window behind the girl, the lavender of a dawn sky served as a backdrop for a snowy expanse of meadow and, beyond that, the steep rise of a majestic mountain.

"Of course he will." An attractive thirty-something brunette in a fuzzy blue house-coat walked into the frame. She was Thayer's wife and the child's mother, Margery. She sipped from a cup as she spoke. "He never gets lost. Reindeer are better than a GPS for —"

A knock, loud and authoritative, sounded at the door.

Margery turned sharply to face it. The cup she was holding visibly shook. Marin's eyes went huge. She jumped up from the chair.

Through the window it was possible to see a helicopter settling down not far from the house.

Margery set the cup down, grabbed for Marin. "Quick, we must —"

Boom.

The door burst open. Armed men in flak jackets poured into the room. Marin screamed and clutched her mother. Margery's arms wrapped around her —

Satisfied, Hanes turned the iPad off. Thayer's face was absolutely expressionless. It told him everything he needed to know.

"That's right — we found them. Did you really think we wouldn't?"

Thayer's eyes rose to meet his. His expression never changed, but there was a deadly coldness at the backs of his eyes that would have had Hanes grabbing for his weapon if Thayer had been less thoroughly restrained.

"We had an agreement. A guarantee of safety for my wife and daughter in exchange for King Priam's treasure. Which was delivered as promised."

"*We* weren't party to that agreement. That was your arrangement with the Germans. Your agreement with us was that you would deliver Nomad 44."

"I've given her to you twice. Physically handed over her incapacitated body in Berlin. Told you where to find her in the US." If possible, the quiet calm of Thayer's tone was even more frightening than his eyes.

"She got away from our kill team last night."

"Not my fault if the people you sent are incompetent."

"She got away the first time you handed her over to us, too."

"Again, not my fault."

"Maybe. Maybe not." Hanes stepped over to a button on the wall, smiled at Thayer and pressed it.

Gushers of icy water shot out of the ceiling and wall to target the man on the bench. It wasn't the first time, but it was the first time that day. Thayer had had a chance to get thoroughly dry, which Hanes hoped made the experience just that much more unpleasant.

Other than closing his eyes against the onslaught, Thayer didn't react. When Hanes was satisfied that he was soaked to the skin, he turned the water off.

Thayer opened his eyes, blinked once and was still. Water sluiced down his face, down his body, ran toward the drain in the center of the floor. His hair was plastered to his skull. A faint blue tinge to his skin bore silent testimony to how very cold he was, but there was no shivering, no teeth chattering, no reaction whatsoever.

The man's iron endurance made Hanes itch to see what real torture could do.

"I want to make myself very clear," Hanes said. "Your wife and daughter are in our hands. Right now they are together and being well treated. We can change that at any time. We can file charges against your wife for aiding and abetting a fugitive, receiving stolen property, money laundering, any number of crimes. Enough to put her in prison for decades, which would, of course, separate her from your daughter. Or we can kill the pair of them, just like that." He snapped his fingers. Thayer's expression didn't change, but the glint in his eyes made Hanes want to step back a pace. He didn't, but he recognized the instinct that had kicked in as the primordial need to survive. "I don't want to have to do either of those things. I don't want to have to hurt a woman and child. But what happens to them depends on you. You have the power to get them released, to give them their lives back. You can even go home to them, and the three of you can live happily ever after."

"What do you want?" Thayer asked.

"I want you to find and kill Nomad 44."

13

Sunday, December 15th

In Paris on a Sunday just about everything was closed. The shops, the supermarkets, even many of the restaurants went dark for the legally mandated day of rest. The wide boulevards with their imposing buildings of finely cut ashlar were thin of traffic as the residents of the City of Light settled in around their tables for the traditional *déjeuner dominical.* Tourists, of whom there were many so close to Christmas, flocked to the seven areas that were officially permitted to be open: the chain-store shopping strip Rue de Rivoli; historic Place des Vosges; the Champs-Élysées, home of the Arc de Triomphe, with its theaters, cafés and luxury shops; Montmartre with its galleries and bookshops; and the Boulevard St. Germain, home to high-fashion boutiques.

Others, tourists and locals, traveled beyond the Périphérique, the ring road that circled Paris, to what was said to be the world's largest flea market, the Marché Clignancourt in Saint-Ouen.

It was just after 2:00 p.m., and Bianca had done just that. She stepped off line four of the metro, which ran south to north through the city, passing through Montparnasse, Notre Dame, Hotel De Ville and Gare du Nord, and glanced around.

No threat as far as she could tell. Didn't mean there wasn't one. Colin swore that the CIA kill team had been called off. His assessment of the situation was that they had approximately another twenty-four hours before the theft and the scope of it could be confirmed, Lynette Holbrook's culpability established (it was the weekend, after all; the red flag of Lynette not reporting to work wouldn't happen until Monday, and even spooks, especially high-level ones, tended to take weekends off), and the appropriate persons or teams dispatched to deal with the problem, i.e., her. Bianca really hoped he was right. Because if he wasn't, well, the phrase *dead wrong* came to mind.

Along with several dozen others, she climbed the steps to street level and joined the crowds walking past the Occo Chicken and the KFC, the flimsy sidewalk stalls with their tourist trap displays of tiny metal Eiffel Towers and Mona Lisa postcards and cheap imported T-shirts, the fruit and flower stands. As always when on a mission, she stayed on high alert, watching her flank through reflections in store windows, flicking glances at windows and rooftops that might provide a vantage point for a sniper, checking out passing vehicles, suspicious pedestrians, anything that might pose a threat. Not that she really expected to encounter trouble at this point: she herself hadn't found out where she was going until just a few hours before she stepped onto the metro, so she doubted a killer was already there before her, lying in wait. But over the years taking precautions had become second nature, and in a situation like this she did so as automatically as she breathed.

From the moment she'd made up her mind to do this, she'd been careful. She'd let Evie know that she would be gone for a while, not by phone or email, which could be monitored, but by having a box of Evie's favorite candy delivered to her at the party with a note that read: "What can I say? He swept me off my feet. See you in a few days. Make my apologies to everybody." She hadn't even needed to sign it: Evie would know who it was from, would know that by *he* she was referring to the mysterious Mr. Tower, and would be thrilled and excited that her friend had at last fallen prey to torrid romance. To let Doc know she was alive, she'd shot him an email under the fail-safe as they'd agreed. The Jeep was registered to another false identity, so she didn't fear having it traced back to her. The items she'd left inside it were a different story, but given the weight of the Jeep, which should have taken it straight to the bottom, the fact that its doors were open and the swiftness of the current, she figured that by the time anyone could hoist it out of the river everything inside it would be long gone. She debated notifying the police that she, in her fake identity as the Jeep's owner, had survived the crash, but since she really, truly wanted the CIA kill team to think she was dead (fat chance, but hope springs eternal) she decided to hold off on that. She assuaged her conscience about the time and trouble that any search effort would involve by vowing to donate a generous sum to the search and rescue squad if she survived long enough to return to Savannah and do so.

Arriving in Paris as Lynette shortly after 10:00 p.m. the previous night, she'd taken an airport shuttle bus to a hotel she wasn't staying in. From that hotel she'd snagged a taxi to a metro station and ridden the metro to a street a few blocks from the hotel in which she meant to register. At that point she took another taxi to that hotel before registering, going upstairs, changing clothes and leaving again, walking the twelve blocks to the small apartment where she had actually spent the night. All of this with Colin trailing discreetly behind as they pretended not to be together, not to know each other, not to so much as be aware of the other's existence on the same planet. Rinse, wash, repeat with minor variations this morning before she'd finally boarded the metro to the flea market.

Bottom line, being Jane Bond was exhausting.

The sun had broken through the morning's rain showers so that the day looked bright and sparkly despite the puddles that still lay on the sidewalks and the sporadically dripping eaves. The temperature hovered around a chilly 42 degrees. Picking up the pace while still making sure to stay with the bulk of the tourists heading in the same direction, she walked briskly past a row of parked white vans abutting the flea market area because, just as a general rule, parked vans made her nervous.

Assassins, kidnappers, robbers, CIA agents — a lot of bad actors did a lot of staging out of parked vans. She'd developed what amounted to an allergy to them.

"Slow down, beautiful. I'm going to the dogs here." Colin's voice spoke in her ear courtesy of a specially designed earring that featured spirals of silver metal dotted with small faux garnets, the largest one of which was an earwig.

"Try to keep up." The transmitter was in a silver-and-garnet ring. Pretending to cough, she brought her hand close to her mouth to reply. At the same time, she sought and found a shop window to check out what was happening with him. The reflection showed her a tall, lean man in a peaked cap sporting a jaw full of stubble, small clear spectacles and a black peacoat over jeans. He'd been on the metro, too, although she'd caught only a glimpse of him, and she gave him full marks for trailing her *almost* invisibly. He fancied himself her bodyguard, which she thought was hilarious although she hadn't (yet) told him so, but she suspected that he was also sticking close to keep an eye on her.

Just in case she decided to go rogue.

Right at that moment, the leashes of a small white poodle and a stocky pug were wrapped around his legs. Bianca listened through the earwig as a stoop-backed elderly woman scolded volubly in French as she worked to untangle Colin from her pets.

She couldn't help it. She smiled.

"Idiot," she said into the ring.

And kept walking. Because waiting around for a man who supposedly wasn't with you to catch up was bad tradecraft. Also because messing with him was fun.

The market was set up more like a blocks-long collection of side-by-side antiques shops than the open table displays and meandering aisles of a traditional flea market, and the goods, which included furniture and art, were on the expensive rather than the cheap side.

Squinting through a replica of Lynette Holbrook's black-framed glasses, transformed into Lynette in every outward aspect from the boxy toast-colored coat she wore with black pants and flats to the mousy brown wig and the prosthesis that filled out her cheeks, Bianca wandered through the booths, keeping her black faux leather shoulder bag pressed tight against her side to safeguard it against pickpockets and thieves, which followed tourists like a dog follows meat and thus were everywhere at Marché Clignancourt. Given her body language as Lynette — head down, shoulders slightly slumped, taking up as little visual space as possible — she might actually be a target, which as herself she never was, so she stayed on guard. All around her, her fellow patrons conversed in French. Her familiarity with the language clicked in, and she realized that she was no longer actively translating what she heard but following various random bits of conversation automatically. She didn't see Colin, but she was confident that he'd extricated himself from his difficulties. Given the absence of shop windows, looking for him had the potential of attracting too much attention, so she didn't.

Her target was Park Il-hyeok. According to the intelligence reports she'd pored over, he visited the flea market nearly every Sunday. Park was an avid collector of antique Chinese ceramics with an emphasis on the Ming Dynasty, and regularly browsed the flea market in hopes that a piece would turn up that he could add to his collection.

This interest of Park's was to be her way in.

There was a particular booth that he favored in Vernaison, a central area of the flea market, and it was in that direction that Bianca headed. All around her shoppers browsed. The chatter was a mix of languages with French predominating. The sound of a woman singing the popular "Dernière Danse" to the accompaniment of a single guitar rose sweetly above the general hubbub. A mouthwatering smell — fresh-baked beignets? — wafted past her nose, reminding her that she was hungry.

Spy now, eat later.

"On your three." Colin's voice in her ear told her that he was, indeed, present, close enough to see her and, presumably, Park. His alert had her looking to her right.

Sure enough, she spotted Park in the three o'clock position, in a booth not far from where she had expected him to be, and recognized him instantly. He was fifty-eight years old, five-nine and wiry, with a round face that belied his build and a short-on-the-sides, long-on-the-top comb-over that featured half a dozen dyed black strands plastered across a bald dome. He was wearing a navy overcoat against the chill over gray dress pants, with a long, fringed scarf of white silk looped around his neck. As she watched, he turned over a porcelain statue to, she assumed, check the maker's mark on its base. A pair of larger, younger men in dark suits who stood with their hands clasped behind their backs a few feet away appeared to be keeping a close eye on him. Bianca knew that he never went anywhere without bodyguards, and assumed that the men were there in that capacity. The bodyguards would protect him and also spy on him, because such was life in the Hermit Kingdom.

There was no way to be sure, but she thought that Park must be heading for the booth he favored. With the goal of beating him to it, she left off pretending to examine the stitching on an antique sofa and started walking that way.

Passing the brasserie Chez Louisette, she discovered the source of both the singing and the delectable smell. The noise and bustle around the small restaurant faded into the background as she eyed the wonderful displays of food on the glass-fronted shelves that formed the eatery's outer wall: trays of pastries, *pain au chocolat,* baguettes presented side by side with small tubs of the wonderful French butter. (Seriously, life-changing butter. Her mouth watered just thinking about it.) Inside the brasserie, she caught a glimpse of waiters carrying plates of roast chicken and *croque monsieurs* and steak frites. Patrons waited in a long line to snag a table.

Bianca's stomach rumbled, reminding her

that breakfast had been a cup of coffee and a protein bar.

"If you're good, I'll feed you when we're done here," Colin said in her ear. Clearly he'd heard her stomach growl. Bianca's lips compressed. This close to the target, acknowledging him in any way would be bad tradecraft, so she didn't.

Skirting the line, she reached the booth that was her goal. Layers of vivid Oriental carpets with the silky sheen of age covered all three of the walls, with the fourth being open to the market. Against the deep reds and blues of the rugs, an antique walnut sideboard held a collection of blue-and-white Meissen china. A pair of enormous gilded candelabra flanked the sideboard. A marble-topped chest heavy with ormolu, a Louis XVI sofa and a gorgeous *trumeau* mirror were among the eye-catching offerings.

Half a dozen shoppers browsed the wares. A thin woman dressed all in black with a deeply lined face and iron-gray hair cut boyishly short ran a handheld scanner over a set of silver flatware on a sideboard. She wore a plastic name tag pinned to her blouse that said Mme. Martin. She was, as Bianca knew from the intelligence reports, the proprietress of the shop.

"Here he comes," Colin said.

Because timing was all, Bianca sidled closer to the proprietress, waited until she actually saw Park approaching, then walked up to the woman. In perfect imitation of Lynette's flat, Midwestern voice (in case Park should subsequently manage to obtain a video of Lynette in which she spoke), she said in French, "Pardon, madame, but I have something —" while pulling a newspaper-wrapped item from her purse.

Mme. Martin interrupted with a gimlet glare and an impatient gesture. "Ah, bah, you Americans, you cannot speak French, none of you. Why do you even try? What is this you are doing? If you are hoping to sell me something, I must tell you that I do not buy from unknown persons."

Park was in the shop. Watching him out of the corner of her eye might give the game away, so she didn't. Instead she trusted in the power of her bait — and, she realized, in Colin's voice in her ear to give her a heads-up if there was something she needed to know.

Having unwrapped the small white porcelain wine cup decorated with colorful chickens, Bianca held it up in such a way that it could be easily seen by anyone in the shop (read Park) and said, in English, "Madame,

I have a Ming Dynasty chicken cup to sell.
I was hoping —"

Park appeared within her line of vision,
his attention obviously caught.

"— you might be interested in it."

"A chicken cup?" Mme. Martin frowned
at it. Ming Dynasty chicken cups were rare.
Bianca had no idea where Colin had obtained it. She doubted very much if it was
authentic. But he had presented it to her as
a means of gaining speech with Park without
anyone, even his bodyguards cum minders,
thinking there was anything odd about her
approaching him. It worked: even as she
feigned looking anxiously at Mme. Martin,
Park came up beside her.

"Bonjour, madame," he said to Mme.
Martin, who responded with an acknowledging nod and a slightly sour "Bonjour,
M. Park." Park then turned to Bianca. "Mademoiselle, I would be most interested in
looking at this, if you would permit."

14

By *this* Park meant the cup. Bianca, purposely hesitant, gave him a dubious look.

"I am a collector," he assured her. Madame grunted corroboration.

Still projecting uncertainty, Bianca let him take the cup.

He held it like it was incredibly valuable, which, if it was real, it was. Turning it this way and that, he examined it, his expression brightening with interest as he brushed a finger over the orange and green and blue painted chickens that decorated it.

When he flipped it over to squint at the mark on the bottom, which had been intentionally blurred with a smudge of soot, Bianca said, "I believe the light is better over there —" she indicated a place where a shaft of sunlight poured in through one of the clear skylights that punctuated the corrugated plastic roof "— if you would care to get a better look?"

As she had expected, he nodded and moved the twenty-some-odd feet that it took to reach the sunlight. Bianca moved with him. When he stopped she positioned herself so that her back was to the bodyguards, who watched with only tepid interest from just inside the booth. Mme. Martin had been distracted by a customer's question, she was glad to see.

Park rubbed at the soot mark with his thumb and tilted the cup into the light so that he could examine the bottom. "This is quite —"

Bianca broke in. Her words were quick, her voice low. "M. Park, please keep your attention on the cup as I speak. I have vital information that I know will be of critical interest to the DPRK and to you, as one of its most senior representatives. It concerns an imminent attack on your country by the United States and its allies." His mouth slackened a little and he shot a startled sideways glance at her. "Keep looking at the cup. You will buy it from me, I will wrap it up in the newspaper I brought it in, and I will include a flash drive that holds a summary of the information I have obtained, along with a way to contact me if you are interested in seeing more. If that is acceptable to you, ask me the price of the cup."

"Who are you?" He sounded both fascinated and appalled. His voice was low. His eyes stayed riveted on the cup.

"My name isn't important. I was doing work for the United States Department of Defense when I came across this information. In my opinion, an attack by my country against yours will lead to all-out nuclear war, which as a human being and a citizen of the world I feel I must try to prevent. Offering you this information so that you can pass it on to your country in time is how I hope to save us all." Her voice, while still barely above a whisper, sharpened and grew more urgent as she spoke. "If you're interested, *ask me the price of the cup. When I tell you, agree to buy it.*"

He wet his lips, swallowed. Then, a little too loudly, he said, "Mademoiselle, what is the price you seek for this cup?"

Ah. She had him. "A thousand euros." A pittance compared to the true worth of the cup, if it was genuine, but an American tourist such as Lynette appeared to be would not necessarily know that. Or if it was a copy and she knew it, she might only want to make a quick buck and get away before the fraud was discovered.

He frowned, shook his head. "That is too much. This may very well be a forgery. I cannot —"

She gave him credit for entering fully into his role, but she wasn't sure there was time for feigned dickering — if it was feigned. Park was reported to be a notorious cheapskate. The bodyguards, in a concerted action that she found troubling, started to close in on her and Park. Whatever the reason for their sudden shift from stasis to motion, it made her pulse bump along a little faster. Although it couldn't be anything to do with her, either as Lynette Holbrook or herself. She was almost positive.

On the other hand, whatever it was almost certainly wasn't anything good.

"Seven hundred euros," she said, summoning an air of stubborn determination.

"Three hundred," he countered as the bodyguards reached him. One of them came close to murmur something in his ear. Park nodded, then said to Bianca, "I must go. Three hundred fifty euros is my final offer. It is all the cash I have with me. As they say in your country, take it or leave it."

Bianca grimaced. "I — Fine. I'll take it." She reached for the cup. "Let me wrap it for you."

"Excellent." He looked at the bodyguard who had whispered to him. "Three hundred fifty euros." He jerked his head in Bianca's direction. "To her."

His tone to the bodyguards was very different from the tone he had used with her. Rougher, more peremptory. It was, Bianca understood, intended to convey his status and the bodyguards' subservient position.

She rewrapped the cup in the newspaper, slipping the promised flash drive in among the wrappings. This one was not disguised as anything; not knowing how tech savvy Park was, they didn't want to risk him not instantly recognizing it for what it was. Along with a summary of the information she had to sell, the flash drive acquainted him with her fifty-million-dollar asking price and details of how the exchange, if he was interested, would take place.

The bodyguard handed over the bills. Bianca tucked them into her purse as Park, clutching the parcel, was hustled away.

"You should have held out for full price," Colin said. "That was a hell of a forgery."

Bianca's lips quirked. She'd *known* the cup was fake.

"You!" Mme. Martin spoke so sharply and unexpectedly that Bianca almost jumped. With Park gone, the woman must have hurried right over. "Go! Do not return to my shop! It is for me to make the sales here, not you. Out, out. Go on."

She made shooing motions with her hands, urging Bianca from the shop. Task completed, murmuring penitent phrases like, "I am so sorry, madame," and, "Yes, I am going," Bianca was glad to comply.

"I'm recruiting her next. She's terrifying," Colin said.

Replying might draw too much attention — she didn't want anyone to notice her raising her hand to her mouth one too many times — so she didn't.

Instead she left the flea market.

If she was going to pick up a tail, this was when it was most likely to happen, as an offshoot of her contact with Park. It was always possible that he was being watched, and that the watcher would try to determine who she was and if she constituted a threat. Or he himself might now order someone to follow her. Add to those possibilities everyone who conceivably might want to kidnap or kill her, either because she was Lynette or because she was Bianca, and her walk away from the flea market was potentially fraught with peril.

The worst thing about it was, there was nothing she could do about it. Her job was to be Lynette, and Lynette would not know, much less employ, anti-surveillance techniques.

She kept her eyes forward and trusted in Colin to have her back. Without, she hoped, giving the least appearance of hurrying, she headed for the train rather than the metro for the return trip into the city.

Never go out the same way you go in. It was one of the rules.

Blending with the hordes of tourists, she left the train at the Eiffel Tower. Despite the temperature and the overcast sky, the park-like lawn surrounding it was jammed with visitors. The walkways along the nearby Seine were packed, too, and the river itself was alive with boats. She walked to the Rue Alasseur and the modest room she had booked there under the name L. Fields. Assuming that Lynette Holbrook would not have a sophisticated system for creating a new identity, and assuming also that she would not be stupid enough to stay anywhere under her own name, Bianca had determined that Lynette's most likely subterfuge would have been to claim a marriage not yet reflected on her ID and register under her supposed married name, which for Bianca's purposes was Fields. That was, therefore, what Bianca had done. As it happened, the hotel was not that picky. They registered her under the name she gave them without question and allowed her to pay cash for the room. As an added bonus, their security cameras consisted of a single pair trained on the check-in desk in the lobby.

"You picked up a tail," Colin said in her ear as she reached Lynette's room, which was small, musty and on the fourth floor. The SVP ne pas Déranger (Do Not Disturb) sign was still on the door. She let herself in. The room was dark except for a shaft of grayish light spilling in through the single window. The piece of paper she'd inserted between the door and the jamb fluttered out onto the floor. She picked it up: no one had been in the room since she'd left. "He's outside staring at the hotel now. No, wait — he's on the move, coming around to your side."

"Where?" She walked to the window and pulled the old-fashioned roller shade down.

"Front entrance being noon, he's moving from eleven to nine o'clock."

That was the side she was on. Easy to think the tail knew where her room was, but another of the rules was *never assume*. After all, if he was at the front of the hotel there were only two ways he could go, and either way he had a 50 percent chance of being right. Bianca turned on the lamp beside the bed and made sure to get between it and the window so that any watcher got a brief look at her silhouette through the shade. Then she moved out of the light and started stripping herself of Lynette's identity, losing the glasses, the prosthesis, switching her Lynette wig for one of flaming red shoulder-length waves. She'd chosen the eye-catching hue deliberately to provide a focal point for any witnesses to her exiting the hotel so that the red hair would be all they'd see or remember, whether in person or if questioned or shown a picture of Lynette by anyone who came hunting for her. Tradecraft 101: one vivid or unusual detail was enough to distract most observers. That detail would almost always be all they remembered.

"Who is it? Can you tell?"

"Best guess, one of Park's. He picked you up not long after you got off the train."

Okay, that wasn't so bad. Nobody had expected Park or the people he would have reported the encounter to not to check her out.

"Got it covered," she said.

She shucked the pants and pulled on a short knit black skirt that she'd worn as an infinity scarf around the neck of the sleek black sweater that had been concealed beneath the boxy coat. She flipped her throwing star necklace — *don't leave home without it* — from hidden beneath the sweater to eye-catching accessory against all that black status, turned the toast-colored coat inside out so that its black underlining was uppermost, and belted it with the black leather belt that had held up her too-large pants to alter the coat's shape.

Rolling the pants into a tube, she tucked them along with the other items she'd discarded into the shoulder bag that, turned inside out, was now a kicky zebra print. Finally she snapped three-inch heels into place onto her flat black ankle boots, and cast an assessing glance around the room.

She didn't want to leave anything she'd been wearing behind in case someone broke in and searched the room. The slacks and blouse hanging in the closet and the items still unpacked in the carry-on by the bed were all Lynette's, as were the toiletries in the tiny bathroom. She'd only touched the clothes and toiletries when she'd unpacked them and she'd been wearing gloves at the time. The suitcase she'd wiped down, just as she would wipe down the room before leaving.

To the right people, using DNA from, say, a stray hair to determine identity was a piece of cake. The key was to make sure the stray hair belonged to Lynette.

She put an almost-impossible-to-detect timer on the lamp that was set to turn the light off at 11:00 p.m., wiped down everything she'd touched and left. If someone broke in and searched the room, all the evidence would indicate that the room had been rented by Lynette, who, taking advantage of her time in Paris, was out for a night on the town. If they waited for Lynette to return, well, it *was* Paris. Random hookups were as popular as the fleur-de-lis.

As a leggy redhead in a midthigh-length belted black coat, short black skirt, black tights and ankle-length black high-heeled boots, she was, she prided herself, unrecognizable as Lynette. Her ID said Alice Dunn, and Alice Dunn she now was. She exited the back door of the hotel and immediately plunged into the stream of pedestrians on the sidewalk. It was dark already — sunset came early in Paris in December — but the area was well lit from streetlamps and Christmas decorations and the glow spilling from shop windows. In the distance, the Eiffel Tower, all lit up for Christmas, glittered alternately gold and silver and red and green against the night sky. It was breathtakingly lovely, even through the fine sprinkle of rain that was just beginning to fall.

Out of nowhere, a warning prickle between her shoulder blades made her breath catch. She was on instant high alert. The sensation came on so fast and was so strong that she almost looked sharply around in an attempt to identify the source. Training kicked in before she could betray herself in that way, but the conviction that she was under hostile observation did not diminish. It was not the kind of feeling that came from, say, Colin's gaze as he watched her back.

This was instinct screaming that she was in danger.

Striding purposefully along, head lowered against the misting rain, there wasn't a whole lot she could do except continue to appear unaware. Knowing that Colin was back there somewhere made her feel a little better, but not a whole lot. He very well might not be aware of the presence of whoever or whatever this was, and contacting him risked alerting them that she was onto them and thus precipitating the very action she hoped to avoid.

The threat felt so real, so immediate, that goose bumps slid over her skin. Covertly she scanned faces, checked reflections in windows. This section of Paris was one that permitted commerce on Sunday, so it was packed. Shop doors opened and closed as people went in and out, meaning that the milling crowd on the sidewalk was in constant flux. She took care to stay in the center of a group of people going the same way she was. Her senses heightened so that she was hyperaware of every little thing: the earthy smell of the rain, the cold dampness of it on her skin, its faintly metallic taste on her lips.

The people closest to her, surrounding her, acted as an unwitting buffer between her and the threat. They were a family of five English tourists in plastic ponchos, two French couples with their heads ducked against the rain, a pair of teenage girls sharing a single umbrella, an old man in a long coat with his dog. She moved with them, matching her pace to theirs. Their chatter, the shuffle of their footsteps, the rustle of their clothing, the hum of the throng on the sidewalk and the more distant growl of the cars in the street, faded to background noise as she listened with almost painful intensity for the snick of a pulled trigger, the hiss of a thrown knife, the telltale sound of a deployed weapon.

Maybe, she told herself, she was overreacting. After all, she knew that she as Lynette had been followed from the time she'd gotten off the train. Could the feeling she was getting be from the tail Park had sent? But she was moving away from the back of the hotel, and Park's tail had been on the right side of the hotel on another street entirely, and he would be looking out for Lynette, not the red-haired sophisticate she'd morphed into. So the answer was, almost certainly not.

Anyway, the vibe she was picking up on was way too menacing for someone whose brief it was to do nothing more than follow her. Menacing as in, *something deadly this way comes.*

That was the thought she was starting to fixate on when a crack of thunder so loud it made her jump shook the street. Right on its heels lightning flashed and the clouds opened up as if someone had unzipped them. Torrents of icy rain poured down. Cries from surprised pedestrians were almost drowned out by the fierce drumming of the rain hitting the hard surfaces of roofs and cars and pavements. Caught in the downpour, people covered their heads, dived for doorways and shops, and darted into the street in a desperate attempt to snag the few taxis among the snarl of traffic.

Bianca pulled the collar of her coat up over her head as best she could and ran.

The apartment was still some ten blocks away. She would be soaked to the skin and half frozen by the time she reached it. *If* she reached it —

"La Chien Rouge on the corner," said Colin's voice in her ear.

Glancing up, Bianca saw the swinging sign with the picture of a grinning red dog above the words *La Chien Rouge* a few doors down. Hard to be certain given the blinding effect of the rain, but it looked like a restaurant and bar. Instant verdict: way better than what was out on the street. Darting toward it, she reached the heavy wooden door, pulled it open and went inside.

15

The smell — booze, roasted meat, wood smoke and wet dog from all the people crowding inside seeking refuge from the rain — was what first struck her, along with the warmth after the freezing wet. Then the sounds — the hum of conversation, clinking glasses, laughter, music. The lighting was low, intimate: a couple of dim chandeliers, multicolored Christmas lights draped around doorways, a corner hearth with a flickering fire, votive candles in glass holders on each table. The walls were white, rough, probably stucco. The floor was dark wood. The ceiling was tall and beamed. A dark wood bar ran the length of one wall. The stools in front of it were filled, and the people who couldn't snag a stool crowded around. Busy bartenders poured without pause. Small tables were crammed with far more diners than they'd been intended to hold. Servers wove among them, taking orders, delivering food and drink. A pair of harried-looking hostesses worked to seat the newcomers.

Forget waiting to be seated. Bianca pushed through the knots of dripping people huddled near the door, walked swiftly away from the big front window toward the back of what seemed to be a combination bar/restaurant/nightclub, spied a tiny two-top in a corner sheltered by a fake ficus decked out with fake gold birds and sat down on a folding metal chair with her back to the wall. Her throwing star was there for the grabbing, and under the cover of the table she pushed her skirt up so that, if necessary, she would have unimpeded access to the knife in her garter belt. With so many people continually coming through the door it was difficult to be sure, but she thought she would know if any of the new arrivals were the source of the danger she'd felt.

Felt: past tense. Her skin no longer crawled, she realized. She no longer had the sensation that she was caught in the crosshairs. Of course, she was inside a restaurant crowded with people, her back squarely against a wall. Her exposure had lessened. Didn't mean the danger had.

"Mademoiselle, are you alone? Tonight everyone must share tables."

Bianca looked up at those words, which were spoken in French, to find one of the hostesses standing in front of her table with a party of three drowned-looking tourists huddled behind her. Clearly they were hoping to join her at her table.

"She isn't alone." A familiar deep voice spoke up in French behind them before Bianca could reply, and Colin stepped around the women. In English, for what she knew was their benefit, he said to her with a smile, "Unless she wants to be. My name's George. May I join you?"

Ah, the chance-met stranger ploy. Anyone who'd watched her leave the hotel and walk down the street alone would hopefully be fooled into thinking she was a lonely single and he was picking her up.

"I'm Alice. And, yes, you may." Bianca looked up at him as he loomed above her, so glad to see him that what felt like a warm little pulse kicked off inside her. Then the realization of how glad she was to see him hit her, disconcerting her, and she frowned instead of smiled at him. By that time the hostess and her hopeful trio had moved away.

"Do you always look this grumpy when you're hungry, or did I do something to make you mad?" His hat and coat dripped water. He took them off as he spoke, dropping his coat over the back of the chair and thrusting his hat into its pocket. The gray thermal crewneck he wore over a T-shirt clung to his broad shoulders. It was dry, but rain had spattered the hem of his jeans halfway to his knees. More water droplets glinted on the ends of his hair, which was curling from the damp, and beaded the black scruff that darkened his jaw. Moving his chair so that he was beside rather than across from her, he sat down, his long legs stretching out under the table. His back was also to the wall: more tradecraft 101.

Bianca cut to the chase. "There was someone on the street right before I ducked in here. I could feel them watching me. It felt hard-core, like a hit in progress." She kept her voice down. The place was so noisy, and there was so much commotion, that she didn't really fear being overheard. Still, because of the whole pin-drop-on-Mars thing, and because dotting all her *i*'s and crossing all her *t*'s was second nature to her, she removed her earrings and set them side by side on the table facing each other. It wasn't showy, it made no noise, but it was effective: both earrings contained tiny listening devices, and small as they were, those two listening devices placed in close proximity to each other would emit a high-pitched screech that was inaudible to the human ear but would be all any would-be eavesdropper with his own listening device could hear.

A quick look around proved disappointing: no one jumped up or cursed or clawed at his ears.

Colin frowned at her earrings. Then his eyes met hers in a moment of acknowledgment that told her he recognized exactly what she'd done and approved. Her feelings about that wavered back and forth between being pleased to be with someone she didn't have to explain things to and disturbed to realize how much they really did have in common. They spoke the same language. Their frame of reference was the same.

Taking off his spectacles, he hooked them into the neckline of his shirt and looked out at the crowd, sweeping the whole with a thoughtful glance before concentrating on individuals.

"You see anybody following you?" he asked.

She appreciated the fact that he didn't press her — *are you sure, could you have been mistaken* — instead accepting what she told him as the cool assessment of a professional that it was.

"No." She shook her head. "But someone

was out there. I'm sure of it."

"They see you duck in here, do you think?"

"I don't know. The rain — it came on so suddenly. Everybody scattered."

The waiter arrived with menus. "Would you like drinks?" he asked in French.

Colin replied in the same language, "A bottle of cabernet sauvignon, please."

When the waiter nodded and left, Bianca said, "Just for the record, I don't drink on the job."

He smiled at her. "Neither do I, beautiful. So what's the best way to convince anyone who might be watching us that we're not on the job?"

Good point. Bianca gave him an aren't-you-smart grimace, opened the menu, glanced at it and switched her attention back to the crowd.

He'd opened his menu, too. "You think whatever you felt out there was directed at Lynette?"

"I've been thinking about that. I picked up on the feeling a couple of blocks from here. After I left the hotel. Dressed like this. I don't see how anyone could have made me as Lynette."

His eyes swept her. "You don't look like Lynette." A slow smile crinkled his eyes, stretched his mouth. "You look hot as hell." Before she could react to that, he added, "And wet." Scooting the silverware that had been nestled on top of it aside, he passed her the white cloth napkin that had been folded in front of him. "Your hair's dripping onto your coat. Pat the ends, take off your coat and we'll grab some food. Kill two birds with one stone. The most dedicated hit man in the world isn't going to stay out there long in this."

He gave a nod at the sheets of rain pounding the big window. Thunder boomed as she obediently blotted the ends of her wig, and they both watched a flash of lightning powerful enough to light up the night. A few people close to the window cried out and jumped away from it. One of the hostesses, looking harassed, hurried over and drew deep red curtains across the window.

Bianca breathed a little easier. Although she knew that a shot fired through driving rain tended to be inaccurate, a crack sniper just might make the attempt.

And people sometimes got lucky.

"Could be a hit woman. Or a hit squad," she pointed out.

"Could be."

"They could go in across the street, somewhere where they could keep watch until I come back out." She slid out of her coat and draped it over the back of her chair. Her purse she kept on her lap. There was too much that was damning, too much that was Lynette in it.

"As long as it's raining like this, good luck recognizing you from across the street. Unless they're in here with us, they're done until it lets up," Colin said.

"You were behind me. You didn't notice anybody following me in?"

"Lots of people. Nobody that struck me as a problem."

The waiter returned with their wine, poured it and took their order. Colin went for Coquilles St. Jacques. She chose salmon.

Your body is your temple. Her father — or, rather, Mason — had said that so often that anytime she thought about eating something that he would condemn as unhealthy she heard his voice in her head.

And listened, because he was right. But, oh, she loved Coquilles St. Jacques.

When the waiter left, they refocused on assessing their fellow patrons.

"See any familiar faces?" Colin asked. Kicked back in his chair with his shoulders resting against the wall, sipping at his wine, he looked casual, relaxed — and seriously handsome. She noticed, gave herself a mental shake and glanced away.

"No." But the room was large, the lighting uncertain, the corners dark with shadows. There was a lot of movement, staff carrying in more folding chairs from wherever they were kept, hostesses seating people, more people milling around the bar, getting up to go to the restroom or do whatever. The music was an oldies mix of American rhythm and blues, pop, rock. At the moment the selection was Michael Jackson's "Billie Jean." A few couples had gotten up to dance in a cleared space in the center of the floor.

"Anybody you know in Paris whose path you might have crossed on the street just now without realizing it?" he asked. The way his gaze roamed the place looked idle. It wasn't. Good technique: she approved.

She'd been to Paris many, many times, as Bianca and a variety of other identities. On this trip, she'd taken good care to stay away from anywhere she'd been or anyone who knew her or any of her identities.

"Nobody who wants to kill me. That I know of," she qualified. "Anyway, that would mean they'd recognized me. In the dark. And rain. Dressed like this. I won't say it's impossible, but it's not very likely."

"No," he agreed. "You never know — US

intelligence might be moving faster than I gave them credit for. Maybe they've already determined what was stolen, nailed Lynette as the culprit, traced her — you — here, spotted you on the street despite the red hair and sent a team to take you out."

"Wait a minute — I thought the whole CIA kill team thing was over."

His lips quirked in the slightest suggestion of a smile. "It's over for you. Not Lynette."

Bianca groaned and dropped her head in her hands.

Colin continued, "Or maybe it's the French. Or the Brits. Or the Aussies. If they know what Lynette did, they'll all be trying to stop her and recover the information she stole. The Russians and the Chinese, on the other hand, would be trying to get that information for themselves. So would about a dozen assorted criminal organizations. Or maybe the last time you were a redhead — let's see, would that be Jennifer Ashley in Bahrain? That girl had some moves — you seriously ticked somebody off and they recognized you just now. After all, the prince and his minions put a contract out on you not so very long ago. Didn't they?"

She looked up. "Yes," she lied. The truth was complicated. And strictly need to know, which he didn't. Ever. "Nice to reflect that multiple people want to kill me under multiple identities. Could be any of them. This is fun."

"We'll figure it out."

"Before I stop a bullet would be good."

"We'll be out of here in under sixteen hours. I think we can keep you alive for that long."

"You don't know how reassuring I find that 'I think.' "

He smiled. As "Billie Jean" gave way to Eric Carmen's "Hungry Eyes," he said, "Your only other exposure will be tomorrow."

When she did the handoff to Park. Bianca wasn't thrilled with the setup for that, but together she and Colin had worked out the way it had to go down. Park frequented a newsstand near his house every morning at 6:00 a.m. sharp before walking to a nearby patisserie for breakfast, after which he went to his office. As he'd been informed via the flash drive she'd given him, if he bought a copy of the *New York Times* along with his usual purchases, she, watching from a distance, would know that the sale was a go and would meet him along the route to the patisserie. He would transfer the money to her account, she would hand over the Chap-

Stick, and the thing would be done and dusted.

The key to making it work lay in keeping Park convinced that she was Lynette, which was the tricky part. Lynette was not a spy. She was not an operative of any kind. She wasn't even a practiced criminal. She would not make sophisticated plans for a drop that would limit her vulnerability. She would do what she had done before: approach Park directly.

Thus exposing herself to danger. Which was why, as Colin had pointed out, she, Bianca, was earning the big bucks.

"After that I'm going home," she said, and was surprised by how fiercely she wanted to. Being an international woman of mystery was getting old.

"Savannah, you mean?"

Before she could reply — or not — the food arrived. Bianca had forgotten how starved she was until the plates were set before them. Her salmon came on a bed of greens and was nutritious and, she had no doubt, well prepared, but she looked enviously at his Coquilles St. Jacques: plump scallops in a creamy wine sauce cooked with cheese and breadcrumbs. The savory scent of it made her mouth water. And her stomach growl.

Noticing, he grinned at her. She switched her attention back to her own plate and they both tucked into their food.

"You know, for a girl who seems as much at ease in Bahrain as Paris, in Macau as Moscow, who speaks at least five languages that I know of fluently, who flimflams the likes of princes and billionaires without batting an eye, a sleepy little town deep in America's South seems an odd choice of a place to call home," he said. "I thought that was just a cover for Bianca St. Ives. Apparently not?"

Bianca chewed, swallowed, before she replied.

"I like Savannah." Her tone was noncommittal. If he thought Bianca St. Ives was just one more cover identity, that was all to the good. She made a show of sipping her wine, but because she was working and the necessity for staying absolutely clearheaded while she did had been drummed into her practically from birth, she was actually, stealthily, tipping her wine a little at a time into the ficus's brass planter. His wine was disappearing at a steady clip, too, but if he was doing anything other than drinking it she couldn't tell. "How, exactly, did you find me there?"

"You really want to know?" He speared a

piece of scallop.

"Yes."

"Take a bite of this and I'll tell you." He held out his fork to her. "Come on, you know you want to." The morsel on the end of his fork looked succulent — but the stare she gave him over it was totally affronted. He laughed. "Baby, talk about some Hungry Eyes. You've been giving my food lustful glances since it got here."

"I have not." But she knew she had. "Fine." She took the fork, ate the bite of scallop — *so, so good* — and handed the fork back to him as "Hungry Eyes" thankfully finished and the music moved on. "So tell me."

"I had ears in when I was following you in Moscow. I heard you say something to your buddy Doc about River Street Sweets. Google that, you get Savannah, Georgia, USA. Piece of cake."

There you go — a pin drop on Mars. The earrings on the table suddenly seemed all-important.

"Have another bite. It'll make you feel better." He grinned at her as he passed over another forkful of scallop. An amused and totally charming grin that had her narrowing her eyes at him before accepting and eating — *mmm, to die for* — his offering.

"So where's home to you?" she asked, refusing another bite with a shake of her head and a stern, I-really-mean-it-this-time look. Accepting her refusal, he ate it himself while she turned with determination to her salmon.

"Carlingford, County Louth. I grew up there."

"Really?" That jibed with the research on him she'd read, but the principle to remember when it came to research was, garbage in, garbage out. As she illustrated all too well herself.

"Yes, really. Mam and Dad, two brothers. I was the middle one. A handful, so my mother tells me."

"I bet." She was entranced by this glimpse into his early life. Families did that to her. "She's still alive? Your mother? What about your dad?"

"My father passed away five years ago. My mother's fine, as are my brothers. I see them when I can." He took another fake (?) sip of wine. "Scholarship to the Royal Military Academy at Sandhurst, army officer, MI6, private contractor. There you have it."

"Married? Children?" She couldn't help it. She had to know.

"No. You?"

That one was easy. "No."

He asked, "What about your family? I've found so many cover stories for so many identities for you that the only thing I'm relatively sure of is that you're American."

"Oh? Why is that?"

"Your accent. When you're just being you and not someone else."

For some reason, the idea that he'd seen her as herself, as well as Sylvia No-Last-Name and Beth McAlister and Jennifer Ashley and Cara Levine and Brenda Smolski and Kangana Batt and Maggy Chance and now Lynette Holbrook and red-haired Alice Dunn, made her feel way too exposed. Almost naked. Not many people had ever managed to get that close a look into her life.

"So where'd you grow up?" he persisted when she didn't reply. "I'm betting it wasn't Savannah. You don't strike me as a born-and-bred Southern belle."

She shook her head. Adopted a playful tone that she hoped didn't sound too forced as she turned the spotlight back on him. "Oh, no, you're not finished. Tell me more. What's it like to basically be —" she hesitated, recalled Doc's description and fluttered her eyelashes at him teasingly "— James Bond?"

He laughed and shook his head. "James

Bond was Her Majesty's Secret Service all the way. I'm a dropout. Fewer constraints, way more money in the private sector. Plus you can pick and choose your jobs."

"Like this one."

"Like this one," he agreed. His eyes gleamed dark gold in the candlelight and were impossible to read as he looked at her.

Meeting them, Bianca found to her dismay that her heart beat faster. She frowned —

"There's a man over there near the fireplace," he said. He leaned closer and picked up her hand. His hand was warm and strong and much bigger than hers, with long tan fingers that looked like they could break her pale slender ones in half with ease. She found the fact that she even registered that disconcerting and did a quick mental refocus. His businesslike tone was at total odds with his gesture, which was outwardly romantic. "He's been watching us off and on for a while. Dark brown hair, long enough to hide part of his face, which is pale and square. About five-ten, stocky. Maybe thirty? Around there."

Bianca fought the urge to glance that way. "Doesn't ring a bell."

"Let's give you a look." Colin stood up and walked around the table, pulling her to her feet. "Come on, sexy Alice. Dance with me."

16

Too easy for someone to steal her purse or go through its contents if she left it behind, so Bianca took it with her. She barely had time to grab her earrings, tuck them *together* — take that, eavesdroppers — into the outside pocket of her purse and sling the strap cross-body over her shoulder before they reached the dance floor and Colin pulled her around to face him.

"He's watching. We need to act like we're hot for each other," he said under his breath.

Maddeningly conscious of a little kick in her pulse, a small hitch in her breathing, at the very idea, she smiled at him, a slow, come-hither smile that had his eyes widening with surprise and then flaring.

The song was Bob Dylan's "Lay, Lady, Lay." She started swaying to its beat, her movements slow, seductive. His eyes dropped to her mouth, then went all heavy-lidded and sensuous as they moved down her body. Finally they came back up to meet her eyes again. Sparks sizzled between them: unwanted, inconvenient, but nevertheless there. The electricity they generated was every bit as tangible as the lightning flashing outside.

He still held her hand. He used it to pull her close.

"You're good at this," he murmured, and wrapped his arms around her. That brought her smack up against him. He was all firm muscle on a six-foot-three-inch, broad-shouldered frame. His arms felt hard and possessive around her. As he danced her backward, she tried not to notice any of that.

Hot. Steamy. Oh, God, maybe this was a mistake.

Keep your game face on.

"I'm good at everything." Full of bravado, she draped her arms over his shoulders and moved provocatively against him. His head bent toward her. His wavy black hair, long-lashed caramel eyes, straight nose with the bump on its bridge, wryly curving mouth, filled her vision, right before he traced the slightest of butterfly kisses just above her left eyebrow. If this was a game of turn-me-on chicken, she was pretty sure that nothing gesture took this round: she caught her breath, barely resisted giving in to a pleasurable shiver and glanced away. They were in the middle of the dance floor now, surrounded by other gyrating couples. She knew he'd placed them there deliberately. He was also keeping his body between her and the possible source of danger, and she knew he was doing that deliberately, too. She was no delicate flower who needed his protection, she wanted to remind him — but, she discovered, somewhere deep inside she found the fact that he *was* protecting her entrancing.

"I'll keep that in mind," he said. His hands moved down until they were almost on her ass. She could feel the size and shape of them just a couple of inches north of being publicly indecent. She flashed him a warning look. He responded with a barely-there, teasing smile. She had to work to keep her pulse rate under control. And her sexy moves firmly on beat.

"You do that," she said. Undulating against him as she was, there was no way to miss the evidence of his arousal. Not that it was a surprise. Being held so closely to him was — not optimum. She was keenly aware that her breasts were being sensitized by the pressure of his chest against them, of the intimacy of their pelvic contact with every bump and grind of the dance, of the elemental yin and yang of their bodies. She was having to exert every iota of her truly legendary self-control to keep it professional, to block out the physical, to not let herself get all hot and bothered, too.

Their eyes met. She could see from the look in his that he was aware she was aware of the effect she was having on him. She only hoped it didn't work the other way.

"They're playing our song," he said, and that was the first time she realized the song had changed. It took her a second, but she managed to focus on the music and listen: Carly Simon's "Nobody Does It Better."

She had to smile. "I thought we already had a song." She was referring to a joke — a sort of joke, a really aggravating sort of joke — he'd played on her when they first met.

He shook his head. "That was Sylvia and Mickey's song. This one's for us."

Us.

Her lips parted. She felt an unexpected flash of pure swoon. *Crap.*

Who would have thought that a simple, two-letter *word* could punch such a hole in her defenses?

Keep it about the job.

"The earrings will work to block a listening device, but somebody close could still overhear," she said, her voice low.

"Thanks for the warning." He bent closer, spoke in her ear. "To the left of the fireplace, in a party of four. Probably put together by the hostess like she tried to do to you." His lips barely brushed the delicate swirls. That slight touch of his mouth on her skin sent a jolt of sexual awareness through her that went clear down to her toes. *Oh no.* She tried to rebuild her own personal, private, internal wall. Didn't know if she succeeded. "Check him out."

He dipped her, his eyes blatantly eating her up as she arched her back and shook everything she had to shake — and shot a covert look at the man in question.

He was exactly as described. And he was indeed watching them.

She'd never seen him before in her life.

Colin pulled her upright, and they swayed from side to side. She tightened her arms around his neck, went up on tiptoe to press her cheek to his. The heat of his skin, the sandpapery feel of his jaw, the scent of rain and man, made her breathing quicken. She wanted to turn her head the little bit it would take to press her mouth to — *Oh no. Not going there. No.*

Bad news: the wall was still breached.

"He's watching us," she agreed. Dear

God, had her voice gone husky? If so —
okay, it had — she hoped he couldn't tell
over the music. "I don't recognize him."

"Not a remnant from your murky past?"

"What murky past?"

He smiled. Because they were cheek to
cheek she felt rather than saw it, in the rasp
of manly stubble against smooth feminine
skin.

"I don't know — the one you won't talk
about?"

She pulled back a little, pulled her cheek
away from his. That left her eyes on a level
with his chin. She registered the sheer
masculinity of that square, black-bristled
jaw and shifted her gaze. It landed on his
mouth: a little too thin, maybe a little cruel
looking. She happened to know from personal experience what it felt like to kiss that
mouth, have it kiss her back. Have *him* kiss
her —

No. No. No.

Keep emotion out of it. It was one of the
rules. This was a textbook illustration of
why: it was the emotional impact of that *us*
that was threatening to do a number on her
life.

"I prefer to focus on the present," she
said, and was proud of how cool and collected she sounded. "And as far as our

watcher's concerned, I don't feel like he's a threat. At least, I'm not getting the same vibe I did on the street."

His arms tightened around her. His lips moved back to her ear. "Then look around, see if you can spot anyone else we need to be worried about."

She *did not* melt against him. She did pull her head away from his mouth, but not obviously, not in such a way that he would know that what he was doing was getting to her. She plugged the gap in her defenses, righted her listing ship and got on with the *job.* With his back between her and the vast majority of the tables, she adopted a glazed expression that she hoped said *I'm so into my partner* and looked over his broad shoulder to cast covert glances at the packed tables.

The next song up was the Mike Reno– Ann Wilson duet "Almost Paradise." Registering that, Bianca almost shook her head. Whoever was in charge of the playlist (God? Probably not) seemed to have a wicked sense of humor coupled with uncanny insight into her life.

With thunder rumbling and torrents of rain still audibly pelting the window, everyone who was inside was staying put. People had settled in, were eating, drinking. The dance floor grew more crowded by the minute. Surrounded by shimmying, shaking, gliding couples, she and Colin danced their way around the floor. She clung to him, matching him move for sexy move. Endured his body curved around hers, his arms holding her so close a sheet of paper wouldn't fit between them, his cheek brushing hers, his whispers in her ear. Endured all that friction. All that heat.

And determinedly kept her mind on her business despite the fact that her blood felt like it was turning to steam.

"Anything?" he asked. The mouth-on-her-ear thing he kept doing was really hard to resist. She had to fight to keep her heartbeat under control, to keep her breathing even, to keep from tilting her head in silent invitation to his lips to explore the sensitive side of her neck. Was he aware? Was he doing it on purpose? Her guess was, yes. She thought about calling him on it, but the last thing she wanted to do was let him know how vulnerable to him she apparently was.

So suck it up, buttercup.

Her eyes collided with those of a man chugging from a beer mug in front of the red curtains. No sooner did their eyes meet than he looked swiftly away. He, too, was seated at a four-top. Short dark hair, beefy build. Dark shirt. It was difficult to see more detail because he leaned back in his chair, which put him deep in shadow.

Deliberately? Impossible to know.

She didn't think she'd ever seen him before.

He didn't seem to fit with the Christmas-sweater-wearing trio of wine drinkers seated with him. But then, the rain made for strange tablemates.

What struck her was how quickly he'd glanced away.

"Over near the window. Four-top, third table from the hostess station," she said in Colin's ear, and described the guy. "We need to get closer so I can get a better look."

"Hang on." He danced her toward where they needed to be. When they stopped to kind of sway in place, his back was once again between her and the possible source of danger. The marshmallowy reaction *that* engendered in her was something she thrust out of her mind. Right now she had more important things to worry about than the possibly calamitous state of her feelings.

Like identifying somebody who maybe wanted to kill her.

"Close as we're getting," he said in her ear. "Look him over."

A fair number of couples still boogied

down between them and their target, providing cover and, if necessary, protection. Human Kevlar, anyone?

"I don't want him to catch me staring at him over your shoulder again. Turn me around so that my back's to him, and let's do a dip."

"You got it."

He turned, then supported her with one hard arm while she let her head and upper torso fall back and shook what God gave her. He slid his thigh between her legs. Then he lifted her hips right up against him and rocked into her. Full contact. Bulge to notch. Unexpected. Impactful. She sucked in air. Her bones threatened to melt. Deep inside, her body took it to a whole nother level: it clutched and began to throb. The wave of desire that washed over her instantly made her weak-kneed and dizzy and so, so *hot.*

She wanted, she wanted —

Oh, hell, no.

Keeping her focus required a Herculean effort, but she did it. Gritted her teeth, swayed to the beat, ignored how hot he was getting her and checked out the target.

Guy was mid to late forties. Brawny. Short dark hair. Face of a bulldog: small eyes, loose mouth, jowly cheeks. He was looking at the dance floor, but not at Colin and her.

She didn't recognize him.

Colin pulled her upright.

She shook her head. He knew what she was saying.

He bent his head, touched his mouth to her cheek. His target, she knew, was her ear.

She felt the warm crawl of his mouth against her skin all over, everywhere there was to feel it, with every nerve ending she possessed. For such a relatively insignificant caress, the effect was phenomenal. Against her better judgment, against her *will,* she was turned on to her back teeth, and not only was it all his fault, not only did she suspect his actions were meant to achieve just that, this was absolutely *not the moment.*

Something was niggling at her.

Turning her head, and not incidentally putting her ear out of reach of Colin's mouth, she directed one more covert glance at the target.

He still wasn't looking at them. Instead, his attention was on the server, whom he was signaling with an uplifted hand.

He was left-handed, she saw, and the ring finger on that dominant hand was missing. What remained wasn't a smooth stump, but a jagged one, as if the digit had been — chewed off by rats.

Four-fingered Franz.

The memory came flooding back: she was ten years old, and she and her father — not her father, *Mason* — were in Paris. They were robbing a bank vault. Correction, *she* was robbing a bank vault, because she was the only one who could fit through the bars of the enormous iron gate that closed off the section of the vault that held the safe-deposit boxes. Mason and the gang he had put together were staging a robbery of the bank itself as a distraction, but the items he was really after were in six of the safe-deposit boxes. Assuming that a silent alarm would be triggered when the cover robbery commenced and the tellers were ordered from their cages, she had three minutes to get in, open the safe-deposit boxes, dump the contents into a bag and get out with the loot before the outer door of the vault slammed down and locked, sealing her inside. She made it, Mason got what he was after, and the crime was officially chalked up as just one more bank robbery. But the salient point was that one member of the gang was Four-fingered Franz. She didn't know if that was his real name, but that was Mason's name for him. That, and the story of the rats chewing off his finger, which Four-fingered Franz had told her with macabre relish when he'd caught her looking at his damaged hand, had stayed with her to this day.

There's no such thing as coincidence. That was something else Mason had said so often that she'd wanted to stick her fingers in her ears.

Now she considered it gospel.

There was no way a known criminal and affiliate of French mobsters was in this particular place at this particular time by chance.

Adrenaline surged through her veins. Tightening her arms around Colin's neck, she went up on tiptoe to whisper, "I take it back. I do know him. He's a career criminal, a member of Le Milieu —" the French equivalent of the mafia "— and I don't think him being here is a coincidence. From what I recall of him, he doesn't have the brains to pull anything on his own, but I think he could be acting as a spotter."

Spotters sometimes worked a hit, keeping up surveillance on the target until the moment was right for the killer to do the deed. The upside was convenience — the hitter only had to show up and carry out the hit, which meant less exposure time, fewer potential witnesses and less chance of being made by the target prior to the hit. The downside was, spotters were potential witnesses, too. Untrustworthy ones quickly wound up sleeping with the coquilles.

Colin didn't so much as miss a dance step. His mouth found her ear again, but this time there was nothing sexual about it.

"Time to go," he said.

"We need to take him out first so he can't let anybody know we're leaving."

Because the notification that they were leaving was probably what the hit man/woman/squad was waiting for. As she had feared, she thought it probable that whoever wanted to kill her was set up so that they could hit her as she exited the restaurant.

"We could try just sneaking out the back door."

"It opens into a courtyard that exits onto the same street. I saw it when I came in," she said. Checking for alternate ways out was something she did automatically whenever she entered a building. This one was less than ideal. Any competent hit man would be covering both exits.

"The other back door."

"Where is it?"

"Kitchen. Exits into an alley."

"How do you know?"

"I've eaten here before. And gone out that way."

That brought a number of questions to the tip of her tongue, but she filed them away for (maybe) later. She was in the grip of a driving conviction that time was of the essence here.

She said, "Even if we go out that way, we still need to take him out before we leave. Otherwise he'll be coming after us himself or sending someone after us."

"Want me to shoot him?"

Men. Genus: Subtle-R-Not-Us.

"No," she said. "I'll handle it, thanks."

Before Colin could respond, she broke free of him and headed directly toward Four-fingered Franz — and the server, an attractive young woman who was bringing him another beer. When the server reached his table, Bianca meant to reach it, too. Because Franz could not possibly know that she was the little girl who'd been in on the bank robbery he'd participated in sixteen years previously, he would not expect her to recognize him, and thus her heading in his direction should not make him overly suspicious. Her cover for approaching his table would be asking the other woman the way to the ladies' room. When the server turned to point it out, she would unobtrusively chop Franz in the G-spot and render him unconscious. It would happen so fast he wouldn't even have time to make a sound.

When the server looked back, all she would see was a man slumped on the table or the floor (depending on how he fell) in what would likely be deemed a medical emergency.

Chaos would ensue. Meanwhile, she and Colin would be hightailing it out through the kitchen.

She was steps away from Franz's table, where the server was handing over his requested beer.

"Pardon, mademoiselle," she began. The server looked at her inquiringly.

A commotion at the entrance brought both their heads swinging around toward it. Bianca's heart leaped as four masked gunmen burst through the restaurant door, pistol-whipping the screaming hostess to the floor and — *Pfft! Pfft!* — shooting a male sommelier who got in their way.

The sommelier crumpled bleeding to the ground. With a jolt of escalating alarm, Bianca automatically registered the weapons as Ceska automatic rifles with suppressor cans. Verdict: not your garden-variety street thugs.

The gunmen stormed into the main part of the restaurant.

"Sur le plancher!" they screamed, ordering everyone onto the floor.

17

Bianca's already quick-stepping heart slammed into overdrive. The server gasped and dropped her tray with a tooth-rattling clatter. Fear exploded through the restaurant. Cries of alarm arose on all sides. Plates, glasses, silverware crashed down on hard surfaces as chaos descended. Chairs screeched as they were shoved away from tables. People sprang to their feet, dived under tables or simply sat, terrified into immobility. On the dance floor, screaming couples ducked down or tried to run away. She saw Colin crouch —

"On the floor!" the gunmen shouted in French again. One sprayed gunfire high, over the heads of the scrambling diners. Even muffled by a suppressor, the rapid-fire chatter of the automatic rifle was terrifying. Chunks of plaster and other debris rained down. People threw themselves to the floor, covered their heads, screamed. A few tried to bolt, caught bullets for their pains. They shrieked and fell, eliciting more shrieks from those who weren't hit. Blood sprayed from convulsing bodies. The burned-toast smell of cordite from the gunfire filled the air.

Not for the first time in her life, Bianca regretted her lack of a firearm. But the covert nature of the job, coupled with the strict French gun laws, made packing heat a nonstarter. She was armed with weapons of her own, though, and there was Colin . . .

Wooden chair legs scraped noisily across the floor mere inches away as Franz jumped up from the table. He was looking at the gunmen, his expression not terrified but — expectant. Was he with them? Was he not? Didn't matter: he was a threat.

She took him out exactly as she had intended, with a silent chop to his meaty neck that had him dropping like a felled tree. Her purpose was to get a known enemy out of the way and clear the decks for engagement with the main enemy even if this wasn't (as she suspected it was) ultimately directed at her. The result was to get one of those automatic rifles swinging around in her direction as a gunman appeared to catch Franz's fall out of the corner of his eye and turned to investigate. Before his gaze could definitively fix on her she shoved the screaming-like-a-banshee server to the floor and went with her.

"Shut up. Stay down," she hissed in French at the server, and closed a hand around her throwing star.

Bang. Bang. Bang.

More gunfire — no suppressor there — erupted from the vicinity of the dance floor, snapping her gaze in that direction. Bullets slammed into the gunmen, who shrieked and dropped or shouted and took cover amid more ground-shaking screams all around.

Colin. She knew it was him even before she saw him, hunkered down behind an overturned table, Glock in hand. Glancing at her, he came up firing and yelled, *"Let's go."*

Oh, yeah. While he had them pinned down. Staying low, she darted toward him, past him, taking care to stay behind him so as not to get in his line of fire. Sprinting toward the kitchen, she leapfrogged it through the seething mass of people rolling and commando crawling and regular crawling and attempting every other means of low-level locomotion known to man as they tried to escape the main dining room. Everywhere cell phones glowed as mass calls were placed to the 112 emergency number.

She would have felt guilty about abandoning so many innocents except she was almost 100 percent sure they would be safer with her gone, that the attack had been staged with the sole purpose of capturing her or taking her out and once she was no longer present the danger would vanish, along with any surviving attackers, like cockroaches in the light.

"Go, *go.*" Colin fell in behind her, both of them bolting past the bar and the dozen people sheltering behind it toward the swinging door to the kitchen.

Bianca was maybe ten feet away from that heavy wood panel when it bounced open. Her heart stuttered in horror as a trio of masked gunmen rushed through it.

"*Ah,*" she squeaked, jumping back and cannoning into the solid mass that was Colin, who, she saw in a lightning glance, had been covering their exit by looking behind them and had to get up to speed on this new development fast. Equally surprised, the lead gunman hesitated a vital second before leveling his weapon at her — and that was all she needed.

"*Eat this.*" A punch of her thumb, a flick of her wrist, and her throwing star spun through the air to lodge in his neck. His eyes went wide with surprise. He made a strangled sound. His gun clattered to the floor. Clutching at the sharp metal plate in his neck, he fell back against his compatriots. Blood sprayed from his neck like soda from a shaken can as the three of them stumbled back into the kitchen and the door swung shut behind them.

So, kitchen exit out.

Bounding forward, she snatched up the fallen weapon — a Desert Eagle 50. Not her favorite semiautomatic pistol. It was heavy at around four pounds and light on capacity with a seven-bullet max. Still, it could do some damage — and what was that thing they said about beggars?

She turned to find a shrieking horde of panicked diners stampeding toward them from the dining room.

"Go out through the courtyard," she screamed at them in French, pointing the way. They turned en masse. Possibly the fact that she was waving a pistol the size of a super soaker had something to do with it.

"This way." Colin grabbed her wrist and yanked her through another door.

This one opened onto a switchback staircase. She could see straight up to the stained-glass skylight awash in rain some seven floors above. Since down wasn't an option, up was the only way to go, so up she went. Fast.

"You want to tell me again how this is better than a CIA kill team?" Bianca threw that over her shoulder at him as they pounded up the windowless stairs.

"They're not as good."

"And you know that how?"

"We're not dead."

"What's this *we* thing? It's me everybody's trying to kill."

He stayed close behind her, on purpose to cover her back again, she had no doubt. The stair silo was well kept. The lighting, dim but adequate, came from brass sconces. Christmas garlands festooned the railings, paintings graced the white plaster walls and waist-high green ceramic planters complete with seasonal poinsettias occupied pride of place on each postage stamp–sized landing beside dark oak doors that provided access to the various floors. The halls all contained apartments, she was sure, as the typical arrangement in Paris was for living accommodations to be located in the floors above ground-level restaurants and shops.

"You've got to get over thinking everything is about you. Although, to be fair, this probably is." His voice was faintly breathless.

"Ya think?"

"So who are they?"

"How should I know? You're the one with all the spook friends."

"These guys aren't spooks. They're criminals."

"Oh, and I know all the criminals?"

"You knew that one downstairs. Not a stretch to think they might be together."

"I have no idea who they are. Well, most of them. Except for that one guy."

From below came the unmistakable sound of a door opening, complete with a sharp blast of chaotic sound from the restaurant that was almost immediately shut off as the door closed again. Bianca stopped dead on the sixth-floor landing. Grabbing Colin's arm as he stopped beside her, she made a silencing gesture. His lip curled as in, *yeah, I figured that out.*

"They in here? Do you see them?" The questions, whispered in French, floated up the stairwell, leaving her in no doubt about who had just entered it.

"No. Listen."

Okay, so the bad guys were six floors below. Bianca deliberately slowed her too-rapid breathing, her pounding pulse, and centered herself for what she suspected was the coming battle. It was all she could do to resist the urge to look over the rail.

Colin stepped away from her — she was

once again impressed with how silently he could move — and tried the door to the hallway.

"Locked," he mouthed.

It was her turn to curl her lip at him. *No duh.*

Cre-e-eak. Cre-e-eak. Cre-e-eak.

If their pursuers were going for quiet as a mouse, they'd reckoned without the venerable wood of the steps. What felt like an icy finger ran down her spine as Bianca realized what she was hearing: the gunmen creeping up the stairs.

The choice was stark. They could shoot it out, thus making sure the bad guys knew where they were as well as attracting every surviving gunman in the building plus a whole host of others, including *gendarmes* and God knew who else with, perhaps, an unhealthy interest in Bianca St. Ives, Lynette Holbrook or any or all of her alter egos, or they could run.

Running got her vote. She and Colin needed to get out of the stairwell. Now. Using her purse as a makeshift holster, she shoved the Desert Eagle into it so that the weapon would be easy to draw if necessary and went for her lock pick.

Before she could get it free the sound of a door opening on the landing directly below brought her head up. It was immediately followed by an exuberant scrabbling and a burst of rapid footsteps.

Bianca sucked in her breath as she realized what she was hearing: innocent bystanders heading unknowingly down the stairs. They were talking — a man and a woman, maybe two kids —

She risked a look over the rail, to find a young couple, two early elementary–age girls and a pug on a leash going down the stairs, and one of the gunmen, apparently attracted by the same sounds that had drawn her attention, craning his neck to look up. He was just a few steps short of the second-floor landing. Another gunman was right behind him.

The young family was toast. No way would the gunmen let them get that up-close-and-personal a look at them and live.

The first gunman saw Bianca at approximately the same time she saw him. His eyes widened. She jumped back, but too late.

"There they are!" the gunman yelled, and fired. *Pfft. Pfft. Pfft. Pfft. Pfft.* Bullets smacked into plaster and wood. Debris went everywhere. The couple screamed. The children wailed. The pug barked hysterically. From the ensuing sounds they all fled back up the stairs. The echo chamber that was the stairwell amplified everything.

Pfft. Pfft. Pfft. Pfft. Pfft.

More shots zinged past as the gunmen stormed upward, firing as they came. Abandoning the landing to race on up the stairs ahead of them was a bad idea: on the stairs, she and Colin made too easy a target. Colin's weapon was in his hand and hers was available with a split-second grab, but of course now they couldn't shoot back: the shrieking family was in the way.

Bianca went with the next best thing. She snatched up the heavy porcelain planter, poinsettias and all, got eyes on her target and hurled the planter over the rail at them.

It slammed into the first gunman. He fell back against the man behind him. The pair of them tumbled down the stairs as the planter rolled after them, scattering deep red Christmas blooms in its wake.

Say it with flowers, Bianca thought with savage satisfaction. She yelled in French, "You! With the dog! Get back in your apartment and stay there!" and turned to find Colin kicking the door open.

It must have been a mighty kick, because the door flew back on its hinges with a crash. Did he run through it? No, he looked around for her.

Her brows snapped together.

"Go." Colin gestured urgently at her to precede him.

"Get them," one of the bad guys yelled in French.

Pfft. Pfft. Pfft. Pfft. Pfft.

The gunmen had obviously recovered. Bullets flew. One smacked into the doorjamb inches from Bianca's head. She bolted past Colin into the hall.

Which was about a hundred feet long and ended in a plain white wall with a tiny window. A red sign with the word *Sortie* (Exit) hung above the last door on the left.

She sprinted toward it, throwing this over her shoulder: "Good to know that chivalry's not dead. But if you keep on hanging back behind me you soon might be."

He was half a step back. Keeping his body between her and danger, she knew. She wavered between finding it cute and maddening.

"Think we could talk about this later?"

Doors lining either side of the hallway were closed. They led to apartments, she knew, and offered no chance of escape. The twin smells of cooking and mustiness because of the rain she could see sluicing past the window assaulted her nostrils. She could hear the gunmen pounding up the stairs behind them.

Standing their ground occurred to her — shades of *Gunfight at the OK Corral*! — but their pursuers were armed with automatic rifles, which meant that she and Colin were seriously outgunned. If fight or flight were the choices, flight once again seemed like the better plan.

"Down," Colin said as they burst through the unlocked door into what was clearly a fire exit. The tight quarters and plain narrow steps were totally unlike the ornate staircase they'd just run up. Since the only *up* option consisted of a single flight to the top floor that offered no more access to safety than the hall they'd just left, Bianca didn't need the instruction: weapon in hand now, she flew down the stairs.

"Up there! Up there!" Shouted in French, that was her first clue that more bad news, as in more gunmen — couldn't be the ones who had been behind them — was heading their way. The second clue — *Pfft! Pfft! Pfft!* — was bullets flying past. Footsteps pounded up the fire stairs toward them. From the ensuing sounds Bianca concluded that there were at least three men.

"Shit! *Up!*" was Colin's take on the situation. They both snapped off shots meant to slow the pursuit. Having already reversed course, eschewing the door they'd just come through because she was as sure as it was possible to be that the other gunmen were at that moment in the hall racing toward it, Bianca swarmed up the single flight of stairs that ended in a door at the top. There was no other choice than to go through it: the staircase ended there.

She prayed it wasn't locked.

It wasn't. She burst through it into a deluge of cold, pouring rain.

18

Dashing out onto what proved to be a flat roof, Bianca was instantly soaked to the skin. A shocked glance around as night swallowed her up and the storm raged around her confirmed the only possible explanation — the seventh floor was smaller than the rest, sitting atop the building like the uppermost layer on a tiered wedding cake. Barreling through the door behind her, Colin checked and said "Jesus" as the pouring rain surprised him, too.

Then they both ran full tilt through it, heads ducked against the onslaught, splashing through puddles, sheltering their weapons as best they could. The roar of the rain muffled the sound of multiple sirens that she imagined must belong to police cars converging on Le Chien Rouge: one more reason to run like hell.

Lightning flashed. Its bright blaze cracking across the sky was terrifyingly close —

how many possible ways could she die tonight, anyway? — but it was enough to show Bianca where the roof ended. The seven-story-deep chasm of darkness between the roof they were on and the next, and the approximately four-foot-wide gap between the buildings, was only a short distance away. She hesitated, slowed —

Behind them, shouts prompted her to cast a hunted glance back. An indistinguishable knot of people burst out onto the roof, backlit by the light from the stairwell so that all she could see was a featureless mass. They separated, cursing as the rain beat into them. She saw that the two groups that had been chasing them had clearly met up and combined, so that now five — count 'em — yes, *five* thugs armed with automatic weapons were after them.

She and Colin had a choice: turn and fight, or leap.

Colin grabbed her hand: *yay* for wordless communication. They sprinted for the edge of the roof, jumped across the chasm as one, then raced away from the edge.

Given the darkness and the rain, it was, Bianca thought, always possible that their pursuers hadn't seen —

Pfft. Pfft. Pfft. Pfft. Pfft.

Bullets whined past, pinging into a metal

ventilation pipe, causing a satellite dish to keel over with a crash, smacking into the concrete rooftop and sending chips flying. They dodged antennae and leaped wires, then as lightning flashed again dived behind a tall brick chimney for cover. The chimney thankfully had a metal cap with an overhang that provided a small slice of shelter from the rain.

They turned as one to snap off return fire around their respective edges of the chimney.

The answering volley slammed into the chimney, the rooftop and everything else nearby. Pieces of concrete flew like shrapnel. Making herself as small a target as possible, Bianca took advantage of another lightning flash to do a hasty recon of their surroundings.

Ahead of them, the edge of the roof was maybe thirty feet away. The problem was, the yawning black chasm between the roof they were on and the next was the width of an alley — about twenty feet.

Bianca's stomach sank. Sopping wet, teeth clenched to keep them from chattering, back pressed flat against the cold brick, she looked at Colin, who was in similar shape beside her.

"Looks like no more roof hopping." He

swiped a hand across his face to clear the streaming water from it. She'd done the same thing moments earlier.

"No," she agreed. Not even for her.

"How many rounds?" His words were nearly drowned out by a clap of thunder.

"Three." Her tone was grim because what he'd asked was, how many bullets did she have left? She knew the answer, because she'd kept careful count. Being caught out with nothing in the chamber at a crucial moment was a good way to wind up dead. "You?"

"Five."

They had eight bullets remaining between them. Given their five pursuers, they could afford to miss or fail to kill or incapacitate with three of their shots. Ordinarily, she would judge that to be doable, but given the rain and the darkness and the fact that their pursuers were loaded for bear with automatic weapons —

Pfft. Pfft. Pfft. Pfft. Pfft.

— and apparently plenty of ammunition, their chances of coming out on top of this particular firefight weren't great. Granted, the ferocity of the downpour was throwing off their pursuers' accuracy to a certain degree, but then, that worked both ways.

"So we've got a problem," he said as bullets raked the chimney and everything else around. The trajectory of the bullets told the tale: the bad guys were slowly advancing on their position. By mutual if unspoken agreement, she and Colin held their fire. At this point, their remaining bullets were too precious to waste. "Short of pulling a Butch Cassidy and the Ninja Kid–style suicide stand, it's looking like our options are try to pick them off one by one or do our best to hold out until the police get here."

The situation was too dire for her to object to him casting her as the Ninja Kid (ha ha, and it went without saying that he considered himself Butch Cassidy) or to find any humor in his lame attempt at it.

"No," she said. "To both."

"You got a better plan, I'd love to hear it."

"Do you trust me?" she asked.

His head turned. He gave her a considering look.

"Oh my God," she burst out when he didn't immediately answer. "I don't mean in some kind of cosmic sense, or as in let me hold your priceless treasure for you because I'm the most honest person you ever met in your life. I mean right here, right now. Enough to jump off this building with me."

"You mean, do I trust you with my life?"

There was a pause of maybe half a beat before he finished up on a softer note with, "Yeah, I do."

Did her heart give a girlish flutter? Maybe. File it under reactions to be sorted out later.

She was already reaching up under her skirt for the escape cord dispenser that was part of her garter belt. His eyes followed her every move. She freed it, held it up. "I'm going to wrap the cord in this thing around the chimney, we're both going to grab hold of the handle, and we're going to run to the edge of the building and jump."

He'd seen her use it to escape — from him — before. The cord's existence was not a surprise.

"How much weight will it hold?"

Bianca smiled. "At a minimum, Doc," she said. "Field tested and guaranteed."

"Good enough."

Pfft. Pfft. Pfft. Pfft. Pfft.

Without the deterrence of answering gunfire, the gunmen advanced with impunity now. She and Colin exchanged looks. He leaned out, slamming them with a spray of cover fire while she wrapped the cord around the chimney and secured it. The last step, detaching the satin garter strap that was the handle and clipping it to the cord, was the work of a second.

"Ready," she said.

Taking her weapon, he snapped off the last of her bullets at their pursuers to slow them down, then jammed her now-empty weapon in his waistband alongside his. They were out of ammo. There was no turning back. With a single look at each other, they grabbed the satin loop, ran for the edge of the roof and leaped into space.

They hurtled down the first three stories in a whoosh and then the immediate burst of their descent slowed, became erratic. The dispenser seemed to sputter, releasing only a few yards of cord at a time.

Then it — *they* — stopped altogether.

"Defective equipment?" Colin asked, faultlessly polite. With both of them holding on by their right hands, they were practically nose to nose.

"This never happens."

Swinging some four stories above the cobblestoned alley, hand cramping, arm aching, barraged by rain, bumping into Colin and the smooth, featureless stone of the building behind them with every gust of wind, Bianca tried to troubleshoot.

The problem with troubleshooting this particular problem was, trouble was right behind them, ready to shoot back.

Shouts from the lip of the roof jerked her

gaze up. The gunmen peered over the edge —

Her heart leaped. Out of bullets, bereft of her throwing star, in a ridiculously exposed position, they were defenseless if their pursuers started firing, which, as soon as they worked out the logistics — the width of the eave made it impossible to simply point and shoot straight down from where they stood — they would do.

Then — talk about your dangling ducks.

"I'd suggest trying to kick our way through a window, but there aren't any," Colin said.

A police car, sirens wailing, lights flashing, sped past the entrance to the alley. Another followed. And a third.

The gunmen popped back out of sight.

It was a reprieve of seconds, she knew.

"It has to be the uneven distribution of weight!" The solution hit Bianca's fear-galvanized mind in a brilliant flash of insight. "Whatever you do, don't let go!"

Wrapping an arm around his neck, she turned loose of the handle — and down they went. She hung from his broad shoulders like a dress on a hanger. He clamped his free arm around her to hold her in place.

They landed on the cobblestones right in front of a group of women huddled together in a doorway in an obvious attempt to escape the storm. Eyes huge, the women gaped at the seemingly out-of-nowhere arrivals.

Letting go of Colin's neck, Bianca slid down his body to hit the cobblestones and punched the button that released her escape cord and brought it snaking back into its dispenser, all in a single smooth movement.

The women stared, goggle-eyed.

"It's raining men," she told them in French, and put a finger to her lips as Colin grabbed her hand and pulled her after him.

They ran together toward the intersection that wasn't swarming with police cars. The good news was, the gunmen weren't going to be following them over the side of the building. The bad news was, the gunmen would be following them.

But right now she and Colin had a small head start.

"They'll be looking for us. We need to get off the street," he said as they reached one of the wide thoroughfares that were so integral to Paris's charm. Even in the teeth of the deluge, a few people still moved along the sidewalk, sheltering under umbrellas and overhangs. Traffic filled the street. She could hear the shriek of sirens, but the sounds were blunted by distance and the drum of the rain. The horror at Le Chien

Rouge, just a couple of blocks over, hadn't touched the people here.

"We can't go back to the apartment," she said.

"I know."

A crowded bar a few doors along had a jumble of customers' coats hanging on pegs just inside the entrance: Bianca could see them through the window.

She tugged at Colin's hand. "In there. We need coats."

They'd left theirs behind in the restaurant. *Leave nothing behind* was one of the rules, but there'd been no time to grab their coats and thus no choice. She wasn't worried about the garment giving anything away or being traced back to her. Siu Siu Tseng, designer to the criminal stars, had fashioned it to look like a perfectly ordinary reversible coat. And treated it with a substance that kept any fingerprints or stray bits of DNA from adhering. But now the missing coats needed to be replaced. Because not wearing one in these weather conditions made them conspicuous, and because the unexpected addition of outerwear could serve to disguise them from those who were almost certainly already coming after them in hot pursuit. Also, because they were wet and cold.

He looked in the direction she indicated,

nodded and followed her inside. When they emerged, she was wearing a scarlet rain slicker with a hood and he was wearing a man's long gray overcoat and a fedora. Plus he was carrying an umbrella, which he opened. She joined him beneath it. As she gripped the umbrella's handle, he put an arm around her: nothing to see here, folks; just two slightly damp lovers splish-sploshing through the rain.

They were now all but unrecognizable as they hurried away from the scene. Bianca was still nervous. She'd thought she was unrecognizable before. Obviously she'd thought wrong.

That nearly unprecedented failure unnerved her.

Who were those guys?

"There. Come on." Pulling her along with him, Colin took off running toward the nearest cross street and a — Bianca had to shield her eyes against the rain to make sure — red double-decker on-and-off tourist bus.

"Really?"

"Sorry to say I'm fresh out of Aston Martins, so, yeah."

It took her a minute: James Bond's signature car was an Aston Martin.

"Oh, ha ha."

They caught up to it at the corner as it

stopped to let a couple off, clambered on board, paid the fare and kept their heads down as they made their way to the back. The bus was nearly full, which wasn't so surprising when she thought of the storm: not many people were getting off to tour the attractions and no one wanted to sit up top.

Escaping by tourist bus had several advantages, she had to admit: it made an unlikely getaway vehicle; its onboard computer system — did it even have one? — probably couldn't be Boston braked; it was dry, and it was warm, which was a godsend considering how cold and wet she was beneath the coat: she had to clench her teeth to keep them from chattering and water ran down her body to form a puddle at her feet.

The downside was, the lumbering, exhaust-spewing, stinky-cheese-smelling bus was slow.

The Arc de Triomphe, where they disembarked, was approximately three miles and a ride across the Seine from where they'd hopped on board. The journey took forty-five minutes.

By the time they were back out on the street, the storm had largely abated. The lightning was no more than an occasional fork-tongued flicker on the western horizon, the thunder was a distant growl, and the rain had slowed to an intermittent sprinkle.

Bianca was so cold she was beyond shivering. The only warm spot on her was her right hand, and that was because Colin was holding it. His hand felt large and strong and *right* wrapped around hers.

She was so cold she was even beyond worrying about the implications of that.

"I'm assuming you have a plan." Bianca was pretty sure he did, because he'd bundled them off the bus. They hadn't talked on the ride — too easy for others to overhear everything that was said. And she, personally, was too cold to chitchat.

"There's a hotel near here. Takes cash, doesn't ask questions."

"You seem to know a lot of places like that."

"Don't you?"

Okay, he had her there: she did. At least a dozen in Paris alone. Problem was, the staff at any of them might recognize her. After her experience earlier, she was wary of trusting in her disguises to keep her safe. Something had clearly gone wrong with that, and until she'd had time to figure out precisely what, the only prudent thing to do was count them out as safeguards. At this point, she and Colin were dangerously close to being unarmed. And in any contest pitting hand-to-hand combat against a bullet — well, she knew what side of that fight she'd rather be on.

"A hotel sounds good," she said. "Lead on."

19

Hand in hand — Hello, young lovers! — and umbrella up to protect them as much from any stray surveillance cameras as from the rain, they walked quickly away from the Arc, which, like the Eiffel Tower, was beautifully lit up for Christmas. The iconic monument to Napoleon's victories was the centerpiece of a traffic-packed roundabout on the west end of the Champs-Élysées, one of the busiest boulevards in Paris. Even in the rain, hundreds of tourists strolled the twelve avenues that formed a star around the Arc. It was a given that she and Colin were by now being hunted like vermin through the streets of Paris, but finding them amid such a throng would — Bianca hoped — be difficult.

She said, "I can't — *we* can't — go back to the hotel where I left Lynette's stuff. We have to assume they'll be watching it, waiting for me to show up again. But we can't just leave her stuff there, either."

"Got it covered."

"How?"

"I'll have somebody call the hotel tomorrow pretending to be Lynette, tell them she had to leave town unexpectedly, have them pack up her belongings and ship them back to her apartment in DC."

"Where she won't show up."

"No. But after what she's done she wouldn't show back up there anyway, if she's smart."

Bianca nodded: solid plan.

"Who were those guys?" She voiced the thought that kept chasing itself through her mind.

He shook his head. "All outward signs point to them being part of some kind of a criminal syndicate, possibly Le Milieu like your friend, possibly something else, but for them to be looking for Lynette the word on her would've had to leak out of the spook community pretty damned fast. Plus right now you look totally different from Lynette. Maybe they had the hotel staked out, saw Lynette go in and you come out, and put two and two together and actually got four. Or maybe somehow they knew to look for you dressed like that."

She frowned. "First of all, that guy was

never my friend. I just happened to recognize him. Second, wouldn't it make sense that they'd want to get hold of the information Lynette stole? *Before* they killed her? Because once they kill her, she's not going to be able to tell them anything."

"You think they were trying to kidnap you? Her?" By that time the hotel, which Colin pointed out to her with a gesture, was within view.

"I don't know. The feeling I got was that they were trying to kill me. But I could be wrong."

"Yeah." He sounded thoughtful. "Your friend — or, I'm sorry, the guy who isn't your friend — from Le Chien Rouge. Who is he?"

She'd known he was going to ask that question. The problem was, she hadn't yet decided what to tell him. Or, rather, how big a lie to tell him. Because of course she couldn't open up with the whole, unvarnished truth. It revealed way more about her than he needed to know — and it brought Mason into it, which led down a path she never wanted Colin to so much as suspect existed.

"Can we talk about this once we're in out of the cold? It's all I can do to keep my teeth from chattering every time I open my mouth."

The look he gave her was maybe a little on the searching side, but what he said was "Sure."

Like most of the buildings in the area, the hotel was made of pale stone. Wrought-iron balconies and gargoyles glowering over the eaves gave the facade a Gothic air. Six stories tall, it had many narrow windows spilling golden rectangles of light across the dark street.

The great thing about working with Colin was, as Bianca noted one more time, she didn't have to spell things out for him. He was *almost* as well versed in tradecraft as she was herself. Countersurveillance was second nature to them both. Cold and wet though they were, there was no need to debate the pros and cons of watching the place for a while before going inside. He accepted the need for it automatically, just as she did. They approached the hotel from the opposite side of the street, strolled past it and, without exchanging a word, ducked into the pharmacy with its flashing green sign on the corner. The one with the big front window that allowed an unimpeded view of the hotel, the street and the area around it.

They emerged some ten minutes later

with power bars and bottled water, a few necessary toiletries and matching *Je heart Paris* T-shirts, along with a high degree of certainty that they hadn't picked up a tail. Still, Bianca kept a wary eye out.

They might have eluded their pursuers for now, but in no way did she feel safe. Every particle of the finely honed sense of danger she'd developed over the years screamed it: the "something deadly" she'd felt on the street earlier was still out there.

And she didn't think the feeling had been generated by the thugs who'd tried to take her out at Le Chien Rouge.

The hotel lobby was small and dim. At one time the building had been luxurious, but it was slightly shabby now. A single desk clerk behind a long wooden counter was the only occupant. A wall-mounted TV blasted away.

"How much is a room for two people?" Colin asked the clerk in French as he approached the desk.

Keeping her face turned away from the clerk, Bianca drifted toward the TV.

That they would share a room was a foregone conclusion, so obvious a piece of tradecraft that they didn't even bother to discuss it. Colin in his role as bodyguard wouldn't have considered any other arrangement, and she in her role as putative victim would be foolish to insist on anything else. To strip the matter down to its simplest form, when an unknown number of bad guys want to kill or kidnap you, two highly skilled operatives are better than one, and it's good to have someone who knows his way around a move or two watching your back.

The clerk's answer was hailed as satisfactory, and Colin, using a fake name and paying cash, checked in. Bianca's attention was caught by an on-air commentator's report on North Korea, a topic in which she'd only recently (as in three days previously) developed an interest. The gist of the story was that North Korea was escalating its nuclear arms capability. The commentator opined that the isolated kingdom's Dear Leader's historic meeting with the US president had been nothing more than a ploy to buy time to finish developing a nuclear weapon that could reach the continental United States. That goal, the commentator felt, was within reach, and once that happened the balance of power in the region, and, indeed, the world, would change forever. With the United States no longer able to unilaterally threaten the Hermit Kingdom with military force, South Korea and Japan would be at immediate risk, and the world would tremble on the brink of nuclear war.

"Did you hear that?" Bianca asked Colin in a low voice as, check-in completed, he took her arm in a loverly way and steered her over to the elevator. Not that she needed to worry about being overheard, as a sidelong glance at the desk clerk confirmed. His bored expression said it all: one more dalliance *amoureuse* among the tourists, and he didn't care. "They say we're being fooled into giving North Korea more time to develop a nuke that can reach the United States."

"We're not being fooled." The elevator arrived. They stepped inside and he punched the button for their floor. "Our side's playing for time, too. That's where what you're doing comes in. While the powers that be make a lot of noise about talking, Operation Fifth Doctrine's being deployed to get the information we need to change the game. Not knowing exactly what we're dealing with gives them the advantage. The thought that we could go in militarily to take out their nuclear weapons and wind up missing some, which might then be fired at the United States and its allies in retaliation, is what's making it so hard for our side to deal with the threat. It's a dangerous game that we don't want to play if we're not one hundred percent sure we can win, and unfortunately, they know that." He slanted a glance at her. "How does it feel to know you're the game-changer?"

"Just peachy keen. You know, if this goes wrong, we might all wind up roasting wee-nies with nuclear fallout." Her voice was tart.

He smiled as the elevator stopped and they stepped out into a long, narrow hall that smelled faintly of cigarettes and air freshener. "I like your faith in the combined abilities of our intelligence services."

"Yeah, well, faith may move mountains, but then, so do nukes."

He unlocked the door and they walked into their room. It was small. It was plain. She spent about ten seconds assessing points of ingress and egress: one tall, narrow window, one heavy wood door. Dark green carpet, white walls, white curtains over drawn blinds on the single window. A gurgling radiator beneath the window. A small dresser/desk combination with a TV on the dresser part and a straight-back chair tucked beneath the desk part. A double bed with two lumpy-looking pillows and a white spread. A nightstand with a lamp. An armchair in a corner with a floor lamp beside it.

A bathroom.

Taking off her coat, she hung it in the closet, snagged her earrings from her purse then dropped the purse on the closet floor, removed the power bars and water (aka breakfast) from the plastic bag, hooked the bag with its toiletries over her arm and headed for the bathroom.

"I'm going to take a shower," she said. She was tired and wired and sick about the innocents who'd been killed and injured in the restaurant and on edge about what would be going down in the morning: the best medicine that she could think of at the moment for all of that was standing beneath endless streams of hot water. He'd taken off his coat, too, and draped it over the TV (more good tradecraft, in case anyone hoped to use the TV as a camera; she placed her earrings side by side beneath the TV as she passed it to foil any unlikely-but-possible listening device) and his hat, and was in the process of pulling his wet crew-neck over his head. As a result, his reply was muffled. Didn't matter: she didn't wait for it.

When she emerged, she was clean and fragrant and *warm,* and he was on the phone. The *cell phone.* It had been a while since she'd stayed in a hotel room in Paris, but she didn't think cell phones were standard amenities.

It had to be his.

"Merci," he said into the phone, and disconnected as she stopped dead, staring at him. His eyes slid over her. She was blonde again, her hair freshly shampooed and blow-dried, and was wearing one of the *Je heart Paris* T-shirts they'd bought in the pharmacy. The red Alice wig and her discarded clothes hung over her arm. Her shoes dangled from her fingers. The T-shirt was perfectly decent — it reached midthigh. Still, by the time his eyes met hers again they had darkened.

She barely noticed, and didn't care.

"Don't tell me you've been carrying that on you. They can trace it." Her voice was sharp. "You *know* that."

"Relax." He put the phone down on the dresser. She saw that it already held a collection of objects he'd had on his person, including their guns. "It's a black phone. A spy phone. Specially configured, totally untraceable. Totally secure."

"You sure?"

"Would I have it if I wasn't?"

The constriction in her chest eased a little. "Who were you talking to? And if you say it's none of my business, I'm walking. You can't trust me, I can't trust you."

"I wasn't going to say that. I called an associate and asked him to leave some weapons and ammo at a dead drop he knows of not far from here. In case you haven't noticed, we're getting low."

She had noticed. "And?"

"We can pick them up on our way to meet Park in the morning."

Okay. That made sense.

He cocked an eyebrow at her. "Satisfied?"

Not entirely, but she nodded. Took a breath. And found that she had recovered enough to register that he was stripped to the waist. The visual hit her like a bucket of water in the face. Black hair curling from the rain. Hard, handsome face. Deeply tan. Totally buff. Wide chest, muscular arms, ripped abs. A large raised scar running across one sculpted bicep. A manly vee of black chest hair.

His jeans rode low on lean hips. His belly button was an innie.

Be still, my heart.

Damn it, *no!*

"I'm going to take a shower," he said, and walked into the bathroom. She got an eyeful of broad bare back as he passed her. "You can have the bed. I'll take the chair."

He closed the door. She looked at it,

blinked, discovered that her pulse had quickened and got mad at herself.

So he was an absolutely gorgeous guy. So he was hot AF. So she'd noticed.

Get over it. Right now she had other, time-sensitive fish to fry. She spread her wet clothes and wig out on the radiator under the window, parked her shoes beside it, listened for the shower — and as soon as she heard it grabbed his phone.

Given her recent experiences, her new live-long-and-prosper motto was *trust, but verify.*

The phone was locked and secured by a touchpad that needed a code, presumably four digits because most codes of that type were. Trying to guess the code was a waste of time. The possible number combinations to find the four correct digits in the correct order was somewhere around ten thousand. And she couldn't be entirely sure the code was merely four digits.

In her purse was a complexion-altering powder foundation that she used as Lynette. Rushing to the closet, she crouched, found the powder and scraped some into her palm. Grinding it into a fine dust between her thumb and forefinger, she sprinkled it over the touchpad. Then she gently blew the powder off.

Bingo. The oils left behind by his fingers caused the powder to adhere to three numbers: 4-6-9.

Three numbers. Hmm.

Obviously he used one twice.

"XMI6," he said behind her. She nearly jumped out of her skin. No point in trying to hide what she'd been doing. The phone, with the powder still adhering to the numbers, was in her hand. She'd been listening for the shower. She listened again just to be sure: it was still running.

She rose and turned to find him leaning a shoulder against the jamb of the open bathroom door. His arms were crossed over his chest. Steam billowed behind him, filling the bathroom. He was still wearing his jeans, which, to be fair, didn't appear to be all that wet. But the point was, he hadn't even gotten undressed.

Indignation stiffened her spine. He'd been expecting her to do what she did. It was a trap, and she'd walked right into it.

20

"You want to check out my phone? Go ahead. Like I said, the code's XMI6."

Bianca fixed him with an accusing look. "You knew what I was going to do. You were *expecting* it."

"I think we've already established that you have serious trust issues. After all we've been through together, too." Colin shook his head, tsk-tsked.

"What about *you*? You turned on the shower then waited to catch me out. Talk about trust issues."

"See, the difference is, mine were justified. Look who got caught with whose phone in her hand."

Her lips pursed. "I didn't *only* want to check out your phone. I was hoping that I could use it to email Doc and tell him to transfer the money Park is going to pay me in the morning out of the account it's wired into as soon as it lands. Not that I think the

money's going to disappear or anything, but
—"

"You could have asked me."

"I was going to."

"Liar." He said it without heat.

If she'd tried to deny it the words would
have stuck in her throat. Instead, she gave
up. "Fine. Call it an occupational hazard.
And, yes, I would like to check out your
phone."

He gestured at it. "Help yourself. Although before you send that email you
should realize that since Doc's a known associate of yours, all his communications,
including his emails, are probably being
monitored."

"Think I didn't take care of that before I
left Savannah?" She made a scoffing sound.
"We have a plan in place for emergency
communications."

XMI6: 9-6-4-6. She whisked the powder
off the numbers with a forefinger, then
punched them in. The phone unlocked.

"Now, wasn't getting the code from me
easier than trying umpteen different number
combinations until your finger fell off?"

Flicking him a derisive look — once she
knew the numbers involved there were actually fifty-four different combinations, which
would have taken her under three minutes *if*

she'd had to try them all *and* use her hack that kept the phone from locking after a certain number of wrong attempts — she hit *recents* in the phone app and a list of numbers came up. The latest was a local number, an outgoing call made eleven minutes ago. That meshed with what he'd told her.

"Look at that," he said. "I was telling the truth."

Her mouth thinned. A quick scroll down the list of numbers told her nothing: she didn't recognize any of them.

"Satisfied?"

Without ringing all the numbers back, there was nothing else she could do, and ringing the numbers back brought its own set of problems with it. Like whoever was on the other end wondering why they were really being called, and by whom, and getting paranoid and suspicious and maybe doing something they wouldn't have done *because* they were paranoid and suspicious — suffice it to say, callbacks to certain numbers could go very wrong.

"Yes." If her answer was grudging, at least she was willing to believe he'd been telling the truth about the call he'd been on.

"You want to email your friend, hit the star and pound keys simultaneously. It'll connect you to a secure internet service. When you're ready to send, hit the plus sign."

She did as he directed and sent her message to Doc. In the meantime, Colin went back into the bathroom and turned the water off.

"No shower?" she asked when he re-emerged.

"Later. When there's hot water again. *If* there's hot water again."

Come to think of it, the steam had stopped billowing in the middle of their conversation. "Looks like a cold shower is the price you pay for being paranoid."

"Baby, it's only considered being paranoid if the person you suspect is trying to break into your phone isn't."

"Like you wouldn't have done the exact same thing." Her tone was astringent to cover the fact that the little pulse of warmth he'd caused her to feel before was back, in spades. The ridiculous reason? He'd called her *baby.* For the second time. For some unknown reason *baby* felt a lot more — personal — than, say, *beautiful,* which he'd been calling her from the beginning, when he didn't know her name. She thought about objecting, reminding him that they were professional colleagues (which was a better way of looking at it than blackmailer and blackmail-ee), but she didn't want to let him know that it had made enough of an impact for her to notice it. Even if it had. No, *because* it had.

He was looking at her, she realized, and realized too that she was looking at him right back. Afraid of what he might be able to read in her eyes, she glanced away. Without really registering what she was seeing, she took in his purloined coat covering the TV, the miscellany of items he'd parked on the dresser, her clothes now starting to steam on the radiator —

Wait — go back. She hastily rescanned the items on the dresser. Her eyes widened, shot to his face. "Oh my God, where's the ChapStick? Did we leave it in the apartment? Or —"

She broke off as, with a twist of a smile, he put his hand over the scar on his arm, plucked at the edge of it and peeled it off. Then he turned it over for her to look at. Inside what she saw was a silicone prosthetic nestled the ChapStick. The section of arm where it had been was now all smooth bronze muscle.

"Fake. Scar." Marveling at the duplicity of it, she shook her head at him. "See why I have trust issues with you?"

"Says the girl with the multiple wigs. And the killer jewelry. And the dead sexy garter belt." He crossed the room, held out his hand for his phone. Working hard to keep from looking sulky, she gave it to him. She didn't like getting caught. It didn't happen often.

"So you ever gonna tell me about that guy in the restaurant?" he asked.

She looked up at him. He was so close she had to do that. She liked that his height meant that she had to do it — and she also didn't like it. Same way she liked but didn't like all those honed muscles, or the scruff on his chin, or the breadth of his shoulders. In short, the man's hunkiness quotient posed a problem. Complications of the sort her unwanted attraction to him could create she didn't need.

"What do you want to know?" As a pre-emptive move to keep any wayward reactions at bay, she turned her back on him, dipping into the closet to fish her Lynette-wear out of her bag.

"How about you start with his name?" He was no longer behind her. Bianca registered that with relief as she stood up, Lynette-wear in hand. He watched her from the center of the room as she headed toward the desk. That still didn't give her a lot of space because it was a small room and he took up what seemed like way more than his fair share of it.

"Franz. If he used a last name I don't remember it." Her target was the desk chair. She started laying out on it the items she would need in the morning to become Lynette. A glance at the dresser told her that he'd placed the fake scar and the ChapStick as well as the phone on it with the rest of his gear. "Or at least, Franz was what he called himself when I knew him."

"And when was that?" he asked.

"A long time ago."

"You gonna tell me?"

Bianca hesitated.

He said, "Let's see, what was it you just said? You can't trust me, I can't trust you? Works both ways."

Tell the truth until you can't: it was one of the rules. "I did a bank robbery with him once. He didn't recognize me tonight, but I remembered him because of his hand."

"His hand?"

"His left hand was missing its ring finger. The stump was — ragged looking. He told me it had been chewed off by rats. That made an impression, and I remembered it when I saw it."

"You must have been pretty young for

something like that to make that strong an impression on you."

"I was."

He waited, but she busied herself with shaking out Lynette's wig and settling it on a corner of the chair back.

"How young?"

She shrugged. "Seventeen? Eighteen?"

"You were part of a gang at seventeen?"

"Bank robbery's not usually a solo activity."

"Who else was in the gang?"

"I don't really remember."

"Bianca."

He hardly ever called her that, either. That was almost worse than having him call her *baby.* She looked around at him: mistake. Their eyes met, and the charge that had been there between them from the first, the electricity — Oh, God, there it was again, sparking away. *Damn it.*

"You can tell me, you know. Anything." His eyes crinkled at her. *Too impossibly handsome.* "I don't judge."

Keep it light.

"Really?" Turning, she made big eyes at him. He nodded. "Okay, then. When I was ten years old —" She took a deep breath and blurted, "I joined a tribe of cannibals. We ate our way through South America, and

320

then I torched their village and ran away."

His mouth tightened. "When we jumped off that building, you told me 'don't let go.' Then you wrapped your arms around my neck and left me holding on for the both of us. You trusted me with your life."

"Don't let it go to your head." Because her pulse had picked up the pace, because her breathing had quickened, because her insides were softening like a damned toasting marshmallow, her tone was brusque. Getting busy with something, anything, else, she turned back to what she'd been doing, shaking out her Lynette pants before draping them over the chair back. Dislodged, the wig fell to the floor.

Before she could pick it up, he retrieved it and held it out to her.

Which brought him close. Too damned close.

She felt the sexy clear down to her toes.

Time to stop this in its tracks.

"Thanks." She restored the wig to its perch and turned with the intention of walking away, only to discover that he was planted foursquare and solid in her path. Shirtless. Brawny. Beautiful. Exuding a whole *Magic Mike* cast's worth of studly vibes. She frowned — up, always with the up — at him.

"Good job with the throwing star back there, by the way. I was looking in the wrong direction, and that guy would've shot us both if you hadn't picked up the slack. I didn't know you had it in you."

"That would be because, like I told you before, you don't know anything about me." She grabbed hold of every ounce of composure she could muster and brushed past him. He caught her arm. She shot him a warning, don't-mess-with-me look, and found that the look he was giving her in return was almost — tender.

Butterflies took wing in her stomach.

Oh, God. No.

"There's an easy fix for that," he said. Trailing goose bumps in its wake, his hand slid down her arm to capture her hand.

"What are you talking about?" In sheer self-defense, something very near to hostility laced her voice. She gave her hand a (not quite full strength) yank. He didn't let go.

"Me. Getting to know you. Here's how it would work. You could tell me things."

"No."

"Nothing earth-shattering. Little things. Like what you eat for breakfast. What your favorite color is. Where you like to go on vacation. If you like to watch sports or the news on TV, or if *Say Yes to the Dress* is more your thing. What makes you happy."

"No."

"You say that a lot." He smiled at her, a heart-stopping smile that did funny things to her insides. "Makes me wonder if you ever say *yes.*"

His eyes captured hers, held. They were golden brown, intense.

She found to her dismay that she didn't even want to look away.

The heat they were generating was enough to make her mouth go dry, make her skin flush, make her think about shedding some clothes . . .

No. No. No.

She tried to come back with something smart, something that would cut through the sexual tension that shimmered like a magnetic field between them. *Keep it light,* she told herself fiercely one more time — but she couldn't.

Just like she couldn't do what she knew she easily could and pull her hand free as he lifted it to his mouth, pressed his lips to its back. That slight touch of his mouth sent quivery tendrils of longing over her skin.

Just — say — no.

"Are you coming on to me?" How blunt was that?

"God forbid." There was that smile again.

She tried steeling herself against it, only to discover, as he turned her hand over to press his mouth to her unresisting palm, that she was fresh out of inner steel. "You ever think that maybe I just want to get to know you better?"

"What's the point? After tomorrow we go our separate ways," she said. He kissed the sensitive skin on the inside of her wrist. *Swoon. Oh no.* "This job will be over."

"Just because the job is over doesn't mean *we* have to be over."

That *we* was what did it: it was the trumpet blast that brought down what remained of her once-mighty walls. The guys she'd been with up until now had always been just that: guys she'd been with. As far as she was concerned, they'd been strictly easy come, easy go. Fungible. She'd always been cool, detached, one foot out the door. She'd never, not once, been even close to getting serious. She'd never been part of a *we*.

The prospect that now, possibly, she was made her heart start to knock in her chest.

Face it, *he* made her heart start to knock in her chest.

Holy hell. This was bad.

"There is no *we*," she said. Her throat was tight, which made her voice come out low and harsh. But she didn't try to move away.

And her eyes — she didn't want to think about what he must be able to read in her eyes.

She was afraid her heart might be in there somewhere.

"Looks like maybe there is," he said, which pretty much told the tale. Then he leaned in and kissed her.

21

She was lost, just like that. His mouth was firm, and warm, and amazingly expert, molding itself to her lips, then parting them and invading with a hungry intensity that sent her reeling. That kiss hit her like a double shot of whiskey rocketing straight through to her bloodstream. She was instantly high, instantly dizzy, instantly weak in the knees. There was nothing she could do to stop herself from being intoxicated by it, nothing she could do to stop every one of her five senses from being inundated by sensation, nothing she could do to stop herself from kissing him back. His mouth slanted over hers as he deepened the kiss and it was *on,* no questions asked, no quarter given. Her heart pounded and her breathing went all ragged and her bare toes curled against the thick pile of the carpet. She didn't know if he pulled her tight against him or she went into his arms, but somehow her arms wound up around his neck and his arms wrapped around her like he was never going to let her go.

He kissed her like he meant it, like kisses were promises and he was making them. She already knew how good he was at kissing, but these were next-level, slow, deep, hungry kisses that made her bones melt. They robbed her of common sense, of resolve, of any vestige of rational thought. If she'd had any idea of calling a halt it got bulldozed by the sheer drugging sweetness of it, by the heat of his mouth, by the intensity of her own response.

Chemistry, that's what they had.

Of the written-in-the-stars, meant-to-be, kismet kind.

Fierce and violent, the storm started up again outside. Lightning flashed, thunder roared, rain pelted down. But as far as Bianca was concerned, the real tempest was right there in that small hotel room with them. The earth moved. Stars trembled. Electricity crackled. The air around them turned to steam.

She'd told Evie he'd swept her off her feet. Turned out, she hadn't lied.

Figuratively, with his kisses, and literally, when he said in a voice gone all hoarse and gravelly with passion, "Just so you know, I

want you more than I've ever wanted anything in my life," and she, blown away by
the romance of it, shaken by the intensity of
her own desire, unwisely answered, "I want
you, too," at which point he picked her up
and carried her to bed.

And she let him. No, didn't *let* him.
Actively, enthusiastically participated, curling her arms around his neck and pressing
her body against his and kissing him like
she'd die if she didn't all the while.

When he laid her on the bed and came
down on top of her, the weight and heat
and friction of his body drove her wild. This
was what she wanted, what she needed,
what she craved.

He was what she wanted, what she needed,
what she craved.

So she slept with him. She wanted, and
she took. It was a mistake and she knew it
was a mistake and she did it anyway. Thus
she deserved the whirlwind that she reaped.
Short version: he rocked her world. Fire-
works exploded behind her closed lids and
her body went up in flames and for the first
time in her life she truly understood what
all the fuss was about when it came to sex.

They did it multiple times, with the same
result: she was swept away on a riptide of
passion that made her lose control, made

her cry out and cling to him, made her reevaluate everything she'd ever thought she knew about herself. A passion so intense that it left her defenseless, vulnerable, exposed.

Finally, exhausted, replete, she fell asleep in his arms.

And then she woke up.

It was, she knew without having to check, close to 4:00 a.m., because her body clock worked like that: she'd meant to wake at that time, and so she did. That gave her plenty of time to morph into Lynette, get to the rendezvous with Park and scope out the scene before the actual meeting took place.

The fact that a whole bunch of people were hunting her through the streets was problematic, but she'd survived manhunts before. Actually, so many times she'd lost count.

All she had to do was get the ChapStick to Park and not die, and her part in saving the world (and not incidentally herself) was played.

By that time her eyes had adjusted to what was kept from being utter pitch blackness by the faint glow of the city at night creeping in around the edges of the closed blinds. Filtered through thin curtains, there was just enough light to allow her to see the outlines of things.

For a moment she lay perfectly still, staring straight up at the ceiling, coming to terms with the reality of the situation in which she'd put herself.

Naked, she lay on her back in the lumpy double bed, with Mr. Tall, Dark and Dangerous, also naked, wrapped around her like a too-warm, too-heavy taco shell as he breathed stertorously in her ear.

Clearly, romance was not dead.

He was sound asleep, which was good.

They'd had sex, which was bad.

His hand was on her breast, his thigh imprisoned both of hers, and his head rested in the hollow between her neck and shoulder.

She remembered how he'd wound up in that position: they'd finished with yet another truly mind-blowing round, and he'd barely managed to shift the bulk of his weight off her before conking out.

At the time, she'd been so exhausted and so woozy with afterglow that shoving him the rest of the way off her had not occurred to her.

Now it did. Only now something more subtle was required.

Slowly, carefully, she lifted his hand from

her breast. Tucking his arm down beside his chest, she slid out from under his sack-of-wet-cement-heavy thigh, and rolled out of bed and to her feet, all to the tune of the rhythmic rattle and rasp of his breathing.

She needed a moment, just a moment, to sort things out on her own before he woke up and she had to deal.

Turning to look at the man in the bed — the smokin' hot, stark naked, total disaster of the man in the bed — she covered her face with her hands and did her best not to totally freak.

She peeked through her fingers. He was still there.

You deserve a break today. Unfortunately, it didn't look like she was going to get one.

What have I done? The classic morning-after question.

The less-than-classic answer: broken one of the rules.

The one that said *keep emotion out of it.*

She was very much afraid — no, she was sure — that she'd done let emotion in.

Lowering her hands, she took one more look, and felt her stomach knot and her blood pressure spike.

Emotion was her Achilles' heel.

No, time to get real.

Love was her Achilles' heel.

Because she'd never really had it, she yearned for it like an addict yearning for crack.

Sex was one thing. A normal, natural instinct, regrettable but, really, no big deal. Although she had a feeling that the kind of physical combustion that had exploded between her and Colin was rare.

But she was afraid — terrified, really — that maybe there was more to it than that. That maybe her extraordinary physical re-action to the things they'd done had its roots in something totally apart from mere sex.

The thought that petrified her was that — maybe — she'd let herself fall the teeniest, tiniest bit in love with him.

Appalled, she examined the evidence from all angles, then sucked it up and stared the cold, hard, immutable truth in the face.

She had.

No. No. No. No. Oh my God, how life-shatteringly stupid can you get?

Wait. Stop. Do not come unglued. Do not lose your shit.

Find your center. Be calm. Reflect.

Remember: for every action, there is a cor-responding overreaction.

Damn, damn, damn! Holy hell! Sweet merci-ful crap!

Clamping down on her own personal welcome-to-the-apocalypse moment as best she could, Bianca found her *Je heart Paris* tee where it had landed on the floor. Pulling it on, she padded over to gather up her Lynette-wear. If anything remained that was certain in her life, it was this: dealing with the fallout from her latest really bad decision would be much easier if she was dressed.

On the way to the bathroom, she scooped up his phone. By now, Doc should have replied to the message she'd sent.

As she passed the bed, Colin flopped over onto his back. She froze, certain he was awake. But his eyes stayed closed, and once the flop was done he didn't move. His breathing quieted, but remained deeply rhythmic.

She could see him just well enough to ascertain that he was still asleep. Her eyes slid over his profile, with its high forehead, straight nose, beautifully cut mouth, determined chin. They lingered on the heavy muscles of his shoulders, his corded arms, his wide chest, his taut abs. The sheet interrupted her view at that point, but it didn't matter: she knew what was there.

Just the thought was enough to make her go hot all over, all over again.

Oh no. No, no.

Instead of hanging around compounding her problem, she tore her eyes away and stole off to the bathroom. Softly closed the door behind her and turned on the light. And immediately got a good look at herself in the mirror on the opposite wall.

Her hair was mussed, her cheeks were flushed, her lips were rosy, her eyes were bright. She looked like a woman who'd just had a really good time in bed, which, in fact, she had, the complications of the aftermath notwithstanding.

The thing that really got her was, she was smiling. The slightest curve of her lips, but it was enough to make her think, *I look happy.*

Because she *was* happy. It had been so long since she'd actually been happy that she almost didn't recognize the feeling.

It's this — thing — with Colin, she thought. *Thing* meaning relationship, her inner precision-meister clarified. Which left her instantly alarmed.

There is no relationship. I can't be in a relationship. There is no place for a relationship in my life.

"In love" just wasn't happening. Not even the teeniest, tiniest bit.

Stay calm, get on with what you have to do,

and maybe the feeling will pass.

Words to live by, she thought devoutly, and put her Lynette-wear and the phone down on the counter by the sink as she heeded her own advice. In something less than ten minutes she'd used the facilities, taken a quick shower, dressed in her Lynette-basic black sweater and loose black pants and pulled her hair back into a ponytail in preparation for the Lynette wig. Her Lynette makeup, cheek prosthesis and the tape for the wig were still in her bag in the closet. Fetching them would require leaving the bathroom, which would almost certainly involve her first postcoital encounter with the current scourge of her existence. The mere thought made her antsy, which was annoying and pathetic at the same time. Seizing on any excuse for delay, she picked up his phone.

She tapped in the code, saw Doc's reply: On it. Short and sweet: her kind of message.

She typed thx and was clicking off when she noticed that a few almost microscopic flecks of powder remained on the screen. Had it not been for the brightness of the bathroom light catching on some of the reflective particles in the powder, she might never have noticed them.

But notice them she did.

The odd thing about it was, the flecks were almost certainly not stuck to where the 4-6-9 keys would be. Probably because by punching those numbers in, twice now, she had eliminated the last traces of the powder adhering to them.

Frowning, she waited until the lock screen reappeared, then discovered that the almost invisible flecks of powder were centered on the 2.

In the course of her not inconsiderable criminal career, she'd come across digital devices with separate codes partitioning them into what were essentially different units. Each code would unlock a different part of the device.

Since the 4-6-9 keys were the only other keys to which powder had adhered, it seemed probable that if there was a separate code, it would include those three numbers plus 2.

Twenty-four possible number combinations. Well under three minutes to try them all. As she started methodically punching in different potential combinations, she reminded herself that it was quite possible that there was an explanation that did not include a bifurcated device for why powder flecks had adhered to the 2.

He could have accidentally brushed a

finger over the key, for example, or something sticky could have dropped onto the screen . . .

Even while she was reaching for various alternative explanations, her heartbeat sped up and her stomach tightened.

A funny thing happened on the way to the love fest . . .

She remembered how quick Colin had been to give her the XMI6 code when he'd discovered her with his phone in her hand.

Because he had nothing to hide? Or because he did?

She hit 4-6-9-2, and the lock screen dissolved into a message page.

Two outgoing messages, three incoming messages.

The first outgoing message, sent by Colin, was a sketchy description of the thugs who'd shot up Le Chien Rouge, with the tagline Identity Check Requested.

The incoming reply read, Pending.

The second outgoing message was a photo of Four-fingered Franz. It had obviously been snapped by Colin while they were dancing in Le Chien Rouge hours earlier. Why obviously? First, Franz was sitting at the table in the restaurant. Second, strands of what she recognized as her Alice wig dangled into the top portion of the photo.

From the angle, and the way the strands were positioned, she felt safe in concluding that, while he'd been dipping her back over his arm and humping her (she could think of no more delicate way to put it), which had probably been done on purpose to *distract her* so she wouldn't notice when he pulled his phone out and started snapping away, he'd been taking a picture of Franz behind her back.

Along with the photo was the message Colin had sent off with it: Identity Check Requested.

In the reply below the photo was a thumbnail bio that said Franz's last name was Marcel and included multiple aliases. The final line included a flag that linked it to another file. That line read: *Known associate of Mason Thayer.*

The third incoming message read: Team in place. Looks like you're getting close. Keep me informed.

The first two exchanges were with an entity called I-24/7, which she knew from harsh experience was connected to Interpol.

The source of the last incoming message was even easier to identify, because the contact info heading it read *Durand.*

Given the context, it wasn't much of a leap to figure out what Colin was supposedly getting close *to:* capturing Mason.

Which he'd been trying to do ever since she and he had first met. She didn't know why she'd ever believed for a moment that it wasn't still on his agenda.

Staring at the name *Durand,* Bianca felt as if every last drop of blood was draining from her body.

From her earliest childhood, Durand had been the hunter and she and Mason — her little nuclear family, as she'd thought of the two of them at the time — had been the prey. He'd been the rough equivalent of the boogeyman for her, and she'd spent a lifetime looking over her shoulder in fear of him. At the faintest hint of his presence anywhere in her vicinity, she'd been taught to flee, hide, disappear. His pursuit had been relentless, and *he had never stopped.* Just the sight of his name on Colin's phone was enough to make the hair stand up on the back of her neck.

Colin knew the threat Durand posed. He knew how she felt. The bitterness of betrayal formed a hard knot in her chest.

She hit the flagged attachment to the first message.

Skimming it, she saw that it was a list of crimes in which Franz was known or suspected to have participated. Eight were marked with asterisks. Those, she saw, were the ones in which he was thought to have worked with Mason, including a jewelry heist two years previously.

Another was the bank robbery she had described to Colin. Only, of course, it had taken place years earlier than she'd implied.

Would he have made the connection?

Surely.

She checked the time on the messages, remembered what time it had been when she'd first picked up his phone.

No doubt about it: the messages had been sent and received while she was in the shower. When he'd forgone his shower to catch her on his phone, when he'd once again started questioning her about the identity of the man in the restaurant, he'd already had the answers.

He'd been checking to see if she would lie to him.

He'd been using her to try to capture Mason.

He'd been in contact with Durand, and Interpol, for almost certainly the whole time they'd been together.

He'd been *playing* her.

Staring down at the phone, Bianca felt the kind of sickening sensation that sometimes happens when you're in an elevator that drops too fast. Her stomach shot into her throat. Her pulse roared in her ears. She went all light-headed. She wanted to vomit.

Then she got mad.

Fingers clenching around the phone so hard she was surprised it didn't shatter into a million pieces, she strode toward the bedroom, threw open the door and confronted the lying, double-dealing, untrustworthy dog who stood beside the bed in the now lamp-lit room fastening what she sincerely hoped were his still cold and soggy jeans.

He looked up when the bathroom door flew open.

"Hey," he said. Once upon a time the crooked smile that accompanied that might have dazzled her. Now it made her see red.

"You lying *bastard,*" she snarled. "Did you really think you could reverse honey-trap me?"

22

Monday, December 16th

"What?" Colin looked startled.

"4-6-9-2," she spit, and hurled the phone at him.

He caught it with a deft one-handed grab before it could hit him. His expression now lively with alarm, he shoved the phone into his pocket without even bothering to look at it and came toward her.

"You had sex with me to try to get me to lead you to Mason. How low, how *vile*, can you get?"

"Wait — hold on. Just calm down. No, I did not. What makes you —"

"I saw the messages on your phone, you asshole." She was so angry her voice shook. "The *hidden* messages, on the secret part of your phone you *hid* from me."

"Need to know," he said, which was the equivalent of waving a red flag in front of a bull.

Steam practically poured out of her ears. "You know where you can shove that."

"You've got it all wrong. I had sex with you because you're gorgeous, and sexy, and I wanted you — want you — so much I was getting half crippled from it every time I was around you. You got under my skin the first time I saw you. You —" He was close by then, and made the mistake of reaching for her.

"Don't even *try.*" She executed a push-up chest strike that knocked him back several feet.

"Damn it, Bianca."

She stalked toward him. "How much of it was a lie? The Five Eyes thing? Lynette Holbrook? The ChapStick? The CIA kill team? All of it? Tell me."

Retreating before her, he held his hands up placatingly. "None of it. Nothing. No lies. Well, maybe an omission or two. But everything I told you is true. Lynette, Park, all of it. You're overreacting."

That was so infuriating she could practically feel her body vibrate like a tuning fork. "I'm *overreacting?*"

"Shh, don't screech. It's just after four in the morning and we're in a hotel, remember? The last thing we need is to draw attention to —"

"News flash, Romeo. I don't give a damn." With the dresser at his back, he was out of room. She kept coming, and got right up in his face. The fact that he was a head taller and almost twice as broad just made him more to want to kill. "Do you get paid extra for seducing women? Or, wait — you're pretty sneaky with a camera. Did you make a sex tape? Are you going to try to use it to blackmail me? Good luck with that."

"Would you *listen*?" This time he succeeded in grabbing her arms. Growling, she used a lightning combination of momentum and a hip throw to put him on the floor. Sneering down at him as he lay grimacing on his back, she turned to walk away.

"Damn it. That hurt." With a quick lunge he managed to catch her ankle and send her tumbling to the floor, too. Luckily, the butt-ugly carpet cushioned the fall. She hit on her side, rolled to her back and just had time to register the unpleasant prickliness of the synthetic fibers beneath her before he threw himself on top of her. Catching her wrists before she could administer the double ear strike that was whipping his way, he pinned her to the carpet with his weight. "Hold it right there. We need to talk."

She gave a snort of unamused laughter. "In your dreams. You really think I'm going to believe a word you say?"

"Like you're a fount of honesty and integrity?" His weight and heat and the sexy smoothness of all those bronzed muscles was newly familiar in a way that acted as the rough equivalent of a match to gasoline.

"More than you." Snapping her heel sideways up toward her butt, she used the strength in her legs to kick her body up with enough force to flip him off her. Freeing her wrists with a jerk, she leaped triumphantly to her feet and aimed an ax stomp at his stomach. He managed to dodge it before springing upright himself.

He said, "You've been lying to me ever since we met."

With both of them now on their feet, they circled each other warily. His breathing had quickened and his eyes gleamed a challenge at her.

She bared her teeth at him. "Not only have *you* been lying to *me,* you've been using me and manipulating me."

"I've saved your ass is what I've done."

"Oh, is that what you tell yourself when you look in the mirror?" Her words dripped scorn.

"Just so we're clear, last night was not a honey-trap. I have never honey-trapped you. You, on the other hand, have definitely honey-trapped me." Without even a flicker of his eyes to warn her what was coming, he lunged, caught her around the waist and propelled her backward until they crashed down onto the bed.

"What?" Throwing chops and elbows, most of which he managed to avoid or parry, she fought to free herself from his attempts to hold on to her. The bed creaked and shuddered, reminding her of — *Don't even go there. "Jackass."*

"Would you *stop?*" Barely managing to catch a knee that was meant for his privates in the thigh instead, he grunted at the impact and once again made use of his superior weight by throwing his body on top of her. She went for his eyes. His hands shackled her wrists, pinning them beside her head. She glared up at him. "Who kissed who and then hit them with a Taser? Who kissed who again and then knocked them out with a drug?"

"Who kissed who on a boat and then handcuffed them to a rail?"

"That wasn't a honey-trap. That was done for your protection. Just like me having a team assembled to arrest Thayer if he shows up around you again is for your protection."

"Bullshit." Snagging his leg with her foot, she executed a sweep that allowed her to

throw him off her. Instead of making good her escape and catapulting from the bed, she flung herself on top of him, straddling him and pinning him in place with an elbow to his throat. From that position, she could have crushed his larynx with ease. Instead she leaned in and exerted just enough pressure to make sure he knew what she *could* do.

His eyes narrowed at her. He didn't struggle. Given where her elbow was, her reaction to that was, *Smart man.* "Thayer's wanted by every major law enforcement agency in the world. Sooner or later, he's going to go down. There's not a doubt about it. And if you're working with him when it happens, you're going to go down with him. And I'm not only talking getting arrested and spending years in prison. I'm talking getting killed, as in shot, hanged, beheaded, whatever, depending on who gets to him first."

"In other words, you're using me to try to catch Mason *for me.* That is *so sweet* — aren't you the noble altruist?" She pressed a little harder with her elbow. He coughed, but didn't try to fight free. Instead his eyes bored into hers.

"Why are you so loyal to him? Does he have something on you? Whatever it is, if you tell me we can make it go away. I'm on your side, baby, I swear."

"You really think I'm going to fall for that?" But the question startled her, made her think. She was loyal to Mason because — despite everything, deep inside she was still bound by the ties of a lifetime, she supposed. Because, no matter how bitter the betrayal, some tiny, unclued-in part of her still thought of him as her father. It was a stark realization.

Which she had no intention of sharing with anyone, much less the lying scumbag beneath her.

"It's the truth. I *am* on your side. I've been on your side from just about the first moment I saw you, when you fell from the ceiling in your sexy underwear."

Her lip curled. "Save it. Think I don't know an enemy when I get seduced and backstabbed by one?"

"If you think I'm your enemy, why don't you go ahead and push that elbow down a little harder? Larynx is like an eggshell. Doesn't take much to crush it."

Their eyes met. In his she read complete confidence that she wouldn't do it. The galling part? He was right. She wasn't going to kill or even really injure him, just like she hadn't really injured him all along. Time to face the terrible truth — she'd been pulling her punches. The other terrible truth was, so had he.

So what did that say about the state of their — *not* relationship?

Short answer: there was a reason *love* was a four-letter word.

Not that there was any question, any longer, of her being even the slightest bit in love with him. Her eyes had been opened in time, which was a good thing, really. Where could it lead — gold rings and picket fences and babies? Given what she was, those were things that weren't ever going to happen for her.

But something like, say, a broken heart had been a dangerously close-run thing.

"Go to hell." She flung herself off him in complete self-disgust, then rolled off the bed and retreated toward the middle of the room. A succession of creaks told her that he was getting off the bed, too. She turned to glare at him.

"I'm trying to catch Thayer because he's a wanted criminal and catching him is my job. I'm trying to keep you safe while it happens so you don't go down with him."

She folded her arms over her chest. "That's the biggest load of crap I ever heard."

"It's the truth." He came toward her. "Just like I brought you into this and hooked you up with Five Eyes because if I hadn't, sooner or later the CIA would have killed you. And speaking of, and referring back to the whole lying-through-your-teeth-every-time-you-open-your-mouth thing, you've never told me anything even approaching the truth about what you did to get a CIA kill team sicced on you. So how about it?"

"Need to know," she said with bite. "And by the way, just so you know, if you ever touch me again I'll break you in half."

An upward quirk to one corner of his mouth told her what he thought of that. But he stopped where he was, thrusting his hands in his pockets and rocking back on his heels as he regarded her almost grimly.

"Look," he said. "There's — something — between us. I don't know — a *spark.* Instead of fighting it, maybe we should try exploring it, see where it leads."

"Screw that."

"You know it's there as well as I do. Last night —"

"You know what? The best thing you can do is forget last night."

"— was special. You are amazing, and —"

"I don't *care.*" Her tone fierce, she broke in again before he could say anything more.

Remembering how they'd been together, the things they'd said and done, infuriated — and hurt. Mustering every inner defense she had, she rejected the memory along with the pain, walled them off, compartmentalized them into something to be dealt with later as she'd been taught. The anger she grabbed on to with both hands, used it as inner Kevlar to wrap around her stupidly vulnerable heart. "Whatever 'special' thing you're trying to make me think is there between us, isn't. It's nonexistent."

"Bianca —"

"We had a one-night stand, and it's over. If it meant more than that to you, I suggest you try calling 1-800-get-a-life."

He opened his mouth as if to say something else, closed it again and ran a hand through his hair. "Bloody hell. We don't have time for this. I know you're pissed at me, and I'm not saying you don't have reason. But how about we put aside the personal for right now and concentrate on doing the job we came here to do? Then we can talk this out."

She met him look for level look. "Fine. If you didn't totally lie about *everything,* if this operation is as crucial as you led me to believe, if me delivering this flash drive to Park will really get the CIA off my back, then let's get going and get it over with. But you can forget about talking later. After the job's over, we — you and I — are done. Got it?"

From his expression she expected an argument, but after the barest of hesitations he inclined his head. "If that's how you want it," he said.

"That's how I want it."

"Then you got it." He glanced at the clock beside the bed. "It's 4:32. We have a little less than an hour and a half before you're scheduled to meet with Park."

Without another word, she retrieved her purse from the closet and headed for the bathroom. When she emerged a short time later it was as Lynette.

He was dressed and waiting for her. His eyes swept her, flickered. The glance she gave him as she walked past him toward the door was cool, remote, professional.

Never look back: it was one of the rules. And as far as she was concerned, that included last night's regrettable interlude with him.

"Let's go," she said.

23

As a little girl who more than once had been left to make her way across the vast metropolis that was Paris on her own, Bianca had learned that the best way to grasp the layout of the arrondissements was to picture the city as a spiral centered on the Seine. Clockwise around the innermost circle were the 1st, 2nd, 3rd and 4th arrondissements on the Right Bank, and the 5th, 6th and 7th arrondissements on the smaller Left Bank. The 8th, 9th, 10th, 11th and 12th formed the second semicircular layer on the Right Bank, while the second layer of the Left Bank was made up of the 13th, 14th and 15th arrondissements. The 16th, 17th, 18th, 19th and 20th arrondissements formed the last outer circle of the Right Bank.

Their hotel was located in the 8th arrondissement. The Champs-Élysées cut through the heart of the 8th from the Arc de Triomphe to the Place de la Concorde, which meant that tourists were as ubiquitous as ants and as a result the area never slept. Cafés were open and people were on the streets even at that early hour. It was cold and slightly misty when she and Colin hit the street, and still full dark. The monuments and Christmas displays were aglow and the streetlights burned, but harbingers of dawn could be seen in the pale ghost of the moon dipping low behind the Eiffel Tower, the "green men" who were already at work washing the pavement, and the garbage vans rattling about their business. The heavenly smell of the bakeries was almost enough to counter the fishy scent of the puddles left behind by the previous night's rain.

Ordinarily, the thought of a fresh baguette spread with that to-die-for butter would have been enough to make her mouth water, especially since she'd given the designated power-bar-and-water breakfast a miss, but her knotted stomach made eating an impossibility. If anyone had known and asked, she would have said that she was too tense at the prospect of the coming job to eat. The truth was, she never got tense before jobs; if anything, she got her Zen on. Her stomach was in a knot because, although mentally she had resolved the emotional turmoil that the previous night's disaster had caused, physically her body had not yet fully gotten with the program.

As much as she hated to face it, somewhere deep inside she was bleeding. The wound was fresh, and would require time to heal.

Nobody ever said life was going to be all sunshine and lollipops, she told herself savagely.

Her rendezvous with Park was to take place in the 4th arrondissement, a relatively short distance that ordinarily would have merited a long walk or a quick metro ride. Given the fact that whoever was hunting her was without a doubt still out there and an unknown number of people, including at a minimum Park himself, whoever he might have told and Colin's handlers, knew the time and location of the meeting, which meant that they knew she was going to be at a fixed point at a fixed time, the streets approaching the rendezvous were liable to be fraught with peril and public transportation to the area would conceivably be watched. Plus, fully trusting in any plan that Colin had had a hand in formulating now seemed foolishly naive. She therefore opted for the safe and simple: she stole a car.

Since she was now Lynette, who would be traveling through Paris alone, Colin was on the other side of the street and a little way behind her when she stopped walking toward the nearby metro stop to jimmy the ancient Audi's door. By the time she pulled away from the curb, he'd caught up.

"I thought the plan was to take the metro," he said as he wedged himself in beside her. He barely fit. His knees pressed against the glove box and his head lacked maybe half an inch of brushing the roof. His shoulders were wider than the seat back. Like most French cars, the Audi was clown-car small, with a manual transmission. It reeked of cheap perfume. The heat sputtered fitfully.

"New plan," she said. Her voice was without inflection. Overt hostility had no place in the working partnership that they needed to maintain until the job was done. Until it came to an end, their association was strictly business, and she meant to keep her side of the equation businesslike.

She refused to even allow herself to take pleasure in how uncomfortable he looked. Well, not very much pleasure.

He said, "Lynette wouldn't steal a car."

"Lynette would already be dead."

"Probably. Still —"

"The time and location of the meeting

with Park might have leaked. And the people from last night are still out there. If they find out about the meeting, if anyone hunting Lynette finds out about the meeting, watching the streets and public transportation leading to it is a no-brainer. A rental car might get pinged, but a stolen car? No way. Getting as close as we can in a stolen car before Lynette joins up with Park on foot makes it far more difficult for anyone to take her out before she even gets to the rendezvous."

He frowned, then gave a slow nod. "Makes sense."

"I tend to do that."

She could feel him watching her, but she didn't look at him. Instead she kept a wary eye out for possible danger as she drove. The mansard roofs and gables and balconies of the centuries-old buildings lining the streets offered plenty of concealment for a sniper. Pedestrians were little more than dark silhouettes moving along the sidewalks: they could be anybody carrying anything. Headlights of the oncoming and following vehicles made it impossible to see inside them. The only good news was, any would-be assassin was equally unlikely to be able to spot them, or to see inside the Audi.

"Parc Marceau," he said as she reached the first of many roundabouts. "Front entrance."

"I remember." As he'd told her on the way down the hotel stairs, it was the location of the dead drop. "Is the *associate* dropping off the weapons part of the team you have lying in wait in hopes of catching Mason?"

"No. Entirely separate."

"Want to explain that team to me? Like how big it is? And where it is now?"

"Six of my men, plus a fair amount of technology, have been combing Paris for Thayer since we arrived." He held up a hand to silence her when she opened her mouth with every intention of blasting him over the fact that this had been taking place behind her back. "Before you get going, let me stipulate that they don't know anything about you being in Paris, as Bianca or as Lynette, or about what you and I are doing. They don't even know that I'm in Paris. All they know is that Thayer is suspected to be here, and their job is to find him."

"My, you do have a lot going on right now, don't you?" *Okay, too much snark. Rein it in.*

"It's called multitasking."

The insouciance with which he said that had her brows snapping together.

"Does Durand know?" Her tone was

brusque.

"That I'm hunting Thayer? He hired me."

"Does he know about me?"

The slight hesitation before he answered told her everything she needed to know.

"Yes. Not that you're posing as Lynette, but that you're working with me."

She would at least have given him a partial bonus point for telling the truth if she hadn't suspected that he'd recognized his own hesitation, known she would put the correct interpretation on it, and thus concluded that an honest answer was his best choice.

Sometimes knowing each other's thought processes as well as they seemed to was a bitch.

"Not to burst your bubble, but an awful lot of people have been trying to catch Mason for an awful lot of years. Nobody's succeeded yet."

He shrugged. "It takes a village."

That was so annoying that Bianca clamped her lips shut rather than reply. She drove the remainder of the short distance to the Boulevard de Courcelles in silence. The entrance to the park was illuminated but unguarded. A few people on the sidewalks, a few cars traveling in both directions on the wide street, but no one who appeared to pay the least attention as she pulled over and stopped in front of the park.

"Tick-tock," she said with a glance at the dashboard clock. The time was 5:16 a.m. They had a little less than forty-five minutes in which to make it to the meeting.

He nodded and got out. The long gray overcoat he wore made him look like a businessman, or a banker. A tall, athletically built one. Frowning, she watched him walk across the pavement, past the classical stone rotunda that marked the entrance, toward one of the massive iron gates that, so many hours before opening time, were closed and locked. Darkness swallowed him up, but she knew what he was doing: retrieving the weapons stash from a trash can beside the gate. Her pulse quickened as a couple with a dog and then two women who looked like they were making for the metro walked past, but they didn't so much as glance in his direction, or hers. Then he was on his way back, a shadow separating from the other shadows. The long duffel bag that now hung over his shoulder could have held anything from exercise equipment to laundry.

Instead, she saw as he got back in the car and opened it to check the contents out by the uncertain light of the streetlamps, it contained top-of-the-line firepower: a Sig

Sauer P226 MK25 pistol and a SCAR-H standard assault rifle plus accessories for both as well as a wealth of ammunition.

She was already driving away as he slipped a magazine into his Glock, chambered a round and restored it to his ankle holster. Then he checked to make sure the Sig Sauer was loaded, thrust it into the holster that came with it and strapped that on beneath his coat. Finally, he slipped the Desert Eagle plus extra mags into his coat pockets, screwed the suppressor can onto the SCAR-H and slipped the weapon back into the duffel so that, when the time came, it could be carried along a street and into a building without attracting attention.

She watched him handling the weapons enviously.

The unfortunate thing about being Lynette was, there was nothing much she could do about any trouble they might encounter. Defending herself in any effective way would immediately give the imposture away. If shit hit the fan, she needed to react as Lynette would. A pistol, for example, wasn't happening because Lynette wouldn't have one or, if she had managed to acquire one, know how to use it properly. Same thing with any kind of martial arts moves. The tools in her garter belt were off-limits, too. And the situation would have to get dire — as in, her life would have to be on the line — before Colin came into play.

Because if Park and crew even suspected that she wasn't Lynette, the operation would fail. And, somewhat to her own surprise, she was discovering that she wasn't going to let that happen. Her own problems, many and varied though they were, paled in significance to the threat a nuclear strike posed to the world. She was committed to doing her part to stop that if she could.

"Here." He passed her a disposable phone that he'd pulled out of the duffel. "This is for you to use to verify the payment, or at least to be seen trying to verify the payment. If the money doesn't transfer right away, don't hang around waiting for it. Once you hand over the ChapStick, get out of there."

"I don't need you to tell me how to do my job." Her voice was flinty. She paused, then added with cold precision, "Park doesn't get the ChapStick until the money shows up in the account. Otherwise, he might get suspicious."

Colin's lips thinned, but he didn't argue. They both knew that the importance of the operation merited taking all but the most egregious risks.

Traffic picked up as they neared the 4th

arrondissement. Driving along the shiny black ribbon of the Seine in the shadow of the gorgeously illuminated Notre Dame Cathedral, Bianca was thankful for the anonymity of the Audi. They were just one of dozens of vehicles speeding through the city in the predawn darkness. At the Pont Louis Philippe she turned away from the river. The Rue de Rivoli, which was where the meeting with Park was supposed to take place, was not far away.

He said, "I'll have eyes on you from the moment you step out on the street. If you need me, sing out."

She responded with a curt nod. They would be in contact via the earrings and the ring. The plan was for him to be in an apartment overlooking her meeting with Park with the rifle trained on the action. When the meeting was over and the ChapStick and money had changed hands, she was to walk to the nearest metro stop, board the train and get off at the Eiffel Tower, where she and Colin would meet and she would be whisked out of France.

From the moment she met with Park, she would be in acute danger.

The Rue de Rivoli was one of the most heavily trafficked avenues in Paris. It was home to world-famous shops, innumerable cafés and restaurants, small parks, the Louvre, the Tuileries and an iconic golden statue of Joan of Arc, among many other must-see attractions. So early in the day, most of the shops and the museums weren't yet open, but the parks teemed with exercise enthusiasts, the cafés and bakeries overflowed with people grabbing breakfast and the sidewalks as well as the street itself were busy with pedestrians and vehicles as commuters headed in to work early to beat the crush of rush hour traffic that would begin in earnest in about an hour. To add to the congestion, an exhibition of some sort seemed to be setting up in the small square around Saint-Jacques Tower, which was almost directly across from the newsstand where she was to meet Park.

By way of the first round of countersurveillance, she idled for a moment next to the curb in front of the Tower under the guise of watching the assembly of what proved to be about a dozen large white tents. What she was really watching was the newsstand, which was open and busy. No sign of Park yet. No sign of anything suspicious. She did a visual sweep of the adjacent sidewalks and street: nothing of interest.

Colin had been doing the same thing. Now he said, "It's twenty till. Drop me off in that alley up there."

Bianca nodded and drove on. Moments later she pulled into the dark and narrow alley he'd indicated, where he got out. The headlights picked up a dumpster, a stray cat and a couple of men walking separately toward the street they'd just left. Nothing out of the ordinary about them, but still she looked them over warily. At this point, an attack could come from anywhere.

Colin slung the duffel bag over his shoulder, then bent down to look in through the open passenger door at her.

"I'll give you the go-ahead when I'm in place," he said. The smile he gave her then was a little crooked, a little wry, and way too intimate for their decidedly not-intimate relationship. "You're the best female operative I've ever seen, but you're not bulletproof. Try not to get yourself killed out there."

Her lip curled at him. "Bite me, fanboy."

He laughed and shut the door. Just as well, because that limited her response to a killing glare directed at his retreating back.

Fortunately, she'd found her center again when, five minutes later, he spoke in her ear: "I'm here."

"Nothing yet." Her voice was crisp, emotionless, as befitted what they were to each other: strictly fellow operatives.

"Same."

By that time she'd parked the car, walked back to Saint-Jacques Tower and stopped at a café across the street from it. From there she could see the newsstand and the area around it. So much hustle and bustle surrounded the setting up of the exhibit, which she felt safe in concluding from the paintings being carried inside the tents must be related to art, that she was, she felt, totally inconspicuous despite (or perhaps because of) the brightness of the stolen red coat she wore. Klieg lights were being switched on inside the tents, making them glow like Japanese lanterns, and tall heaters had been delivered and were being hooked up. Generators hummed, and workers were in the process of festooning the small iron fence around the square with bunting. As she watched, a trio of white delivery trucks with the words *École des Beaux-Arts* scrawled in large electric-blue letters on their sides pulled up to the curb in front of the tower. The *École* was one of the premier art schools in Paris, and she assumed that the trucks contained more items pertaining to the exhibit.

"Your coffee, mademoiselle," the server said in French.

"Merci." Bianca took the steaming cup. More as a cover than because she had any desire for coffee, she sipped from it as she turned away from the counter to cast a searching glance up and down the street. Traffic, both vehicular and pedestrian, grew heavier by the minute. Half a dozen patrons browsed the newsstand. None looked familiar. None looked suspicious.

There was no sign of Park.

Colin said, "Two lookouts in place, almost certainly from Park's camp. One standing by the Pascal statue. One seated to the right of the newsstand. Black puffy coat, newspaper."

Bianca spotted the men in question, the one bundled in a black parka, the other sitting on a bench with a newspaper. Both discreetly scanned the area around the newsstand.

"I see them," she said. For Park to have lookouts in place was only to be expected. They were a precaution on his part rather than a threat to her. The type of operative she was watching for would not be so easily spotted.

"Here he comes. Across the street, passing the giant nutcracker beside the hat shop."

By *he,* Colin meant Park: Bianca saw him exactly where Colin had said he was, walking purposefully along the sidewalk past Le Chapeau Parfait, bodyguards trailing.

Her final act as Lynette was at hand.

Her senses immediately heightened. Everything from the pale stone of the soaring Tower to the shiny hoods of the cars to the mostly grays and blacks of the coats of the pedestrians on the sidewalks to the bright colors of the magazines in the newsstand's racks grew more vivid. Snippets of conversation, shuffling footsteps, the rumble of traffic, the jingle of money changing hands, all clarified and separated into individual tracks of sound in her head. She could feel the weight of the crisp winter air against her cheeks. The smell of exhaust and cigarettes and coffee grew sharper. She took one more unwanted sip of coffee — the brew was hot and newly bitter — pitched the remainder and stepped out of the café to get a better view.

Park reached the newsstand and went for the rack of international newspapers against the back wall. She could feel adrenaline surge through her veins as she watched him pick up a copy of the *New York Times.*

"It's a go," she said into the ring. Giving Lynette's black-framed glasses a one-fingered push up the bridge of her nose, she headed across the street. Instead of using a crosswalk as anyone on the watch for her might be expecting her to do, she navigated her way through the flow of traffic, weaving between the cars.

"I've got you." Colin's steady tones were those of the consummate professional she now needed him to be. Knowing that he was watching, that he had her covered, made her feel safer.

Until it didn't.

Even as she reached the sidewalk, even as Park saw her and approached, *New York Times* tucked under his arm and bodyguards in tow, she felt that horrifyingly familiar cold tingle between her shoulder blades.

Without taking her eyes off Park, without looking around, without altering her Lynette body language by so much as the stiffening of her shoulders, she went on instant red alert. As surely as she knew that the sun rose in the morning, she knew that whoever had been stalking her just before she'd ducked into Le Chien Rouge was out there on the Rue de Rivoli right at that very moment, and he had her in his sights again.

24

"You have that which you promised me?" Park greeted her as she fell into step beside him. Blending in with the steady flow of pedestrians on the sidewalk, they walked away from the newsstand. A pronounced crease between his eyebrows was the only visible sign of discomposure Bianca could see on his round, placid face. He wore the same overcoat as before, but today's scarf was a Burberry plaid. His bodyguards kept just far enough behind so that their conversation could not be overheard.

"I do. Do you have the money?" It was hard to stay completely focused on what she was doing when her Spidey-sense was going haywire. In front of, behind, above, beside — she could not pinpoint the source of the danger. But the sensation was acute enough that she felt it on what was almost a cellular level. Using her peripheral vision and every reflective surface available to her, she scanned the sidewalks, the shops, the cars, the square.

Dozens of people streamed in both directions, heading to and from the metro, filling the cafés, milling around the square, window-shopping, stopping to take photos. Vehicles clogged the street. Windows, balconies, roofs, even the Saint-Jacques Tower itself, overlooked her position. She wanted to alert Colin, have him search the crowd for — what? Something, someone *wrong.* As Lynette, with Park so close, she could not. To contact Colin would risk blowing the operation.

Abort. Abort. Abort. That's what her mind screamed. But the mission was too important, and too close to being completed. And besides, since she had no idea where the source of the danger was, which way would she go to escape? She might walk right into it.

Park said, "Fifty million is too much. I will give you twenty."

Bianca's head swiveled toward him like something out of *The Exorcist.* Her eyes met his with such ferocity that his widened. *Are you kidding me?* hovered on the tip of her tongue, but she remembered her Lynetteness in time.

"This is not a subject for negotiation," she

said. A family of chattering Germans spilled out of a café just ahead of them. Taking Park's elbow, Bianca sped up to shelter among them. More bodies equaled a more difficult target.

"Twenty million is a great deal of money." Frowning, Park lowered his voice in deference to the proximity of what he almost certainly didn't realize was their human shield. "And it is all I am authorized to pay."

If she'd been conducting the sale as herself, that was the moment when she would have turned and walked away. But given that Lynette was inexperienced and frightened and on the run, and she herself could practically feel the hot breath of whoever was hunting her tickling the back of her neck, she was at a real disadvantage. She needed to get this done and get gone.

Traffic had stopped to permit pedestrians to cross to the square via a crosswalk. Leaving the Germans to go on their way, Bianca steered Park into the crosswalk, where a large number of people were, to judge from their conversation, on their way to help set up the art festival.

Zig when they expect you to zag.

She pulled the phone Colin had given her out of her pocket. "Make the transfer." As she agreed to the lower price, it was all she could do not to talk through her teeth.

He pulled out his phone and turned it on, thereby, she gathered, indicating his willingness to follow her instruction. Then he hesitated. "First you show me what I am buying."

If she showed Park the ChapStick, there was little she as Lynette could do to prevent him, or his bodyguards, from wresting it from her. On the other hand — oh, happy thought! — she could make a huge outcry that would attract all kinds of attention, and that was something he would do much to avoid.

The pedestrian signal flashed a warning. Traffic started to edge into the crosswalk. Slowing down to avoid a hot-pink couturier's van, which totally jumped the still-red light to roll in front of them, she said, "Here," and allowed him a glimpse of the ChapStick, which, because she was Lynette, she kept loose in her coat pocket.

Staring down into her pocket at the ChapStick, which was the only thing in it, he frowned and said, "Twenty million for a —"

Boom!

The square exploded in front of them in a huge blast of heat and fire and sound.

The force of it slammed into Bianca like a freight train, picking her up, hurling her backward. She screamed as, wreathed in a tsunami of flame, the pink van flew toward her — and then everything went black.

The carnage would have done a slaughterhouse proud. Dozens of dead and wounded littered the ground. Blood was everywhere. Body parts and bits of clothing and miscellaneous items like menus and hangers and automobile tires hung from balconies and awnings and the small, ornamental trees. Overturned vehicles blocked streets and sidewalks. Emergency workers ran to and fro, triaging the injured, shuttling victims on gurneys, providing first aid. The truck that was the source of the explosion still burned furiously. Shouting firefighters wielding gushing hoses battled the blaze. Thick gray smoke billowed toward the lightening sky. The acrid smell stung noses, made eyes water. The shriek of arriving and departing ambulances echoed through the canyon of scorched buildings, making it necessary for the reporter from BFM TV, France's number one news channel, to shout into her mic to be heard.

". . . *un attentat terroriste,*" (a terrorist attack) she said to the camera. *"Personne ne prend la responsabilité."* (No one is taking responsibility.)

There was more, but Colin, striding past the TV crew to search inside yet one more small shop that had had its front window blown in, tuned it out. He was cold with fear as he checked out an obviously dead woman impaled by window shards. She was the right shape and size, with brown hair — his heart thumped, his mouth went dry, his breathing stopped. A glimpse of the woman's face allowed him to breathe again: *not her.*

A paramedic crouched beside a second woman, blocking her face from his view even as he did a lightning-fast scan of the premises. That the second woman's face was hidden didn't matter. It had taken him no more than a glance to ascertain that neither of the other two female victims in what, as it turned out, was a boulangerie was Bianca.

So far he'd found no trace of her. Or Park. Or the bodyguards.

Terror clawed at his insides, fighting to be released. It was all he could do to keep it in check. Losing his head would do no one any good, least of all her.

At this point, all that was known for certain was that one of three trucks supposedly from L'École des Beaux-Arts had not been. Loaded with explosives, it was a ringer sent to park behind the two that were legitimately from the school. It had blown up just as Bianca, with Park and the bodyguards, had been crossing the street toward it. At that precise moment, his view of her had been blocked by traffic. Through his rifle scope, he'd been scanning the area immediately behind her for possible danger. The wall of flame had blasted into his field of vision a split second before the force of the explosion had knocked him on his ass. It was strong enough to shatter the partially open window he'd been set up behind, to shake the building, the block. He'd rushed to the scene, arriving within minutes. The chaos had been so complete that even now, some forty minutes after the blast, he still had no idea whether or not she was alive.

All he knew was that he couldn't find her. And he was sick with dread.

Was she trapped beneath an overturned vehicle? Had she been blown into a building where she was even now lying injured? Had she already been whisked away to a hospital by a first responder?

Or was she dead?

That was the thought he couldn't stomach.

If she was conscious, she would have contacted him. Unless, of course, there was a problem with communications, which was always possible depending on where she was and in what condition.

If she was alive, wherever she was, she was in danger from more than any injuries she might have suffered. Disguised as Lynette, with Lynette's papers, injured and possibly unconscious, she was a sitting duck for the many and varied entities that wanted her dead.

Was she the target of the blast? It was possible that she wasn't, but his first, instinctive thought was, *There's no such thing as coincidence.*

What were the chances of there being a terrorist attack at the exact moment when an on-the-run young woman wanted by what seemed like half the world walked past?

"Major." Hailing Colin by the rank he'd held when he'd served under him, Angus Wilson strode toward him.

A tall, sturdy, thirtysomething Scot, Wilson was one of his men, part of the Cambridge Solutions team he'd had in place in Paris to hunt for Thayer. In the aftermath of the explosion, as finding Bianca had turned into the most urgent thing in his existence and, for her, a matter of life or death, he'd summoned them to assist. Telling them she was an associate of Thayer's, he'd shown them her picture as Lynette and set them to searching.

Instantly on the move, Colin had just reached him when Wilson added, quietly so as not to be overheard, "We've got something."

His heart lurched. He didn't want to reveal how personal this was, not to his men, not under the circumstances when supposedly the woman he was looking for was nothing more to him than a job, but as he walked with Wilson across the ravaged square he found that he was sweating. Their goal was a tight group composed of three more of his men — and a van that had clearly, from the damage to its side, just been set back up on its four wheels.

A hot-pink van. The color was impossible to mistake. He clearly remembered that it was one of the vehicles that, seconds before the explosion, had blocked Bianca from his view.

Recognizing it, he felt his gut twist. His heart pounded like he'd been running for miles. Gritting his teeth, he braced himself for whatever was getting ready to come his way.

Another of his men — Nester Davis — was crouched beside a figure sprawled on the pavement, partially covered by a blue rescue blanket.

Colin heard a roaring in his ears.

Davis pulled the blanket back.

Colin blinked at the inert body of a man in gray cords and a tweed jacket. His first thought was, *Not Bianca,* accompanied by a composure-shattering upsurge of relief. Then Davis grabbed the bushy white beard that covered the lower half of the man's blood-smeared face and yanked it off.

"What the —" Colin stopped, stared.

"We found Thayer." Fake beard in hand, Davis confirmed what Colin had just realized. "And he's alive."

"It wasn't us." Hanes's voice was tight with strain. His fingers clenched around the secure phone he held to his ear. It was just after 7:00 a.m. Paris time, and as he cast his eyes skyward in a silent request for divine intervention, he found himself, ironically enough, looking at the steeple of Saint-Germain-des-Prés church rising majestically against the dull gray of the early morning sky. Rushing in his rented VW Polo from his hotel room to the scene of what the TV stations were all screaming was Paris's latest terrorist attack, he'd been caught in traffic on the Rue Dauphine in the 6th arrondissement. The vehicles around him had ground to a complete and total halt just about the time Wafford had called, demanding to know what the hell Hanes had done.

"Thayer's in the middle of it." Wafford's growl underscored how supremely unhappy NCS's deputy director was with the turn events had taken. It was somewhere around 1:00 a.m. in Virginia, where Wafford's home as well as his office was located. It seemed probable that he'd been at home, in bed, when the bomb had gone off. It also seemed probable that he was aware of what was happening because he'd had someone continually monitoring Thayer's whereabouts, just as Hanes himself had been continually monitoring Thayer's whereabouts. Monitoring that was made possible by the grain-of-rice-sized tracking device that Hanes had forced Thayer to have injected between his left thumb and forefinger before he was released to find and kill Nomad 44.

Because you didn't pull the trigger on a Hellfire missile without some means of tracing its flight.

Maintaining tight self-control, Hanes said, "I'm aware. I repeat, it wasn't us."

"Was it *Thayer?*"

"No, sir." He prayed that that was true. He was at least 95 percent sure it was — but with Thayer, one never knew.

"Then who the hell was it?"

"I don't know."

"Was Nomad 44 the target?"

Hanes hated what he had to say next. "I don't know."

"What do you know?" It was a snarl.

"That there was a bombing, that according to Thayer's tracking device he was at the scene when it happened and is still at the scene, and that his last report, which came in at 23 hundred hours last night, was that he was zeroing in on Nomad 44. That the news reports are saying it's a terrorist attack, although that has not been confirmed. That I'm heading for the scene right now, as are the men I have with me in Paris."

"Was Nomad 44 at the scene?"

"I'd say it's probable."

"Another thing you don't know."

"Yes, sir."

"Well, *find out.*"

"Yes, sir."

"Hanes. There can be no autopsy on Nomad 44."

"I understand."

"Then get your ass in gear and clean up this goddamned fucking mess," Wafford roared, and disconnected.

Hanes said a few choice words under his breath, shoved the phone back in his jacket pocket and applied the heel of his palm to the horn.

". . . a bloody *cock-up*." Bowling's voice lost none of its plumminess when employed at full volume, Colin discovered as the director of GCHQ bellowed at him over the phone he pulled a little away from his ear. "Where the hell is she?"

"That's what I'm trying to find out." Colin's voice was carefully even. He was watching his men bundle Thayer into an ambulance as he spoke. Not that he'd told, or meant to tell, Bowling that. Not until he'd gotten a better grip on what had happened. He wouldn't have answered Bowling's call at all if he hadn't hoped against hope that somehow Bowling, who had eyes and ears everywhere, had had word of Bianca's whereabouts. Which, as it turned out, had not been the case. Although Bowling's sources *had* come through for him with the information that Five Eyes' newest asset was missing in the explosion that was already the lead news story around the world, prompting his call.

"I don't need to remind you that this job is *vital*." The faint crackling sound that accompanied that was, Colin felt sure, Bowling chomping on one of his ubiquitous

382

cigars. "I don't like the feel of this." There was the slightest of pauses. "A report from Big Bird's nest said MH1 is dead."

Big Bird was Edward Mulhaney, head of the American NCS, Big Bird's nest was Mulhaney's office, where Bowling apparently had a mole, and MH1 was the code name assigned to Lynette Holbrook. The real Lynette Holbrook. Colin's blood ran cold.

"Confirmed?"

"I trust the information." Another faint crackling sound.

"What happened?"

"She was considered a liability."

That said it all: Lynette Holbrook, having obtained the information that made Operation Fifth Doctrine possible, had been killed to keep her from compromising it. He knew how it worked: as an asset, she was disposable once she was no longer useful. Didn't stop him from feeling sick at his stomach about what had been done to her. His anxiety over Bianca, already through the roof, catapulted into the stratosphere.

Bowling said, "How much do you trust MH2?"

MH2 being Bianca. He knew what Bowling was asking: Could she be missing because she'd sold out to another player?

"One hundred percent," Colin replied.

"Your arse," Bowling warned, meaning that if Colin was wrong he could expect a nasty rebound. Then he added, "Keep me informed," and ended the call.

25

The well-equipped unit was as much a jail as a medical facility. A clandestine treatment center designed to provide care for top secret military prisoners, it was run out of the officially closed former Val-de-Grâce hospital. Colin's history with the people who ran the place went all the way back to his MI6 days. It was there that he'd had his men rush Thayer, rather than handing him over to paramedics on the scene and, later, the gendarmerie, who would hold him until whatever agency won custody could arrive to pick him up. So far, no one outside Colin and his men on the scene, which meant no one in officialdom, knew that the legendary Traveler had been captured at last.

Not even Durand. Not until Colin had decided that Thayer was of no use to him.

At that moment, some seventeen hours after the bombing, Colin stood beside Thayer's hospital bed looking down at the man he'd pursued for months, the man Durand had spent a full two decades hunting. Besides being shackled wrist and ankle to the titanium bed frame, which was, in turn, bolted to the floor, Thayer was encumbered by an IV, a catheter and so many gauges attached to so many monitors that the preeminent sound in the room was their beeping.

He was concussed, stitched up, badly bruised and groggy-eyed from medication.

He was also sixty-four years old, grayhaired and clad in a limp blue hospital gown with his head propped up on a pair of fluffy blue pillows.

Elite assassin, master criminal — or just a tired and injured old man?

Getting it wrong was not a mistake Colin was planning to make.

"You were following her. Why?" There was steel in Colin's voice. He was beside himself with fear, although he was doing his best to conceal it.

Bianca had seemingly disappeared off the face of the earth. None of the hospitals had a record of having admitted anyone named Lynette Holbrook, or Bianca St. Ives, or any of her other aliases that Colin had been able to remember. A physical search of every single hospital to which victims of the bombing had been admitted had failed to turn up any trace of her. She was not listed among the fatalities, nor was her body in the temporary morgue that had been set up. Surveillance footage was no help: the cameras around the square had been disabled, probably by the perpetrators of the atrocity, and none of the cameras in the surrounding streets had picked up any sign of her in the aftermath of the bombing.

Park and the bodyguards remained missing as well.

Was it possible that Bowling had been on the right track, and she'd sold them out to someone and disappeared? Or, in a scenario that he considered slightly more likely, that she'd taken advantage of the chaos to run, to cut all ties with her former existence and start over again with a new name and identity somewhere else?

He was as certain as he could be that the answer to both questions was no.

His biggest fear was that she was dead. The police continued to search for additional victims. The medical examiner's office was cataloging body parts.

Just thinking about that made him sick as a horse, so he didn't.

If she hadn't run away, and she wasn't dead, she was in terrible danger. The third credible possibility was that someone had grabbed her. If that was so, they would kill her as soon as they got what they needed from her. Every minute that he spent trying to find her was the minute she could die. That was the thought that was driving him insane.

Thayer's eyelids drooped as if to signal that he was on the verge of falling asleep. "As I believe I've told you several times before, I was simply out for my morning constitutional. I had no idea she was even in the area."

Colin held on to his fraying calm with effort. He knew Thayer was lying — hell, Thayer knew he knew he was lying, and didn't care — and what his every instinct urged him to do was beat the truth out of him. But number one, Thayer was old, number two, Thayer was injured, and number three, given the kind of man Thayer was, even beating him to a bloody pulp was unlikely to get him to give up any information he didn't want to give up.

Looking around at Davis and Charlie Parrino, whom he'd assigned to stand guard over Thayer with the added instruction that they were not to take their eyes off him even if they were 100 percent certain he was dead, he said, "Give us a minute, please."

Because he was about to embark on a

negotiation that no one except the other party to it needed to hear.

His men left the room.

Thayer's lids drooped again. He didn't quite yawn, but he looked like he was about to.

Colin kept his voice even. "She's incredibly loyal to you, do you know that? Won't tell me or anyone else the first thing about you. Incentives, threats, nothing anybody's come up with yet has made her turn on you. I don't know what you are to her, or what you've done to deserve that, but how about you reciprocate a little bit? Anything you can tell me about what happened to her or where she is could save her life."

"You're the cop." Thayer's response was unexpected. He was looking at Colin with a spark of interest. "From the casino in Macau."

Where Bianca had staged a distraction so that Thayer could escape.

"That's right."

"How the hell did you end up with Bianca?"

The easy way Thayer said her name spoke to the long and deep-seated familiarity that Colin had known existed between them. He still didn't like it.

"You answer my questions, maybe I'll

answer yours."

Thayer's lids drooped again. "As I've said every one of the umpteen other times you've asked me, I wish I could help you out, but I can't. I don't know where she is, or what happened to her."

Colin could feel an angry pulse begin to beat in his temple. "You know, I can choose who I turn you over to. I can go with Interpol, or four of the Five Eyes countries — for the most part they're nice and civilized. The Americans and their CIA — not so much. Then there's a prince in Bahrain who's offering the kind of reward for you that would set me up for life. I hear he's a big fan of beheading people he doesn't like. And let's not forget —"

A tap on the door presaged Davis's entry. Looking apologetic, he held out a cell phone. "Sorry, Major, but an urgent call's just come in for you from the home office. Miss Trainor says it's about the lady we're looking for."

Colin's instinctive frown at being interrupted vanished in a quick upsurge of hope. Helen Trainor had been the first employee he and his partner, John Hart, had hired when they'd gone into the spy-for-hire business. An elegant, posh-voiced, silver-haired sixtysomething, she ruled Cambridge Solutions' headquarters in London with a rod of iron. She never called him in the field. If she was doing so now, something of earth-shaking importance was up. Stepping forward, he took the phone from Davis and dismissed him with a brief "thanks" and a gesture asking him to close the door behind him as he slipped back out into the hall.

As Davis complied, Colin spoke into the phone. "Rogan here."

"I have a Dr. Zeigler from the States on the line who says speaking to you is a matter of life and death." Helen sounded as untroubled as if she was placing an order for takeout. "Shall I put him through?"

It took him a second to cobble it together: Dr. Zeigler was Bianca's Doc.

"Yes."

Helen said, "Dr. Zeigler, I have Major Rogan for you. Please go ahead."

"Doc?" Rogan said.

"What are you doing in Paris?" Doc demanded without preamble. His voice was shrill with distress. "The boss is in North Korea!"

"*What?* How do you know that?"

"She activated the locator beacon. You know, the one she has in her —" he seemed to get briefly tongue-tied "— garter belt. She never activates that. Never since I've known her. It's only for the most extreme kind of emergency."

"Let me talk to him."

At the unexpected nearness of the gravelly voice, Colin almost jumped. Grabbing for his weapon, he whipped around. Thayer — damn it to bloody hell, he'd broken his own rule and taken his eyes off the man — stood — *stood* — not three feet away. Shackle free. Minus IV, catheter and gauges. Barefoot, barelegged, baggy hospital gown slipping off one shoulder. Eyes clear and 100 percent awake. Holding his hand out for the phone.

The sight poleaxed him. Even with his weapon in hand, he felt off balance.

"If I wanted to kill you, you'd be dead," Thayer said impatiently. "Let me talk to him. I know how that locator beacon works. You don't."

Obviously he'd heard both sides of the conversation.

"Step back, Thayer. And get your bloody hands up," Colin managed, and said to Doc, "Hang on."

"Is that *Mason Thayer* there with you?" Doc sounded shocked. "Jesus, man, look out." He added something that Colin, preoccupied with keeping Thayer covered, missed.

Thayer sighed. "I'm Bianca's father," he said. At what Colin felt must be his own stunned expression, Thayer nodded at the phone and added, "Ask him." He raised his voice, directing his next remarks to Doc. His voice, Colin noted, was completely different now. Smoother, tougher, American. "Hey, there, Miles. Thanks for the lift in Macau, by the way."

"Yeah, that's him," Doc said unhappily before Colin could even form the question. "It's true. He is. Her father, I mean."

Thayer said, "If she activated that locator beacon, she's in real trouble and she's asking for an extraction. You want to save her life, give me the damned phone."

Colin hesitated, looked the man he'd been doing his best to bring to justice for months in the bright blue eyes and felt the pieces of the puzzle he'd been trying to assemble since he'd first laid eyes on the hot blonde in the lethal underwear fall into place. He'd succeeded where so many others had failed. The rewards of capturing Thayer, both monetary and to his and his company's professional reputation, would be immense. He had the prize Durand had been seeking for a large part of his working life within his grasp, thus fulfilling his promise to his friend and mentor. And he was thinking about turning him loose.

Durand would go apoplectic if he knew. And the call he was getting ready to make in regards to Thayer might be dead wrong.

Colin did a lightning review of everything he knew about Thayer, then went with his gut and handed him the phone.

26

Tuesday, December 17th

If Hell was cold and smelled of urine and vomit and damp, then the place where Bianca opened her eyes was Hell. She lay on her side on a filthy stone floor. Stone walls splotched with dark patches of — something — met her gaze. The corner where she lay was deep in shadow. The room itself was dimly lit with artificial light. Her head ached, her mouth was dry, and her body felt like one giant bruise.

Someone tapped her cheek with an icy finger. It wasn't the first time, she realized, and realized, too, that those soft taps were what had brought her back to consciousness.

"Please. You must wake up. They will come for you soon."

The voice was female. A scared whisper, not threatening. Bianca turned her head. The cheek-tapper was kneeling beside her, leaning over her, tapping anew.

Black hair, chopped short and matted. A round face. Anxious dark eyes. It was a girl, late teens, twenty at the most. Skinny. Dirty. Arms covered with bruises and goose bumps. Dressed in the tattered remains of a T-shirt and shorts. Chained.

The chain was what snapped Bianca back to some semblance of real awareness.

The girl had what looked like a dog's choke collar fastened tight around her rubbed-raw neck. A heavier chain ran from that to an iron ring set into the wall about two feet from the floor. It wasn't long enough to allow her to stand up.

What —

The girl spoke again, softly and quickly. "You said some things while you were unconscious — you are American? Maybe they will let you go, trade you. If they do, if you get out, you will tell my family that you have seen me, please? I am Irene Choi. I was kidnapped in August from the streets of Seoul, walking to my mother's house."

Bianca blinked. She heard the words, but their meaning did not quite compute. "Where are we?" Her throat was scratchy, which made her voice whispery, too.

"This is Hwasong."

"Hwasong?"

"Kwanliso Number 16."

It took Bianca a moment — her head swam, and thinking seemed to require an enormous effort — but she was able to translate *kwanliso:* it was Korean for penal labor colony. With a flash of horror, she realized that Kwanliso Number 16 was one of the notorious prison camps of North Korea. Which meant she was in *North Korea*.

Did not *see that one coming.*

A burst of frantic memory recalled Park, the explosion, the pink van hurtling toward her. Everything before that, almost nothing after. She had clearly been knocked senseless. The van must have protected her from the worst of the blast while somehow failing to hit her, probably passing over her as she lay unconscious in the street. Subsequently she'd been kidnapped — by Park? Or, more likely, someone in his orbit, because who else would take her to North Korea? She recalled, too, a brief window of hazy lucidity when she came to in the belly of what she thought was a cargo plane and was given something to eat and drink, and then injected with a substance that sent her plunging back into darkness. Another fragment of memory in which she'd been in a vehicle on a rough road tried to take shape in her mind.

It was superseded by the surprising realization that the girl was speaking to her in English.

"It is in North Hamgyong," the girl continued. "The mountains hide it." Her already low voice got even softer, so soft Bianca had to strain to hear the words. "The former Pungyye-ri nuclear test site is nearby. Mount Mantap is nearby." The mountain that had collapsed as a result of North Korea's nuclear tests: Bianca remembered that. "It is rumored that much secret work for the military is carried out here. Important people visit, and sometimes we are taken out to see them. There are more than 20,000 prisoners here. No one is ever released, no one has ever escaped. If you are brought here, you die here."

"You speak English," Bianca said. She wasn't quite hitting on all cylinders, but she was getting there. One thing she knew for sure: the situation was *bad.*

"Yes. I am *Hanguk saram* — from South Korea. I go to college at St. Louis University. I came back for the summer to visit my mother. My grandfather is General Ri Yang-ho. His son, my father, is dead. I am his only grandchild. He defected from North Korea, and they grabbed me to make sure he stays silent about what he knows. They make me make videos pleading with him to come back or I will be killed. Of course, if he does come back we will both be killed. Please, you must get word to my mother that I am alive."

Bianca nodded. "How long have I been here?"

"Not long. They went to eat their midday meal. I heard them talk among themselves — they will be back for you when they have finished. Did you understand what I said to you? I am Irene Choi. I must get word to my mother —"

"I understand," Bianca said. "You are Irene Choi, and you want me to tell your mother where you are if I get out of this place."

"Yes." Irene darted a fearful glance around. "I am not the only one. There are five of us. They call us special prisoners. Right now we are of use to the regime. When we are not, they will kill us."

Bianca grimaced and tried to sit up. Her head pounded unmercifully, but that wasn't what stopped her. Her wrists were shackled, and the chain connecting them was fastened to the same iron ring that Irene was tethered to.

She frowned at it. It was a heavy chain, with solid links. Just as the shackles around her wrists and the chain linking them were solid and heavy.

This just keeps getting better and better.

The chain's length was too short to allow her to sit up, much less stand. She had to recline on one elbow. She looked around. A single incandescent bulb hanging from a long wire nailed to the ceiling provided the only illumination. There were no windows, and a solid-looking metal door was the only exit.

"What's your name?" Irene asked.

Bianca already had her mouth open to reply when she remembered. "Lynette," she said. And immediately did a quick inventory to see if that was still operable.

The wig, thanks to the truly world-class measures she employed to secure it, had stayed in place, as had her cheek prosthesis. Her glasses, earrings and ring were gone. Her red coat was gone as well, and she felt a pulse-quickening shot of alarm as she remembered the ChapStick/flash drive in the pocket. Had it made it to North Korea with her, or had it been lost along the way? There was no way to know, which meant that worrying about it was useless, so she pushed it to the back of her mind and continued to take stock.

She was dressed in her Lynette-wear of

black crewneck and loose black pants. Her shoes were missing; she was in (torn) stocking feet. The stockings were attached to her garter belt —

The hazy memory that had been trying to surface succeeded. During her brief period of consciousness in the bumpy vehicle she'd managed to activate the locator beacon in her garter belt. Of course, the only person left to monitor it was Doc, and what he could do about getting her out of this she had no idea — if the signal was even getting through. If he even saw it.

Colin — he would be wild with worry. Or would he? Maybe — *Stop.* She refused to think about Colin any more. All her energy had to go to dealing with the disaster at hand.

"What did you do?" Irene's tone was a mixture of curiosity and pity.

Irene meant what had she done to wind up at Hwasong, she knew. Bianca shook her head. She was still gathering information about the room — actually, calling it a room was a misnomer; it was more of a stone dungeon with a wooden ceiling — and had just discovered that she and Irene weren't the only people in it. A large, cylindrical metal tank stood in the corner opposite them. A rubber hose fed into its open top from a faucet attached to one of the many PVC pipes that crisscrossed the ceiling. That particular pipe must have been a water pipe, because the tank was full almost to the brim — and the young man standing in it was submerged to just below his nose. His mouth was underwater, and if he lowered his head by even the slightest degree his nose would be, too. She knew he was chained in place, or secured in some way. It was classic torture: if he slumped, or worse, if his legs gave out so that he couldn't stand anymore, he would drown. What could be seen of his face was ghostly white. His hair was dark and wet and clung to his skull, his face was long and cadaverous, and his eyes were wide and full of despair and looking right at her and Irene. Bianca was reminded of Edvard Munch's *The Scream.*

"That's David," Irene said, seeing where her gaze rested. "He's one of the Americans. Tim —" She nodded at what Bianca realized to her horror was a wooden cage hanging from the ceiling. It was maybe four feet by four feet, with slats in the front. Inside was a man. He was folded up on himself like a paper clip, and appeared to be either unconscious or asleep. "— is the other one. They're college students, too. They came on a tour from China, and got arrested for an act of disrespect to the Supreme Leader. They're here at Hwasong because they can be used as bargaining chips with your country. But the guards hate Americans, so they are being treated very badly."

"Where are the others?"

"They took the preacher away this morning: Mr. Stevens. See that?" She pointed to a slanted wooden platform built into a corner of the room. It had an iron bar at the higher end, metal rings at each corner of the lower end, and a watering can and a stack of towels sitting on top of it. "They waterboarded him first. He was unconscious when they carried him off. I don't know if he'll come back. He's from Scotland, and he came as part of a group, too. He left a Bible behind in his hotel room when he tried to leave the country. They arrested him at the airport. And then there is Lee." Irene nodded toward what looked to Bianca like an empty corner. "He's in the hole. He —" Even as Bianca realized that what Irene was nodding at was the iron grate set into the stone floor and that Lee, whoever he was, must be imprisoned beneath it, there was a sound outside the door.

"Oh no! They're back — they've come for you. I'm truly sorry. Don't tell them we talked. Be brave. I'm sure they won't kill you."

Bianca's heart started to pound as the door, groaning, was pulled outward. Bestowing a quick, commiserating pat on Bianca's arm, Irene slithered away toward the wall, where she curled up in a tight little ball, facing it.

Two soldiers came in. Stern-faced and compactly built, they were neat in their uniforms of brown belted tunics, pressed trousers and black-billed hats. She registered their weapons — a holstered revolver, a sheathed knife and a baton — as one grabbed her arm, his fingers digging in hard, while the other pulled a set of keys from his pocket and unlocked the chain securing her shackles to the ring.

"Nyeon," the one with the keys said to Irene, whose cringing body was apparently in his way. Bianca's Korean was rusty, but she came up with the translation, *bitch,* at just about the time the soldier kicked Irene in the back with his boot. Hard. Irene jerked and cried out, while Bianca, in full-on frightened Lynette mode, was hauled to her feet and dragged from the room.

It opened into a corridor that had heavily armed and smartly uniformed guards stationed along it on both sides. From the absence of windows, the dank smell, and the fact that the set of metal steps she was being taken to led only upward, she concluded that she was in a basement. The guards stood at attention with their backs to the walls, staring straight in front of them as she was frog-marched between them. They were perhaps an arm's length apart, and there were — she counted — ten on each side, so twenty in all, plus the two propelling her along. That seemed like an excessive amount of security for the four beaten-down prisoners plus herself in what, given the fact that there were no other doors opening off of the corridor, appeared to be the only holding room. Maybe the security was there for another reason?

There *was* another reason, she discovered as she reached the top of the stairs. After one of the guards announced their presence with a quick knock, she was taken through a door into a large room that, after the gloom below, seemed almost painfully bright. Blinking at the harsh daylight pouring in through a wall that was mostly windows, she found herself looking at a middle-aged man in a uniform featuring golden epaulets and a chest almost entirely covered with glinting, police-badge-sized commendations.

Talk about your full medal *jacket.*

His presence was the reason for the excess security, she was sure.

Without releasing their grip on her arms, her escorts stopped and saluted.

The officer ignored them. He stood in front of the wall of windows and the impression she got was that he had been looking out when they entered and had just turned.

"I am General Yang," he said to her in heavily accented English. "You are?"

"L-Lynette Holbrook," she squeaked, and he nodded as if that confirmed what he already knew. Frowning, he looked her up and down.

Her heart still pounded, and she didn't try to calm it because it served her purpose. She hoped he could sense Lynette's fear. With her shoulders slumped and her head hanging in terrified Lynette style, she nevertheless managed a surreptitious glance around. It was a one-story building, a long, low office bungalow with the basement below. The walls were white, the floor was some kind of gray composite. A coat tree in one corner held a long brown overcoat and an oversize officer's hat, which she assumed belonged to Yang. Banks of computer equipment took up almost all of the long wall on the right side of the room. An arrangement of a couch and two chairs was grouped beneath an oversize, glass-fronted photo of the Supreme Leader on the left wall. A second, closed door, also on that wall, led she knew not where.

To the guards in his own language, Yang uttered a harsh "Bring her here."

She was taken to him. With a jerk of his head he dismissed her escorts, who retreated to stand at attention with two more guards stationed in the back of the room.

Bianca was left alone to make herself as small and cowed looking as possible in front of what was obviously, in his world, an immensely powerful man.

"You are just in time," he said. His tone was pleasant enough as he turned to gesture out the window. It was tinted, so that although they could see out no one could see in. "Look."

She looked. And in that look she saw many things. Closest to the building, a black limousine. She thought it must be the general's car, and from the fresh tire tracks in the light dusting of snow that covered the pavement in front of the building concluded that it — and he — had arrived not long before. She saw scraggly, denuded trees and a ten-foot-tall barbed wire fence and snowy hills rising in the distance. Just beyond the parking area — the bungalow and the parking area were on a slight rise, so she was looking down on the scene — she saw a flat field with dark bare dirt showing through a sparse sprinkling of snow. Hundreds of prisoners in brown coats huddled in a semicircle around the edges of the field. Dozens of armed guards surrounded them.

In the center was a man tied to a pole. He was gagged, but not blindfolded. His hair was reddish-brown, his skin was pale, he was of average height but very thin. He looked to be about fifty years old. He wore a torn and filthy white shirt with tan trousers. His feet were bare.

In front of him stood a squad of guards in a straight line.

A light snow fell. The sky hung low and gray.

"That is Mr. Howard Stevens from Scotland," Yang said. "To all the questions he was asked, he told only lies."

In the field, the line of guards snapped rifles to their shoulders.

Bianca's heart stood still as she realized what was happening. Helpless to do anything else, she watched in sickened silence.

A fusillade of gunfire rang out.

Stevens jerked, then went limp, sagging against the ropes that held him to the pole.

His shirt bloomed red.

Yang took her arm, turned her away from the window.

"Now we will talk," he said.

27

Bianca went cold, inside and out. The man gripping her arm was a ruthless murderer of not just that poor man, but probably thousands upon thousands of people. She had no doubt at all about his ultimate plans for her.

As Lynette, she visibly trembled with fright.

As Bianca, she now deliberately slowed her pounding heart and calmed her thundering pulse.

Focus. The stakes of this game were her life.

Yang walked her toward the computer bank, the centerpiece of which was a large upright monitor on a desk-like counter. The monitor was flanked by an open laptop to which it was connected and a series of small black canisters, which, she realized, were the computers themselves and to which the monitor was also connected. A line of smaller monitors was mounted above. Bianca saw that the ChapStick was plugged into a USB port on one of the canisters, and secretly cheered. The upper monitors all displayed a gray screen with a red star in the center. The laptop appeared to be running some sort of security check, which made her do the mental equivalent of holding her breath: *Please, God, let whoever had configured that flash drive have done it right.* The consequences if the ruse should be discovered would be beyond dire. The large monitor, which was state-of-the-art, had documents and maps displayed on the screen in various windows.

"You will tell me how you came to possess this flash drive," he said.

She haltingly recited Lynette's story.

"So you stole the information from your country to give to mine because you thought to prevent a nuclear war?" The look he gave her was inscrutable.

"Yes."

"You lie!" He shouted it while banging his fist on the desk.

She jumped, and, when he grabbed her, shrank away from him. Without warning, he slapped her so hard in the face that her head snapped to one side. The blow was stinging, stunning. It caused tears to spring to Ly-

411

nette's eyes, made her knees wobble and then, as he used his strength to force her to the floor, give way.

The blow awoke in Bianca an icy rage. The physical pain in her cheek was sharp and burning. The mental pain of enduring such abuse, of weeping and cowering in the face of it, was far worse. It killed her that she had to swallow it, refrain from retaliating, keep her anger hidden.

As Lynette, she was on her knees in front of him, lips trembling, tears slipping down her cheeks, shaking so much that the chain linking the shackles on her wrists jangled. His hand slid beneath her chin, jerking her face up so that she was forced to look at him. It was all she could do to keep any trace of Bianca from showing in her eyes. But for the sake of the operation, and for her own sake as well, because, after all, the name of the game was to get out of there alive, she made the smart choice and went full-on Lynette.

Pretend to be weak, that he may grow arrogant: Sun Tzu.

"Please — please don't hurt me."

Satisfaction gleamed in his eyes. "If you think to fool me, you will suffer. Now you will tell me the truth. Why did you steal this information?"

Lynette's eyes were wide with fear as they met his. "I *did* want to prevent a nuclear war. I did. I did." His free hand lifted threateningly. She burst into more terrified speech. "And I hated my boss and I couldn't afford to quit my job. I wanted enough money so that I never had to work again. And — and this was the only way I could think of to get it."

"Ah." His hand lowered. "And how did you decide to offer it to Park Il-hyeok?"

"I found his name in the documents. I ch-checked him out online and saw what I thought was a way to approach him. And Paris is easy to get to."

The laptop beeped. Yang released her chin, straightened and looked around. With a stab of fear, Bianca looked, too: it was obvious that the security check had done its thing.

"Ah," he said. "Good."

From that, and the green bar that ran the length of the screen before disappearing, Bianca concluded that the security check had found nothing awry.

While she breathed a silent sigh of relief, he looked away from her to nod at the soldiers in the back of the room. Bianca tensed as one of them started forward, but as it turned out, his goal was the second

413

door in the room. Opening it, he went out, leaving it ajar. She saw a small entryway with a door that led out to the parking lot, which she could see through the tinted window in the top of the door. Then from somewhere on the other side of the entryway Park — Park! — limped into view. Clad in a stained blue dress shirt and rumpled gray trousers, his hair disordered, his face ashen, he jerked away from the soldier who'd been sent to get him, crossing the entryway and walking into the room on his own. He seemed to be having difficulty with his left leg. Bianca wondered if it had been injured in the explosion or in some other way since.

The soldier following him in shut the door and retreated to stand at attention with his fellows at the far end of the room.

Park stopped dead upon seeing General Yang. "You — *here?*"

"As you see."

"Why was I brought to this place?" Park's voice shook. Then he seemed to regain some of his mojo. He stood taller, bristled. Bianca realized then that the men were speaking Korean. Her command of the language seemed to have kicked in, because she understood what they were saying without effort. "My work in Paris — I have much that is happening right now. I —"

"Your work in Paris is over."

"That's not your decision to make."

"Ah, but it is. Because of your posting outside the country, you may not yet have been informed: our beloved Supreme Leader has recently honored me by appointing me head of the RGB. You serve under *me* now."

The RGB, or Reconnaissance General Bureau, was the much-feared intelligence agency that managed the country's clandestine operations, Bianca knew.

Park paled. Bianca had no way to be sure, but from his reaction she suspected that whatever previous relationship he'd had with Yang had not been the happiest.

"I congratulate you," Park said.

Yang inclined his head. "Thank you."

"I do not understand the way I am being treated. I — I brought in this intelligence coup for our country!" Park gestured at Bianca, the only indication he gave that he'd seen her. "And for this I am repaid with a bomb blast and a kidnapping?"

"We were not responsible for the bomb blast. The RGB has information that the Hanguk were responsible, in an effort to keep this most valuable information from reaching us." The Hanguk referred to South Korea, Bianca knew. "As for the kidnapping, it was carried out in the interests of our country. I personally wished to assess the seller of this information for myself, before I brought it to the attention of the Supreme Leader and other senior counsellors. But I must say I am surprised you would call being brought here a kidnapping. A loyal servant should consider it a repatriation."

"A loyal servant! That — that cannot be in question. Our revered leader has no more loyal servant than I." Park's eyes darted around the room as he spoke. He clutched his hands together in front of him.

"That may be so. You will tell me of your interactions with this woman."

In quick, nervous sentences, Park told of their meetings, concluding with, "I had her story investigated. I am convinced that what she told me is true. Everywhere, with all their resources, they are looking for her. The information she brought is of great value to our country. We are fortunate she came to us — to *me* — with this."

"Very fortunate," Yang agreed, but there was something in his tone that sent prickles of foreboding racing over Bianca's skin. "What was the amount you agreed to pay her?"

For the first time Park looked dismayed.

"Twenty million US."

Yang's expression said that he already knew this. Bianca instantly thought of Park's bodyguards. "Yet you requested fifty million. A large discrepancy."

"I — I bargained with her to reduce the price. I did it for our country. To save money for our country!"

"Yet the entire fifty million was given you. And you made no mention of your plan to bargain to reduce the price."

"If I succeeded, I was going to give the rest back! I would never have kept it! It was in case she would not agree to the lower price! I could not know that she would." He wrung his hands as he spoke. "I would have returned the rest as soon as the transaction was concluded! You cannot doubt it!"

"And yet you said nothing of the possibility." Yang's voice was almost gentle.

"I saw no need! I would have —"

"Returned it. So you said. But we can never really know, can we?"

"We were interrupted! The bomb —"

Yang made a gesture silencing him. "I am aware that because of that most unexpected occurrence the transaction was not completed. Which brings us to the small matter of your name on a certain list in this material we have acquired. You are indeed unfortunate that because of the bomb you had no time to examine for yourself that which you purchased before it came into my possession."

"What — what are you talking about? What list?"

"A list of those who pretend to be loyal while taking money from other countries to betray our interests. Of those who operate as double agents. Of *traitors,* Park Il-hyeok."

"What?" Park went white, held up a hand, stumbled back. "No, no —"

Yang pulled his sidearm free, jerked it up.

"I am innocent!" Park screamed.

Bang.

Blood and hair and brain matter exploded out of the back of Park's head, splattering the picture of the Supreme Leader that hung on the wall behind him. Park crumpled to the floor, blood puddling in a thick red pool around his head. The raw meat smell of it filled the air. A horrified witness, Bianca experienced a surge of adrenaline so strong that it was all she could do to stay meekly kneeling as Lynette. There was no time to feel any guilt because the information she'd brought had caused Park to be killed, no time to get her stone-cold warrior mode on, no time for anything except raw reaction.

Would Yang turn the gun on her next?

Heart pounding, pulse racing, she did a lightning assessment. She could spring up, shackles and all, take Yang out with a blow to the nose or chin, grab his weapon, shoot the four guards — and then, with whatever firepower she could manage to acquire along the way, try to fight her way past the twenty guards remaining in this one building and the no doubt hundreds of guards on duty outside while breaking out of a heavily fortified, supposedly escape-proof prison — and then battle her way across North Korea.

Or she could play out her hand as Lynette. Even the Terminator had some limitations.

She went with Lynette. Slumping forward, shoulders shaking, she rocked with distress — and, through her Lynette bangs, kept a wary eye on Yang's gun.

Yang made a peremptory gesture at the guards. "Get this mess cleaned up."

They hurried to obey. He walked toward her while holstering his gun.

Okay. He was not going to shoot her right at that moment, it seemed. Her heart still thudded, her pulse still raced, she was still wired to the max — but she was powering those reactions down.

Keep your game face on.

"Look at me." Yang stopped in front of her. He'd switched to English for her benefit, she realized.

Lifting her head, she looked at him. All terrified, traumatized Lynette.

"You will be taken back to the cell. You will try to remember everything you read, everything you heard, everything you saw while you were typing in these documents. We will do a comparison, you and I, between what you remember and what is actually on the flash drive you so kindly brought us, just to make sure there are no inaccuracies. And you will select one of your fellow prisoners. In an hour you will be brought back here, and if I am satisfied with what you have remembered, all will be well. If I am not —" He smiled. It was an expression of such cruelty that *Bianca* felt a chill. "The person of your choice will be executed. Then we will try again. You will have another hour, make another choice. This can go on all day, until the only one left is you." He gave a small shrug. "It is time to clean out the filth in the basement anyway. Who knows when inspectors will request to visit?" He clapped his hands, a sudden sharp sound that made her jump and the guards look around. He pointed at two of them. "You. And you. Get her out of here."

The guards moved with alacrity, grabbing her painfully by the arms, lifting her shivering, shrinking Lynette self from the floor and taking her away.

28

So. She had always wanted to fight a death-defying battle against impossible odds.

Not.

But here she was. In the process of having the shackles on her wrists chained to an iron ring in a stone-walled, windowless torture chamber she shared with four weakened, despairing and captive strangers, one of whom she was supposed to single out for death.

Outside the metal door, twenty armed soldiers lined the hall. One floor above, between her and the only door to the outside that she had seen, lurked an armed, murderous monster and four more armed soldiers. It could be that there were even more armed people on the premises, so the possibility for an unpleasant surprise was there.

Beyond the building were enough armed guards to keep 20,000 prisoners in check.

Plus she knew not how many ten-foot-tall, electrified, barbed wire fences, checkpoints, guard towers, locked gates.

And the whole of North Korea.

Her available weapons? The switchblade in her garter belt. Her martial arts skills. Anything she could steal or jury-rig.

Hmm.

She was hungry, hurt, increasingly homesick. She couldn't even begin to allow herself to think about Colin, because there was so much conflicting emotion there that it just took up space inside her that she needed to use for something more immediately productive, like survival. She didn't have the same close family ties that most people did — she was pretty sure Mason didn't count — but Evie, Hay, Doc, even Guardian Consulting, all mattered to her. Her *life* mattered to her. There were so many loose ends, so many things to look forward to, so much she had yet to do.

The thought of leaving it all behind was unbearable.

The thought of what might happen to her if she died was even worse. Did genetically enhanced supersoldiers have a shot at the hereafter just like everybody else? She didn't know, but she did know that she wasn't yet ready to find out.

But if she didn't figure something out, fast, everything could end right here. *She could end right here.*

Panic was useless, so she didn't. Instead, while Lynette, now chained to the wall, huddled shivering on the cold stone floor and the guards left with much noise — stomping feet, groaning door, lock banging into place — Bianca set herself to problem solving.

And came up with a plan.

That thing they said about necessity being the mother of invention? Mortal terror apparently worked, too.

Hashtag: Never say die.

"Are you all right? Did they hurt you?" Irene, having kept to her fetal position against the wall until the guards were gone, scuttled over to touch her shoulder with a tentative hand.

"I'm fine." Abandoning her Lynette persona as being of no further use, Bianca sat up. "A man named General Yang is here. He's the head of the RGB, and he told me to pick out one of you to die. If I don't remember something well enough to suit him, which I'm betting I won't, he'll kill whoever I choose. He also said that it's time they got rid of the filth in the basement. I'm fairly certain he means to kill us all. Today.

424

And the guards will be back to get started in less than an hour."

Irene gasped. "Oh no! No —" She broke off to watch with a combination of fascination and horror as Bianca pulled the guard's key ring from her pocket. "Where did you get those? What are you doing?"

"We're going to escape." There were other methods she could have used to get out of the shackles — if all else failed, she'd been trained to dislocate her left thumb so she could pull her hand free, and she had her lock pick in her garter belt — but she really was pain averse unless pain was absolutely necessary, and time was of the essence here. Anyway, her pickpocketing skills had allowed her to lift the keys from the guard with a minimum of risk, and the keys would, she hoped, enable her to free not just herself, but Irene and the others, too.

No man left behind and all that.

"We — we can't. No one has ever escaped from Hwasong. They shoot you if you try. And — and — it's not possible." Irene's increasingly agitated whisper faltered as Bianca unlocked her own shackles with two quick twists of one of the keys. Catching the chain so that the metal wouldn't clang as it hit the stone floor, Bianca set the discarded shackles down and held the key

425

up in front of Irene's now saucer-sized eyes.

"They're going to kill you anyway. Do you want to at least try to get home to your mother or not?"

"Yes. Oh, yes." Irene's agreement was fervent. As Bianca unlocked the chain that tethered her to the wall, the girl was visibly trembling. "But how? There are many more obstacles than just these chains. We cannot even get out of this room. There are guards. They have *guns.*"

At this point, her plan was strictly *need to know.* And Irene didn't. None of them did.

"You're going to have to trust me. And do exactly what I tell you."

Gently, Bianca pulled the choke chain away from Irene's neck and set it down. Then, as Irene clutched at her raw and bruised flesh, she stood up.

Irene looked up at her. "But what can you do about the guards?"

Bianca was already on her way to the wooden cage. "I have a plan, okay? Help me get the others."

"What about Stevens?" Irene scrambled to her feet and hurried after her. "Do we just leave him?"

"He's dead. Yang had him executed by firing squad. While he and I watched through a window."

"Oh no!"

Suspended from the ceiling, the cage was about three feet off the floor. The kid folded inside was conscious; he looked at her with quick fear as she unlocked and opened the door.

"I'm here to help you," she said. "Do you think you can get out of there on your own?"

"I'm — not sure." His voice was barely audible, more a breath than a whisper. He had a black eye and a swollen lip and a bruise on his cheek — and that was just the damage she could see. Clearly he'd been beaten, and he was wedged in that cage like a sausage in a casing.

Irene said, "Tim, we're going to escape."

Tim — that was the kid's name. The other one, the one watching wide-eyed from the tank of water, was David.

"How?" Tim asked.

"I don't know," Irene said.

"Hold it steady," Bianca instructed Irene, and when the girl grabbed hold of the cage and braced herself, she reached in to catch Tim by the arms and help him wrest himself out.

The moment he tried to stand, he collapsed.

"My legs," he groaned. Irene made a distressed sound and crouched beside him.

427

Both of them rubbed his legs. Watching them, Bianca was reminded that they'd been in this hellhole for some time together. It looked like they'd gotten close.

Bianca frowned. "Are they injured? Broken?"

Tim wasn't tall — maybe five-nine — and he was emaciated. His clothes — the shredded remains of jeans and a sweatshirt — hung on him. His hair was a dark blond shoulder-length bird's nest of tangles. He looked to be maybe twenty, twenty-one. His features were sharp, pinched, and where he wasn't bruised he was pale. She judged that when he wasn't being brutalized he was a good-looking kid.

She was really, really hoping they weren't going to have to carry him.

"I think they're asleep," he said, referring to his legs.

"Work on that," Bianca told the pair of them. "And be very quiet." To Tim she added, "You need to be able to walk." To Irene she repeated, "He needs to be able to walk. Soon. The guards could come earlier than they said."

Her internal clock told her they had about forty minutes left. If the murderous monster stuck to the schedule. It was possible that he wouldn't.

Irene looked scared, but nodded. Tim said something to Irene, and as Bianca left them Irene replied. The murmur of their low-voiced conversation — from what she could tell, it pretty much consisted of Irene recounting what Bianca had just told her and Tim exclaiming — followed her as she hurried toward the kid in the water. Getting him out was potentially trickier, depending on how he was secured. One problem was that the tank held a huge amount of water and was relatively close to the door. What she wanted to be careful about was letting any water escape that might creep out into the hall and alert the guards that something was up.

She turned to take a good look at the door. It was less than three feet wide. Metal, probably iron. Opened outward into the hall. Locked, if she remembered correctly, by an iron bar on the outside.

The good news was, opening it took some effort and made a lot of noise. The guards weren't going to sneak up on them.

The bad news was, the guards didn't have to. They weren't going anywhere.

They were trapped.

Grabbing the towels from the waterboard platform, Bianca was relieved to see that Tim was up and walking, although he leaned heavily on Irene. Working with careful speed, Bianca stuffed the towels under the thankfully narrow crack at the bottom of the door. Then she reinforced the towels with a tarp that was kept rolled up beside the platform, spreading it out on top of the towels. Presumably it was used to shield someone or something from getting wet during torture. She only hoped that it plus the towels formed enough of a seal.

"I'm coming," she reassured David, whose eyes were bright with alarm as he watched the goings-on around him. Well, he had reason. If the guards came before they were ready, the pitched battle that would result might well end in a slaughter — theirs. And situated as he was, he could neither fight nor hide. But water leakage was a concern, and she wanted to delay any chance of it for as long as possible, so David was stuck until she was ready.

She held up a "one minute" finger to David and crossed to the grate over the manhole in the floor. Unlocking the chain that secured it in place, she lifted the heavy iron cover and looked down at the individual inside.

He was looking back up at her.

He'd been huddled on the floor of what proved to be a shallow, concrete-lined pit.

Black hair, black eyes, as ragged and skinny as the others and maybe even younger, Bianca saw at a glance. Never taking his eyes off her, he slowly, warily straightened to his full height, which was maybe five-four. That brought him head and shoulders out of the pit.

Lee, if she remembered his name correctly.

"What is this?" he asked Irene, who had walked Tim over to the pit. He spoke in what she guessed was his native Korean, although his accent belonged to the North rather than the South.

Irene replied in Korean. "We are going to escape. Are you coming with us?"

"Escape is impossible," he said. To Bianca's relief he managed to clamber out of the pit on his own. He was dressed in a black shirt and brown trousers, both of which were dirty and torn. He tottered a little as he stood upright, and she understood his legs were wobbly from his ordeal.

"Why is he here?" Bianca asked Irene in English as she carefully replaced the pit cover, because there was no point in letting anyone know that she was conversant in Korean unless she had to.

"He is the nephew of Tran An-Kor, one of the Supreme Leader's top advisers. Lee is being used for leverage over his father, so that his father, who is the brother of Tran An-Kor, is sure to tell everything he knows."

Bianca nodded. "See if you two can help Tim climb up onto the pipes, and then get up there yourselves. We all need to be on the pipes, as close to the ceiling as possible."

"Why?" Irene and Tim asked in mystified unison, while Lee demanded a translation from Irene.

"Just do it. I'll explain in a minute." Already moving back toward David as she spoke, Bianca listened as Irene, for Lee, translated what had just been said and told him about Stevens, and then as the two of them continued to talk in Korean.

"Who is she?" Lee asked. "Why should we listen to anything she says?"

"An American. Her name is Lynette. She came last night. She says she has a plan."

"She is a woman."

Irene shrugged. "She stole the guard's keys and freed us all. That is more than any of us could do."

"They killed my uncle yesterday, and my cousin," Lee said. "The guards told me. Today they will kill my father. They will come for me at any time. If this escape does not work, I am dead anyway. So I will take a chance."

"I am taking a chance, too," Irene said, and Lee nodded.

"What are you two talking about?" Tim demanded of Irene. He was still whispering, but his whisper sounded stronger now.

Irene translated as she and Lee boosted Tim up onto one of the pipes that crisscrossed the ceiling. Glad to see that it was sturdy enough to bear his weight, Bianca turned her attention to David at last.

She was acutely aware of the ticking clock.

As she'd feared, getting him out of the tank involved a lot of water spillage. His hands were cuffed to a ring inside the tank, and despite rolling up her sleeves, she got wet herself getting to them. Once the cuffs were unlocked it was easier. He was able to use his hands and arms and, with her help, managed to pull himself out.

After he dropped to the ground, David steadied himself against the tank and stood for a moment sucking in air. Water poured off him. Now that he was on his feet she saw that he was about five-eight, bone-thin, and, like Tim, dressed in jeans and a sweatshirt. Both garments were soaked, and he was shivering.

"None of us even has a gun" was the first thing he said, through chattering teeth.

"Outside in the hall are twenty armed

soldiers." Bianca crouched to examine the plug at the bottom of the tank. "And that's just a start. You really think you can shoot your way out of here?"

He grimaced by way of an answer. "Then what are we going to do?"

"You're going to strip down to your underwear and climb up on the pipes." Pulling the plug out would be easy. The question was "What happens to the water when the guards drain the tank?"

"It floods the floor. They let us sit in it. Eventually it goes away." David was stripping off without argument, she was glad to see. Probably he was glad to get out of his sopping, freezing clothes.

"How long does it take?" She pulled the plug. Water shot out.

"A couple of days before it's all gone. Why are you doing that?"

Good — that meant there wasn't a drain somewhere she didn't know about.

The puddle around the tank started spreading across the floor.

"I'll tell you when we're all up on the pipes." Straightening, she saw that the other three perched above them like birds on branches. They watched the firehose-worthy stream of water with apparent fascination. She looked at David. "You need a boost?"

she asked, and offered her linked hands.

He looked at her, clearly considering. Then he stepped into her hands and from there managed to jockey himself up beside the others.

The floor was already awash. Quickly she rolled up her pants, knotted them above the knee to keep them there. Rushing now, splashing through cold, ankle-deep water, Bianca unhooked the cage and set it down because she didn't want anything besides them attached to the pipes. Then she leaped, grabbed hold and pulled herself up to straddle the large water pipe that fed the tank. Detaching the hose from the faucet, she turned the water on full force.

The gushing sound alarmed her — the last thing she wanted was for one of the guards to come investigate the sound — but there was nothing she could do about it besides hope that it couldn't be heard through stone walls and an iron door, or that it wouldn't be investigated if it was.

The pipes were sturdy PVC, and formed enough of a canopy to keep them all up near the ceiling. The seal she'd created from the towels and tarp seemed to be working. Between the emptying tank and the pouring faucet, the water reached a depth of about two feet in minutes and was rising fast.

"What is her plan?" Lee asked in Korean. He sounded alarmed.

"Lee is asking what is the plan," Irene said. She, too, sounded uneasy.

"You going to try to drown them?" David looked down at the swirling, murky water. "Or us?"

Tim said, "Filling the room up with water isn't going to keep the guards out, just so you're aware. The door opens outward, so when they pull it open it will just gush out."

"I'm counting on it." Bianca was busy removing the last of three nails from the ceiling. She looked around at them, Irene and Tim close together, David sitting cross-legged on a pair of pipes, Lee crouched in an elbow section like he was prepared to jump at any minute. It hit her: they were *kids.* And she was all that stood between them and a horrible death. "All right, here's the plan. We —"

A sound outside the door silenced her and galvanized them all. Sitting bolt upright, going quiet as mice when a hawk passes over, they stared at the closed door in horrified anticipation. Fear vibrated in the air. Hurriedly finishing what she'd set out to do, Bianca watched the door along with the others. Her heart knocked in her chest. Her stomach twisted. If this didn't work —

A series of loud metallic clangs followed by a harsh scraping sound told them that the lock was being lifted. Next would come the grating noise of the door being dragged open —

"We're dead," David said with conviction.

"Shh," Irene hissed.

There it was: the grating noise. Bianca's breath caught. Her pulse raced. The door began to move —

"Do not let any part of your body touch the water," Bianca warned as the door, aided by water pressure, burst open.

A man cursed in Korean, and she got a glimpse, just a glimpse, of the two guards holding on to the edge of the door as an explosion of water rolled past their legs.

She turned off the faucet, cutting off the flow. Then she dropped the light bulb, still glowing and attached to the long brown wire that plugged it into the socket in the ceiling, into the water below.

29

They died silently. Not a scream, not a shout. The two guards she could see were instantly stricken, unable to let go of the door as the current passed through their bodies. Eyes wide and mouths agape, they shivered and shook, then fell back into the water with a splash. Multiple splashes from farther along the corridor seemed to announce that the wave of electrified water had done its job, although Bianca's view of what was happening was limited by her position on the pipe.

Gripping her switchblade now in case it came down to hand-to-hand combat, she waited in tense silence for any surviving guards to start shouting, shooting, doing whatever they needed to do to summon reinforcements.

Nothing.

"Fucking awesome," David whispered after a moment.

Bianca rolled an eye in his direction.

"That was some sick shit," Tim concurred.

Okay, they were kids.

"Are they dead?" Irene stared fearfully down the corridor. "Really?"

"I would guess so," Lee said in Korean. "Or they would be making noise."

"Don't anybody move until I give the okay." Tucking her switchblade into her waistband for easy access, she looped the short rubber hose that had been attached to the tank around the wire and pulled the plug from the socket: current broken, electricity off. In theory. She dropped the cord, stared down at the water. There was no way to carefully test to make sure the water was safe that she could think of, and anyway, time was once again of the essence.

What she didn't want was to have the guards who remained with Yang coming downstairs to see what was taking so long.

Making sure her pants were still rolled up — the last thing she needed was to be slowed down by the sodden, dragging hems of Lynette's baggy pants — she dropped down into the cold water, which lapped hungrily around her ankles.

She didn't die.

Letting out the breath she'd been holding, she turned to look at the group on the pipes.

"Okay, we need to move out. I'm going first to make sure the way is clear. Give me a minute and then follow. For us to get out of the building without raising an alarm, we all need to be dressed as guards. Each of you strip off a guard's uniform and put it on. Hat, weapons and all. And get a uniform for me. And boots. Be as quick and quiet as you can, and then come upstairs. Understand?"

They nodded. From the way they were looking at her, she now had their absolute respect.

Heading into the hall, Bianca stopped briefly in the doorway to survey what lay before her.

The good, the bad and the parboiled.

The guards — twenty-two of them, she did a quick head count just to make sure — lay where they had fallen, some facedown, some on their backs or sides in about eight inches of water. Their bodies overlapped in many places.

First order of business: make sure they were all dead.

Picking her way among the bodies, she armed herself with a pair of their service weapons, which were Ruger P semi-

440

automatic pistols, checked to make sure they were loaded and functional, and added a pair of handcuffs. Then, satisfied that the guards were, indeed, all dead, she started up the stairs.

Behind her, her fellow escapees were already starting to yank uniforms off corpses. There was no time for her to do the same. Every minute the guards didn't return with her as their prisoner multiplied the danger.

At the top of the stairs she knocked on the closed door as the guards had done earlier, then opened it, stepped inside — and, with a pistol in each hand, shot the two surprised guards point-blank.

Then she whirled to target Yang.

He'd been leaning over the large computer monitor when she'd entered, apparently engrossed in the documents on the screen. At the sound of gunfire he spun around, but he was just that crucial few seconds too slow. She had the drop on him before he so much as touched his gun.

"Did you send for me, General?" She spoke in English. The time to reveal that she was conversant in Korean was not yet. The noise of the shots being fired concerned her for fear they could draw anyone else who might be in the building to the room, but not a great deal. After all, he'd shot Park and no one had come. "Here I am."

She gestured at him to get his hands up, which he did. The shock in his eyes as he looked first at her and then at the dead guards behind her brought a grim smile to her face.

"You — you — what is this? Where are my guards?" he asked her in English.

He meant the ones he'd sent for her, she knew. She didn't bother to answer. Instead she said, "Take your gun out, put it on the floor and kick it over to me. And I'd be very careful, if I were you. Killing you would be the most fun I've had all day."

Blinking rapidly, he did as he was told. Tucking the second Ruger in her waistband, she scooped his gun up without ever taking her eyes off him.

"Who *are* you?" He stared at her like she'd grown a second head. "What do you want from me?"

"Turn around, put your hands on the counter and spread your legs."

He complied, and she walked up behind him.

"You are an agent! Were you working with Park?" His head turned sharply to his right. She thought he stared at something although she couldn't tell exactly what, and then he grabbed the ChapStick that still stuck out of the side of the computer canister like a wart on a frog and in pulling it out answered that question for her. "What have I done?"

Forget frisking him. She chopped him in the G-spot. Not too hard, because she was going to need him to be able to walk in a short period of time. But hard enough to drop him to the floor, where he lay unmoving. She retrieved the ChapStick from where it had fallen as he collapsed, and looked at it thoughtfully. He'd risked his life to pull it out. He wouldn't have done that if he hadn't feared its purpose, which was, as he'd probably suspected, to infect the system with malware. If she plugged it back in, it might continue infecting the system with malware. On the other hand, if it hadn't done its thing by now, it probably wasn't going to happen, and leaving it behind was a giant red flag that begged for further scrutiny from whoever's job it was going to be to make sense of what had happened in this building. From Yang's reaction, she felt confident that he was afraid the ChapStick had done something which horrified him. That made her think that it was, indeed, connected with the central system, which was good enough for her. In the end, it was a judgment call, and she made it. She tucked the ChapStick away into a tiny secure pocket in her garter belt. It was going with her.

Then she frisked him. And cuffed him. And closed the laptop on the desk and put it into the black leather messenger bag that was stored beneath it. She suspected that it was Yang's personal laptop and bag, but it really didn't matter. Colin had said that any device that had been connected to the central computer system once the malware was installed would be able to connect to the internet and reveal all that system's secrets once it was taken beyond the borders of the air-gapped DPRK. She was going to take that laptop beyond its borders.

Assuming she made it out.

The kids sidled into the room, giving each other lots of side-eye and wearing uniforms as instructed. Irene handed over the one they'd brought for her. They looked scared, and as they glanced around and took in the dead guards and Yang on the floor they looked even more scared.

"If we're caught, we'll be torn apart by starving dogs," Lee said in Korean as Bianca pulled the uniform on over her clothes, stomped her feet into the boots and transferred the weapons, except for the one in the holster on her belt, to her pockets. None of the uniforms fit well, but it didn't matter. All they needed was to look the part briefly from a distance.

Irene tittered nervously at Lee's remark.

"What did he say?" Tim demanded.

Irene translated.

"He's not joking," David said.

"Tim, David, search the guards' pockets for car keys," Bianca intervened before they all ended up freaking each other out. She assumed — hoped — from the way those guards stayed with Yang that they were his personal guards and one of them was his driver. "Irene, you and Lee get the overcoat and hat from the coat tree."

They complied. Bianca smacked Yang into wakefulness and hauled him to his feet while they did, and was pleased when David came up with a set of car keys.

"Who knows how to drive?" she asked. She was forced to support Yang as he swayed woozily, so at her direction Tim draped the overcoat around his shoulders to hide the fact that his hands were cuffed behind him and Irene plopped the hat on his head.

They all replied with variations of "I do."

"I need to sit in back with Yang to make sure he does what we need him to do," she

445

said. "Whoever drives is going to have to pretend to be Yang's usual driver. Drive slowly to the front gate, stop for the guards, and if they want you to roll down the window then that's what you do. Irene, translate for Lee. Tell him he's my first choice because he speaks the language and looks the part."

Irene translated, and Lee said, in Korean, "I can do that. I can answer their questions, too. To everything I'll just say, 'I serve under General Yang.' "

Irene translated. Bianca nodded at Lee and gave him the keys.

"David, I need you to support Yang on his other side. Tim, you go in front of us and open the back door, then stand back with your head bowed, very subservient. You'll get in the back with David, Yang and me. Irene, you'll ride with Lee in the front. From the time we leave this building to the time we get in the car, anyone who looks our way can see us, so it's crucial that we all keep to our roles and pretend to be soldiers under Yang's command. Is that clear? Irene, translate for Lee."

As she did so, everyone nodded.

To Yang, whose eyes appeared unfocused and who was still unsteady on his feet, she said very softly, "General Yang. I have a gun in your side. If you make one wrong move I will kill you instantly."

He blinked rapidly and inhaled, which Bianca knew meant that he was regaining his faculties. Best to get him in the car before that happened.

Whether he understood what she'd just said to him or not, she had no way of knowing.

"Everyone, make sure your hats are on tight. Ready? Let's go."

30

With Lee and Irene in the lead, they hurried across the entryway. A quick sideways glance as they passed through was enough to reassure Bianca that there was no one else in the building; the room on the other side of the passageway, the one from which Park had emerged, was a holding cell.

The cold wind slapped them in the face as soon as they stepped outside. After the first shock, Bianca found it invigorating. From the deep inhalations on the part of the others, they did, too. She remembered that they'd been imprisoned for months, and this was probably the first fresh air they'd breathed in all that time. The slight smell of sulfur it carried reminded her that what had once been and might still be a nuclear testing site was nearby.

In commendable soldier mode, the group stepped smartly as they went down the stairs and covered the few yards to the car, a black Mercedes limo. Even as she kept a firm hold and a covering gun on Yang, Bianca reconnoitered their surroundings.

The parking lot opened onto a narrow, blacktopped road that ran between perhaps a dozen warehouse-like buildings set on either side of it before intersecting with another, wider road. That road, she thought from the height of the twin watchtowers that she could see above the buildings about a mile along it to the right, led to the front gate. Her deduction was reinforced by the large crimson-and-blue DPRK flags flapping atop each tower, and the direction taken by the ten-foot-tall barbed wire fence just beyond the parking lot. The field where Stevens was executed was now the scene of some sort of marching exercise by what looked like an entire platoon of soldiers. It was way too close for comfort. The only good news was, their backs were turned: they were marching *away.* At the precise moment her gaze fell on them, a shouted command from one of their officers caused them to execute a perfectly in-unison about-face and come high-stepping it toward the parking lot.

Great. Chalk up one more opportunity to die.

The cold air was having an effect on Yang, too: his head came up and his eyes were brightening. It wouldn't be long before he was in full possession of his faculties. She only hoped they made it into the car first. One yell and they were screwed.

Her grip on his arm tightened warningly. She jammed the gun a little harder into his ribs. Just in case.

They reached the car. A beep told her that Lee had unlocked the doors.

He snapped to sudden stiff attention beside the driver's door. Beside him, Irene did the same thing.

"Sir," he said to Yang in Korean, and saluted smartly. Irene saluted as well.

Out of the corner of her eye Bianca saw a work detail of prisoners rolling cut logs across the frozen earth and loading them on a truck parked nearby. The work detail wasn't far from the northern edge of the parking lot, but until she'd looked around they'd been out of her sight. They were under the supervision of a pair of guards. Curious glances were cast toward the crew beside the limo before eyes were hastily averted. She silently applauded Lee's quick thinking.

Yang's head turned toward the prisoners.

Tim opened the rear door. Bianca all but shoved Yang into the car, applied quick, light pressure to his vagus nerve to keep him docile for a few minutes longer while she considered what best to do with him, then took the seat opposite. The others piled in. The doors closed. The rear compartment was configured into two luxurious bench seats facing each other. Tim took the backward-facing seat beside her. David was next to Yang, facing forward. Lee locked the doors, started the car and began to drive slowly out of the parking lot.

"You think they noticed us?"

"We're never going to make it."

"Tim, tuck up your hair."

"Stop talking in English," Irene said.

"I think we turn right at the intersection to reach the front gate," Bianca said and Irene translated.

Lee said in Korean, "I know where the front gate is. I made a note of it when they brought me in. Then, I was thinking I would escape. After a week in this place, I thought I never would."

Bianca pulled off Yang's overcoat, then fastened his seat belt around him so that he was locked tightly in place next to the window. Just in case they had to roll it down to prove to the guards who was inside. He moved slightly and groaned. His head rested back against the seat. He blinked once, twice, then closed his eyes again and went still. To hide the fact that his arms were pulled behind him, she draped his coat over him as if he'd done it because he was cold.

"How far?" she asked.

"Maybe two kilometers."

Irene continued to play interpreter as they spoke.

"You have controls to the rear windows up there. Practice rolling Yang's window down about a third of the way." Yang's window rolled down and up a few times. Blasted with cold air, he blinked and stirred again, but then when the window stayed up he stopped moving. If he was coming to, which he should be by now, he would be feeling groggy and disoriented. It would take him a little bit to get up to speed.

"Good job," Bianca said. "If the guards ask to speak to Yang, that's what you do. Roll it down, wait a beat, then roll it back up again. We want to limit his exposure as much as possible. And before we stop at the gate, be sure to close the passenger partition."

Lee agreed.

Workers and guards were everywhere, busy outdoors despite the cold. A smattering of snow lay on the ground. Neat fields gave way to what looked like an industrial area. Trucks and heavy equipment rumbled down pitted roads. Beyond the warehouses, buildings were arranged around squares, as in small villages. The camp itself nestled in a valley surrounded by mountains. It would, Bianca judged, be almost pretty if it hadn't been hell on earth for the people trapped inside.

The limo reached the intersection, turned right.

Lee said something that Bianca didn't hear. Irene repeated it for Bianca's benefit. "We will soon be approaching the gate."

Fear thinned Irene's voice. Immediately the atmosphere inside the limo changed. Dread hung heavy in the air.

Bianca looked around. All the miles of ten-foot-tall, electrified barbed wire fences that surrounded the prison centered on this: a red metal gate blocking the road ahead. Sentries paced back and forth in front of it. A pair of guardhouses stood on either side. Tall watchtowers rose behind the guardhouses. There would be riflemen inside, Bianca knew, positioned so that they had a clear shot at anyone attempting to pass through the gate.

Her heart started to beat faster. Her pulse rate quickened.

"We are approaching the last connecting road before we reach the guardhouse. If we are going to turn aside, I must do it there," Lee said, and Irene translated.

That must have penetrated Yang's fog, because he lifted his head and looked around as if not quite sure where he was. He tried to shift positions, and suddenly seemed to realize that he was confined. He started to struggle. Bianca gripped his leg above his knee, hard, and squeezed. He yelped and jerked his leg away.

"Stay still," she ordered him in English.

Their eyes met. This time she knew he recognized her. He looked around again, and she saw from his expression that he was still a little foggy but that his situation was becoming clear.

She could chop him again, but if the guards wanted to see him before allowing them to pass through the gate, finding him unconscious in the back seat might prove problematic. What they wanted was as little scrutiny as possible.

"Trade seats with me," she said to David. They traded seats so that Bianca sat beside Yang.

"You are trying to escape," Yang said to her. "You will never succeed. You will be recaptured, and you will die a thousand painful deaths. All of you will."

"If we die, you'll die first. Right here in

454

this limo."

"Do I go or do I turn?" The note of urgency in Lee's voice was even more intense in Irene's translation.

An ugly glint in Yang's eyes warned of trouble. She needed a bit more time to decide how best to deal with him. On the other hand, the longer they drove around inside the camp the more likely it was that someone would discover the dead guards. Then they'd have no chance of getting out of there.

Forget Russian roulette. The game she was playing here was called 101 ways to die in a God-forsaken hole a million miles from nowhere.

"Go," Bianca said, and showed Yang the Ruger. "One wrong move, and you're dead."

The limo kept going straight, started to slow —

"The guard's coming out. I'm getting ready to brake," Lee said, and Irene translated with a touch of hysteria.

"Here we go," David said.

"Oh, Jesus," Tim muttered.

Lee said something under his breath that sounded like a prayer. That, Irene didn't translate.

Yang smiled.

Bianca thrust the gun beneath his coat

and jammed it hard against his privates. He gave a pained grunt, and his eyes shot toward her.

"One wrong word out of you, and I blow it off," she said. Then as the car slowed in preparation for stopping she threw the words he'd said to her earlier back at him. In Korean. So he knew that if he spoke out of line to the guards she would know. "If you think to fool me you will suffer."

The passenger partition rolled shut just as the car stopped. The tension in their closed compartment was so thick you could stir it. David and Tim sat bolt upright. Bianca could almost hear their hearts hammering. The partition had a smoky tint, but she could see through it. A guard in his puffy billed hat leaned down to peer through the tinted driver's window. Lee rolled the window partway down.

Lee spoke before the guard could say anything. Because of the panel, Bianca couldn't hear what he said — she imagined something along the lines of "I serve General Yang!" — but she saw the guard's reaction. His eyes widened. He snapped a look toward the rear of the car. How much he could see of who was who and what was what in the passenger compartment Bianca didn't know.

She had to assume that if she could see the guard, the guard could see her. And Yang.

Yang took a breath. She could sense it: he'd figured out he had nothing to lose. He was going to flop around. He was going to yell.

She ground the gun harder into his privates.

The guard stepped back.

The window rolled up.

The gate opened.

The car drove through.

An hour later, when they were safely out of the valley and climbing up through the mountains, Lee pulled the car over on Bianca's orders.

There wasn't a choice. It had to be done. Telling the others to stay in the car, she dragged a protesting, struggling Yang from his seat, marched him to the side of the road and shot him dead.

One bullet, through the heart, as she'd been taught. The mark of a professional. He didn't suffer, which was more kindness than he'd shown his many victims.

Bianca was turning away when Lee, having emerged from the car, passed her to stare down at the general's body.

She reminded herself that he might be a kid, but he'd seen far worse.

He lifted his hand, which she saw with some dismay held a gun. He pumped three shots into Yang's body.

"For my father," he said. "And my uncle. And my cousin."

Then he turned and walked back to the car.

31

Wednesday, December 18th

A wooden fishing shack on a low ridge overlooking the meandering Tumen River was not the ideal place to spend a snowy December midnight. But there they were, eight of them, freezing their asses off on the Chinese side of the river despite the fire blazing away in the metal stove in the center of the one-room structure. On the other side of the water, the lights of the North Korean city of Musan emitted a pale glow a few miles away.

Colin was freezing his ass off more than most, because he was outside in the pitch-dark walking up and down the edge of the windy, barren bluff doing his best *Lion King* imitation as he struggled to find a signal so he could use the state-of-the-art satellite phone that allowed him to talk to Doc. He needed a satellite phone because Doc was in one of Thayer's safe houses, a presumably cushy apartment in London with presumably central heating, working the highly sophisticated radar equipment that had been installed there.

Thayer, damn him, was inside the fishing shack by the fire.

Colin's men — he'd brought along all six that had been with him in Paris, on the theory that he might need firepower — were down on the riverbank, scouting around for any sign of Bianca. Before they'd lost contact with him, word from Doc had been that she was on the move — in a vehicle, judging by her speed — heading across the mountains in the general direction of Musan. Then she'd turned off the main road onto a smaller road that led north along the river.

Then they'd lost her signal.

Then they'd lost Doc.

Sources in the region had directed them to this, the narrowest part of the Tumen River. On a dark night like this, with the river frozen, it was the best place in a hundred miles to cross, they said. Anyone attempting it who knew anything would come here.

Despite the dozens of armed guards patrolling the banks on the other side.

The question was, did Bianca know that

this was the place to come?

Over the course of what had been an eventful day chasing a temperamental signal across a couple of continents, Thayer hadn't shown a whole lot of fatherly concern.

"She's resourceful. She'll figure it out" was what he'd said when Doc had relayed the news that her locator beacon indicated that she was near the village of Hwasong, in all probability locked up in the notorious prison camp there. His amusement at the anxiety Colin hadn't quite been able to keep hidden would have annoyed Colin if he hadn't been so, well, anxious.

And if he hadn't had more important things to worry about.

The initial relief of knowing she was alive had given way to a horrible, gnawing fear that she might yet die.

Then Doc had relayed the news that she was out of Hwasong and traveling north.

Colin had come up with various contingency plans to go in and get her if she didn't show up somewhere safe within a few hours. For a small military force, which was what he and his men basically were, to breach the borders of a country like North Korea could cause a major international incident if it should be discovered. The bigger problem was, once inside North Korea he would almost certainly lose the connection with Doc, which would make locating Bianca like finding a needle in a haystack.

"You do that," Thayer had said, settling down in a folding camp chair by the metal stove. "Me, I'm just going to wait right here."

Suddenly the tiny green light on the satellite phone that indicated it had found a signal lit up.

Colin looked at it for what felt like a full minute before his brain registered what he was seeing.

Ironically, he'd turned back and was now just feet away from the shack.

"Doc, you there?" he said into the headset he quickly put on.

"She's coming toward your position." After more than an hour of no contact, during which Colin had felt himself developing white hairs, Doc's voice was as clear as if he was talking from a couple of miles away. Doc knew their position because Thayer, whose cool competence Colin had actually found pretty impressive even if his concern for his daughter was lacking, had outfitted himself with a tracking device that allowed Doc, once tuned in to the proper frequency, to track him, too.

Colin pictured them as two bright blips

on a dark screen. Or vice versa.

"How far?" he asked, clipping the phone itself to the holster he wore over the black parka that was all that was keeping him from sprouting icicles.

"A couple of miles. On the other side of the river. I've got coordinates."

"Hang on. Let me get to the map." Which was inside the shack. "We've got her signal back. She's only a couple of miles from here," he told Thayer as he entered.

Thayer was sprawled out in the chair with his booted feet close to the stove and his hands laced over his stomach, and at the news the only thing that moved were his eyes, which flicked a look at Colin.

"Told ya," he said.

Busy pinpointing the coordinates Doc was giving him on the map he'd already pinned to the wall, Colin didn't reply.

Boom.

Colin's head came up. The explosion was distant, but it was definitely an explosion.

"That'll be her," Thayer said, and stood up.

The man was outfitted in an arctic parka and pants. He zipped the parka, grabbed the rifle that had been resting beside him, slung it over his shoulder and headed out the door.

Colin snatched up a pair of night-vision goggles and followed.

Thayer was standing just outside the shack looking across the river, where a huge blaze burned about half a mile from the riverbank. Whatever was going up was big.

"How do you know that's her?" Colin asked.

Thayer glanced at him. "Diversion," he said. "She likes to blow things up."

"She's right across the river from your position," Doc said. "Heading toward you."

Thayer started down the bluff. The camo he wore blended so well with the snow-dappled, frozen mud that he practically disappeared in the dark.

Colin started down, too, adjusting the channel on his headset so he could communicate with his men as well as Doc.

"The package is on the way. Rendezvous at Point A," he said. Point A was a dilapidated wooden dock that extended a short way out into the frozen river.

When he got to the dock, his men were there. They were all wearing night-vision goggles. Colin put his on as well and looked toward the opposite bank. Not that there was much to see, except a curving ribbon of river that was shiny black with ice beneath a light frosting of snow. The scruffy pine woods that covered much of the mountainous northern region reached almost to the river. Except for the fire burning fiercely in the distance, everything was dark and still. If guards were on patrol, he couldn't see them.

Maybe the diversion had worked.

"We've got her heading toward the river," Colin told them. "Get ready to provide cover fire as necessary."

Thayer stood off by himself, using a pair of binoculars to scan the opposite shore.

Colin spotted what he at first thought were shadows moving among the trees across the river. Then the shadows emerged from the woods and headed toward the ice, and he realized that he was seeing people. In multiples. Like, five.

What?

No matter. It had to be her.

"Doc, I got a visual," he said into the headset, not wanting interference if he needed to communicate with his men. "I'm turning you off."

"Say hi to the boss for me."

"Will do."

He turned off Doc's channel, unslung his rifle, said "Heads up" very quietly into the channel he had left, pointed to the dark figures now on the ice and gave his men the *go* signal.

They headed out.

The ice was slippery. Running was not an option. Weapons at the ready, Colin and his men advanced toward the group that was slip-sliding toward them. They were being super quiet, as were he and his men. He frowned as they got closer. What he was seeing were soldiers in uniform.

He knew the exact moment they spotted him and his men: four of them slithered to an ungainly stop.

The fifth checked for a second, then kept coming, motioning at the others to follow.

Bianca.

It didn't make him particularly happy to realize that he would recognize her anywhere. Even across an icy river in the dark in a North Korean soldier's uniform.

His gut had twisted itself into knots shortly after the explosion in Paris. He felt it untwist now, and knew he had a problem that went way beyond the gastrointestinal.

A whole different part of his body was involved.

Bang. Bang. Bang. Bang.

Rifle fire from the North Korean shore exploded through the night. Bright muzzle flashes flared in the darkness. Judging from their position, the diversion had worked.

466

The shooters ran through the woods toward the river at an angle that suggested they were returning from the blaze.

"Return fire." Colin gave the order over his headset, and started firing himself as he and his men skate-speed-walked across the ice toward Bianca and friends.

She and her party skated toward him even faster. Then one of them slipped and fell and another stopped to help.

Bianca whirled, and started returning fire with a pistol to cover her fallen friend.

Colin's heart seized up. All alone out there in front, she made a hell of a target. He cursed, rapid fired and skated faster. Her friends picked themselves up and slip-raced toward the advancing line of his men.

Two went past, snaking in between Wilson and Parrino. He overtook the other two, the one who'd fallen and the one who was supporting, and, still firing, reached Bianca, who was snapping off rounds and skating backward at the same time.

Nice trick if you can do it.

She looked over at him as he fell in beside her. She didn't look surprised, so he was guessing she'd recognized him across the crowded ice, too.

"Next time I'm going with the CIA kill team." She had to raise her voice to be heard over the gunfire.

"Good to see you, too, beautiful. You blow something up over there?"

"A car. Some propane tanks. A barracks."

"Doc says hi."

She smiled.

They caught up to his men, or, rather, his men caught up to them. A slip-sliding backward skating retreat while engaging in an all-out firefight with an enemy was new for him. He never wanted to have to repeat it.

Once they reached shore, the opposing gunfire stopped. Just stopped, like someone had pulled a plug.

They were on Chinese territory, and safe. Unless someone decided to break the rules, or sell them out, or just plain hated foreigners. Which was a problem more often than he cared to think about.

"What happened?" he asked her. Surrounded by his men, with her friends being swept along with them, they were beating a hasty retreat back toward the shack, where the SUVs they'd taken from the airport waited.

"Long story. We did it, by the way. I think. The head of the RGB plugged the flash drive into a computer that I'm almost positive is part of their military computer network. A laptop was connected to the same computer at the time." She patted what he saw for the first time was a black messenger bag that hung over her shoulder. "I've got the laptop. And the ChapStick, too, by the way."

She handed the bag over.

He slung it over his own shoulder and smiled at her. "You're a hero."

"Yeah, that's me. Saving the world, one ChapStick at a time."

One of her friends fell back and said to her, "Lee is scared. He said if the Chinese catch him they'll send him back and he'll be killed."

Colin was surprised to hear a girl's voice under that uniform. In the dark, it had been impossible to tell.

"That's not going to happen." Bianca sounded strong, sure and protective. She looked at him. "This is Irene. She was kidnapped from South Korea last summer. Her friend Lee is North Korean. His family was executed and he wants asylum some-place safe. The other two are Americans who were imprisoned for disrespecting something or other. They just want to go home."

"Imprisoned?"

"In Hwasong."

"Sweet Jesus, did you bring prisoners out with you?"

Irene said, "She helped us escape."

By then they'd reached the top of the bluff.

Bianca stopped dead. He looked around to see why, and found that she was looking at Thayer, who was sitting on a flat boulder not far away.

Her face was wiped of all expression.

"You should have told me he's your father," Colin said.

She flicked him a look. Then she said, "Need to know."

"You know, I'm starting to hate that phrase."

"You and me both." She seemed to take a breath, then said, "I need to go talk to him. Take those four — they're kids — and keep an eye on them, would you? Make sure they stay safe. Go ahead and load up or do whatever you need to do, and I'll be with you in a minute."

"Yeah," he agreed.

"Hey," she said. He looked at her. "Thanks for coming for me."

"Anytime." He cast another look at Thayer — a dark shape among other dark shapes, he was as unmoving as a statue — and walked away.

32

She'd never wanted it to come to this.

But as soon as she'd seen Mason sitting there in the dark, she'd known.

Four-fingered Franz was the tip-off.

What were the chances that one of Mason's longtime flunkies would be watching her in a restaurant she'd just happened to duck into right after she'd felt the deadly weight of an assassin's gaze on her back?

At the time she'd thought he was acting as somebody's spotter.

Now she knew whose.

There's no such thing as coincidence.

Mason had taught her well.

Now it was time for her to use what she'd learned. Against him.

She had a Ruger in her pocket. She'd counted her shots. Three left.

She only needed one.

He wouldn't even know what hit him. No fear, no pain.

Slipping her hand in her pocket, she aimed the weapon. And stopped walking. With Mason less than three feet away. Point-blank range. Her finger was on the curve of the trigger. She'd discarded her Lynette wig and the cheek prosthesis hours earlier, so she was herself again.

Facing him.

He sat there looking at her. It was too dark for her to see his expression. Which was good.

He said, "You can't do it, can you?"

Ah. He knew. She inhaled, felt the trigger against her finger.

"I couldn't do it, either," he said. "I had you in my sights in Paris. Twice. And out there on the ice. I didn't take the shot."

"What about Berlin?"

"I gave you the code. I knew you'd figure it out."

Her finger dropped away from the trigger.

"They have Marin and Margery," he said. "The CIA. They shot down my helicopter in Macau, captured me, found them. They let me go to kill you. It's the only chance Marin and Margery have."

"My life for theirs."

"Yep."

They looked at each other for a long moment. Marin was seven years old. Until the

472

shocks of the last few months, Bianca had thought of her as her baby sister. The truth was a cold bitch, but feelings, she discovered, weren't that easy to switch off. There they were, settling like a stone in her stomach.

"Then I guess you better kill me."

"That was the conclusion I reached, too," he said, and stood up.

33

Friday, December 20th

Hanes set the chopper down in the flat, grassy field he'd chosen for the exchange. Strapped into the rear seats were Thayer's wife and child, sedated so he didn't have to worry about them doing anything to complicate the situation, like try to run off. Anyway, he really didn't like the idea of a child being scared or hurt, and this was the easiest way to avoid that. However this went down, the little girl wouldn't know anything about it.

"It's done." Thayer's words had dropped like bricks over the phone when his call had come through yesterday. Hanes thought he had detected emotion in them, which coming from Thayer was something that he treasured. He only wished he was going to be allowed more time with the man — breaking him was high on his wish list — but a deal was a deal.

This area not many miles outside the mountain village of Sagada, in the Philippines, had been chosen for the exchange. The CIA kept a safe house nearby, and it was remote enough that there would be no witnesses.

A blue Nissan sedan came into view, speeding along the narrow blacktop road. He had no doubt it was Thayer. The car was an obvious rental, and tourists rarely came this way.

He got out of the chopper in anticipation, made a gesture signaling to the pair of snipers he had stationed in the woods bordering the field to get ready. They were there because this was Thayer, who was about as trustworthy as a rabid dog. Not that he wanted to shoot the man. Too messy, and then there would be the wife and child to deal with.

The Nissan pulled off the road and bumped across the field until it stopped beside the chopper. Thayer got out. It was a warm, sunny day, and the man was wearing aviator shades and a polo shirt and looked like he was on a damned vacation.

Except for the gun in his hand.

"You've got rifles trained on you," Hanes said as he approached, to forestall any misunderstandings.

Thayer smiled. "So do you."

Hanes figured it was a bluff, but — this was Thayer. He couldn't be sure. The man had connections all over the world. Thayer waved in the direction of the woods across the road. A glint of something — a mirror, a flashlight — blinked in answer.

So, not a bluff.

"Where is she?" Hanes asked.

"In the trunk."

"Open it."

Thayer punched a button. There was a beep, and the trunk opened.

Hanes walked over and looked in. A blue body bag was jackknifed into the trunk. From the look of it, whatever was in there was in a position no live human could assume. The smell hit him, made him grimace and settled the matter. There was no mistaking the stench of death.

He unzipped the bag.

The smell rolled out, enveloped him, choked him. It was all he could do not to gag.

Trying not to breathe, he took a good look.

Even dead, bloated, with shiny, purplish skin that looked like it might burst at a touch, there was no mistaking her: Nomad 44.

A blackened, dime-sized hole between her

eyes, the crusty brown of dried blood matting her hair.

He hated what he had to do next: he checked the side of her neck for a pulse.

Her skin felt cold, spongy, a decaying casing for an overripe body.

No pulse.

He withdrew his hand, zipped the bag up, closed the trunk, stepped away. And breathed.

Then he slowly and carefully ran the wand-like bomb detector he'd brought with him over the vehicle.

"What did you do to them?" Thayer asked. His tone was ugly. He'd been looking the helicopter over, searching for signs of sabotage, Hanes had no doubt, and had found his family.

"They're sedated, asleep. They're fine."

"They better be." The menace was unmistakable.

Hanes said, "Give me the key." Thayer had pivoted and was employing the same kind of military-approved bomb detector Hanes had used on the car to check the helicopter for a bomb.

He wouldn't find one. Not that the thought hadn't occurred to Hanes. But there'd been zero chance that Thayer would simply climb in and take off without taking that elementary precaution.

Finished, Thayer came back around to the side Hanes was on, tossed him the key.

Without another word, Hanes climbed into the car, made a U-turn and headed back toward the safe house. The prize in the trunk needed to go into the freezer he had ready for her, pronto.

Too bad he hadn't thought to specify, when he'd told Thayer to bring him the body, that he wanted it on ice.

In the rearview mirror, as he drove away, Hanes watched the helicopter lift off.

34

As soon as the car bumped into motion, Bianca came out of that body bag like a greased pig. The overpowering smell of the dead marsupial that was in there with her was enough to suffocate her. But needs must, as the saying goes.

She and Mason had made the assumption that Hanes would drive the body back to the safe house, and they had had the road prepared accordingly. She had five minutes before the Nissan reached the overturned truck that had spilled a load of mangoes across the roadway. A small section of the pavement had been left clear — they didn't want the car to stop altogether, just in case Hanes decided to take that opportunity to look in the trunk again — but to get around the obstacle he would have to go partway into the tall grass along the verge and that would require him to slow way down.

At which point she would exit the trunk.

Doing so required that she first unscrew the false bottom Mason had had installed while she was being transformed into the bride of Frankenstein. Their criminal contacts in the Philippines weren't extensive, but those connections they did have did excellent work, as both she and the car proved. She didn't have a lot of room to maneuver as she undid the screws, and the dead animal they'd scooped up from the roadside to seal the deal stank horribly, but she managed it.

When the car slowed, she was ready. She hit the button on the back side of the custom body bag that would cause the human-sized blow-up doll rolled up inside to inflate, so that at first glance anyone looking into the trunk would assume that there was still a corpse in the bag. Then she dropped out of the opening in the bottom of the trunk, hit the tall grass beside the road (they'd calculated that perfectly) and scrambled into the woods as the Nissan continued on down the road.

She had a rendezvous to make. Putting her head down, she ran through the woods, pulling off her wig, peeling away the layers of latex skin that had allowed Hanes to check her pulse without feeling anything, shedding the bloated body suit that had made her look swollen with decomposition. She tucked all those items in the shoulder bag she'd brought, because leaving the discards behind in the woods was just not good tradecraft. Then she wiped her face with (several) makeup removing wipes.

By the time she reached the field where Mason was supposed to pick her up, she was dressed in a black tee and leggings, and her blond hair, which had been coiled up under the disgusting wig, was loose. She settled a headset into place, adjusted the position of the mic.

The helicopter came swooping down out of the sky, right on schedule. As it came toward her, Mason leaned out of the pilot's door. He, too, had a headset on.

"Can't stop." His voice crackled in her ear. "Grab a runner and jump on."

"What?" That wasn't part of the plan.

But he was coming toward her, flying low, the runners about eight feet above the ground, and she could tell by the way he was flying that he was serious. It was a small helicopter — a B407, she thought — and as maneuverable as a mosquito.

She turned and ran in the direction the helicopter was going, and when it passed over her she jumped up, grabbed a runner, hauled herself up on it, slid open the door and climbed inside.

"What the hell was that?" She glared at him as the helicopter soared back up into the bright blue sky and she pulled on her seat belt.

"I can't stop."

"What, no brakes?" Her tone dripped sarcasm.

He smiled. "I have a little bead of a tracker in my hand. They wouldn't let me out to chase you down and kill you without it. Hanes can keep tabs on where I am. Which is why we flew into Manila separately, and why I had you get yourself and the car ready without me. Right now, he's probably watching me flying away into the sunset. And if I stop for something, he's going to wonder what."

"You could have told me that earlier."

"Need to know."

"From now on, whatever it is, assume I need to know," she said with bite.

"My, somebody rolled out of the wrong side of the trunk. Speaking of, you still have the slightest hint of *eau de varmint* about you."

"Thanks for noticing." She glanced into the back seat. Marin and Margery were securely strapped in, leaning against each other, the child's head on her mother's shoulder. It was obvious they were asleep, equally obvious they'd been drugged. "Once Hanes finds out he's been played, he's going to be coming after you with both barrels. Me, too. You need to stash them someplace where they won't get caught in the cross fire again."

"See why I taught you to keep emotion out of it? My family's in danger because of me, and I'm hamstrung in what I can do because of them."

Funny that it still hurt to have him so casually confirm that he considered Marin and Margery his family, which by extrapolation meant she was not. Or actually, now that she thought about it, not funny at all.

She glanced out — they were flying over acres of forests, and the treetops were an interesting mix of greens below. The road they'd come in on, the one Hanes was presumably still driving along, cut through all that green like a line drawn by a graphite pencil.

"You could've killed Hanes back there. Why didn't you?"

"Because I don't know what tricks he may have up his sleeve. And I want the girls tucked safely out of the way before I start an all-out war."

"I've got her." It was Hanes's voice, a

tinny, distant version coming out of nowhere, and to hear it so unexpectedly made
Bianca jump. "She's dead. Nomad 44 is
dead."

Her eyes slewed to Mason. He caught her
gaze, tapped his watch. Which was not a
watch at all, she saw, but a receiver.

"I bugged the car," he said. "Little insur-
ance policy."

Bianca said, "You could have told me."

She read *need to know* in his face, but
before her head could explode Hanes said,
"In a chopper. Heading toward Manila."

Bianca realized that Hanes was referring
to Mason, and what they were listening to
was his side of a cell phone conversation.

There was a pause, and then Hanes said,
"Yes, sir."

Neither she nor Mason spoke. They were
listening too intently.

Hanes said, "I've taken care of it. About
four minutes from now, the chopper's going
to be hit by a missile. I've already called it
in. The drone's in the air."

The hairs stood up on the back of Bianca's
neck. Mason's hands tightened on the
controls. There was no mistaking what
they'd just heard.

Hanes said, "It doesn't matter if they set
down. The drone's programmed to target

him."

"The tracking device," Mason whispered. Face paling, anger tightening his mouth, he looked down at his hand.

At just about the same time, Hanes said, "He was injected with a tracking device. There's no way it's missing him."

Mason's face contorted, and then he heeled the helicopter around.

Bianca grabbed the side of her seat. "What are you doing?"

Hanes said, "Yes, sir. I'll do that." From his tone it was a sign-off.

Mason said, "I'm heading for the safe house."

"What? Why?" Bianca shifted in her seat so that she could see him better. "We have to get that tracking device out of you *right now.*"

Mason shook his head. "If he misses me with this, he'll just keep coming. One of these days he's going to succeed, and he's going to take Marin or Margery — or you — with me. This stops now. I'm taking *him* with me."

They were flying back the way they'd come, only he'd maxed the throttle and now everything beneath them was a blur.

"What?"

"When we get to the safe house, you're

485

going to take over the controls. I'm going to jump down onto it. He thinks you're in his car, which he'll pull into the garage. Whoever he was talking to — his boss, I'm betting it's Wafford — thinks you're in the car. The missile hits the house, the house blows up, Hanes is dead, I'm dead, everybody — the *CIA* — thinks you're dead."

"You're not really going to let them kill you." The horror in her voice made it as much a question as a statement.

"I'll see what I can do. But this is an opportunity not to be missed. It'll take out Hanes, and you and I will be officially dead."

"But —"

It was too late. The safe house was in sight. It was small, painted yellow, and had a red tile roof complete with a stovepipe and skylights. No sign of the Nissan in the driveway. But the door was closed on the attached garage, and since there was no sign of the car on the approaching road, she assumed it was in the garage and Hanes must have already arrived. Bianca cast a terrified glance out the window, searching the sky for a drone.

But the thing about drones is, once you see them, you're already dead.

"Get ready to take over the controls,"

Mason said.

"What about *don't be a hero?*" She almost screeched it. It was one of the rules.

"I'm not being a hero. I'm doing what has to be done." The helicopter dropped; they were coming up on the safe house. Mason undid his seat belt and opened his door. Warm, jungle-scented air rushed in, along with the *thwap thwap thwap* of the rotor blades. Eyes wide with horror, heart jackhammering, she undid her seat belt. He looked at her. "Get over here. Bring me in low."

She scrambled into the pilot's seat, grabbed the controls — and he swung out onto the runner. Breathing like she'd just run a marathon, she brought him in low.

"Bianca —" He had to shout to be heard over the rotor. She looked at him. His silver hair whipped skyward. His eyes blazed bright blue. Her stomach lodged in her throat. "Take care of the girls. And get the hell out of here."

He jumped, landed on the tile, scrambled for a foothold, found one.

And she sheered the helicopter away.

35

Hanes heard the crash, and walked into the living room to see what that was about. Until that moment he'd been wearing a headset, listening to the guys in the control center at the base monitoring the drone. Once that was taken care of, he would have Nomad 44's body put into the freezer. But she could wait. He had no real animosity toward her, while he hated Thayer from the marrow of his bones. He didn't want to miss the missile's moment of impact, even if he was only hearing about it, not seeing it.

All in all, it was shaping up to be one of his better days.

The sight of Thayer crouched in his living room in the middle of a sunburst of broken glass hit him like a gut punch. He stopped, did a double take, sputtered, "What the hell?"

Thayer's hand was bloody, his mouth was bloody, and even as Hanes gaped at him he took off at a dead run, spitting something bloody out before making a leap at the picture window at the far side of the room.

Thayer was still in flight as Hanes made the connection: bloody left hand, bloody mouth, bloody spit, *tracking device.*

He felt a thrill of horror.

He turned to run.

Boom.

36

Sunday, December 22nd

Wafford lived in a big stone house just outside of Alexandria, Virginia. It was impressive, with a pillared portico and lots of mullioned windows and a set of wide concrete steps leading up to the door.

Bianca shot him as he went up those steps. Right through the kneecap. Lowering her Win Mag as he screamed and fell, she emerged from the cover of a glossy green magnolia to stride across the immaculately kept lawn toward him. The grass was brown and crisp with cold beneath her feet, but there was no snow.

No witnesses, either, except, perhaps, for the half-dozen horses grazing disinterestedly in a nearby field. No one to see a young woman in a black coverall with a black knit cap pulled down over her blond hair. The big stone house was the centerpiece of a hundred-acre farm. Usually it hummed with activity, but on this, the last Sunday before Christmas, all the help had gone home.

His wife was away. As always, Bianca had done her research. Wafford was home alone.

She was there to kill him. Enough of running scared. Time to take the battle to the enemy. One thing that had become clear to her since the CIA kill team had shown up in Savannah was that the only way she could live her life in peace was to stamp out everyone who thought she had no right to live. Before he'd leaped from the helicopter, Mason had said that since Hanes had reported her dead and the house her corpse had supposedly been in had been blown up with a missile, she should be safe. She didn't think so. Because too many of the people who'd hunted Nomad 44 had found out about her life in Savannah, and she didn't just want to live, didn't want to run and start over again and spend the next however many years looking over her shoulder and praying that she wouldn't be found.

She wanted the life she had made for herself as Bianca St. Ives, and she was prepared to do whatever she had to do to make sure she could have it.

It was survival of the fittest. And from now on, thanks to what they'd made her, that would be her.

"What — what do you want?" Wafford was crying, groaning, clutching his wounded leg as he tried to crawl away from her up the stairs. Twilight was falling; the dying light threw a soft golden glow over the steps. She walked up them after him. The Win Mag was slung over her shoulder now. A pistol was in her hand.

"I want names," she said. "I want to know the names of everyone who was involved in the Nomad program, everyone who knows Nomad 44 exists, everyone who's been hunting me."

Whimpering, he turned his head to look up at her. The light fell on his face. It was twisted with pain — and, as he recognized her, fear.

"My God. Hanes told me you were dead." He seemed to choke.

"Hanes is the one who's dead." His death, in the fiery explosion that had consumed the safe house, had been confirmed. His charred remains had been found. Bianca knew, because Doc was an internet wizard who could find out anything. It was he, for example, who'd found out that Tim and David were at a hospital in Berlin being checked out before they were flown back to the United States, that Lee had been granted asylum in South Korea, that Irene

492

had been reunited with her mother.

It was he who had found out that Colin had returned to London and his business.

And that the ChapStick had actually done its thing.

So far, Hanes's was the only body that had been found in the ruins of the safe house. But the excavation, and the forensics that went with it, was ongoing.

Was Mason alive? Was he dead?

She didn't know.

That was one thing Doc couldn't seem to find out.

"I want names," Bianca said again. "You didn't decide that I needed to be eliminated on your own. Who told you to go after me?"

His whimpering deteriorated into sobs. He writhed, clutching his knee. "It's my job, you have to understand. I was given an assignment to carry out. I — It wasn't about you. I had *no choice.*"

"I'm going to ask one more time, and if you don't tell me I'm going to shoot out your other knee." Her voice was fierce. "Who told you to go after me?"

"Oh, *God.* Hal Woodbridge."

The powerful Senate Majority Leader, currently gearing up to make a run for President of the United States.

Pfft.

The silenced round sang right past Bianca and went straight through Wafford's heart. He collapsed without so much as a gurgle. Bianca whirled, her firearm at the ready.

Standing about ten feet from the bottom of the steps, lowering his Beretta, was Mason. Something inside Bianca that had been stretched taut as a bowstring ever since he'd stepped off that runner now relaxed.

"That was the name I was looking for," he said. "You can leave the rest of this cleanup operation to me. Go home, live your life."

"How did you know I was here?" Because she'd been careful. No one did.

"I didn't. I just decided I'm tired of running from them. Let them run from me." A glimmer of a smile curved his mouth. "Like you did, hmm? Well, they say great minds think alike." He started to turn away, looked back. "Thank you for getting Margery and Marin safely to England, by the way. I've got them squared away."

He turned to go.

"Wait." Such a quick, almost casual encounter. He'd been her *father.* One question had been burning in her mind ever since she'd learned the truth. She'd never meant to ask it at all, but –– it just came out. "Why didn't you kill my mo — Issa and me, all those years ago?"

He turned back around, looked at her. She found that she was holding her breath, waiting for him to respond. His face was expressionless, and she thought he wasn't going to.

Then he said, "She was tiny, you know. Issa. Maybe a hundred pounds. Big dark eyes. She looked like she'd fall over if you breathed on her hard. And young — nineteen. But she was smart. It took me a while to track her down, and when I did that little thing had the balls to come at me with a fire extinguisher. She blasted that foam at me and snatched you up — you were a baby, bawling your head off in one of those bassinet things — and ran. It was a rented room, up a flight of stairs, and she slipped going down the last few steps and fell. I was coming after her by then, and I saw her fall. Only instead of putting out her hands to save herself, she twisted around to try to protect the baby she was carrying — you — so she hit hard on her back. When I got to her she was lying there looking up at me, kind of stunned, with you still cradled in her arms. The fall had knocked the breath out of her, but with me standing over her she managed to suck in enough air to say, 'Please don't hurt the baby.' Not 'please don't hurt me' but 'please don't hurt the baby.' She was looking up into the face of a ruthless killer and she knew it and she begged for you. She was so brave, and so fierce in defense of you. I couldn't do it. I knew if I didn't they'd send somebody else, so I told her I'd protect the two of you and I did. Until they killed her."

His voice went heavy on that last.

Bianca wet her lips. "You kept me."

His mouth twisted. "She loved you so much. There wasn't anything else I could do. By then she'd made us a family, had you calling me Daddy. It was the damnedest thing, the way that worked out."

"You loved her." It wasn't a question. She knew him well enough to divine the answer from what he'd said.

"I did."

She couldn't ask it. But he must have seen the question burning in her eyes: *Did you love me?*

"You were such a smart kid. You grew on me. I started to teach you things, and you learned everything I threw at you and more. I could see your potential. The DNA thing they'd done to you — when they sent me after you they'd made it sound like you were some kind of mistake that needed to be erased. But in every way that counted you were just a little girl. You thought I was your father, and after a while I felt like your father."

A sudden tightness in her throat made it hard to speak. There was so much she wanted to say, but emotion wasn't something they did. Bottom line was, she owed him. She'd never before realized how much. "You saved my life, and you raised me. Thank you."

"No thanks needed. I said I felt like your father. I still do," he said. Then, without giving her a chance to answer, he lifted a hand in farewell, turned and walked away into the gathering dark.

37

Tuesday, December 24th

Bianca stepped inside her condo, locked the door and inhaled the familiar scent — plus pine — with pleasure. It was shortly after 8:00 p.m., she'd just finished having burgers with Doc after declining to accompany Evie to a party at her mother's house, and she was looking forward to spending the rest of Christmas Eve in luxurious solitude, with a hot bath and maybe Netflix for company.

In one corner of the living room, the Christmas tree twinkled merrily. Otherwise, the place was dark.

A gaily wrapped package on the coffee table in the living room caught her eye. The tag on it, in letters big enough so that she could read them from where she stood, said *Bianca*.

It hadn't been there earlier.

Hmm.

She and Evie, and Doc, and Hay, had all

exchanged presents at the office. Evie had ended up giving Hay a framed, autographed picture of the Georgia Bulldogs baseball team, because the autographed bat she'd originally gotten for him had, um, died.

Bianca crossed to the present, looked at it, sat down on the couch and started to open it. The tag was just that: a tag. The only thing on it was her name.

It had been professionally gift wrapped. The paper gleamed gold, the ribbon was sparkly white.

Inside was a beautiful polished rosewood box with a hinged lid.

She lifted the lid.

It was a music box: a melody tinkled out.

The tune was "Nobody Does It Better."

She sucked in air.

Then looked up as a tall dark shape stepped into the doorway that led to the bedrooms and leaned a shoulder against the frame.

Colin.

She was so glad to see him it was ridiculous. Her heart made like the Grinch's and expanded three sizes.

"Evie let me in," he said.

Because she'd told Evie he'd swept her off her feet. Because Evie thought they were having a whirlwind romance.

Because Evie hated the idea of her being alone on Christmas Eve.

"What are you doing here?"

He smiled at her, that charming, crooked smile that did bad things to her good intentions.

"We have another job," he said.

ACKNOWLEDGMENTS

What would a book be without the publishing team behind it? Not as good, for sure. I want to thank my wonderful editor, Emily Ohanjanians, who has done such a fabulous job with these books; Margaret O'Neill Marbury, for her unflagging support; Meredith Barnes, for keeping on top of book tours and publicity; and everyone at MIRA Books. It's a privilege to work with such dedicated, talented people!

I also want to thank my agent, Robert Gottlieb, who tirelessly looks out for me, and the team at Trident Media Group.

I want to thank my husband, Doug.

And last and most important of all, I want to thank you, my readers, for sticking with me all these years. You're the best!

ABOUT THE AUTHOR

Karen Robards is the *New York Times, USA Today,* and *Publishers Weekly* bestselling author of fifty novels and one novella. She is the winner of six Silver Pen awards and numerous other awards.

The employees of Thorndike Press hope you have enjoyed this Large Print book. All our Thorndike, Wheeler, and Kennebec Large Print titles are designed for easy reading, and all our books are made to last. Other Thorndike Press Large Print books are available at your library, through selected bookstores, or directly from us.

For information about titles, please call:
(800) 223-1244

or visit our website at:
gale.com/thorndike

To share your comments, please write:
Publisher
Thorndike Press
10 Water St., Suite 310
Waterville, ME 04901